CROWN YOUR HEAD WITH IVY

A J RICHARDS

First Edition

Book Cover by oliviaprodesign

ISBN 978-0-473-59575-3 (Paperback)
ISBN 978-0-473-59576-0 (eBook)
ISBN 978-0-473-59577-7 (Kindle)

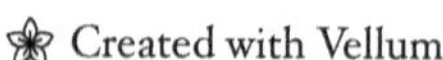 Created with Vellum

This novel is dedicated to L.G.
who taught me the connection explored here.

alia and I swayed in the back of the taxi as it drove along the dark city streets towards the art gallery. I leaned my forehead on the cool glass of the window and watched the glow of streetlights flashing by.

"Shhhh," said Talia, and she pulled a plastic water bottle out of her handbag. She elbowed my side and then passed the bottle to me, glancing at the driver in the front seat. "This is pretty much your last chance!" she hissed.

I sighed but reached out for the bottle, taking a good mouthful of the wine that she had hidden in it. The wine stung my throat as I gulped it down. I shivered and blinked.

"Yeah, that's the stuff Pene. When was the last time you got to let loose, huh?"

"It's been a while," I had to admit. The wine I had drunk at home while Talia did my hair and makeup had gone to my head far too quickly, and this mouthful was only going to make my dizziness worse. I fell forward, nearly hitting the seat in front of me as the taxi pulled to the curb.

"Here we are ladies, that'll be sixty three dollars."

"What! That's simply robbery! You sir, are a scoundrel!" Talia spoke with wide open eyes and mouth, as though she had never been so scandalised by anything anyone had ever said to her before. The sight made me giggle and hiccup.

"I am that, but the price is the price," winked the older man.

Talia glared at him and pulled a card out of her purse to pay.

"Thanks muchly ladies, have a great night," said the driver as we climbed out.

Talia stood on the pavement and took another drink from her bottle then held it out towards me. *Why not,* I figured. *What have I got to lose?* The wine burned in my stomach and I grimaced. All around us, dark buildings hunched over in the cold air. I began to wish that I had worn more clothes. *It's not supposed to be this cold at this time of year, is it?* My stomach bubbled and my chest burned.

"Come on. I want you to meet some people!" Talia began to stride towards a queue of people outside an otherwise perfectly ordinary white building. I looked up and down the street. Buildings rose around me like cliffs, all grey and divided up into dark rectangles of unlit windows. The queue was the only source of light and colour that I could see anywhere along the street. A few lonely trees stood in their small squares of dirt along the pavement, barely taller than my head and fenced in by metal gratings.

I studied the queue as Talia and I tottered closer. I couldn't quite believe what I was seeing. The makeup that they were wearing was darker and more intense than anything I would have considered for myself. Their faces were divided into clear sections, bright colours. It was incredible how they were drawing attention to every inch of their face, instead of trying to camouflage themselves into the preferred standard.

"They look amazing," I whispered.

"Don't let them hear you say that," laughed Talia. "They'll pull you into a dialogue about external appearances that could last the entire evening! Come on, let's see who's here already."

Talia swept past the line of people, all of them chatting behind a slack rope that was strung along the storefronts, and led me to an otherwise nondescript set of double glass doors at the front of the queue. Brilliant green light billowed out from the doors and washed over us. The people at the front of the queue raised their eyebrows as we walked right past them. I was sure someone would complain or say something sharp at our expense, but the biggest outburst we had to deal with was a skinny young man with extremely tall hair shaking his head.

The bouncer stepped forward with an unimpressed expression and one raised hand. His black collared shirt and jacket shifted uneasily on an obviously strong and bulky physique.

"Evening ladies. There is a queue, you know." It wasn't a question.

"I know, and we don't mind waiting," said Talia as she leaned forward towards him, drawing him in to her conspiracies. "Is Frederick here yet? He told me that he couldn't wait to show me his piece."

The bouncer narrowed his eyes, but he pulled out a clipboard from behind him somewhere and ran a heavy finger along it. About a third of the way down the paper his finger stopped and I heard his surprised puff of breath.

"Alright, it says here that Frederick has a name down for entry. What's yours?"

"Talia."

The bouncer shook his head and for a moment I was worried that he would send us to the back of the line, but then he unclipped the rope and waved us towards the doors.

"Thank you so much," gushed Talia as we walked by and pulled open the doors.

Inside the gallery was full of sound and light. Spotlights spun and changed colour, flashing from deep reds to virulent greens and boisterous purples, illuminating every wall and corner. Groups of people were clustered throughout the space, laughing and giggling together, beer and wine and spirits in their hands. The buzz of conversation fought with the buzzing atmospheric music that ricocheted off the walls, and I felt my breath quicken.

"This is a lot," I said into Talia's ear. She reached out to squeeze my wrist.

"You'll be okay. It's just been awhile since you've had so many people around you. Shows you haven't had a proper night out in far too long! But this is fun, this is living! You need a little danger every now and then, to get your blood pumping, to remind you that you're alive. And look at the art!"

She was right, the art was pretty overpowering all on it's own. Giant paintings of abstract shapes and colour shouted from the wall. Sculptures were placed throughout the concrete rooms, twisted and unnatural shapes dominating the space. Old furniture and metal was repurposed into architectural shapes, or visions that didn't look as though they could hold their own balance. And yet they stood on the floor, with real people walking around them, peering at them. *How can such unreal objects exist in the real world?* Each one held my gaze. I wanted to know about the people who could imagine these strange visions. What did they think these were? What did they want me to see in them? What visions could I see, and how could I share them with the world?

Talia walked back over to me with a glass of wine. I hadn't even noticed that she had moved off to the bar, so entranced had I been by the art all around us. I took the glass subconsciously, and sipped at the wine within. The lights in the gallery were beginning to flare around the edges, a rainbow halo in my vision. I put a hand on my diaphragm as my heartburn flared.

"Do you see what I see?" I asked.

"What is it that you see?" smiled Talia, taking her own sip.

"They are all so unusual. They fascinate me." I turned to look at my friend and felt overwhelmed by the size of her eyes.

"I see it," she said, looking back at me.

"Talia, you *are* here! George said he'd let you in. You naughty thing, why didn't you come to find me?"

The voice that cut through the hubbub of the gallery belonged to a tall skinny man with a mop of black curls, wearing a close cut floral shirt and tight bell bottom jeans. I would have sworn that he had stepped directly out of the seventies, weird thick moustache and all.

"Frederick, darling!" Talia held out her arms as though she was going to hug him, but instead they each kept their arms out as they kissed the air near each other's cheeks.

"Who is this that you've brought along?" He asked as he stepped back from Talia. He looked me up and down and then smiled. Apparently I measured up to his standards, and I didn't know whether I should be offended by that idea or not.

"This is my friend Pene, I've known her forever and she is amazing! You'll love her. This is the first proper night out she's had in years!"

"Years! Mercy, have you been locked in a fairy tale tower!" he asked me.

"No," I laughed. "My husband and I have a young daughter and it's just difficult to get out."

"Difficult you say, and yet your husband is away hiking all weekend! I think you've been scared of getting out, of finding out what you really want," Talia declared.

I wanted to look away from Talia's gaze, but I felt like that would be giving in to something, and so I kept my gaze firm. She smirked and turned back to Frederick.

"Now, what is this piece that you are so determined to show me?"

"You have to see it!" Frederick's eyes sparkled. "I've been trying out some traditional veristic stuff, and it's so much fun. Come, come!"

He led us through packed hallways and alcoves, past people wearing black leather and buckles, long rainbow-patterned form-less coverings, and everything in between. Smiles and laughter followed our passage, and I wondered if they were judging me as I passed.

I tried to avoid looking at anyone else as we walked. I tried to focus on the conversation between Talia and her friend, but they had moved on to discuss people who they were inspired by, or perhaps they were just exchanging gossip about the artists that they knew in common. In any case, my wine diffused mind quickly lost focus on their conversation and I glanced into a particularly dark alcove just as we went by.

Inside this space I couldn't see any artworks. The wall was lined with dark curtains, and a few deep purple fluorescent lights outlined their edges. Shadowed figures were in that room, moving slowly around one another. That purple light revealed the curve of a hip, or reflected off long straight hair. Limbs moved into the shadows, and heads leaned in over dark forms that slunk around one another. I realised that I had stopped, with one hand on my stomach, and the other at my mouth, one finger tracing along my lower lip.

I gasped as a hand touched my shoulder.

"What are you looking... Oh I see! You getting into performance art now are you?" Talia stepped closer and squeezed me in a hug around my shoulders.

"Performance art?"

"Yeah, this group like to do this sensual, dangerous thing." She bobbed her head from side to side, looking a little like a snake as she did. "I can never remember what they call themselves. Empathy? Emphasis? Something like that?"

"Yes, something like that," said Frederick from the other side of her. His face was twisted in disgust. "Please let us move on, I find this group distasteful."

As we walked away I licked my lips and asked him why.

"They just have nothing else to say. It's always darkness and teeth and slow-moving naked bodies." He shook his head and scratched at his moustache. "And I've heard that they are always trying to recruit others, and convince them to invest in the troupe. Sounds like a scam if you ask me!"

He whisked us around a corner and then spun on the soles of his feet, swinging an arm out to direct us to his destination.

"In here!"

The room that Frederick had led us to was lit with a calm white light, maybe a little dimmer than regular daylight, but not by much. After the gloom of the previous rooms, it was blinding. We were much further from the music now, and the thump and buzz through the walls was muted. The artworks here looked like old traditional pieces, portraits and landscapes.

"I didn't think that this was the kind of gallery to include these sort of paintings," I said.

"I know," gushed Frederick. "It's such a twist!"

We walked around the walls, admiring the paintings that were displayed. Most were about as wide as my arms outstretched, and almost as tall. The figures in the paintings were lovingly detailed, their minute eyes and lips given excruciating detail. *How long must it have taken to create these,* I wondered as I leaned in closer to examine the surface of the paintings. Tiny flicks of the paintbrush gave life to fingers that gestured with the delicate accuracy of fairies. Some of the paintings held larger figures, often gods or monsters or heroes. In one, a minotaur towered over an armoured man who was shielding a woman who gathered gossamer strands of string around herself.

"These are stunning," I said. Frederick nodded his head.

"It is nice to see something a bit different to the rest of the gallery isn't it? I feel like it really demonstrates the breadth of skill the artists here possess."

I coughed to try and settle the burn from the wine in my stomach and then asked "Do all the artists do a piece in this style?"

"No, but most of the artists have a piece in this area of the exhibition. It was an invitation from the gallery owner, to see if we could find inspiration in some restrictions."

I looked at another landscape, a sweeping bay, with large headlands overlooking an untamed shoreline, a long canoe being paddled across the waves in the middle. The view was so carefully detailed that I could recognise the beach immediately. I had been there for family Christmases for years while I grew up, though it must have been nearly a decade since I had visited it. The artist had done a fantastic job of imagining the trees and birds that would have thrived around the bay, before the seawall had been built to one side, and apartments grew up on the other.

I took a step back, about to find Fredrick and ask where his own piece was displayed in this area, and walked into someone.

"Oh god, I'm so sorry," I blurted out, clutching at the thin stem of the wine glass in my hand and trying to cup my other around it to catch the drops that sloshed up it's sides.

"It's no problem, you didn't get me with the wine," said a cheerful sunny voice that slid into my ears like warm honey, spreading warmth down my neck and across my shoulders. I felt my cheeks begin to flush even before I looked up to see who it was that I had walked into.

The woman standing close to me was possibly one of the most stunning people I had ever seen. It was hard to determine what made such an impression on me, what feature was drawing my breath from my lungs. Her hair was dark and long, pulled forward and twisted into a rope that fell over her shoulder and all the way down to her slim hips. Her eyes were large and creased in the corner with a smile that was open and inviting. There was no smirk, no judgement in that face, simply curiosity about me.

"I really am sorry," I managed to splutter.

"And it really is no problem," emphasised the woman. "My name is Kallista. What's yours?"

"Pene," I replied, then licked my lips and sipped at the remains of my wine. *Is my hand shaking? Oh god, I need to get a hold of myself!*

"It's lovely to meet you Pene," said Kallista, holding forward her own wine glass to toast me. I lifted mine until it clinked against hers, watching the thick red wine in her glass roll around the sides in response. "Are you enjoying the art?"

"What art?"

Kallista laughed, with one hand wrapped across her stomach and supporting the other holding her glass.

"Oh, obviously, um-"

"Hello Kallistsa." Frederick seemed to appear out of nowhere at my side. Talia walked up behind him, a strange look on her face. She looked confused and somehow sad, but I wasn't sure why.

"Hello Frederick!" Kallista's eyes and mouth widened as she saw my host. Then she grinned and tilted her head to look up through narrowed eyes at him. "What have you been hiding from me?"

"Absolutely nothing Kallista." Frederick wasn't smiling, or angry, or upset. His face was as still as stone. I wondered what was the problem he had with this woman. Now that she had turned to address him I noticed she was wearing a floor length backless dress the colour of a thick forest. It was so dark that it was almost totally black but the green glowed through, as though from beneath the surface, like a light beneath deep ocean water.

Talia stepped closer to me and tucked her arm through my elbow.

"Come on," she said quietly into my ear.

"Alright," I replied softly, confused. I spoke louder as I said my goodbyes to the new woman.

"Perhaps I'll see you again another time Kallista?"

"Indeed, that sounds delightful," smiled Kallista. "Here." She pulled a white rectangle of cardboard out of a small purse hanging by her side. "This might help that happen." She passed it over to me.

I took it and glanced over it before I tucked it away. It had her name and phone number on it, but not a lot else. "You're a mortgage broker?" I asked.

"Amongst other things." Kallista winked at Frederick and

then leaned forward to kiss him on one cheek. "Lovely to see you Fredrick. Don't be a stranger now!"

And with that, she slipped off through the crowd, her hips swaying like a serpent.

"Why were you acting so weird?" I asked as Talia and Fredrick bustled me further into the exhibit.

"Oh, Kallista is..." Frederick waved his hands in circles as though the movement could conjure the right words from the ether directly into his mind. "Well, you saw the performance artists?"

"You think she's a scam artist?" I looked across the crowded space, trying to find her again. *How can they say that about her, she seemed so friendly and happy? I can't believe that she's some sort of scam artist.* There was no sign of the dark green dress.

"I mean, she comes across as a really nice person," said Talia with a serious expression. "But I've known friends who have got involved in her circles and..." She trailed off, grimacing.

"What is it that you both are having trouble saying out loud?"

Frederick sighed. "She ruins people's lives Pene. They end up with very few possessions, and often with no relationships left from before they became part of her circle."

"Why is she here?"

"She is a creative person, and anyone can pay the entry fee." Talia squeezed my arm. "And us artistic types can be inspired to take part in some silly things if we're not careful."

"Like the Empathy performance artists," I realised.

"Yeah, I guess. Now, come on. Let's see what it is Frederick made and then we can go and get another drink."

It turned out that his work was one of the sculptures sitting in the middle of a room, not a painting at all. He had carved a strange little figure out of white stone. It was barely three feet tall, and it's entire lower half looked like an animal. It's legs were covered in tufts of thick fur, and I was surprised to find broad hooves at the bottom of its reverse-kneed legs. Above the waistline of fur, a stout pot belly stuck out, as round as a balloon. It's arms were as chubby as toddlers arms. The stone was carved to resemble thick flesh and reminded me of Tilly's arms when she had just learned how to walk.

The strange boy was holding a set of small tubes in one hand, near its face. That face was split by a gigantic grin, and thick hair that curled down from it's crown and around two tightly coiled horns on either side of it's head, like a ram's. It was incredible how real the figure looked. If it wasn't made of white stone I would not have been surprised if it had started dancing and playing music right there in the middle of us.

"That's awesome Frederick," breathed Talia. "What an achievement. The way the skin around the hands is creased." She shook her head and whistled. "I'm in awe."

"Thank you darling, I am quite happy with how it turned out. It's a Pan, one of the ancient mythological creatures of the forest, dancing and playing music."

After admiring the statue in closer detail for a few minutes, we agreed that it was time to top up our drinks and turned to leave, whereupon I nearly walked into someone else.

"Pene! How much have you drunk, you lush!" shrieked Talia in delight.

"Oh my goodness, I'm sorry," I yelped as I tried to dart backwards.

"No problem," murmured the person. This time it was a woman a few inches shorter than me, wearing heavy black velvet. She was larger than Kallista, and wore bright red glasses beneath long black hair that curled slightly where the ends sat on her shoulders. She nodded at me and then moved past us, her hand on the arm of a tall man with a huge chest and long wavy hair of his own. He wore torn jeans and faded work boots. As he passed, he nodded at us as well.

Talia looked at me and shrugged, and then motioned that we could leave. As we did, I could overhear the woman speaking to her companion.

"Look Peyton, it's a satyr. But all the danger has been stripped away from it."

I glanced back, and then gasped. The stone figure was staring straight at me, a scowl twisting it's features. It was like an imp now, a small creature glaring at me between the figures that clustered in the concrete rooms. I blinked and grabbed Talia, ready to point to the creature, but as soon as I touched her and turned back, I saw it was back in it's dancing position, smiling into the world. *What was that? I was sure that it was looking at me.* I swallowed heavily, which made my stomach roll. *I think I've drunk too much.* My mouth felt sticky as I pushed my tongue through it, and my neck felt tight. I pinched the bridge of my nose. *Way too much. I should slow down.*

CHAPTER TWO

I managed to convince Talia to get me a soft drink at the bar, though she made no attempt to hide her disappointment. We spent the rest of the evening walking from one small group of artists to the next, enquiring about their pieces. Talia expounded on her own ideas, though none of them were suitable for this gallery, as she worked with large rainbow coloured murals on the sides of buildings most of the time. After an hour or two, I reached over to touch her shoulder. I was feeling like a young child lost in the woods, shadows all around me and eyes reflecting the moonlight as they watched me. It was like all these people were dangerous animals, hiding behind the trunks and in the leaves. Talia brought a hand up to touch my fingers as she turned away from her conversation.

"I'm really sorry to be a nuisance," I said in a low voice, trying not to let her friends overhear me. "But I'm getting tired and I think I'm just going to go home." My feet were aching, wedged into heels much higher than I would usually wear, and my temples were beginning to throb. I was sure that I had drunken far too much wine. My heartburn was bubbling like a pit of lava in my stomach. To make things worse, I was worried that I was beginning to sober up and the hangover was already beginning to send nails into my skull. Talia sighed.

"Babe, I'm sorry. I thought you'd like meeting all these people."

"I have!" I nodded to emphasise my point. "It's just that I'm not used to being out so late these days, and..." I let my voice trail off. I was afraid that I might say something that insulted the gallery and the artists, though all I was trying to say was that I was tired.

"Look, we'll get you home as soon as you want. But the burlesque is going to start really soon, and that will be a hell of a show! Why don't you come and find a seat, so that you can rest those lovely legs of yours, and we'll call a taxi after the show?"

I considered the idea, genuinely weighing up the idea of just bowing out of the evening now. But Talia looked so excited, and the idea of getting to see some burlesque performers did sound enticing. She had often told me about the sensual shows that she had seen, and I had always wanted to be there to see one.

"Alright. Let's watch the show."

"Eeee!" squealed Talia, and she leaned in to kiss my cheek. Within a moment she had said her farewells to the group she had been speaking with and we had moved through the gallery to one of its largest rooms.

The walls were still covered in a medley of jagged artworks and bold colour, but there were far fewer sculptures in this room. Rows of simple plastic chairs had been lined up either length of the room, and were already beginning to fill with people clutching their drinks and heads bowed together in conversation. Talia led me over to a pair of seats in the second row.

"Shouldn't we sit in the front?" I asked.

"I mean, we could," shrugged Talia. "But I've seen some of these performers before, and there's every chance that the front row are going to regret their seating choice before long."

We chatted briefly about some of the artists that Talia had been talking to. I got her to explain how she knew them, and tried to get her to explain what they were working on, but very few actually seemed to be making paintings or sculptures. Most of them were more interested in video pieces, or performances that interrupted everyday life outside a gallery.

Over her shoulder I saw the woman with the long braid and the slim green dress come swaying into the room. Again, I was struck by her, by the way her eyes seemed to take in everything, by the way she seemed ready to smile at everything. Talia clicked her fingers in front of my face and I shook my head, surprised.

"What are you-?" she murmured as she turned to see what was behind her. "Oh, Kallista." She turned back to me with a frown bending her brow. "Pene, what's with you. You're not usually like this."

"I don't know what you mean," I lied. Truly, I was just as confused as Talia. I could tell that this woman had formed some sort of immediate hold over me, but I liked men. In fact, I liked one man, my husband. The thought of Otis, off in the hills and bush somewhere, probably with aching legs and a grumbling stomach, while I sat in this room with wine and beautiful women wandering past made me feel guilty. The acid in my stomach bubbled and I grimaced. *I'm not used to having so much wine, it's gone to my head.*

Talia sighed heavily. She didn't believe me, but what else could she say? Behind her, Kallista caught my eye and smiled. She lifted her hand slightly in a wave and then kept walking along the seats, ending up at the far end of the room. *That's probably for the best,* I thought, though I couldn't suppress a flash of disappointment.

As I watched Kallista strolling to her eventual seat, I saw a ray of light flash red as it passed through some distinctive glasses, only a bit further along the row of seats on our side of the room. It was the other woman I had nearly walked into. She was sitting next to the man she had been with, her head leaning against his shoulder, and his arm around hers. They looked comfortable.

. . .

THE LIGHTS LOWERED. The music faded. For a long second we all sat in shadow and silence, then someone in a bright gold jacket and top hat came storming out between the seats, clutching a microphone to their face. Their makeup was thick and a red beard bristled from their chin, but beneath the jacket they were wearing bright red underwear over fish-net stockings, and their hips were extremely shapely.

"Welcome to our gallery everyone, are you having a wonderful night?"

The crowd cheered in response.

"That's what I like to hear! Now, usually I would do you a bit of a song and dance, maybe crack a few quips, just to show you all that I can. But tonight, I think we all want to see the show, am I right!"

There was a mixed response this time. Some of the crowd cheered that, yes, they would quite like to get on with the show, while there was also a noticeable "aw" of disappointment.

"Is that my fan I hear grumbling in the audience?" asked the presenter, lifting a hand up to cup around their ear as if they could barely hear. They bowed deeply and then smiled as they stood. "Never fear! If you all treat the performers well, I've got something planned as a bit of reward at the end. You do know how to treat performers well, don't you?"

The crowd cheered again, louder than before. A few whoops and whistles burst out of the noise.

"Yes, exactly! With that, let's bring out Candy Berry!"

The presenter rushed off as a woman dressed in a gigantic red and white dress made of lollies and sweets came out. She had blue hair and bright red lips, and her eyes sparkled as she bobbed her hips and twirled between the rows of our seats. Her smile was infectious and I began grinning. People in the seats around us were clapping in time with the poppy music. I was entranced by the way her hips shifted as she danced, and by the broad smile on her face. She looked so happy to be performing and it made me feel happier just to see her.

As the music continued, Candy started removing one item of sugar themed clothing at a time. I began sitting forward on my seat as her licorice belt was unbuckled and pulled around her waist and then dropped to the floor beside her. After that, her lollipop bra followed, and then her creme skirts were slowly discarded until she was almost naked. She stood in just a set of bright blue garters and underwear, spinning red and white sequined tassels on her breasts and held candyfloss in either hand over her head.

I felt warmth in my cheeks, and my pulse was pounding. The curve of her breasts being lifted by her outstretched arms looked soft and inviting. I desperately want to reach out and run my fingers across the smooth skin of her stomach and hips and thighs. But then she bowed to us, gathered up her clothes and skipped away off the stage. I leaned back in my chair, chewing on my lower lip. *What's come over me,* I wondered as I tried to catch my breath. *I shouldn't get so drunk, it's making me feel all messed up. We should go soon.*

Before I could say anything to Talia, the next act came out. This time it was a pair of men dressed in cowboy hats, leather chaps, and all the accoutrements one might expect of an old school western. They had on dark jeans, white shirts, six-shooters that I assumed must be fake, all of it. They began miming along to voices in a pre-recorded scene that had clearly been taken from one of those old movies, or perhaps even chopped together from multiple sources. The lines had their characters start arguing, the two performers flinging off jackets and shirts as they prepared to fight, and then "accidentally" tearing away each other's pants as they tussled. Again I began sitting forward, feeling a pleasing warmth spreading through my shoulders and face. These men were lithe, with defined muscles in their legs and arms and stomachs. Watching them lay hands on each other, their fingers pressing into each other's skin, was getting me excited all over again.

Eventually the two were standing between the two sections of seats that faced each other, wearing only their chaps, a small black g-string each, their gun belts, and hats. They stood, muscles tense and glistening, hands poised over their pistols. I was staring at the ass of the man nearest our seats. It looked perky and ripe, and I just wanted to reach out and run a finger-nail down it. I bit my lip.

A clock began tolling, and when it reached twelve, the two drew, a toy cap went off in one gun, and the other man threw himself to the ground. The winner flexed his muscles like the winner he was, and for one moment I wanted to be standing there next to him, letting him know that I thought he was an incredible champion, my arms wrapped around his strong waist. Then, they bowed and left as well.

"Are you having a good time?"

After the cowboys had left, the presenter stormed back on stage waving their arms in the air to generate even more cheers and whistles. After the noise died down, they gave a short speech about the gallery, thanking the owners and some artists by name. They managed to make a few good jokes, but wrapped things up before anyone grew too bored.

"Alright, I said I had something special for you prepared, in case you treated our performers well. I think you have treated them exceptionally well, so, let's bring out Monday and Terry!"

As the presenter swept out this time, two other people walked in. One was a young man wearing a black and white hori-zontally-striped shirt beneath a leather vest, and an eye patch. The woman wore a large triangular hat, a floral skirt, and a woolen shirt over the top. They were both carrying swords. Together, they reached the center of the room, turned to us, and bowed. Then they stood, turned to the seats on the other side of the room, and bowed again. After they stood now, they lifted their swords and took up fencing positions. They lunged together and started yelling something into the air as they smashed their swords at one another.

I listened for a while over the clash of the swords.

"Is that... Shakespeare?" I muttered.

"I think so. Hamlet?" answered Talia.

And then one of them swiped at the other, and some sort of special effect must have been used, because red liquid began spraying out from a fake wound and over the front rows. I leaned back and shrieked, and I wasn't the only one.

"Oh shit!"

I knew it wasn't a real wound, or real blood, because the sword had actually not come within two feet of the person on stage. That, and the way the liquid sprayed out in an absolute sheet of red, raining down meters away, in a non-stop curtain.

The two continued their fight, resulting in two more fountains of fake blood erupting over us in the audience, and then one falling to their knees in death. The crowd around me was shrieking in laughter, cheering and some also just shrieking as red liquid dripped off their nose or chin.

"What on earth is this?" I asked Talia.

"You don't recognise it?" Talia grinned at me and nudged me with her elbow. "They just did the duel from the Addams Family movie! That was so good!"

I watched as the couple stood, bowed to both seats again, and then calmly walked out, leaving puddles of red water all across the floor. Members of the crew had already started pushing the liquid aside with mops and were throwing down sand or something similar as grit on the floor. The crowd was whooping and cheers rang in the small space. The presenter in the gold jacket came back out and lifted their arms in the sky.

"Did I tell you or what!?" they yelled.

I THOUGHT that the show was going to continue with other acts, but the late hour coupled with the fact that I had stopped drinking meant that I simply couldn't keep my head up any longer. I was finding it harder and harder to stay focused, although the men and women that were performing were all beautiful in one way or another. I blinked and let my head fall on Talia's shoulder. She leaned her cheek on the top of my head.

"Shhhh," she whispered, wrapping an arm around my shoulders and she lifted her hand to push the hair out of my face. "It's nearly time to go home."

I grunted happily and tried to keep my eyes open.

Together we made our way out of the gallery, leaning heavily against one another. As we wove among the crowd, I was unable to make out any individual face or figure. I couldn't focus properly, as though even my eyes were too tired. Faces stared out of the shadows towards me, and bodies waved like wheat in a field. I tucked my face into Talia's shoulder. I noticed a square of white light in front of me and groaned as it blinded me. It was the screen of her phone. I tried to wave it away, but she just laughed and pulled the phone out of my reach. She was calling a taxi, or texting, or using an app, or doing something that was far too complicated for me to process right now anyway. I staggered along next to her, trying to follow a narrow path between treacherous roots.

We were outside, and the cold night air made my cheeks tingle. I was able to stand up straight, breathing in deeply and feeling refreshed by the cold air in my lungs. *When did we get out here,* I wondered. I turned to look behind us. The door to the gallery was dim, and silhouettes were outlined by the lights that flashed against it. *I don't remember coming through that door at all.* It was a pleasure to feel my thoughts moving more normally in my mind though.

"I'm feeling better already."

"Glad to hear it! Still, we'll get you home soon." Talia took my hand and squeezed my fingers. She didn't let go.

The car arrived and we tumbled into the back seat, giggling as we tried to find our seatbelts. The driver had already started the car moving, and so we were thrown from side to side a little as we got the belts sorted. Talia fell against me, her head on my chest, and I felt a flash of warmth run through me. I looked down on her, as she moved her face off my breasts and turned to look up at me. Her eyes were large, and her lips so red.

The car lurched around a corner and she was pulled back to her side of the car. I laughed and then pushed my fingers through my hair to pull it away from my eyes, and she laughed too.

The ride back to my house took longer than I thought the ride out to the gallery had taken. *That's what happens when you drink too much,* I told myself. *Now you're exhausted and running out of energy, and the ride is much less interesting. You'll be lucky if you just don't fall asleep!*

It was like I was psychic. I was already losing the fight to keep my eyelids open.

I was floating in a sea of molten stone. It pressed against me, and it was dark and light all at once. All sound was muffled beyond it, except the slow slap and thump of the sea shifting around my body. It's heat sank through my skin, my cheeks, my ears, my fingertips, and suffused my flesh with a quiet fire. The liquid stone shoved me, slowly, shifting my position. My breath was coming shorter now, quicker, and the heat was entering my core. I felt a pressure that was going to build until I exploded.

Cool air blew on my face, and the sea receded. I gasped and opened my eyes, sitting up from where I lay, on Talia's lap. I looked around us. She was looking down on me, having just opened the taxi door.

"We're home babe," she whispered.

"Mmmm," I grumbled, sitting up and rubbing my eyes. It was hard to think properly. I still felt so warm. I blinked and managed to undo my seatbelt as Talia paid for the ride, and then clambered out and stood on the footpath while the car drove off. Talia came up beside me and slid her arm around my waist.

"Come on, you need to get to bed."

We walked up to my front door. I could feel every inch of her arm on my back and side, I could feel each of her individual fingers and where they were placed on me.

I dug my keys out of my tiny purse and pushed the door open. I turned to thank Talia, but my head kept swaying and whatever I said, it mustn't have come out as sensible words, because Talia laughed gently and then followed me inside. She guided me through the kitchen, down the hall, and into my bedroom. My skin was beginning to feel as though it was burning, pinpoints of fire from her fingertips on the back of my arm. I collapsed onto the bed and rolled over. Talia stood above me.

"I'll be back in just a second. You should probably take your dress off and get under the covers." Her voice was rough. I watched her leave and groaned as she left the room. Darkness washed over me again.

A body moved on the bed next to me and I reached out towards it. I opened my eyes and it was Talia, back again.

"You left? But you're here?"

"I brought you this." She lifted up a plastic mixing bowl that she must have found in my kitchen. "Just in case."

I reached out to her shoulder. Her face was so close to mine, lying next to me on the bed. "Thank you."

I looked at her face, so near, her lips slightly apart. I lifted my head off it's pillow, towards her. Then I thought of Otis, asleep in his hut far away, legs aching from his hike. I shook my head and pulled away. Talia jerked her head away from me.

"I should go," she whispered. I nodded as I sank bank onto the covers.

The last thing I heard of her before sleep dragged me down was a quiet voice saying "Goodnight babe." A cacophony of dream and memory rose up like a twisting cloud around me and I sank inside it.

CHAPTER THREE

In my unsettled sleep, I dreamed memories of the week that had been, of my life that had been interrupted by a night out with my best friend. A life that had been functioning perfectly well, though very predictably.

The last week had passed in an interminable blur. Somehow each day had felt exactly the same as the one before it, stretching out forever, and yet they had passed frighteningly quickly. I would wake in the morning and then wake up my daughter Tilly so that she could start getting dressed for Primary School. The same arguments would arise, she would declare that she didn't know where her shoes were, and then we would turn the house upside down before finding them tucked behind the shoe shelf near the front door, like always.

Otis would help, by making me a cup of tea and a bowl of porridge, and toast for Tilly. He usually put together a lunchbox for her too, which meant that I was the one who had to try and tame her hair into a ponytail while she either cried that I was hurting her or declared that she wanted a triple inter-woven braid. I never had time to do a triple inter-woven braid.

Then she would claim she had already cleaned her teeth and I would ask to smell the minty toothpaste on her breath. She would breathe at me, leaving me gagging, as she had never actually brushed her teeth. So we would march to the bathroom and I would have to supervise her brushing to ensure that it actually occurred.

Otis had left by the time I walked past my now cold mug of tea and bundled Tilly into the car, ready to take to school.

A noise roused me and I groaned and then rolled over, pulling my duvet tighter around my shoulders.

SOMETIMES OTIS WOULD TELL me that he wished he could spend more time at home, like I did, because he thought he could use the break. He was a nice man, and I loved him, so I only ever rolled my eyes when he said such things, instead of kicking him in the shin.

After dropping off Tilly and exchanging domestic stories with the other parents who clustered by the school gates, I would arrive home in time to unload the dishwasher, stack it again, bring in the last load of laundry so that there was room to hang out the next load, so that the machine was empty and I could fill it with the next one.

Each day had different chores, but I couldn't tell which I did when. One day was all about paying off the power and water and internet bills, amongst others. Another day involved me cleaning all the windows and trying to fix Tilly's torn uniform.

Eventually I would return to school to pick Tilly up and exchange more fascinating stories with the other parents while we waited for the children to be released. One day of the week, I think it might have been Wednesday, Tilly had an after school Gymnastics class, so I would drive her to the large warehouse that had been filled with padded gymnastics equipment and sit in the small office drinking slightly oily cups of tea while the children shrieked and tumbled around the mats and boxes.

I rolled over in my bed and pulled my pillow over my head, relishing the cool material on my hot skin.

• • •

AFTER A LONG TIME hiding in the warm sanctuary of my bed, I found my dreams slowed down enough that the memories they were replaying no longer ran inside each other, and I could remember what had happened over the last few days more clearly.

"Are you sure you don't want to come with me Pene?" Otis asked as he pulled a handful of clothes out of the drawers in our bedroom and piled them on top of the bed. I shook my head and laughed.

"You mean come out into the cold nights and muddy trails around the bush? No thanks! And even if I did, It's too late now, isn't it?"

"I mean, sort of." He shrugged then smiled. Those green eyes lit up the room as they sparkled over his grin and I had to smile back at him. "But we could give it a go. Maybe I could smuggle you into the huts in my backpack?" The backpack in question sat on the floor next to the bed, a large grey rucksack covered with pouches and zips.

"Might be a slight squeeze getting me in there," I snorted and then left him sorting out what he was going to wear on his trip. My husband was treating himself to a two night hike with some guys he had known since he was in school. It was going to involve walking for hours through the bush to a small wooden hut where he would have to eat pre-cooked meals and suffer a complete lack of showers, before doing the same the next day. And then, after all that, he would have to hike back out to the cars so he could come home. I walked down the hall to the kitchen. The idea of setting out in the wild, with no real idea what was going to happen, it just made me shiver. *Nope, there is no way I want any part of that, it sounds dreadful! I'm not changing my mind now!*

"How's he going?" asked our friend Talia. She was sitting at the kitchen counter on a tall stool. She held a glass of pale yellow wine in one hand. In the lounge beyond, my six year old daughter Tilly was watching cartoons as she finished off a bowl of instant spaghetti and mushy meatballs for dinner.

"He's doing fine," I grinned. "Still trying to convince me to go along. Like I want to put myself through that!"

Talia laughed, and the way she smiled was like a painting. "No, you're definitely better off staying here with me babe," she agreed. She lifted the wine bottle and shook it in my direction. "Have a glass of wine with me?"

"Thank you, but I won't tonight." I placed a hand on my stomach. "I've been getting heartburn, and the alcohol just makes it worse."

"Your loss," sighed Talia as she topped up her glass. "So, what are we going to do this weekend? There's a gallery opening tomorrow night that would be amazing! John and Sveta and Elodie are all putting out some new pieces and they've hired some burlesque performers that will take your breath away. Frederick said he was expecting me."

"You think that I'd be that impressed by the performances, do you?"

"I know that I was, last time I saw Elodie perform!" Talia fanned herself with her hand and made a whooping noise. Otis came into the kitchen and leaned against the counter.

"Saw who perform?" he asked, reaching over to pick up a cracker from a plate on the counter. Half a round wheel of camembert was left on the plate, next to some cherry tomatoes and basil leaves. "And why are we all in here when we could be enjoying the evening from the deck?"

"I considered taking my wine out there, but the boards are so warped that the chairs keep wobbling." Talia frowned. "Sorry to say."

Otis nodded. "Yeah, it's getting pretty bad." He shrugged the deck aside for now. "Who were you talking about watching?"

"Burlesque performers," smiled Talia, proffering the wine

bottle to him as well. "I'm trying to convince Pene to come with me to an art gallery event tomorrow night."

Otis waved aside the wine. "That sounds like a great idea Pene. You're always saying that you don't get out and meet people much anymore."

"What? I do not!" I considered my recent weekends and how much time I spent putting Tilly to bed and then watching TV shows about forensic teams solving crimes. "Hmmm, maybe I do need to get out."

"See!" grinned Talia. "Apparently 'you're always saying!'"

"I guess so," I had to admit ruefully. "But an event like that will be full of artsy types, with weird visions and ideas." I pursed my lips. "I haven't done anything that interesting in years."

"Suddenly you have a problem with artsy types," said Talia, pretending to be offended.

"Oh shush you. You know I love you. Besides, what would I do with Tilly?"

"Leave her with my parents," said Otis, covering his mouth to avoid spilling cracker crumbs across the counter. "That was what I said we should do if you had decided to come on the hike, remember?"

I did remember, and the thought made my shoulders slump. Every time that I had to deal with Otis' parents Annika and Larry, my heartburn got worse. Somehow, even when they were trying to be helpful or supportive, they always managed to say something judgemental. It was as though they were automatically disappointed by my existence. I had to fight to convince them that I wasn't as bad a wife and parent as they thought I was. I certainly didn't like dropping Tilly off with them for any length of time, both to avoid dealing with them myself, and because of how they might influence her young mind.

Talia noticed my expression and giggled. "Oh Otis, you know your wife has issues with your parents." She reached over to him and pushed his shoulder. "Stop causing trouble!"

He shook his head and patted Talia's hand, but then spoke

directly to me. "Babe, I know that you find them difficult sometimes, but if it got you a night out wouldn't that be worth it?"

I took a deep breath. "I think I'd be much happier just spending the weekend with my daughter actually."

"Alright," he nodded, with raised eyebrows and frowning lips. "Whatever will make you happy."

Talia reached across the counter and held my hand.

After dinner we put Tilly to bed and hugged Talia goodbye at the door. Alone with each other for the first time that day, Otis and I made our way into the bedroom. I moved to go straight to our small ensuite, but Otis grabbed my arm before I could get far. The movement made me turn back to face him, just inside the doorway to our room. He reached out and put his arms around my waist, pulling me close.

"I'm about to go away for a few nights," he murmured as he drew closer and lowered his lips to my neck.

"Oh yes?" I put my arms around his shoulders, enjoying the familiar way his fingers pressed into my sides. "Is that why I can't go to brush my teeth, is it?"

Otis lifted his face off my collarbone and rolled his eyes at me. "Your breath is fine!" And to prove it, he pressed his lips against mine and kissed me. I smiled under his embrace and returned the kiss, feeling his tongue edging along my lips, returning the movement with my own. I could feel his whole body against mine, and it was beginning to make me feel warm and relaxed.

Together we stumbled back towards our bed, pausing to pull our clothes over our heads and push our jeans to the floor. I lay down on top of the duvet and reached up to turn off the light switch above the headboard. Only a soft orange glow from Tilly's nightlight in the hall illuminated us now, outlining the curves of my body on the bed. I looked up at my husband as he stood naked above me, lit as though by orange flames. His cock stood out from his body, and the spark in his eyes made me bite my lip.

Then he tripped against his backpack as he walked around the bed.

"Dammit," he yelped.

I giggled, and pressed my arm over my breasts. I suddenly felt more exposed than I had moments before. He growled at me and then clambered up from the floor and lay beside me, leaning over the top of me. His arms framed my shoulders and his hip lay against mine, leaving his hardness pressed against my skin.

"Oi, this is supposed to be a very romantic last night before I leave you for a great journey," he said in a deep rumble.

"Oh, you are the most romantic man in the world," I laughed and I reached up to pull his head down to mine, meeting his lips again. He climbed further on top of me, and I opened my legs to him, sighing as I felt his heat slide over my pussy. The heat seemed to transfer from his hardness into me, beginning a core of warmth inside my self that grew and spread through my body. I felt my muscles relax as we kissed and his fingers sought my entrance. They pushed against my lips and I could feel myself open to him.

Then I gasped as he moved up and sheathed inside me, one motion that sent a wave of warmth rushing across my skin. Otis leaned back, looking down on me as he shifted back and forth, slipping in and out of me. I squeezed my legs around him as the warmth built, clutching my fingers into his shoulders. Just as the heat blossomed from my stomach and shot out to my fingers, toes and the tip of my nose, Otis shuddered and groaned.

He relaxed on top of me, exhaling slowly before slipping out of me and rolling over on the bed.

"I will miss you for the next couple of days," he said, as he shifted the duvet and rearranged his legs and body under it's covers.

I leaned over and kissed his shoulder. "I'll miss you too."

. . .

AFTER OTIS LEFT in the morning, I sat in the kitchen with a mug of tea, enjoying the way the liquid warmed me from the stomach out. My phone buzzed on the counter next to me. I picked it up and smiled when I saw that it was a text message from Talia.

im not taking no for an answer leave tilly at the In Laws!

I smirked as I tapped out my reply to her.

I would prefer not. we will just watch a movie and have a pizza

my head is killing me. How could you let me drink so much? You owe me

I had to laugh. *How was it my fault what you were drinking? You were the one who stopped by our house with a bottle of wine, we didn't even suggest it to you! Besides, what did you get up to after you left our house?* I thought of Talia, and where she would be right now. I could picture her lying in her bed with her eyes closed as she tried to ignore her hangover and prepare for another night out. I felt nerves squirm in my stomach. *I suppose I could use a night to let my hair down,* I considered.

Alright I'll see if they are free

:D xoxoxox !!!

I had to laugh at the string of symbols that Talia sent me. I could just imagine her grinning and squealing in her bed. The image made me smile.

"Come on Tilly!" I called out as I turned around on the stool. She looked up from her bowl of chocolate cereal at the dining table behind me. "How would you like to stay with Grammy and Gramps tonight?"

She squealed in delight at the idea. *I guess that makes that decision easier,* I thought. The rest of the day passed quickly. Tilly and I cleaned up the house and hung out some washing. We coloured in together for an hour, listening to her favourite pop songs. Then I helped her pack a bag with some clothes and pajamas and books, ready to visit with her grandparents. As I drove along the road towards their house, I had to ask myself where the day had gone. *Didn't I just make this decision five minutes ago?*

As we drove up Otis' parents house I felt my throat tighten. However, I managed to settle my nerves by the time we pulled into the driveway and climbed out of the car. I stood in front of their home, a two story townhouse shaped like giant concrete lego pieces glued together. A single bush, manicured into a sphere not much taller than Tilly, stood in it's perfectly circular ceramic pot by the letterbox.

"Are you sure you don't mind staying here tonight sweetheart?" I asked, trying not to move my mouth too much as we walked. I couldn't bear the idea of Annika watching me from behind a twitched aside curtain. She would assume I was trying to poison her granddaughter against her, I was sure of it.

"I like spending time with Grammy and Gramps. They let me stay up late."

I groaned and rolled my eyes, but squeezed her hand in mine.

"If you don't feel good, you make sure you ask to call me. I'll come and pick you up, no worries. Remember, you're my number one!"

"Okay monkey mumma."

I smiled at my little sweetheart and then lifted my hands high and started making ook ook noises as I chased her along the rest of the path to the front door. She shrieked in delight as she ran.

Annika swung the door open before we had even come halfway up the grey and white speckled concrete steps.

"Hello darling," she said. As she always did, she spoke with her mouth curved up at either side, in a manner that some might have mistaken for a smile, but her eyes remained slack and unfeeling. I wondered if her pretence worked on other people. She reached a hand out and gathered Tilly in by her side.

"So why aren't you able to take care of your daughter tonight?" she asked me, never once looking down at Tilly.

I gritted my teeth and forced myself to smile.

"My friend Talia has asked me to come to an art gallery opening with her actually. It should be really fun."

"Oh yes, I imagine it would be fun. Don't worry Tilly," she said, now turning and crouching slightly, placing a hand on each of Tilly's shoulders. That strange smile appeared on her face again. "We'll try to find a way for you to have fun, while your mum gets to go gallivanting around an art gallery!"

"Thanks Annika," I said, forcing the words out from my stiff cheeks.

"We'll see you tomorrow darling. Bright and early, yes?" Annika's eyes were large and dark.

"Certainly, of course you will." I shifted my attention to Tilly. "I love you sweetheart! See you in the morning."

My daughter grinned at me and then Annika was pulling her inside and swinging the door shut. I stood alone on the steps for a moment, trying to sort my thoughts, and then I snorted, turned, and stalked back to the car. *She didn't even say goodbye, or ask me in for a cup of tea, or anything.* I slammed the door shut and started the car. *Screw her. I'm going to go and have a proper grown up night out for a change!*

By the time I got home, Talia was sitting at the kitchen bench with a glass of wine in her hand. The sight made me jump as I walked into my house.

"How did you do that?" I exclaimed. *Did I leave the door unlocked? I could swear I just unlocked it as I came in?* I looked at the keys, still in my hand. Talia giggled.

"I still know where the spare key is, and I locked the door after me. I'm a responsible house guest after all!" She brushed her tightly coiled hair back over her shoulder. She was wearing a black dress that clung to her body beneath thin straps over her shoulders. Her skin looked creamy smooth. "Now, are you going to join me in a glass and get ready to come out?"

I looked at the wine in her glass as she swirled it slightly. It was as golden as sunlight and sparkled in the setting sun's light that peeked through from the lounge. Something about the sight made me wary.

"I don't know if I need a drink just now. I did tell Tilly that I would come back and pick her up if I had to." A small voice in the back of my head wondered if I had said that to make her feel better, or to give me a way to bail out on the evening for myself. *I can't do that to Talia though! No, I made that promise for Tilly.*

Talia pursed her lips. "Fine! But come on, let's find you something stunning to wear. You're going to meet so many interesting people tonight!"

Talia gathered me into my room and started pulling dresses out of my wardrobe, flinging them onto my bed. Each one was accompanied by murmured commentary. "Yes, that will show off your boobs well... That one is so slinky... Oooo, we could put your hair up with this, your neck would be on display then." The pile grew larger and larger.

"Um, I think that's enough options isn't it?"

Talia turned back to look. There was a multi-coloured mound on the bed now, so big that it looked as though someone else was lying there. "I suppose it's a good starting place. Alright, try one on for me." She flung herself down on the bed next to the mound and lifted her wineglass to her lips. Her eyes watched me over the lip of the glass.

"Are you just going to lie there?" I asked. I crossed my arms over my stomach and pursed my lips.

"That is absolutely my plan, yes," she grinned and bounced herself on the bed a little.

"Ugh," I sighed. Then I turned my back to her and took off my clothes, leaving my bra and underwear on. I reached out backwards, surprised at how self conscious I was in front of my friend. *It's not like she hasn't seen me get changed before*, I thought to myself. *Why is it different now that she is laying on my bed with a wine? It's so quiet in here.* One of the dresses found its way into my outstretched hand.

"Thanks."

"Oh, it is definitely my pleasure."

The first dress I tried on was one I hadn't worn in years, not since before I had had Tilly. I pulled at it's panels and seams, trying to get it to sit correctly on my hips and stomach, but I couldn't make myself feel quite right. I glanced over at the mirror and grimaced. *Look at the way it bunches up! This is terrible.*

"This is no good, I can't fit it any more."

"You fill that dress exactly the right way!" exclaimed Talia. She looked me up and down as I pressed my hands across myself, trying to hide behind them. "But if you aren't comfortable, I'm sure one of these others will do." She shoved her hand into the pile and pulled out something blue from deep beneath its surface.

After a few more dresses, and many more frowns from me, I ended up with a long dark skirt given texture through an embroidered floral pattern, and a top that looked somewhat like a corset, but only in style. It didn't actually constrict me and so I was okay to wear it and yet I could also breathe.

"Look at you now! Hair and make up next!" Talia licked her lips and raised an eyebrow. "And a wine?"

I looked at myself in the mirror, turning my head from side to side to get different views of myself. I put my hands on my hips. Talia stepped up behind me and slung a hand around my shoulder.

"You look stunning babe."

"Oh go on then," I said. "Let's have a wine!"

CHAPTER FOUR

aking up on Sunday morning after the night at the gallery took a long time. The memories of the last week were still flooding my head, and it was hard to recall what had happened during my night out with Talia. I showered, and spent much longer than normal allowing the hot water to sluice through my hair and run down my body. My head was not sore, a fact that made me immensely grateful, but it felt as fragile as an eggshell. If I moved too quickly, I knew that it could shatter.

I dressed and reluctantly went to face Annika again while I picked up Tilly. My mother-in-law had begun to interrogate me about what I was doing to keep her son happy and taken care of, and I only managed to extricate myself from that situation by agreeing to bring the family to her house for dinner on Tuesday.

Then I got to spend the rest of the day with my daughter. We had done some gardening, planting some basil and broccoli and cherry tomatoes in our small garden in the backyard. I had examined the deck as we had walked by it. *Those planks are definitely too old,* I told myself. *We do need to fix that.*

By the evening I sat waiting for Otis. The sunset was stunning outside, and I wished that I could go and enjoy the pink and orange view as I cleaned the kitchen after making dinner.

Instead, I kept scrubbing the pots and setting them to dry on the rack by the sink, watching the colour slowly fade on the walls. After cleaning up, I sat at our dining table next to the kitchen bench, and looked out the broad window above it at the stars beginning to pepper the sky overhead. I picked up a cup of tea in a heavy green mug and sipped at it. The drink spread through my mouth and down my throat, creating a pleasingly warm space in my stomach. Having a warm core made me feel more comfortable.

It was getting late, but I didn't want to go to bed without my husband. The house just hadn't felt as comfortable without Otis' presence. I felt intimately aware that Talia was the last other adult that had been in the house.

The door rattled, switching my attention from the stars to the world closer by. The door swung open and Otis stepped in. My heart leapt and I smiled. His cheeks were stubbly and his hair had that 'I haven't been washed in too long' sheen. He hauled in his hiking pack with him and rolled it onto the floor next to the door, crouching down to unlace his heavy boots.

"Welcome home sweetheart," I said, taking another sip of my tea. "How was it?"

"Amazing, you should have seen it!" Otis looked up at me, his eyes glowing bright. "The hills fell away in these long swooping rolls, and from the ridgeline you could see the ocean glittering. It was totally amazing."

He stood up and walked over to where I was sitting, reaching out to put his hands on my shoulders, and leaning down to kiss me. My nose wrinkled a little at his smell, as it wasn't particularly fresh, but I was so happy to have him home that I just accepted it. I returned the peck and then pushed him back with a smile.

"It sounds gorgeous. Did you take some photos?"

"I did, but I really wish that you would come along with me. It's not the same, seeing it on a flat little electronic square instead of with your own eyes."

I shook my head. "It just isn't going to work that way yet. Maybe another time."

Otis ran a hand through his hair and grimaced. "Eurgh. I'm going to go and have a shower. Maybe you could join me? It's been a long few days since I've been able to hold you in my arms." He reached out for me again. This time I did push him back.

"Stop it!" I finished the last mouthful of my tea and stood up, taking the mug around the kitchen bench to put it in the sink. "I'm already clean and ready for bed. I'll see you when you get there."

He smirked and nodded then followed me through the short hallway to our bedroom. While I pulled back the duvet on our bed and crawled between the soft inviting sheets, Otis continued into our personal bathroom. I heard the shower begin to run as I lay with my eyes closed. Just as sleep crept around me, I felt Otis climbing into bed behind me, wrapping his arms around my shoulders as sleep wrapped my mind and pulled me down.

IN THE MORNING Otis woke up early and prepared some breakfast for himself and Tilly. Tilly munched on the toast he put on her plate, one slice covered in a thick layer of crunchy peanut butter, the other smeared with marmite. She chewed and watched animated animals chasing each other around a strangely two dimensional landscape on the tablet that was propped up in front of her on the low coffee table in the lounge.

I stumbled out into the kitchen blinking the sleep out of my eyes and rubbing my hand through the tangle of my hair. Otis rushed over and handed me a cup of tea, steam spiralling from the dark brown surface of the liquid. He leaned in to give me a quick peck on my lips, so quickly that I was only just beginning to pucker my lips after he had already planted the kiss and moved on.

"Good morning sweetheart, here you go. I'm going to have to

head out pretty much straight away, I heard on the radio that there was an accident on Kauri Road, so things are going to be pretty backed up."

He grabbed his work satchel off the dining table and stuffed a plastic container of leftovers from the fridge under his arm. "Oh, and while I was away I was talking with Timothy, and we thought that it would be a good idea to take out a loan and renovate the deck. Let's talk more tonight."

And with that, he scurried out the door. It banged shut, leaving me standing with my tea in a silent kitchen. Tinkling music bubbled out of the lounge.

I guess I'll catch up with him tonight, I told myself as I started collecting Tilly's school things from around the house. My tea grew cold on the kitchen bench as I pulled her uniform out of the drawers, and found her schoolbag. It wasn't hanging on the hook in her room where it should be but bundled into a corner of the garage where she must have flung it as soon as she jumped out of the car last week.

Once she was dressed and ready, I kept drinking my tea, lukewarm though it was. I kept half an eye on the time as I flicked down my social media feeds on my phone. One of my cousins had shared a series of videos featuring people falling off bikes and skateboards. *One I might have understood, but seven? Far out Ellie, that's a lot of laughing at people in pain.* I switched off the screen and hustled Tilly into the car, ignoring her complaint that she hadn't finished the latest episode of whatever cartoon nonsense it had been.

"You can finish it after school, now come on."

As I buckled myself in and glanced in the rearview mirror to see if Tilly had followed my instructions, a white van drove past the driveway. It had a ladder strapped to the top, and a peeling magnetic sign stuck to the side. The sign was some sort of pun involving building and construction. The man driving the van was sitting high in his seat. Something about his expression caught my attention. He was staring ahead of himself. His gaze seemed focused, narrow, as though nothing existed in his world. His skin was dark and tough from working out in the weather, and his hair was gathered into thick dreadlocks that were bundled behind his head. I could see the muscles in his arms shift as he turned the steering wheel, and I felt my pulse quicken. Then he turned sharply and looked out of the mirror at me with intense blue eyes. I gasped, but then the van had driven on and I couldn't see him any more.

"Are you ready to go?" I asked Tilly, watching the van continue down the street. I pressed one hand to my chest, trying to calm my heartbeat. *Where did that come from? What is happening to me at the moment?*

"Yes mum, let's go."

I dropped Tilly off at school, only stepping out of the car long enough to pull open the door for her to hop out and let me give her a big hug before she strode off into the school. A breeze rustled the hair on my neck and I shivered, then turned. The streets around the school were lined with trees and hedges, their leaves rustling in the gentle wind. Rooftops peered over the top, and small children in red uniforms were walking along the footpaths. Nothing seemed out of place. I couldn't see anything unusual, but I felt as though something was watching me.

I stood there, trying to figure out what was causing the uneasy feeling on the back of my head. Shrugging, I climbed back into the car and began to drive away. As I glanced into my rearview mirror, I thought I saw a tall dark figure standing by the entrance to the school and looking at me. I slammed my foot on the brakes and focused on the mirror, but there was nothing there

I went home, filling the rest of my day with cleaning, and laundry, and logging in to my university's online learning portal. I watched a lecture from my Business professor and took a look at the readings they wanted me to get through. Try as I might to keep myself occupied, I couldn't concentrate. Memories of Kallista smiling and weaving away through the gallery kept coming to the top of mind, and the feeling of lying in the dark-ness with Talia next to me made my neck prickle. Blue eyes glowed in my memory. I wished Otis had been able to stay awake longer, or had taken the day off. I felt like I needed him here with me.

Thankfully, the afternoon rolled on and I had to go and pick up my daughter from school. I stood outside Tilly's classroom with all the other parents here to pick up their kids. I knew them all reasonably well by now, enough to know their names and some of the big events in their lives. Janine was standing next to me, explaining why her husband James was finding it hard to run his independent accounting business right now. I had to admit, it wasn't the most interesting conversation I'd ever been a part of. *I wonder if this is how Talia feels when Otis and I talk about buying vacuum cleaners and stuff?*

"But it must be such a blessing to be able to do the renova-tions in your bathroom Janine?"

Thank you Trudy. Janine hadn't explained the exact dimensions of her new vanity to us yet today, and we all know that a build up of that level will simply lead the average woman to burst.

I sighed and smiled and looked over Janine's shoulder. The sun was high and the sky was blue. Why wasn't I happier about it? *Oh god,* I thought. *Otis and I spent a lot of Friday night talking about fixing the deck. Talia must have been bored out of her mind!*

The bell rang and my smile became genuine. The shrieks of the children as they came swarming out of the rooms like ants from an upturned nest were like the finest music to my ears. *Here comes Tilly!*

"Mummy mummy mummy, you'll never guess what we did today!" my daughter shouted as she careened across the concrete, constantly on the edge of tumbling. She leaped into my outstretched arms and nearly tipped me over backwards. Without pausing, she clambered up to my shoulders, sending me further off balance with her gigantic school bag. Finally, with her face millimetres from my own, she stared into my eyes with her own giant serious brown irises. "We made butterflies," she declared.

"That sounds glorious," I laughed. I helped her down and took her by the hand. "Tell me all about it."

As we walked away, waving at the other mums and children, Tilly did. She expounded in great detail the life cycle of a butterfly, wrinkling up her face at the gross part. "Did you know that caterpillars all melt away when they are in a cocoon? Isn't that disgusting," she spoke with relish.

"I didn't!"

The afternoon passed slowly. Tilly wanted to help make dinner, which involved pulling all the pots and pans out of the cupboard and dropping them on the floor, and tipping half a jar of flour into a mixing bowl.

"Come on sweetheart, do you have to do that?"

"Yes, I'm making cake!"

My temples throbbed but I squeezed my eyes and continued. "Why don't you go and do something else? Do you have some homework? Your room probably needs cleaning?"

"Can I watch TV?"

"Sure, why not?" It was easier than trying to clean up the rest of this mess while she just made more. Tilly rushed off to the lounge and switched on the TV while I started piling the pots back into their cupboard. At first I tried to put them back into order, with the largest bowl at the bottom, and the ceramics to one side. I rammed the last bowls back in and hoped that they wouldn't crash to the floor when I next opened the cupboard. In the meantime, there was a load of laundry on the line out the back of the house, and if I didn't have it in soon then I wouldn't have time to iron Otis' shirt's before I had to get started on dinner. One long deep breath and then I heaved myself off the tiles and headed out to get on with the next chores.

I was still standing over the ironing board, lost in clouds of steam and the intermittent hiss of the iron discharging when Otis got home.

"Hi ladies!" he called out from the door, shrugging off his suit jacket and stepping out of his work shoes.

"Daddy!" screamed Tilly as she burst off the floor in front of the TV and darted out of the lounge and across the kitchen to the front door. Otis pulled her up into a huge hug, laughing as he did. I smiled at the sight. *Where did the girl get these reserves of energy?* It was barely six in the evening and I was as exhausted as if I had been lugging sacks of rocks all day. I put the iron to the side and switched it off.

"Hey babe," I said as I walked up to Otis and planted a kiss on his cheek. "How was your day?"

"Oh, pretty usual," he said. He put Tilly down and walked over to the fridge, pulling out a green bottle of beer and popping the top quickly. He sucked down a mouthful and then gasped happily. "All the better for having come home to a lovely welcome and a beer though!"

And then he was off to the lounge, pulling out his phone. Tilly skipped ahead of him, sinking back onto the carpet and allowing the red cats in her cartoon to shout at her once more. I picked up the iron and switched it back on.

"What would you like for dinner," I called as I continued getting the creases on his collars sharp.

"I don't mind," he replied.

Steam belched from the iron and lifted around my face, leaving tiny wet drops on my face.

MY SHOULDERS ACHED as I gathered the ironing and hung it all in our bedroom closet, folding the pants over the horizontal wooden bars on the hangers. A twist to the left, with my hands on the closet door frame, and I felt my spine click and settle into a new position, relieving some of the tension that had developed in it over the day. I reached up to squeeze the back of my neck.

"Will dinner be far?"

I snorted and felt my brow frown. "Um, excuse me?"

"I was just wondering," asked Otis from the lounge. "I've finished my beer and I was thinking I might start looking up builders and mortgage brokers to see if we can extend the mortgage to cover getting a new deck. I'll be in the office, alright?"

"I guess so." I came down the hall and stood in the lounge, with my hands on my hips. Tilly was still lying on her tummy on the carpet, her head propped up and staring at a crab wearing exercise gear on screen. Otis was laying back in his chair, with a smile on his face.

"You didn't think that maybe I could use a beer?" I asked.

"Sure?" Otis looked confused. "You could have a beer if you want? They're in the fridge, right?" He stood up out of the chair and began to walk out of the lounge past me. I remained where I was standing. Otis paused and looked at me with a curious shake of his head.

"I'm about to make you dinner, you know?" I asked him.

"Yes," he nodded. His eyes slipped left and right, as though looking for more information. "And that's why I thought I'd go start making plans for the deck?"

What is it that he doesn't get here, I wondered. Shaking my head and sighing, I stepped aside and let him go.

Why doesn't he pay attention to me, I asked myself as I chopped carrots with a heavy knife. The blade thunked into the wood of the chopping board. *He didn't really ask about my day at all. He didn't offer me a beer. Am I just like those other boring mums, caught up in my husband's life? Are bloody deck renovations the most exciting thing that I have to look forward to?*

I couldn't help but remember how Talia's breath had felt as she lay on the bed next to me in the darkness. My cheeks began to flush and my stomach tightened. I returned to the carrots, chopping them faster and harder.

After dinner came bathtime for Tilly while Otis played some games on the X-Box. I sat down on the couch, curling my legs up beneath myself and huddling into the large hoodie I was wearing. My phone became a gateway to another world, a world that looked bright and warm and entertaining. My old school friend Rachel was posting photos from a recent holiday in Bali. Warm beaches, tropical jungles, and her skinny tanned bikini body smiled out at me as I scrolled down and down the stream.

We had been so similar at school. We were inseparable, always at the beaches at the same times, taking the same classes. We'd even kissed most of the same boys during weekend house parties, at the same time more than once. And now, she was living a life that seemed so far away from my own. *How does that even happen?*

"Hey babe, Tilly's done with her bath."

"What?" I glanced up from the phone to see Tilly dripping all over the carpet, naked and wet from her bath, carrying a towel in her arms. Otis' lips were pursed tightly together as he twisted the controller in his hands, focusing on the character on the TV screen.

"I guess I'll take her to get her pajamas on and go to bed then?"

"Cheers babe," murmured Otis without looking at me.

Tilly kissed him on the cheek and said "Good night dad!" before I led her back through the hall to her room.

Posters of fairies and elves covered the walls. I dressed Tilly quickly in a pink fluffy set of pajamas. Toilet and teeth, then a Mr Men story, and Tilly's eyes drifted shut and her soft snores began to rise in the dark room.

I lay on her small bed and stared at the dark ceiling. *What have I achieved today?* I felt tired already and I just wanted to crawl into bed myself. But that felt like a total surrender, a failure to use my time for myself. *Now what?*

Back in the lounge, Otis was still playing his game.

"Hey sweetheart, Tilly's asleep. What do you want to do tonight?"

"What do you mean?"

"Shall we watch a movie together or something?"

"Oh." Otis twitched the controller as he paused the game,

then looked at me. "Yeah, we could watch something. What were you thinking?"

I smiled and sat down on the couch next to him.

"I saw this new series on Netflix, maybe we could watch that before we go to bed."

"Sure."

And so we did, spending an hour watching a TV series about a group of young mothers who all had dysfunctional relationships with their partners and their young children. Otis wedged himself into the corner of our couch, and I nuzzled into the gap beneath his shoulder. It felt nice to have his arm draped across my shoulders, his fingers grazing my collarbone. *Yes, this is what I've been needing all day.*

As we watched the show I laughed a lot, but Otis didn't seem to find it as funny as I did. When it finished, he gently pushed against me so that he could get up.

"What did you think?" I asked as I stood up and stretched as well.

Otis waggled his hand and tilted his head left and right. "It was fine I guess. Most of the characters were kinda annoying though."

"What do you mean?" I switched off the lights in the lounge and followed him down the hall to the bedroom. He was already taking off his work clothes and so I began pulling off my hoodie and leggings.

"I don't know. I guess I just didn't find it funny that they were so horrible to their families."

I lay down on the bed with my hands together on my diaphragm. "I suppose they were." The mattress squeaked as Otis crawled over next to me, one hand reaching over to run fingers across my belly.

"I think it was meant to be so outrageous that you laugh at it," I said as his fingers slowly twirled around my belly button and began to trace down towards my legs.

"Yeah, maybe that was the point," said Otis. He began to

press his fingers through the hair between my legs, softly moving closer and closer. My breath began to get faster. His fingers felt warm on my skin.

He leaned down to where I lay and kissed my lips as he continued to rub his finger up and down. I reached out to him, searching down his stomach towards his cock, sliding my hand along it where it lay hardening on his thigh. The skin was smooth and warm, and as I wrapped my hand around it I could feel it grow firmer.

"Are you ready?" he asked.

"Sure," I said, widening my legs. He rolled over and rested his elbows to either side of my head, his hot hardness just outside of me. I could feel his cock bend as he began to slide inside. I winced a little as one of my lips was caught and pulled, but a quick adjustment and we were ready to continue.

Otis leaned down and kissed me again, then smiled. He began to thrust, bucking his hips back and forward. I felt my breasts bouncing and winced again, until I grabbed them with my hands so that I could try and hold them still. Otis' eyes were closed and I could see that he was mouthing some words as he moved, though I couldn't figure out what they were.

Otis' belly pressed down on me and I felt him filling me up. I wondered whether he would mind if I kept watching the TV series without him. Otis grunted and stiffened, and I squeezed my legs against his sides as he came inside me. The warmth spread out beneath my belly. Otis sniffed and widened his eyes as he pulled himself out of me and rolled over.

"Phew, that was a good one." He grinned and reached over to pat my stomach. I could feel the remaining warmth of him begin to seep out of me and I reached under my pillow to pull out an old tee shirt that I normally slept in. Before the duvet got stained, I tucked the tee shirt under my bottom.

Otis stood up and pulled on a bright blue pair of boxer shorts with Garfield on. He blew me a kiss, then headed off to the ensuite. Moments later I heard the tap running and a scrubbing sound as he brushed his teeth.

After he had cleaned up and returned to the bedroom, I took my turn to prepare for bed. I had to pull out a fresh tee shirt from my drawers. By the time I had pulled it over my head, Otis had turned out the lights.

"Are you asleep yet sweetheart?" I asked as I lifted the duvet and shuffled my legs down into the warm space beneath. Soft snores were all I received in reply. I chuckled and slid my arms around Otis as I snuggled into bed.

"Good night sweetheart."

CHAPTER FIVE

The next morning Otis was up and dressed for work early, still chewing on a slice of toast as he called out to remind me that I had agreed to go over to his parents for dinner that night, before he swung out the door and drove off. Tilly was hooked on the same cartoon as usual, and complained about having to put on her uniform for school, but I got her strapped into the car on time.

After I dropped her at school I went to visit my great-aunt in the retirement home. She was beginning to lose her memory, the poor dear, and so I spent a lot of time reminding her who I was and sipping on a cup of tea. Then I went to pick up some food parcels and used kids' clothes that were being passed on to mums in need in my community, then I went to drop off the parcels.

As I drove through my errands, I thought about Otis' idea to renovate the deck outside. *It's probably a good idea really,* I decided. *We should talk to someone about getting money together for it.*

Pulling into my street I noticed that the house a few doors down from ours had some scaffolding and framing up around the garage. *I wonder what they're doing to the place,* I thought, and I slowed down as I drove past. Standing under the structure, one hand grasping the pole over his head as he leaned against his arm and spoke into his small black cellphone, was the man I had seen in the white van yesterday. He had to be one of the most attractive men I had ever seen.

His face was long, rugged, but with extremely soft blue eyes that were staring at the sky. His hair was a mess, a tangle of long thick brown dreadlocks, tied loosely together into a tail by one of the dreadlocks. His job meant he was wearing heavy dusty workboots, shockingly small shorts that exposed his long and toned legs, and a basketball vest. His skin was darkened from the sun, and his muscles were compact and defined. I felt my mouth go dry and then shivered. It took effort to stop looking at this man and to guide my car back into my own driveway.

As I got out of the car I could see over its roof, along the footpath, to the house. The builder had his back to me now, but I could see he was carrying some sort of bulky equipment. The set of his shoulders told me that it was heavy. There was a loud bang and the tool did something to the side of the house. I wished I was close enough to watch the muscles in his shoulder tense and shift as he handled it.

My cheeks felt warm as I gathered the groceries inside. I put them on the kitchen bench and then leaned against the counter. The benchtop felt cool beneath my hands, and for a moment I wanted to lie my face on it, to try and cool down my skin. But, as I leaned against it, I found that the pressure from it's corner was just pushing back against the ache between my legs and I wanted to relieve the pressure immediately.

I stepped quickly through the hall and into my bedroom, slipping my hand down the front of my pants, my fingers searching out my clit as quickly as I could. I collapsed onto the bed face down, pressing my fingers against myself, and I tried to loosen my clothing with my other hand. The builder filled my thoughts, pushing out all other sensations. All I could see were those blue eyes. All I could hear were of my own gasping breaths. All I could feel was my skin tingling where I imagined his rough hands might hold me.

With my eyes closed, I felt as though I was completely hidden from the world, somewhere private and safe and quiet, like a shadowy grove, deep in the forest, tucked away from paths and tracks and wanderers. A breeze tickled my collarbone as I imagined the dappled sunlight that would trace over me, the look in his eyes as he leaned over me.

I pressed harder, biting my lip and panting. I spun over on to my back, arching as I tried to explode myself. My stomach tensed, my legs pulled up. Finally, the build up between my legs reached a crescendo and I felt a wave of blue sensation wash down my body. I slid my hand back out of my pants, rubbing my wet fingers together and looking around for somewhere to dry them. Eventually I just wiped them on the side of my shirt.

Where did that come from? I stared at the ceiling of my bedroom. *My husband's bedroom,* I reminded myself. With that thought, I felt a small knot of guilt in my stomach. *I'm a married woman, I shouldn't be thinking of other men like that! I need to talk to him properly about Talia too.* I imagined the builder's thighs again, the strong line between his sun-darkened skin and the paler flesh beneath. My hand began to creep down my stomach again.

No! I pulled my hand back and clasped it to my other. *I need to find something else to fill my time.*

With distraction as my new goal, I hung out a load of laundry on the clotheslines and washed the dishes, cursing the broken dishwashing machine. Then, finally, I sat down on the couch with another cup of tea and turned on the mothers TV series again.

It was so good to laugh! I found myself drawn in to the petty upsets and over-wrought dramas of the characters in the show, whooping as they yelled at members of the public who had crossed them, and cackling when their children broke priceless heirlooms. *Why doesn't Otis see how hilarious this is!*

By the time the episode finished, I glanced up at the clock on the wall. Nearly time to pick up Tilly again. I sighed. *I guess that's all the time I get today.*

Waiting outside the classroom at Tilly's school, I felt a little uneasy. It was as though all the other parents around me could see the way I was feeling, the heat and tightness between my legs that kept me shifting my stance and pressing my thighs together, as though I could smother the flame and put it to rest. I thought my session on the bed would have dealt with the issue, but all I wanted to do was go home and do it all over again. I wondered what the builder's dreadlocks would feel like, dangling down from his head over me, brushing along my naked skin.

I coughed and shook my head, shifting my weight from one leg to the other. I was here to pick up my daughter!

The school bell rang and children came bursting out of their rooms, shrieking and squawking like a flock of seagulls that had found a loaf of bread. The sight made me smile. But Tilly wasn't one of the first out like usual. As the other children leaped into the waiting arms of their mothers and fathers, I walked closer to the classroom, wondering where she might be.

When Tilly emerged, she was engaged in a deep discussion with a young boy with long messy hair. The two of them looked as serious as professors, and they were making short, contained gestures with their fingers at one another. The sight made me laugh.

"Hello my little number one! Who's this?" I asked as the two approached. My daughter lifted her eyes to me and blinked, as though surprised to see me there.

"Oh! This is Percy!"

The boy shook his hair out of his eyes as he looked at me. He smiled a little, softly and shyly, like a baby rabbit.

"Hi Percy! Are you guys in the same class?"

"Yup!" said Tilly.

"How come I haven't seen you before?" I asked Percy, trying to entice some words from him too.

"I just moved here," he murmured.

"He just moved here," repeated Tilly, in a voice like bubbles. "He used to live somewhere else, but he just moved here and now he comes to our school, and Mrs Cantlon said that I should be his buddy and show him around the school, and do you know something mummy, he is so so clever! He knows all about dinosaurs and birds and fish!" She beamed.

"Wow, that does sound very clever! Welcome to the school Percy, I'm sure you will be very happy to be here."

"Can he come over to our house for a playdate please mum?"

"Oh, sweetheart, we have to meet his parents first. They would get worried if they didn't know where he is, wouldn't they?"

"My mum's just over there," murmured Percy, and he pointed behind me.

Mum turned out to be a short woman about my own age, wearing a long black dress and lots of rings and silver necklaces. She had red glasses on and her black hair fell in small waves around her shoulders. She seemed extremely familiar. As we walked towards her, I felt my throat clench. *This is the other woman I nearly ran into at the gallery on the weekend!* I was sure of it. Her build, her hair, those red glasses. I had nearly bowled her over near Frederick's statue. *Oh crap, I hope she doesn't recognise me,* I thought. I pursed my lips. *Or that she at least forgives me.*

"Hi there," I said, stepping closer and holding out a hand. She smiled and took it in her soft hand and shook gently.

"Hello. My name is Tara. Was that your little girl I heard talking to Percy?"

"Yes, my name is Pene, and this is Tilly." I felt relief spread down my shoulders. *She doesn't seem to recognise me at all!*

"It's lovely to meet you Tilly." The woman crouched down so that her face was level with the children. "And did I hear you say that you wanted Percy to play at your house?"

"Yes please!"

Tara's mouth turned down in a sad face, but her eyes still seemed glad. "It's so kind of you to ask, but we have some appointments this afternoon and I need Percy with me. Maybe we can arrange a playdate for another time?"

"Yes please." Tilly leaned forward and placed one hand on Tara's knee, and I had to cover my mouth as I giggled at the sight. Tara smiled again and stood up to face me.

"I am sorry that we can't do anything today. It would be lovely to make some new friends in the area. I sometimes get stuck at home in the evenings and wonder what I should do with myself!"

"How about we trade numbers," I offered. "Then these two can arrange a day soon."

"Sounds lovely," agreed Tara and so we each handed over our phone to the other and typed in our numbers.

"I look forward to hearing from you," said Tara as she took Percy's hand and began walking out of the school.

"You too!" *That went well. It would be nice to have some more friends for Tilly.*

I took Tilly home and sat down to do her reading homework with her. As she worked her way through the book, pointing at the words and sounding out each letter, I found my thoughts drifting. I would look out the window of the lounge and see the wooden fence around the backyard. The grain would make me think of the builder's dreadlocks and my cheeks grew warm again. I refocused on my daughter, encouraging her to try each word. The sun was shining down from a clear blue sky and the colour made me think of the flash of blue I caught from the builder's eyes, making me shift in my seat. I hadn't managed to see whether he was still working on the house down the road as we pulled into the driveway. I found myself thinking of quiet glades again, wondering how sheltered our backyard would be.

"Good girl Tilly, you did so well!" I said as she finished the book. Tilly clambered down from her perch and tucked the book back into her school bag.

"Can I go watch the TV now?" she asked.

"I suppose so," I said. As she ran over to the coffee table, I shifted my thighs backwards and forwards, sighing at the slippery feeling that was growing. How was I supposed to deal with this? My daughter was sitting only a few feet away from me. Could I take the time in my bedroom? Or would she come and interrupt me. The thought of Tilly walking in on me in my bedroom while I was touching myself made me groan. I couldn't risk it.

So, instead, I sat on a stool by the kitchen counter and started swiping through social media feeds on my phone. Jokes and selfies slipped past on the screen, but my attention was on the heat that still begged for my attention.

I tried sending a text to Tara, in case that might help distract me.

Hi Tara Pene here. Would you like Percy to come to our house tomorrow?

I stared at my phone, willing a response to come as soon as possible.

"Hello girls!" Otis' voice burst from the front door as he strode inside.

Oh thank goodness, I thought. I got off the stool and began walking around to my husband, reaching out to him, but Tilly came running in from the lounge and beat me to him. She grabbed her father around his legs, and started telling him about all the fun things she had done in school that day.

"... know that a butterfly comes out of a cocoon, which is what a caterpillar becomes, because caterpillars are actually babies that turn into butterflies and we made some out of toilet rolls and..."

I caught Otis' eyes and ran my bottom lip against my teeth. I could feel the heat in my eyes, and the sensation felt as though it was dripping out across the surface of my skin, craving contact, craving his hands to touch me.

He blinked and patted Tilly on the head. "Hey gorgeous, that all sounds so cool! But I think I need to talk to mummy for a moment, okay? Why don't you go back to the lounge?"

"Okay!" she yelped as she spun and dashed back to the tablet in the other room.

Otis stepped towards me and I leaned into his arms, moaning gently as they surrounded me, his hands pressing into my sides and the small of my back. I felt his chest press against my breasts, his breath on my neck as he leaned in to kiss me.

It was a deep kiss, and I returned it. I drew on him like fresh water in the desert, my fingers catching in the belt loops of his pants and pulling him closer. He pressed forwards, forcing me to step back. I felt overwhelmed by him, and I loved it. His tongue slid along my lips, tickling but enticing. One of his hands shifted back from my side and moved up to cup my breast, squeezing and sending a throb of desire through my body.

"Take me to bed," I whispered.

"Sure!" he growled in reply. The tone of his voice sent a shiver across my scalp. He grabbed my hand and led me to the bedroom, where he spun around to face me, kissing me again. He leaned back to breathe in and then blew out slowly. He had both hands on my shoulders, holding me slightly away from him. "Where has this come from?"

"Shhhh," I said, pressing a finger to his lips. I moved the finger down his chest, slipping it between the buttons in his shirt and running my fingernail through the patch of hair that was underneath. One by one I popped the buttons open, trailing my fingernail over his stomach and ruffling the rougher hair that led below. Now my finger was hooked over his belt, the tip brushing against the black tight coils that I knew were hidden beneath his pants.

I leaned in to kiss him again, then moved my lips lower. I kissed his neck, his collarbone, his chest, pausing to catch his nipple between my teeth. He gasped in surprise and clutched the back of my head, but I kept moving before he could realise what had happened. As I approached his belt, my lips and tongue tracing across his skin, I was unbucking and unzipping his pants. Just as my chin reached them, I was able to pull them down, taking his underwear with them, revealing his cock, standing straight out from his body.

I kissed the base of his shaft, his hair brushing my cheeks, and drew one hand up his legs, scratching his thigh before running my fingernails along his balls. Again, the surprised gasp from above made the heat in my pussy spread through my core and out to my limbs. I drew my tongue up him, then wrapped my lips around the head. My fingers gripped the shaft, slowly moving up and down, squeezing slightly, while my tongue and lips teased more groans and moans from my husband. His fingers pulled through my hair, pulling my head further down on his cock.

"Mummy, daddy? Where are you?"

"Oh shit!" yelped Otis, and he pulled his cock away from me so suddenly that I spluttered. I blinked and fell forward onto my hands, and then looked up as Otis fell over on our bed, tangled in the pants around his ankles. His cock waved in the air for a moment before he tumbled off the other side of the mattress. The door behind me creaked as Tilly pushed it open. I turned and managed to force a smile onto my face.

"Hi sweetheart. What's the matter?"

"I'm getting hungry. What's daddy doing?"

I turned to see, and found that Otis had poked his head over the bed but kept the rest of his body hiding below it. He smiled awkwardly and shifted a little. I assumed he was trying to get dressed while half lying down, without looking at himself. I shook my head.

"Daddy is just getting changed."

"That's silly daddy, you should stand up when you're putting on clothes, or it's too hard."

"Uh... Yeah..." Otis' eyes widened as he nearly fell sideways, but he caught himself. "I just think it's better if I get dressed this way right now sweetheart. How about you go back to the lounge and we'll be there soon?"

"Okay."

Tilly walked out again, leaving our bedroom door wide open.

"Where were we?" I said, rising from the floor and putting my hands to the bottom of my top, ready to lift it over my head.

"We were somewhere really good," said Otis, standing up himself. I frowned as I saw that he had pulled his pants back on already. He began rebuttoning his shirt. "But I don't want Tilly to catch us in the middle of that! What would we say to her? Let's just get on the road to my folks' for dinner."

I felt my mouth drop open. "Really?"

"Yeah, I think that would be best. But my god, your mouth is amazing!" Otis came around the bed and leaned over to peck a kiss on my cheek before heading out the door.

I stood in the middle of the room, a fire raging inside, still tasting him on my lips. *Fucking really?!*

CHAPTER SIX

We gathered Tilly into the car and set off for Otis' parents' house. He drove and I sat in the passenger seat, squirming as the vibrations in the car set me off. I could feel my nipples pressing out against my bra, and it was all I could do to stop myself reaching over and grabbing my husband's cock while he was driving.

At the front door to their house, with my thoughts swirling, Otis reached out for the door handle.

"Shouldn't you knock first?" I asked, placing a hand over his arm to stop him.

"It's my parent's house," he blinked. "Why wouldn't I just go in?"

"You can't just go into someone's house," I explained. Why didn't he understand something so simple? You can't just barge in on people, even if they might be expecting you. There are rules about this sort of thing!

He shrugged, but at least he knocked on the door.

Luckily we weren't waiting long before his mother Annika opened the door.

"My dears, it is so lovely to see you!" she gushed and she

swept forward to hug her son and bent over to grab Tilly's head and give her a kiss on the forehead. "Come in come in come in!"

She spun and rushed off into the house. Otis followed, as did Tilly. I normally would have gone straight in, but this evening I was feeling off balance. Even Annika's facade was making me feel unsettled. I knew that this was how she acted in front of her son, and other people, I had come to expect it of her. She knew the role she was supposed to play for them. I had long ago become used to this treatment. But it stuck in my throat tonight anyway.

I took a breath and turned around to look across the neighbourhood. The stars were beginning to come out in the darkening sky. As I looked down the street, I thought I saw someone walking along the footpath, a tall figure but completely silhouetted. As I turned back to catch a better glimpse of them, I'd lost them completely. The footpath was empty.

"Pene?" called my husband's voice from inside.

"Coming," I answered. I set my shoulders and headed in, shutting the door behind me with a thump.

"So, we hear that you are hoping to renovate that little deck area of yours?" asked Annika as I arrived in the sitting room where the others already were. A fire was crackling in the large black square of the fireplace. Otis had been given a glass of wine already, and his father Larry lifted a bottle in my direction. *Clearly someone's been chatting already.* I raised a hand to refuse the glass, pressing the other to my stomach..

"Thank you, I'd prefer some juice if that's alright."

"No problem," he replied, and moved off to the kitchen to find me some.

"Yes, we have been thinking about it. The planks are beginning to curl and pull out the nails," I told Annika, taking a seat. I tried to ignore her comment about it being a small area. This house had two decks, each much larger than ours, one by the master bedroom upstairs, and the other containing a barbeque, a pizza oven, and a spa pool; all just outside the main lounge.

"Goodness, that's dreadful. With children who could be stubbing their toes and tripping constantly? You must take more care."

I paused and licked my lips. "Thank you. No, we realised that it could be dangerous and that's why we thought that we-"

"I'm so glad to hear that you will fix it. Do you have enough money to do that?"

I glanced at Otis, who was sipping at his wine and playing with some small plastic dolls with Tilly. "I mean, not really, but we had a thought that we might be able to refinance the mortgage so that we can borrow a bit more-"

"Oh my, getting into more debt. Is that wise?"

Again, I had to pause while I caught up with Annika's comments. Just as I began to open my mouth, Larry came back into the room.

"Here you are love, orange juice." He handed me my glass and then went to sit in a large easy chair near the fire.

"Pene was just telling me that she and Otis need to take on a lot more debt," said Annika. I clenched my teeth and tried not to roll my eyes.

"Why would you do that?" asked Larry. "With a young daughter, and you not working, is that really a fair burden to place on Otis?"

I tried to catch Otis' eye, hoping that he would say something about how I worked really hard on the house, or maybe mention that I was working towards my business degree from home, and how it was worth so much to us for me to be available for Tilly but infuriatingly he just kept his head down and the dolls in his hands.

Despite my attempts to explain our position, the conversation pretty much stayed that way, even through the delicious dinner of vietnamese stir fry. In fact, Annika managed to ask me if I had made anything like it recently, and when I said that I hadn't, she actually asked me if I had ever learned to cook. *If there weren't moral codes that said I shouldn't throw my dinner over my mother-in-law you'd be dripping with fish sauce,* I thought to myself, though I found the idea extremely tempting.

On the drive home, I stared out of the car windows at the streetlights regularly passing by. Their dim orange glow washed over me in waves.

"You're quiet tonight," said Otis.

"Oh, really? I'm the quiet one now?"

"What do you mean?"

"I mean, you couldn't have kept your mouth closed better if it had been welded shut."

"What?"

"You didn't think you should step in and defend me from your parents at all?"

"They were just trying to help."

I leaned my forehead on the cool glass of the window next to me and stared out into the night. *If you think that that is how to show that you care about someone, I'm amazed you have any friends left at all,* I thought. I considered talking to him about what had happened after the gallery with Talia. I even considered telling him how I had felt about the builder down the street. But I couldn't bring myself to right then.

I WOKE up the next morning with purpose bubbling in my veins. *You think we live in a shack huh? You think that we aren't taking proper care of our child, by not having a properly upgraded deck, do you? We're going to fix that deck and believe you me, we can afford the loan to do it!*

I sat in the kitchen as Otis whirled through and off to work. As he left I wondered if we would ever get a chance to talk, for me to explain to him that confusing feelings had been swirling in me and that I wasn't sure what it meant. I knew that we needed that time, but I didn't know when we were going to get it. *Tonight,* I decided firmly. *I must speak to him tonight.*

I told Tilly to go put her uniform on and brush her teeth as I pulled my purse along the bench closer to me. Rummaging past bills, notes, and keys I managed to find what I was looking for. A small rectangle of white cardboard, with Kallista's name and contact details on it.

I punched the numbers into my phone and then paused. *Is this really a good idea Pene?* Frederick had a pretty low opinion of this woman, and Talia thought she was really bad news. I stared forward at my purse sitting in front of me, without really seeing it's white shape as I was lost in my own thoughts.

Then, licking my lips, I hit call. A chirpy voice answered after only a couple of rings.

"Hello! Kallista of Echetes Brokers. How can I be of service?"

My throat felt dry, and I had to cough to clear it before I could reply. *I've called her far too early in the day, she's probably barely awake!* "Hello Kallista! My name is Pene."

"Hi Pene," came the cheerful reply. There was a moment of silence. "How can I help you today?"

"Oh!" I blushed and crouched down slightly on my seat. "Um, we met at the art gallery the other night?"

"Wonderful!" Another pause.

I could feel the blush growing up my neck from under my shirt, as I waited too long in silence before replying again.

"Yes, and you mentioned you worked in finance, and my husband and I are thinking of doing some small renovations, and so I thought maybe we should talk to you about if you could help us with that?"

"That sounds great, I would love to come and chat with you about your position and your needs. If you give me your email address I'll send you a checklist of documents that we'll need, and then I can come around this evening if that's alright? Are you both free?"

I blinked. "Um, yes, I suppose we are."

"Excellent! Send me your address and I will come by for a conversation. Would about eight o'clock be okay?"

"Yes, that should be fine."

"Great! See you tonight!"

I hung up and looked down at my phone before tucking it back into my purse. *That woman exudes positivity and confidence, even through a phone call,* I thought.

The morning sun streamed onto my back. *I guess that's happening now.* I took a moment to text her our address, and then sent another text message to Otis, letting him know the plan.

thanks babe that sounds great he replied.

I drew a deep breath. *Yes. I am working towards things we both agreed to. I'm not allowing myself to go heading off in some direction that he doesn't know about.* I decided to make Otis a teriyaki steak for dinner. *It's not because I feel guilty,* I told myself. *I have nothing to feel guilty for. I thought of Kallista because I'd just met her, and it makes sense to talk to her about renovations.*

Just as I was about to tell Tilly to go and get in the car so that I could take her to school, another text message came through.

Hey babe Im free for lunch do you want to catch up?

It was Talia. At first I smiled, but as my thoughts of the weekend caught up with me I stopped smiling. What did she think of everything that had happened? I hadn't even had a chance to talk to Otis. *Still, she has been my friend forever.*

sure Let me know the time and place

I made myself some toast and gathered Tilly into the car, setting off on my day.

TALIA SENT me another text just after I had dropped Tilly at school, telling me to meet her at a café in a nearby gardening centre called Diamond Gardens. It was only twenty minutes away, though the morning traffic made it take a bit longer for me to arrive. Walking in through the gigantic ceramic pots and smelling the earth, fertilizer, and floral perfumes that floated on the air made me feel as though I was searching through ancient overgrown ruins, looking for a lost explorer or a wise mystical hermit. The scents were thick and made me feel light headed.

As I walked through the stacks of plants and tables of seedlings, I was shocked by a goat staring out at me from a collection of broad, low, dark-green shrubs. *Why is there a bloody goat in the shop?* I kicked a foot out at it, to try and scare it off. I half expected it to clatter away from me or, worse, to lunge at me and try to chew on my clothes. When the goat didn't react to my foot, I took a cautious step closer. I reached one hand out to brush its fur. My fingers made contact with a rough concrete surface.

"Holy cow," I said out loud, totally caught off guard. "It's a fake!" I pushed on the concrete statue, tilting it off balance and then allowing it to resettle. It's solid hooves clonked against the broad concrete slab that made the floor. *That is so incredibly life-like. How did they achieve that,* I wondered as I moved further into the rows of leaves.

I pushed aside a broad green leaf bigger than my face and saw the tables and seats of the café revealed beyond it, spread out amongst their own bushes and shrubs. Talia was leaning back on a chair by the nearest table, basking in the sunlight with her eyes covered by huge broad dark sunglasses and her face raised to the sky.

"Hi there," I said as I came over to sit with her.

She lifted her head and turned towards me, grinning as she took in my presence. Her whole face lit up as I walked over. Her skin glowed in the sunlight.

"Hey babe!" she exclaimed. She stood up and walked around the table to give me a huge hug, squeezing me tightly. "How are you recovering?"

"I've had quite a headache, but I'm hanging in there," I snorted and then squeezed her back.

"I bet you have!" She shook her head, as though I was some incorrigible party animal.

"Hey, it's not my fault! I don't go out drinking much anymore, that pain was on you!"

Talia took off her glasses and stared at me with wide innocent eyes. "I'm sure I don't know what you are trying to imply!?"

Laughing, we took our seats around the table. Talia began to talk to me about a new motif in her artworks, taking her spray painted wall murals into a more fluorescent space-whales-hippy sort of image, moving on from the tropical waves and landscapes she had been known for.

"Will the surf wear shops be as keen for you to paint them up like that?" I asked as I sipped on an iced chocolate that was rich and luxurious. "Obviously some of them would be pretty hippy friendly, but there's plenty of chain shops that have a very set image that they want to portray."

Talia waved my question aside and screwed up her nose. "I've done so many of those stores, I think I need to find a better way to make money from my art anyway."

"You could always go back to selling canvases. That was going pretty well for you."

"It was fine," she sighed. "But I enjoy the murals so much more. I get to express much bigger ideas and emotions."

"I do enjoy seeing your ideas spread out across a wall for the world to discover," I had to admit.

"Thanks babe!"

"Actually, I saw a goat statue in the bushes back there that you'd probably love. It's no mural, but it was just an incredible piece of work."

"Really?"

"It was so lifelike, I totally thought it was a real goat wandering through the shop. It reminded me of Frederick's little guy."

Talia laughed, her face glowing.

"I'll show you it when we leave," I said. "The eyes were absolutely stunning. How do you paint concrete and capture that shine, the sort of wetness of an eye?"

Talia tilted her head. "That sounds awesome. I'd love to capture real lifelike eyes in my murals."

I told her that Otis and I were going to meet with someone about getting the money to renovate the deck outside the lounge. Talia opened her eyes wide and mouthed 'thank goodness', but let me keep talking. I made sure to evade her questions about who we were meeting. *There's no point in admitting that I'm meeting someone she thinks is terrible,* I told myself. She giggled and reached over to clutch my hand.

"Listen to you! You sound so settled down and domestic!" She grinned, her teeth flashing.

"Well, yes. We are very settled down." I leaned back a little. *What's wrong with being settled down?* I didn't know what I was going to say about that, or even how I felt. I did know that it was nice to sit and talk with her.

"Oh babe, I don't mean anything bad about it!" Talia leaned closer, bringing her other hand up to join her first, cradling my hand in hers. She squeezed my fingers. "It's just funny to remember our drinking days, staying out til dawn with all sorts of people, dancing to techno in fields surrounded by cows, and then to imagine you renovating a deck in the suburbs." She smiled again, to show it was meant as a light hearted comment, but I was still unsure what to think.

"I mean, I remember those days fondly too. But I met Otis and we are trying to build our life together," I said slowly.

"Totally! And Tilly is wonderful!"

"You're just jealous," I concluded, trying to wrap the topic up with a joke. "You wish you had a place to call your own."

Talia laughed, but her eyes looked tighter than before. "Yes, bunking with hippies and living from a paint streaked suitcase can be exhausting."

"You are at our place often enough, that it almost counts," I said, trying to smooth over any ruffled feathers. "And you know that we love having you around." She smiled.

"I do love coming around to be with your two."

There was a moment of silence as we looked at each other. I coughed and decided to try changing the subject.

"Can you tell me any more gossip about that woman from the gallery? Whose lives has she ruined?"

Talia smirked and dug her phone out of her handbag.

"You know I can! I first met her at that retreat in the Cook Islands I went to about a year ago. Have I showed you the photos?" Talia pulled her phone to her chest and tilted her head backwards. "Oh my god, you have to see them! It was utterly empowering." She sighed, her chest rising and falling beneath her hands. "But that's not the point. That woman was there, and so I got to meet her during the various workshops that were being put on."

"That doesn't sound bad. If she was there for the same reasons as you..."

"I didn't think so either, not for the whole week we were there. Everyone got along so well, and there were massages, and swimming beneath waterfalls, and evenings around the fire on the beach looking for ourselves." She sighed again, closing her eyes in ecstasy. "It really was wonderful."

It was my turn to be jealous. "Yes, yes, you liked your island holiday, but what did Kallista do?"

Talia stuck her tongue out at me before continuing.

"When we got back, we had all connected on such a level that we decided to make a group chat, so that we could all stay in touch. At first, it was fine, and we all kept the same ideas going and it was like the retreat was living on through us.

But then Kallista started mentioning that she already ran a group that explored some of the same ideas that we had been discovering at the retreat."

"Oh, so she does work like that Empathy group? Sucking people into her ideas?"

"I mean sort of. First of all, it was weird, because she hadn't mentioned it at all during the retreat. We were supposed to reveal everything to each other, it was part of building trust and truly connecting. But she didn't tell anyone about the group."

"Maybe she thought that the organisers would think she was trying to steal their ideas?"

"It's still undermining the purpose of the retreat though."

I nodded and sipped the last of my ice chocolate.

"And then, you know, some of the people from the retreat said that they were interested in coming along to her group."

"Did you?"

Talia squirmed on her seat and lowered her eyes.

"I was interested, but luckily I saw what happened to the others and never actually went."

"So what *did* happen?"

"They stopped talking in the group chat. I saw one woman in person, and she seemed happy, but she said that Kallista's group was very personal and she wasn't allowed to discuss it with people outside the group."

"That seems strange." I frowned.

"Exactly, and I heard from the husband of another woman that she had started acting out and spending all their money. He said that he thought they would be getting divorced soon if nothing changed. That was enough to keep me from getting involved."

We sat at our table in silence, letting the sunlight wash over us as I thought about it all.

"She seemed like such a friendly person," I said.

"Yeah, she is lovely to talk to. But there's something strange going on with that woman."

Our conversation dried up a little after that. We hadn't discussed what had happened on my bed on Saturday night, and I decided that I didn't want to. Talia was one of my best friends, and if anything were to happen to these sort of get-togethers then I would be heart-broken. Better to just let things continue as they were.

We got up to leave, and hugged again. Talia made me promise to see her again soon. We walked together for a short distance, because I wanted to show her that goat statue that had scared me under the bushes earlier, but for the life of me I couldn't find it anywhere.

"Maybe someone bought it?" she suggested, and I had to nod and accept that was probably what had happened. She reached over and squeezed my shoulder and then set off for the other exit.

I walked out through the foliage, ducking under the hoses spraying a mist over everything. I felt as though I had been to see an oracle, the mouthpiece of a god, and it had bestowed knowledge upon me. The only problem was, I had no way of knowing whether the knowledge it had given me was of any use to me.

CHAPTER SEVEN

As I drove home, I wondered what was going on with Talia and myself. She hadn't mentioned anything about my bedroom and I had almost begun to think that maybe I had imagined it. Realising just how drunk I had been made me blush, and I rolled down my window so that the fresh air from outside would cool my cheeks. *But I hadn't imagined how happy she had been to see me, or the way she reached out to me so often, had I? Were all of those things the actions of a friend? Am I just reading too much into things?*

I had never considered looking at another woman as any sort of romantic possibility, but the way Talia had been behaving was making me re-evaluate my own feelings. And the way Kallista made me feel. I remembered the way her eyes had shone in the dim gallery when she looked at me, the way the corner of her mouth had risen as she smiled. *Oh god, that's definitely something I haven't felt before.*

But I was a married woman! I loved my husband and we owned a house and we even had a daughter together. I couldn't even begin to contemplate this, it was totally unreasonable. I wasn't the sort of woman to have an affair. *And even if I was as tempted as I'm trying to deny I am,* said a quiet guilty voice in the back of my head, *Otis is a good man and I wouldn't want to hurt him like that.*

I really hadn't realised just how dangerous Kallista seems to be. I indicated around a roundabout, getting closer to home. *It really does sound like she is the eye of a pretty chaotic storm.* I thought about the new information Talila had given over brunch. *Maybe it's not actually Kallista's fault though? I mean, maybe those people had just become busy, or decided to take on new commitments. Things happen, lives change. Is it really fair to blame one woman if someone else makes a decision about how they are going to live their life?*

I pulled into our driveway and left the car outside the garage. I glanced down the street as I walked towards the front door. The large white van was sitting by the curb a few houses down. I bit my lip and felt my blood rush, but I shook my head, pushed open the door and rushed inside.

I closed the door behind me and leaned back, letting the cool wood slow my pulse. I closed my eyes and took a deep breath. *I need to think about something else for a while.*

I sat down in the lounge and pulled my laptop out from it's spot on a small table on the side of the room. I unfolded the screen and logged in, going straight to my online learning portal. I lost myself in the forum for an hour or two, adding comments about our readings, replying to other students who I had never met in person. It was a great distraction and I could feel tension evaporating from my shoulders as I worked. I pulled up a pdf that the professor had told us to read and began typing up some notes about the chapter so that I would remember the key points.

Before I knew it, I glanced down at the corner of the screen and noticed that it was nearly time to go and pick up Tilly from school. I stood up and stretched, twisting my back from one side to the other to loosen muscles that had begun to cramp up from hunching over the laptop for so long.

Now that was a productive day, I told myself. I couldn't help but smile as I put away my computer and gathered up my keys on the way to the door. *It always pays to stay focused on what's really important.* I locked the door behind and turned around. The builder was standing on the footpath in front of his van down the street.

I paused and took in the view. He still looked amazing. I just wanted to walk over and reach out and run my fingers along the curves of his muscles, to press against them and see how strong they were. He was on his phone, looking down at the ground and walking in a slow circle. He lifted his eyes and looked straight at me.

I jumped and started looking around, as though I was trying to spot a bird or someone who had called me. I could feel my cheeks beginning to glow and I hoped that he wasn't able to tell from so far away. I scurried over to the car and unlocked the door, throwing myself in and turning the car on before I'd even managed to sit myself on the seat properly. *Shit,* I thought as I drove away. *I need to get a hold of myself!*

The crowd of parents were all standing outside the classrooms when I arrived. Janine was explaining that getting a loan for a renovation was a long and tortuous process, but luckily her husband was something of a financial wizard and so they should have their finances in order very soon, and then they would be able to continue work on their new bathroom. I snorted but then had to lift my hand to rub my nose, pretending that I had sneezed. Janine had glanced over at me and, although I thought her talk about her renovations was silly, I didn't want to upset her.

"How are you Pene?" asked Trudy. She was still in her skintight athletics gear from whatever exercise she had done that day. As I began to answer, I wondered if she had actually come from a workout or if she was just wearing the clothes. *Oh my gosh, she might just wear that as her regular casual clothes,* I realised. I was impressed and horrified. The leggings outlined every curve of her legs and butt, and I couldn't imagine wearing the same!

"I'm doing well, " I answered. "Actually, Otis and I were thinking of doing some renovations ourselves."

"Really?" said Janine, with raised eyebrows. "What were you thinking of getting done?"

"Our deck in the backyard is getting old and the planks need replacing." I shook my head a little. I didn't want them to think we were doing anything really big, it was really just a little maintenance.

"Good luck sorting out the loans. It's a nightmare, it really is." Janine reached out to clutch my shoulder, as though she could pass her luck to me through body contact.

"Actually, we've got a woman coming to meet us tonight who works arranging this sort of thing. Fingers crossed she can help make it easier."

Janine widened her eyes and then smiled wider. "Of course, fingers crossed!"

Thankfully, the bell rang then and children began swarming out of the classrooms like ants from a nest. Shrieks filled the air and we were surrounded by small children weaving bikes through gaps between people that made me flinch. *Holy crap, watch it,* I thought more than once.

Trailing behind the others in the class came Tilly. She was smiling and had both hands gripped onto the shoulder straps of her bag. She walked straight over to me, took my hand and said "Come on mum, let's go" in a bright voice.

I looked down at her. In all respects I would have said she was in a good mood, but something felt off. I squeezed her tiny hand in my own.

"Are you alright sweetheart?"

"Yeah, I'm fine," she said.

"You know, you can tell me if something's wrong," I added carefully, trying to entice her feelings out of her.

"Yeah. It's just," she began to say and then stopped. I squeezed her hand again. "It's just that Percy said that he didn't like the book I was reading today."

Really? Is that all? I felt a smile begin to stretch into my cheeks and had to rein it in.

"Oh sweetie, it can be tough when your friends don't understand why you like something."

"He said it was babyish."

"Oh love, that's tough." *Shit,* I thought. *I still haven't heard from Tara about having some sort of playdate. How am I going to deal with that?*

"Tilly," I asked slowly. "Would you be sad if we had Percy come over to play?"

"No," she said, turning her serious wee face up to look into my eyes. "I still like him. But we need to work out our differences."

I tried not to laugh as I nodded. "That's very grown up of you sweetie."

Tilly nodded.

I looked back up as we made our way out of the school grounds, moving with the people that were all sweeping out of the gates and pathways. But then I saw someone moving against the current. They were shorter than a lot of the other parents around them, so it took a moment to be sure who it was behind all the heads and shoulders, but then I saw those distinctive red glasses and knew. It was Tara. *She must be running late.*

The crowd kept us walking so I couldn't move closer and say hello, but I lifted a hand to wave at her as we passed by. She didn't even turn her head. Her forehead was creased and she was frowning. *Did I do something to her? She still hasn't replied to the text message I sent her. Was it too presumptive to ask? Even though that's what we said the other day?* I kept walking, frowning myself now. People could be so confusing. *Maybe Percy and Tara aren't going to be as useful as new friends for me and Tilly as I had hoped.*

I helped Tilly with her homework once we got home, trying not to think about the builder, or Kallista, or Talia. But that meant my mind wandered over to worry about what I might have done to upset Tara, and that was no good either. I tried to fold the laundry instead, but that just left more time for my thoughts to fester.

When Otis came home, I rushed over to him and wrapped my arms around him, pressing my lips into his. The feeling of his body against mine, his hands gripping on my shoulders, made my thoughts clear instantly. All that filled my mind was the sensation of his tongue, his breath, his fingers. I slipped my arms down from his back towards his arse.

"Babe, babe!" he chuckled as he stepped back from me, pulling my hands away before they could grab him. "Tilly is just over there! Besides, I've only just got in, I'm exhausted" He tried to grin at me, but I couldn't help glaring at him.

"Some men would be glad of a wife so happy to see her husband," I told him.

"I am, I am!" He raised his hands in defense. "But I really do need to unwind a bit."

I blew air through my lips. "Fine."

Seeing as my husband was in no mood to help me out, I decided to start preparing dinner for us. I peeled potatoes, and prepared a marinade for the steak. I finished quickly, but now there was pressure between my legs. I shifted my hips, trying to relieve the pressure without needing to go and jump on my husband.

As I pulled out the pans and pots that I needed, Otis came back through to grab a beer from the fridge, walking past me with his back to me as he did so. Normally I might have been annoyed, but I was intensely aware of his arse pressing against me as he slipped past. I wanted to reach back and grab it. Instead, I boiled the potatoes and fried the steak.

"Tilly, can you set the table please?"

She grumbled about it, but she turned off the TV and came through to the dining space next to the kitchen. She pulled out some plates and placemats, arranging them on the dining table, then returning for cutlery.

"Are you ready for dinner babe?" I called.

"What's that?" came Otis' voice. "Uh, yeah, sure!" He came in from the lounge as well, frowning at his phone.

"What's the matter?"

"Hmm?" Otis looked up, with surprise broadening his eyes. "Oh! No, nothing. I just can't figure out where the next 7 goes on this blasted sudoku."

He sat down at the table next to Tilly, reaching over to absent-mindedly tousle her hair without looking up.

Dinner was served and eaten in relative silence. Tilly offered a few comments about her day and Otis showed plenty of enthusiasm. I chewed on my meal as I watched my husband and my daughter. They were so important to me, and yet they could be so frustrating. I loved them the same way that I loved my hand or my ears. They were simply a part of me, part of my self, and I didn't think about what it might be like for them to be gone. Should my ears hurt, or my fingers get broken, I'd still want them as part of me. I smiled at the jokes Otis was telling Tilly.

After dinner Otis offered to clean the dishes, and so I got Tilly into her pajamas and tucked into bed. She ran back into the kitchen to kiss her daddy goodnight after she had brushed her teeth, and thankfully fell asleep without too much tossing and turning. I made my way back out to the lounge, where Otis was waiting.

"I'm ready to put my feet up now," I said, slumping onto the couch next to Otis. I leaned into his shoulder and he shifted an arm around me. He leaned his head over to press against the top of mine.

"Long day was it?"

"Not really," I admitted. I had been busy, but it wasn't the business of the day that had left me feeling worn out. It was the way my thoughts had circled around the same ideas all day, people who I found myself entranced by, even though I didn't want to be. The pressure that I had noticed when Otis came home, that pressure had been growing all day if I was honest. It was an ache that had centred on me, a tight pressure between my legs that had kept my nerves on edge and my senses over-come. Only now, after all the domesticity of bedtime for Tilly, did I finally feel like I was relaxing from that heightened state.

"We have a few minutes now to just be comfortable," smiled Otis, looking down at me with shining eyes. He squeezed my shoulders and began to run his fingers down my arm. "In fact, if Tilly really is out to it, then maybe we could-"

There was a knocking at the door. I had to smile ruefully.

"Apparently we don't have as much time as you thought!" I said, detangling my limbs from his and standing up again. I arched my back and pushed my arms to the ceiling, enjoying the sensation of my muscles pulling and stretching.

"It's a nice view," he grinned , his eyes firmly focused on my backside. I slapped it and wiggled it at him.

"Come on then!"

Together we bundled out of the lounge and through the kitchen, giggling as he tried to grab my bottom and I slapped his hands away. We were wrapped in each other by the time we got to the front door. Otis leaned in and kissed my neck, pressing his face into my soft skin, and I soaked up his attention.

"Alright then, I guess we'd better have this meeting then!" He sighed and stepped away. I felt cool where he had touched my skin and sighed too.

CHAPTER EIGHT

Otis reached out and pulled open the door, revealing Kallista, spotlit by our kitchen lights, framed by the darkness of the night beyond her. She was still one of the most stunning women I had ever seen. She was a little taller than me, willowy thin, with long long brown hair. Her eyes looked as though she was laughing at all times, they carried such a light in them. She was wearing a black dress that hinted at the curve of her hips. She stepped in confidently and kicked off her heels by the door, holding out a hand to me.

"Good evening darling! It's so lovely to see you again! And this must be your lovely husband? My name is Kallista! I've been so looking forward to seeing you both tonight!" Her hand slipped around mine, soft and warm and the contact sent an electric shock up my arm. I felt my cheeks grow hot.

"Hello, why don't you come in," I managed to say, gesturing for her to come and sit at the dining table.

"Certainly, certainly!" said Kallista, turning to shake Otis' hand enthusiastically as well. I could see by his wide eyes that he was as gobsmacked as I was.

Kallista turned and slid into a seat at the table, the movement pulling her dress against her hip and outlining her legs. I followed and sat down. *Since when did I look at other women's hips? Since when did it make me feel this way!?*

"I understand that you guys are hoping to get some more money from the banks?" Kallista smirked and leaned forward towards us, like a co-conspirator in some sort of scheme. It made the smooth skin by her collarbone look exposed, above the inviting scoop of her neckline.

"We don't want to rob a bank," blurted Otis. *Was that a joke, or has she messed with your mind too,* I wondered while I turned to stare at my husband.

"That's a shame, I've got my safe cracking equipment in the car!" Kalissta's eyes managed to shine even brighter when she was laughing somehow, it was unnerving.

Otis chuckled half-heartedly, and leaned back in his chair.

"Alright, but enough kidding around," she continued. "Let's talk about serious matters. Do you have any wine?"

"What?" My head was spinning as I tried to catch up with her train of thought. "I think we might have a bit of sav in the fridge? One of my friends left it after she stopped by last Friday."

"What a scoundrel!" Kallista raised an eyebrow at me and pursed her lips in mock horror. She reached out and laid her hand on mine. "Can I have a glass love? I find that it makes the work feel less like work, and working in the evening is a curse otherwise!"

"Sure." I began to rise out of the chair, but Kallista snapped her fingers and beckoned Otis towards the fridge, leaving her other hand on mine.

"What are the menfolk for if not serving us, eh?" She winked at me and I lowered my eyes. *She holds a conversation like some sort of whirlwind,* I thought to myself as Otis stumbled into the kitchen and gathered some glasses. *How does she hold so many thoughts in her head at once. I can't believe how much she's affecting me, I have to try and control myself. I'm a married woman!* I straightened my back a little. *Oh god, she's still touching my hand!*

"Here we go," said Otis, returning with three glasses and a

tall pale bottle of wine. He unscrewed the lid and poured three glasses. I considered refusing, I wasn't sure how well my heartburn would go after the last weekend. But in the end, I decided that it would be strange to be the only one not having a glass. Kallista lifted hers and swirled the golden liquid inside, holding it up to the light. She pressed her lips together and hummed.

"I generally prefer red if at all possible, but we make do with the materials to hand. Do you have any tissues or cloths?"

"Would paper towels do?" I asked.

"Yes, perfect."

"I suppose that I'm the one who has to get them?" asked Otis, but he was smiling as he said it and he moved back to the kitchen quickly.

"Great, thank you," enthused Kallista as she took the paper squares from Otis when he returned. *I've never heard someone sound so happy to be given a paper towel,* I thought. *I wonder what she needs them for?*

"Cheers, it's lovely to meet you, and I hope this evening gets us all what we want!" She held her glass up for us to toast, and so Otis and I joined in, clinking the rims of the glasses together and then taking a sip. Before she sipped from her drink, Kallista tipped her glass, pouring a splash of the wine onto the wooden table. As she lifted her glass to her lips, she dabbed up the wine using the paper towel in her other hand. I glanced at Otis, but he looked just as confused as I did.

"Ah," she sighed after swallowing her sip. "That makes everything just a little bit better, doesn't it? Alright, what do you need this money for?"

We spent a short time explaining the plans for the deck to Kallista, getting out pieces of paper to draw diagrams of what we were thinking and jotting down the early costs that Otis had worked out so far. She asked some questions about our incomes and we printed off some statements for her to check. All through the conversation she teased us and made jokes, her laughter strong and joyful. I could never get past the sparkle in her eyes that revealed the pure happiness that must fill her. I sipped at my wine slowly, taking care to be aware of how my stomach was handling it, while Kallista drained her glass quickly and asked Otis for another.

"I think that I have everything that I need now," she said eventually, and a pall fell over us as she spoke. *But if you leave then we won't have your laughter here anymore,* I wanted to say. I wanted to tell her that she should just move in and never leave. She was like a fireplace, cozy and enticing, and I wanted her installed in my home for my pleasure. But, that was ridiculous, and so she stood up and gathered her things. I admired the strength in her arms as she put all the papers into her little business case and then sucked in a sharp breath as she smoothed her dress down her sides. She twisted and looked down the length of the dress, now pulled against her chest, hips and leg.

"How do I look, presentable?"

"Mmm hmmm," I said. My stomach was beginning to feel tight again. Kallista winked at me again.

"Excellent. I do hate to step outside looking a mess." She grinned. "I look forward to being in touch to let you know if we can arrange you some more money! I'll have to come and have a wine with you on the deck once it's fixed!"

"Red of course," burst in Otis, stepping alongside her to the front door.

She leaned in and gave him a quick hug with her hands on his arms and a peck of a kiss on his cheek. Her lipstick left a dark red smear on his skin. "Yes, red please!" She turned to me, holding out both arms for a full embrace. "Pene, I think you and I should catch up for a coffee one morning." She held onto my shoulders slightly longer than I expected as she stepped back. "Have a wonderful evening you two! See you later!"

And then the door shut and there was silence.

· · ·

"SHE WAS A LOT, WASN'T SHE?" said Otis, pushing his fingers through his hair and widening his eyes. "Lovely, but so much personality!"

I stepped closer to Otis, hanging my arms around his shoulders.

"You didn't like her?" I asked, surprised.

"Oh, she certainly knew her stuff, I'm sure she will get us a good deal."

"That's not what I meant," I said, moving closer so that our bodies were pressed together.

"Um, is this a trick question?" asked Otis. His face was beginning to glow. "I mean, uh, she was a quite attractive person."

"Mmmm hmmm," I murmured, leaning in to run my lips against his, softly kissing him.

"You, uh, don't mind the idea that I think she was attractive?" he murmured between soft kisses.

I shook my head. "I thought she was good looking too. I've been noticing a few pretty people around recently." I felt my heart pounding. *How would he take that? I don't know if I could tell him who I had been noticing yet.*

"Oh really?" he grinned. "Shall we go back to the bedroom?" he suggested, his hands on my hips, his fingers squeezing slightly.

"Why go somewhere else?" I asked. Then I moved one hand off his shoulder and lowered it to the front of his pants, holding on to his shape and beginning to rub my hand up and down. I smiled as I felt his cock begin to grow hard under his clothes, and as his breath moaned into my ear.

I undid his pants with that hand, placing my other on the back of his neck and drawing him closer to kiss him strongly. He kissed me too, pressing himself against me, clutching at my back with one hand. His belt cracked as I drew it out and dropped it to the floor with a clatter. I could feel him straining for release, and I removed his underwear quickly, dropping to my knees. I reached out for him, wrapping fingers around his length, opened my mouth and pulled him inside.

I stretched my mouth wider, enjoying the sounds that drifted down from his mouth to me. I let my tongue move along the bottom of his shaft, moving back and forwards, building a rhythm. His fingers in my hair guided me, faster then slower, deeper then pausing. I grabbed his backside with my free hand, enjoying the feeling of muscle tensing as he leaned into my movement.

It was like we had walked together far into a secluded corner of the world, and discovered a glorious waterfall, a tower of water that plummeted endlessly before us, power and beauty all tangled into one twisting deluge. It made me want to dive in, to feel this new sensation wash me away and carry me to places I had never been.

My teeth grazed his sensitive skin, and I pressed my fingernails into the soft flesh of his buttocks. I could feel him beginning to pulse and I knew that he was close, but I wanted my own pleasure as well. I couldn't let him finish before me, I knew that he wouldn't have the energy to provide me with satisfaction otherwise! So I slid his cock out of my mouth and stood, running my hands up his hips, tucking them just under his work shirt.

"Let's get that off, shall we?" I asked before undoing the buttons. Otis nodded and began to tug at the bottom of my shirt as well. There was a moment of tangle and confusion, but then he was standing naked in our dining room, and I was stripping my own clothes away.

He kissed me again as he undid my bra, slipping the hooks free with one hand as his tongue explored my mouth. I groaned as his hand cupped my breast and his fingers passed over my hard nipple. I was so ready that even a simple nudge on that center of sensation sent a quiver of heat up to my head and then down my spine. I could feel the heat in my pussy and I could barely stand as I began to squeeze my legs together and turn my hips. Otis pinched my nipple between his thumb and forefinger, squeezing the hard pebble and making me break away from his kiss with a gasp.

"God, what's come over you today," asked Otis. "You're amazing!"

He slid a hand across my stomach and beneath the waist of my pants. The angle was difficult, but he pressed further, brushing his fingers through my hair and seeking out the waiting heat of my pussy. His finger slipped between my lips, rubbing across my clit, and I almost melted through the floor.

"Oh god," I groaned. Otis' finger pressed deeper, curling to penetrate me, slipping inside me. I could feel my wetness spread as he slid in and out of me, his fingers pushing against my sides. I hung from Otis' shoulders, panting in time with his hand as he rubbed inside, his ready hardness pressing against my side.

Before I completely collapsed on top of him, with legs like jelly I turned to the kitchen bench.

"Fuck me Otis." I leaned over the bench on my elbows, my hands behind my bowed head. Otis stepped up behind me, pushing my pants to the floor and pulling my hips towards him. Slowly, he pressed his hard cock against my entrance, then shifted and slid all the way. I could feel his body against mine, my body filled up by him, reaching every part of me. I closed my eyes and groaned at the feeling of him. One hand lay on the small of my back, while the other gripped my hip and Otis began to thrust.

Single solid thrusts, one by one, each time punctuated by a slap of skin on skin. I felt the sweat on my brow run down my nose and drip onto the kitchen bench. Each thrust made my breasts leap and brought me one step closer to my pinnacle. Otis' fingernails began to claw into my skin and I arched my back, lifting my head to the lights above us.

"Keep going!" I breathed, as one hand came forward, along my side, and reached around to take hold of my breast, squeezing it hard. Otis' lips met my shoulder as he hunched over me, and he could hold himself back no more. His thrusts became faster and faster, my hips pressing back to meet his. Our breaths kept pace, shallow and fast, our skin flushed with the pleasure that was building.

Higher and higher we climbed, scaling the rocks beside the waterfall until we could see the whole world laid out below us. When we reached the crest together I felt Otis pulse and release inside me, matching my own wave of satisfaction, a wave that washed the tension from all of my muscles at once and left me slumped on the cool kitchen bench, leaving me exposed.

Otis pulled himself away, which startled me out of the reverie that had come over me.

"Mmmmm," I purred. "That was just what I've been needing all day."

"Anytime you need more of that, you just come and let me know." Otis smiled like a cat that had cornered a mouse, full of pride. He pulled his pants back up, but without the belt they hung off his hips a little. I examined his body, the way his chest shone with a thin film of sweat, the flush in his cheeks, the way his eyes sparkled.

"I love you Otis," I said.

"I love you too," he said, coming over to hold me and kiss me again. This was a softer kiss, less urgent. I relaxed into his lips.

"Come on," he said as he stepped back. "Let's get to bed."

I gathered my clothes from the kitchen floor and followed him to our room.

I LAY in bed longer than usual the next morning. I was dreading beginning the day. I just knew that as soon as I swung my legs out from under these blankets, I would have no time for myself between the routine of breakfasts and school uniforms. Instead, I tried to check my phone for as long as possible. There was a text message waiting for me from Tara. *She must have sent it at some point when I was busy last night,* I thought, licking my lips as I remembered the way my husband had made me feel. Then I grunted. *Huh. She ignored me for so long, and even refused to wave at me in person, but now she texts? What's with that?*

Hi Pene, lovely to hear from you! Percy would love to play with Tilly soon, but we are busy today. Would Tilly like to come over on Saturday?

She included her address.

I lay back on the pillow and listened to Otis in the shower. The water pattered like rain, a soothing white noise that made me want to turn over and go back to sleep. Although my first impulse was to refuse, just because I thought that she had been treating me in a peculiar way, I had to admit that I wanted to encourage more friendships for Tilly. But the idea of going to someone else's home made me feel uncomfortable, but I couldn't figure out why. *Why do I want the children to come here? What's the big deal? Is it just that I'm annoyed at Tara?*

In the end, despite my misgivings, I couldn't think of a reason to make Percy come to our home, and so I replied to the text and let Tara know that Tilly would love to go to their house. Then I began scrolling through my social media, looking for any interesting news from my friends. Rachel was the most prominent figure again, with a series of photos of her in a beautiful yellow and orange sarong sitting in a bar in Bali, drinking something that looked very fruity.

"Mum!" Tilly yelled from the other room. "I'm hungry!"

I sighed. Still, at the age of six, Tilly struggled to get herself sorted in the mornings. I rolled out of bed, checking that the long tee shirt I wore to sleep was pulled down far enough for modesty, then walked out. Tilly was sitting on the floor in front of the TV. *She certainly learned how to find her favourite cartoons soon enough!*

Nevertheless, I got busy preparing her some peanut butter toast, and then I made some toast for Otis who was rushing through as he pulled on his clothes. He spun past and grabbed his breakfast, then pecked my cheek, before sticking the toast in his mouth and moving on.

"'Anks 'abe," he said, his cheeks twitching towards a smile around the food in his face, crumbs spilling to the floor. He finished buttoning his shirt and reached up to pull the toast out so that he could speak properly again. "You're a legend. Catch you later!" And he was out the door, bustling into his car.

"Love you too sweetheart," I said, smiling and shaking my head. All he needed to do was wake up about ten minutes earlier and he wouldn't start his days in such a calamity. I picked up Tilly's plate of toast and took it over to her.

"Alright love, here's your toast."

"Thanks mummy." Tilly didn't even glance away from the screen. She stuck her hand out to the side and patted around the floor until she found the plate, picked up a slice of toast, and began chewing. I reached over and ruffled her hair.

"You're welcome. Hey, I have some special news for you!"

"Mmm."

"Tilly, you need to look at me."

"Oh." She turned. "Why, what's wrong?"

"Nothing wrong. Do you remember your new friend Percy?"

Tilly nodded. "He was so clever, and he's from somewhere else." She sighed. "It's sad that he was mean to me."

"Yes, well, maybe he has changed his mind? You see, his mum and I thought that you two would like to have a playdate in a few days!"

Tilly finally looked away from the cartoon on the screen and focused her wide eyes on mine. I could practically see the gears turning as she processed this information. Then she nodded "Yes!" she declared, with serious eyes. "That would be great!"

"I'll take it that you like this idea," I laughed.

"Oh it's the best idea, mummy. You're the best·mummy in the whole world."

"I think I am too," I grinned.

CHAPTER NINE

*P*reparing Tilly for school took another twenty minutes, but then we were heading out the front door ourselves, pausing to check that she had her shoes, then going back inside so she could go to the toilet, then asking her where her shoes had gone. As I stood at the doorway, holding the front door open as Tilly sat on the floor and tried to get her little black shoes on, I glanced down the street.

There he was.

The builder must have just arrived to work on the house. He was standing next to his white van, parked on the side of the street, covered in black markings. I couldn't quite see what they were at this distance, but those long dark dreads fell in a rope down his back and he was wearing a vest that showed off the strength in his arms, even from here. He pulled some gear out of the van, and whipped a leather work belt around his hips. I bit my lip.

Something tugged at my top, and I jumped.

"Mummy, we're going to be late, hurry up!"

I opened my mouth to answer my daughter, and to explain that perhaps it might be her fault that we would be late, perhaps she should be more organised herself, but then I realised that it would just be wasted breath. As I backed the car out of the driveway I stole a peek at the white van in my rearview mirror, but I caught no glimpse of the builder.

After dropping Tilly off, I wondered what I was going to do with the rest of my day. Oh, there were chores and errands that I could have worked through, but nothing that couldn't wait. I felt like getting out and doing something different, something that was just for me. As I walked out of the school towards my car, I reached my hand into the back pocket of my pants. They were the same ones I had worn yesterday, pulled on in a rush, and because there was totally at least one more day left in them. Kallista's business card was still there, tucked away after I called her. I pulled it out and turned it in my hands.

She'd be busy today anyway, I told myself. *A woman like that must spend half her day in the gym, and she clearly has a lot of clients to meet.* Despite those thoughts, I texted her.

Hi Kallista, Pene from last night here. I was wondering if you would like to get a coffee?

I opened the door and got into the driver's seat. My phone buzzed.

Sounds great! Are you near Avagadro's? I can be there in an hour

I SAT at a table in Avagadro's, sipping nervously at my glass of water. A waiter came by to ask if I wanted to order a coffee and I rushed them away, though I tried not to seem rude about it. *Was this silly? Why was I meeting with this woman for coffee, didn't I have my own friends to see? Actually, I don't have any friends to see today,* I reminded myself. Most of them were working, with no children, so they weren't exactly free for coffee at ten a.m. on a whim. And the few who did have children lived further away than I could justify travelling. *No, Kallista is the best chance I had for actual in person conversation with somebody today.*

But would she even come? I'm just some random woman that she had a business meeting with, she doesn't really know me from a bar of soap.

"Pene! How delightful to see you! I'm so glad that you texted me!"

Kallista was striding into the café, wearing multi-coloured activewear leggings and a bright fluorescent orange top that drifted around her like a golden mist. Her face was shining and a smile covered it. She gathered me into a hug before I had finished standing up and then was in her seat before I had recovered enough to say hello.

"I knew as soon as I saw you that we would be fast friends," she declared, leaning forward with her arms making a triangle and her fingers clasped together beneath her chin. Her dark eyes were large and happily watching me. "So, have you ordered yet?"

"Uh no, I haven't. I was waiting for you to get here."

"Never bother waiting for me!" She leaned back and waved off the comment. "I'm far too unreliable." She winked at me and then turned to address a waiter who was clearing another table. "Excuse me sir, but we are ready to order."

I was amazed. If I had said that, it would have come across as presumptuous and rude. But somehow Kallista managed to make it sound reasonable for him to drop what he was doing and attend to her needs.

"I hope I didn't interrupt something?" I said.

"No of course not, I would have said. Why do you think you interrupted something?" She tilted her head a little, like a curious sparrow.

"You're wearing very different clothes than you were last night. I wondered if you were going to the gym or something?" I gestured at the bright outfit.

"Oh I see!" Kallista laughed. "No, I wear this sort of thing most days. My clients usually see me after their working day, so I'll get dolled up in the afternoon if I need to. Sometimes I have meetings during the day, but I can plan ahead for those. I'm much more comfortable like this!" And she hopped up from her seat to give me a twirl, the movement lifting the edge of her orange top slightly, like a dress. Her leggings shaped her thighs and calves precisely and I had to press my lips together.

"Thank you," she said to the waiter who was standing next to her with his mouth slightly agape. She leaned closer to him. "I just want a flat white please." She raised an eyebrow at me. "Or is it late enough for a wine?"

"Wine? Oh, I don't think that I could do wine so early." I answered.

"Spoilsport," she pouted, but her smiling eyes told me that she didn't truly mind. "Alright, so just the flat white for me. For you?"

"I'd like a cappuccino please," I told the flustered waiter, who nodded, repeated our drinks back to us and then made his way back to the service counter. Kallista tucked herself back into her seat.

"Am I interrupting anything for you?" she asked.

"What? How would you think you are interrupting something? I was the one who asked you to coffee."

"Yes, but one never knows. After all, you look..." She gestured at me meaningfully. "*Exactly* the same as when I last saw you." One side of her mouth pulled back in a grin and her eyebrows lifted suggestively.

I clicked my tongue in embarrassment. "I know, it's one of the perils of spending so much time in the house. I often end up just wearing whatever is comfortable for weeks on end."

"There's nothing wrong with being comfortable. You should be proud that you know what you like."

"I don't know if it's actually what I like. I'd say it's more like I just end up wearing whatever I wear."

"I see you as someone who knows what she wants," confided Kallista. Her long hair was settling forward, a loop beginning to cover an eye, and she pulled it aside and behind her ear. "And that's why I said I thought we should see each other again. That's why I'm so glad that you texted me today."

"You are?"

"Of course I am!" She chuckled while the waiter returned and placed our drinks down on the table in front of us. Kallista lifted hers in long fingers, sipping from the mug and rolling her eyes in ecstasy as she tasted the frothy dark liquid. She lowered the cup back to the table. "I want to introduce you to something."

"Some thing? So, like, an animal or an artwork?"

"No."

"It's just that when someone says 'introduce you' they usually mean a person, so when you say 'thing' it just makes me wonder what you mean." I could feel my cheeks growing warmer with embarrassment as I tried to explain myself. To cover my awkward comments, I took a sip from my own drink. It was absolutely delicious.

"Oh I see! No, it's not a person or an animal or anything like this. I guess you could say that it's sort of like a club."

"Oh okay." I was suddenly suspicious. *This is just what Talia was warning me about.* I could feel my stomach sinking. "Do I have to invest anything?"

Six months ago, I had come to a similar coffee with a mum from Tilly's school who had seemed like someone I could be friends with. She had tried to get me to invest in her small business, a business that seemed to entirely consist of convincing others to sell health products and buy their stock from myself. When I'd asked the woman if it was a pyramid scheme she had seemed offended and said "Absolutely not! Those are get rich quick schemes, where people just lose their money! My mentor in the business has the latest Mercedes and makes thousands of dollars a month!"

"So, he got rich quick?" I had asked. Then, ever the one to poke the sleeping bear, I'd added. "How much have you had to invest in your stock so far?"

The mum hadn't even finished our coffee together, leaving me with the bill for her muffin. Now she avoided me in the playground at school. I didn't want to have a similarly disappointing experience now.

"No, you don't have to invest anything," said Kallista. "I'm not here to scam you out of any money. This is more of a club for people with similar interests. It's really a women's only club that has casual meetings every few weeks."

"Like a social club or something?" *This sounded a bit different to what Talia had talked about. She had seemed convinced that Kallista was taking advantage of people, but how bad could a social club be?*

"Yes, exactly like that!"

I nodded and felt a small flicker of guilt in my stomach. I knew all about the little social groups that cropped up amongst bored people, especially those who had young children making schedules difficult. I had tried to join a bookclub at the insistence of my mother, but I had found that I had nothing in common with the women in it. You would have thought that reading the same book each month would have been enough, and then I could have had conversations with them about the books, but somehow the conversations always ended up being about the families of the other women. They all had children who were older than Tilly, and so they spent a lot of time discussing things much more interesting than doll's dresses and cartoons.

When we had discussed the books, I had felt a little out of my depth. One woman, Shelley, must have had a degree in literature or something, she kept saying things like "The protagonist was outlined using stereotypes from the genre, but the details of her relationship with her parents kept her from being a cliche," or "I was waiting for the antagonist to reveal themselves as such, but I believe that the setting itself became the antagonist, which allowed for a more natural relationship between the main character and the characters she encountered." I had often walked away with my brain feeling over full, just like I had after lectures during my first attempt at uni.

That first time trying to get through university had been

alright because I was training for something and spent time decompressing what I had just learned. There was no way that I was going to spend time reviewing my notes after a social book club! And so, after a few meetings, I had made some excuses and then never returned. I had tried a mum's coffee group when Tilly was a lot smaller, but that had gone no better. Somehow I had managed to reach this stage of my life with no solid groups to be a part of.

I didn't want to tell Kallista this. She was so bright and enthusiastic, and I wanted to get to know her more. I felt as though having this woman in my corner would help me feel as bright and energetic myself. But if I told her that I was no good at social groups, would she just cut me off? The thought made me preemptively sad.

"So, what's the group about? What do you do?"

"That's the secret, isn't it," smiled Kallista again, before draining her cup. "Mmmmm, that was really good. Maybe we could get a wine together next time." She pushed the cup aside. "There aren't a lot of rules for this club, but one of the rules is that we aren't supposed to share what happens during the meetings with outsiders, not even our friends or romantic partners. However, we are welcome to bring along those who are curious! Would you say that you are curious?"

"I might be." I couldn't lie. The idea of doing anything with this woman was a little bit exciting. I had the feeling that she could make a round of mini-golf into an adventure! "I really need to know more about it."

Kallista pouted. "Is my word not good enough for you?" She giggled. "Okay. How about if I tell you that this group keeps me going. This group is what gives me the power and positivity to deal with the modern world. How does that sound?"

I had to smile in return. "That sounds pretty good."

"Excellent! As it turns out, there's a meeting next Friday night. Would you like to come along?"

Friday? It was already Wednesday. Would I be able to get out for the evening at all? "I'd like to but I'll have to see if I can get a babysit-ter. Two days isn't a lot of time for that." I shrugged, unsure whether I was annoyed or grateful. *Even an evening of being sold some sort of investment might be bearable in this woman's company,* I told myself.

"That's what your husband is for, surely? Anyway, it's not two days, it's just over a week. Not this Friday, the next one. I'll text you the time and the address. If you make it, I'll be waiting by the front door, and if you can't, I'll understand. Just bear in mind, we don't let late-comers in. You'll see why."

Kallista stayed for another 20 minutes, letting me talk about Tilly and how she was doing at school. She made a happy little chirp when I described how happy Tilly was to make friends with the new boy in class, and she asked questions about what Tilly enjoyed most. It was the most satisfying conversation I had had in months. Eventually she glanced at her phone and apologised.

"I will have to get going sorry, I do have some places to go today. But this has been really wonderful. I hope we can do this again, and I really hope that you can make it to the meeting on Friday! I really do think that you will get a lot out of it. Say hello to Otis for me!"

"I will, thank you."

With a whirl of colour, Kallista came around the table to give me a huge hug, and then I was standing alone next to the table in the cafe.

"Wow. She's got a lot of personality," said the waiter as he began to collect the used mugs and spoons from our table. "Do you find it overwhelming?"

"No, it's exhilarating," I said.

THE REST of the week passed slowly, fulfilling the usual routines. I hung out the laundry, cooked dinner and logged into my busi-ness course every day at 10.30am. I read the online papers, interacted with my fellow students on the message boards, but everything I did felt full of colour. I knew it was my eager anticipation of more time with Kallista that was exciting me, but I relished the sensation.

My giddy mood dimmed when I saw Tara again while we were picking up the children on Friday. This time she had to walk past me in order to leave with Percy. I wondered how I should react to her. Should I pretend I hadn't seen her, the same way she had done to me on Wednesday? She had seemed so friendly, but then so cold. *As far as I know, Tilly and I are coming over for a playdate tomorrow, surely I should say something?* I decided that it would be easiest to focus on the crowd, to pretend that I was looking for Tilly. That way we could avoid any awkward moments.

"Pene! How lovely to see you!" said Tara as she approached. She smiled and stepped in closer.

"Oh hello Tara! I didn't see you there!" I smiled as though I had only just seen her. *Now what do I say?* "Hello again Percy, how are you?"

"Good," murmured the boy, shuffling in closer to his mother.

"He's really looking forward to having Tilly come over tomorrow," said Tara. She lifted a hand to pat her son's hair. "And I'd love it if you could stop by for a cup of tea too. Maybe you could stay for awhile when you drop her off?"

The question surprised me. I had thought that she didn't like me, that I must have done something to offend her. Why was she suddenly being so nice?

"That sounds lovely, I'll have to see if I have time." I answered, trying not to commit myself to anything.

"Oh good," said Tara and she reached out to touch my upper arm as she continued walking. "Come on Percy, we'll have to get going unfortunately. Have a good day Pene, I look forward to spending some proper time together!"

I watched her go with slightly narrowed eyes. *What's your deal?*

"Hi mum!" yelped Tilly from behind me. I spun and picked her up for a huge hug.

"Hello sweetheart!"

THAT EVENING, as I was waiting for Otis to get home from work, I caught myself drumming my fingertips on the kitchen bench. Tilly was in her room, and I could hear her singing softly to herself as she played some sort of game with her tall and skinny plastic dolls. Only weeks ago I had felt as though my life was exactly where I wanted it to be, I had everything that I had been hoping for. My husband was wonderful, I was making good progress with my studies, and our home couldn't be better. But then I had gone out with Talia and remembered a world that I had nearly forgotten. The deck needed attention, proving that the house was not as perfect as it seemed.

Is something wrong with me? I wondered. *Shouldn't I be satisfied with all this?*

Before I got too maudlin, Otis came rushing through the door with a gigantic smile and gathered me into a hug. Tilly came running out of her room to greet him as well, and the love that wrapped around me lifted my heart. I grinned back at my husband and kissed him firmly.

After putting Tilly to bed, Otis and I stood in our bathroom, brushing our teeth, in our pajamas. I watched him in the mirror, white foam frothing out of his mouth as he brushed thoroughly. He spat into the sink and wiped his face.

"So, how was your day love?" he asked. "I didn't really get a chance to find out, what with Tilly being so enthusiastic."

Now was my chance. Now I could tell him that I was excited to go out with a woman who inspired me for the evening. Now I could tell him that I had almost kissed my oldest friend in the world. But how would he react? What if he was disgusted with me? What would I do? The thought of his face wrinkling up in horror at my confessions made my stomach cold. I couldn't stand that.

"I met Kallista for coffee this morning."

His brow wrinkled slightly. "Who?"

"The broker from last night."

"Oh yes, of course! That's nice. It was more of a social coffee than business I guess?" He filled a glass of water from the sink and carried it to his bedside table.

"Yes, exactly."

"Cool. She seemed like a heck of a person! So, are you making a new friend, are you?"

"I hope so," I admitted as I pulled down the blanket and climbed into bed next to him. "She's invited me to a social event thing next week. On the Friday night. You'll have to sort dinner for yourself and Tilly, and get her to bed."

"That's fine. How nice, you get a night out!" Otis lay back against the pillows, stretching one arm around my shoulders and tucking me in close to him. He smelt warm and of something soft, like rosemary. I wondered what he had been doing with his day. "Just remember I'm off on Saturday morning for a day hike."

"I will," I replied.

CHAPTER TEN

The next morning I woke up with purpose, ready to tackle the day in the most positive way I could imagine. I got myself showered and dressed and made a large breakfast of bacon, scrambled eggs and hash browns for the whole family. Otis stumbled out of the room as I laid the plates on the dining table.

"Wow, babe, this is great," he mumbled as he scrubbed at his eyes with his knuckles.

"You're welcome!"

I gave him a kiss on the cheek and went into Tilly's room to wake her. It was unusual for her to sleep in, normally she would have switched on some cartoons long before I managed to rouse myself.

"Alright sweetheart. We've got a playdate with Percy in a couple of hours," I said as I walked into the room. "Get up, get dressed, and come and eat the delicious breakfast I made you."

"Breakfast?" came a confused small voice from somewhere inside the twisted blankets and sheets.

"Yes, breakfast. And we need to get this house ship shape so we're ready to go as soon as we can!"

The morning passed in a blur of showering, cleaning the

windows, and vacuuming, interspersed with bouts of putting away Tilly's toys, although she seemed to pull out other toys just as quickly. Before I knew it, I had texted Tara to say we were on the way and bundled Tilly into the car.

Tara's house was very close to the school. *You wouldn't even have to cross a single road between here and the classroom,* I realised as I parked next to the curb outside the house. There was a walkway between some of the houses only a few hundred meters down the street that would lead almost directly to the school. The house itself was old, with battered weatherboards cladding the sides and rust showing on the corrugated iron roof. The driveway dipped down the hill, and a short flight of steps led on to a covered deck. Tilly and I walked up.

As we reached the top, a voice came from the dim space under the deck's roof.

"Tilly!"

Percy came running along a deck lined with old shelves and boxes. I glanced into them as we followed Percy back into the front room. They seemed to be filled with art supplies, paints and brushes, charcoals and canvases.

"Welcome to my home Tilly," smiled Tara as we walked inside. She stepped forward and took my hand to shake it. "And you too Pene."

I smiled in return. The house was much darker inside than I would have expected. It was a lovely day, the sun was out, so why was it so dim? *And why is she still wearing those red glasses?*

"It's a pleasure to be here," I said, and I followed Tara to a set of comfortable chairs and sat down.

"Shall I get us something to nibble on, or a drink?" she asked, hovering next to me.

"I mean, I wouldn't say no!" I laughed.

"Give me one moment."

Within a few minutes she had returned with a wide plate covered in crackers, hard cheese, small tomatoes and a small bowl of relish. She left it on the low table between our chairs and then hurried back to her kitchen to fetch a jug of orange juice and some glasses.

"Nothing like a simple platter to occupy the hands," she said as she crunched down on one of the crackers and sat in the other seat. The children had already vanished off through the doors to some other part of the house. Their giggles echoed back to us.

"Yes, this is delightful! You didn't have to go to so much trouble" I was impressed by the food that Tara had laid out. *Have I misunderstood something? She was avoiding me the other day, wasn't she?*

"I don't mind," she smiled. "I don't have guests often, so I want to make sure I treat them properly. How have you been?"

I was about to reply with a simple "Fine" but decided that I wanted to keep my positive mood going. Instead of backing down and avoiding the issue, I wanted to keep the air clear.

"Things have been pretty good actually, but I must say I was hurt when you ignored me the other day."

"Oh!" Tara's eyes widened. "When was this?"

"Outside the classroom at school." I picked up a cracker and spooned a small amount of the relish onto a cracker, crunching down on it. "After I got your text, I assumed there must have been some sort of mistake, but at first I thought I'd offended you somehow!"

"I know what must have happened," nodded Tara. She sighed. "I mustn't've seen you. You see, I'm legally blind."

"Oh." I sat and tried to process what she had said. "What?"

Tara laughed at my inelegant reaction. "I have been since I was born. I have a rare condition and I can't see very far ahead of my face. I can't see colour either."

"But you..." I trailed, worried that I might ask a question that might offend her.

"I do so well?" Tara shook her head with a smile as I nodded. "People say that a lot. When you don't know any other way, you do whatever you can. It's just normal for me. So I'm sorry that I missed you in the crowd at school, but please do call out and come over to me if you think I may have missed you. I've been looking forward to you and Tilly coming over all week!"

I should have realised, I thought. *The way she sometimes focused elsewhere when we were talking, walking to school instead of driving, the glasses.* "You have?"

"Absolutely! I was hoping that the kids would get on well and we could hang out some more. We have only come to the area recently, and I do find it difficult to make new friends."

"I think that's a danger associated with being a young mother, not blindness."

"It doesn't help," she grinned.

"It reminds me of a show I was watching with my husband the other night." I proceeded to explain the mothers show I had enjoyed to Tara, and she instantly understood the reasons I found it so funny. She cackled when I told her about the mother who was wearing fine clothes for an evening out with a potential client and only discovered a streak of baby vomit down the back of her clothes when she got home afterwards.

"Did the client congratulate her on her avant garde style," gasped Tara with a hand at her mouth.

"Yes!" I shrieked, stamping my feet in joy. "You know they did! But first she spent, like, an hour in the bathroom trying to scrub it out and making it worse!"

"I have to see this show! What else have you been up to since that evening at the art gallery?"

"Nothing really. Lots of domestic things. I've just been invited to a social group meeting next week though, I'm looking forward to that!"

"Excellent! What was the group?"

I paused. *Kallista said not to share this with anyone. I can't believe I've broken the first rule already. What am I supposed to do now?* I decide to try and bluff my way past, so that Tara wouldn't ask too many more questions. I started trying to think of other things that I could mention. Maybe I could ask her if she had a partner who was always heading out doing their hobbies like Otis and his hiking?

"Do you know, I don't even know what they call themselves yet!" I laughed and sipped at my juice. It was crisp and cool. "The woman who invited me said that it's a group that empowers her, that helps her keep going with her crazy schedule and succeed in her life." I picked up another cracker. "Honestly, I am slightly worried that she's going to sell me something."

Tara's eyes narrowed, and her lips pursed slightly.

"Oh yes," she said. "So next week would be your first time attending?"

"Yes, exactly. Why?"

"There's some less than typical groups in this neighbourhood." She picked up a small tomato and popped it into her mouth. "I've been approached by a couple of them. I wondered if it was one of them."

"Didn't you only just move into the area? How have you discovered these groups?"

"I spent a lot of time trying to figure out who I was when I was younger, and I got involved in all sorts of groups. Usually not for long before I realised that they weren't for me. But, it means that I am known in certain circles. I had one young man knocking on my door before we had finished unpacking our dishes!"

That sounded intriguing. What sort of circles would this woman be known in? I looked around the sitting room for clues. A tall bookcase stood on the far wall, and as I looked closer I realised that the shelves were carved to mimic the appearance of bones. Some paintings hung in elaborate frames on the walls, but the portraits within were slightly unnatural. Their eyes were a little too big, or the face was too long.

"Have you joined any of these groups?"

"No."

"Why not? Are they scams or something?" My worries from the night before returned. *Was Talia right, was Kallista going to try to take my money? Oh god, were they more dangerous than that somehow?*

Tara ran a hand through her hair, pushing it back from her face.

"No. Not exactly. I mean," she sighed and paused, gathering her thoughts. "I'm familiar with other groups like these, and I've been part of them before. It's not like I know these specific groups very well. I found that the majority of them are, for the most part, just a group of people getting together to do something fun for an evening. Basically, a hobby group, like old men who make models of warplanes, or a knitting circle. But somehow, there are always a few who get really obsessive, and they can be trouble to have in your life. Remember the other night at the gallery?"

"What about it?"

"Did you see that group in the dark room, doing all their slow sensual almost-nude dancing?"

"Yes I did!"

"They're mostly harmless. You might want to watch your money around them, but really they aren't doing anything truly dangerous. They call themselves Empusa, and they want to believe that they are vampires."

"What?"

"I know, it may seem strange to you. But that's what many of these groups do, they try to revitalise something that has become a child's game in the modern world, mythology and stories. They were all powerful and dangerous real ideas at one point in history. There's a whole range, Wiccan circles, those Empusa are a local one, and I've heard of a group trying to bring back Bacchic Mystery!"

I shook my head. "This sounds like one of those nice hobby group sort of meetings to me." *Wait, what does she consider truly dangerous if not a bunch of artists pretending to be vampires scamming people out of their money?*

"I'm sure it is," Tara smiled, though it wasn't as wide as it had been before.

I need to talk about something else.

"Actually, there was one other thing that has been a bit of a highlight in my week." I explained to her how I had developed a bit of a crush on the builder down the road, and how it had spiced up my time with my husband. Again, her response was less enthusiastic than I had imagined.

"Just a bit of fantasy fun, is it?"

"Of course. I haven't even spoken to the man." *Good grief, this is turning into a downer.* I was beginning to regret telling her my stories at all. She was able to ask a single question that deflated my sense of fun in a moment, making me feel as though I hadn't really thought about the consequences of my actions. "I'm not going to cheat on my husband or anything!"

"No, of course not."

"Come on," I tried to convince her. "You've had fantasies about other people before, right?"

She nodded, and smiled.

"There's nothing wrong with a bit of imagination, is there!"

She nodded again, though the smile slipped.

"I guess I'm just worried about your meeting. Some of the groups that approached me are very good at encouraging you to pay more attention to your whims and emotions than to thinking things through. I would worry that they might encourage you to do something that was not in your best interests."

"I am a grown up," I told her. I bit down on one of the small tomatoes and enjoyed the way it burst between my teeth.

"And so am I, but I've had trouble in my relationship before when I allowed myself to focus on my emotions to the exclusion of other thoughts."

I ran my tongue across my teeth, catching the small tomato seeds, swallowing the last of its juice.

"Are you married?" I thought of the large man she had been with at the art gallery. *Was that him?*

"Yes. Early on in our relationship, I kept some important secrets from my future husband, because they were so intense that I didn't think he could handle them. At first I would just avoid the topics, and then I actually lied to him about it. Thankfully, once I broke down and explained myself, we were able to work things through together, but that was after months and months of fighting that nearly ended us."

"I'm not going to divorce my husband."

"I don't think you want to. But I know the groups that approached me when we moved here. Have you told your husband about this crush of yours?"

"What's that got to do with anything?" I cut a slice of cheese and laid it on a cracker.

"I'm sure it's nothing important. But if you don't want to tell him, maybe you know it is more than a crush?"

"I will tell him." I hoped that I wasn't sounding like a petulant teenager, simply denying everything that the other person was saying. "We've been very busy lately. I know that he trusts me and he loves me."

"I'm glad to hear it." And she did sound happy about it. She even smiled. "Just be careful with that group. Some of them can break down the trust you build with your husband. Do you think it's a religious group?"

I crunched on the cracker. I shook my head slightly, then paused. "I wouldn't have thought so, but she did say that the group inspired her," I said slowly.

"That doesn't really narrow it down unfortunately, they could all seem like some sort of spirituality focused group, especially at first." Tara was almost speaking to herself. "Just be careful. Intense emotions can be hard to control."

Thankfully I managed to pull the conversation away from my upcoming meeting and onto our children's teacher. Tara thought that the teacher was very pleasant, but that she was not exposing the kids to interesting enough ideas.

"It's all very well for them to play with balloons all day, but has she actually taught them anything about buoyancy or static electricity?"

I giggled and leaned forward in my chair.

"Tara. They're six. You know that right?"

"I suppose," she frowned, and then chuckled as well.

Tilly was much calmer than usual for the rest of the weekend. She was happy to have spent so much time with her friend, and did as she was told with a bright "yes mum!" all through Sunday.

I was feeling quite buoyant myself. Every morning was one day closer to seeing what this mysterious meeting with Kallista was all about. One day closer to spending more time with that firecracker.

I dropped Tilly at school on Monday morning and then headed home.before I knew it it was midday. I still didn't have to go pick up Tilly for a few hours. There were chores that I could do, but I didn't want to deal with them yet. I felt as though mere housekeeping and cleaning would be a letdown in comparison to the activity and enthusiasm of Kallista. How was I going to get through the week? The anticipation would kill me! I considered logging in to my online business course, but the idea of opening my laptop and typing in passwords was exhausting just to think about. So I turned off the car and then sat in the driver's seat in the driveway. *What should I do with myself now?* A movement out of the corner of my eye caught my attention.

The builder was outside the house down the street again.

I opened the car door and climbed out, letting it swing shut behind me as I began to walk back out the driveway and down the path. Without thinking about it, I soon found myself leaning on the fence of the house down the street, watching the builder.

He had a nail gun in his hand and he was using it to blast nails into some paneling that he was sticking up onto the wooden frame of the structure. I figured that he must be rewalling the garage. The heavy tool made the muscles in his arms taut, and he was shining with the work he had been doing all morning.

"Hi," I called, then grimaced. *How pathetic was that?*

The builder turned to me and let the nail gun drop a little lower in his arms. He sniffed and then pushed his dark sunglasses back over his head, shifting his work earmuffs back as well. His eyes were bright and blue.

"Sorry?" he asked.

"Um..." I wished that I was somewhere else, anywhere else. "I just said hi."

"Oh." The builder blinked and looked around the street. "Hi?"

We both stood, looking at each other. I became very conscious of my clothes. I hadn't worn anything particularly exciting today, just some old jeans with paint splashes on, and a plain tee shirt. I found myself thinking of Kallista. Now there was someone who dressed to leave an impression. I wished that I had thought to go inside and get changed into something else, something with a low neckline perhaps. *But then, if I'd gone inside, would I have had the nerve to come back out?*

"Was there something that you needed?" asked the builder.

Oh thank god, he thought of something to say, I thought. *Lord knows, I'd been drawing a blank.*

"My husband and I have been thinking of renovating our deck," I began, immediately regretting having mentioned Otis. "And I wondered if you could give me a quote, or any advice."

"A deck? Yeah, I'm sure that I can do that. Where do you live?"

"Number 64, just down the street that way." I pointed. "Would you come over to take a look?" I felt a warmth start to grow between my legs at the thought of this man coming into my home.

"Yeah, I'll come by." He hefted the nailgun, using it to gesture at the panelling. "I'm pretty busy with this, but I'll try to come over at the end of the day or something?"

"Sure, yes," I replied, already disappointed that he wouldn't come over straight away.

"Cool. My name's Nic, what's yours?"

"Pene."

"Nice to meet you Pene, I'll catch you later."

"You too."

Then he pulled his earmuffs and glasses back into position and returned to his work. I walked back to my house in a daze. What was I doing? Was I really going to try and take advantage of this builder? I had spoken and acted on impulse, allowing my instincts to carry me along and never stopping to actually think about it.

No, you must be grown up, I resolved as I walked inside. You have a life that you have set up and that you love. You can't let yourself be carried away with emotions and feelings and fleeting passions. It was one thing to look at someone and think that they seemed attractive, but it was quite another to invite them into your life! I tried not to think about Friday night and how I was bringing Kallista into my life as well.

I'm not really doing anything wrong, I thought as I walked into the bedroom and lay down. *We really do want a builder to have a look at the deck and see if they can do the work. And besides, last night Otis had seemed excited by the idea that I'd found somebody else attractive.* I began to slide my jeans over my hips and off the bed, running my fingers back up my thighs after I had. *And he had clearly been turned on by Kallista, and that had turned me on.* My breath grew shallow as I ran a finger along the edge of my underwear, tickling my own skin.

I breathed faster and faster as I teased myself, with thoughts of Nic filling my head. His face swum above me, and his eyes stared down at me as my fingers edged under my panties, rubbing at my clit. Then a memory of Kallista entered, walking with an inviting sway of the hips, and pushed aside the builder. As I rubbed harder and faster, the two faces blurred into one another and I couldn't hold one image in my head.

As the pressure built and I was close to climax, my head was filled with the idea of both Nic and Kallista being here in the room with me. It was so real that I could almost feel their fingers on me, their breath in the air. Then I imagined Otis walking into the room, and my orgasm gushed from me, leaving me panting and shivering on top of the bed.

It's just a bit of fun. Just a bit of a fantasy, I told myself.

After I caught my breath and got changed into some clean clothes, I tried to occupy my mind by doing the laundry and the dishes, killing time until I had to go and collect Tilly from school. It was hard to forget all those eyes in my mind though.

CHAPTER ELEVEN

*S*tanding outside the classroom with the other parents, I found that I didn't know what to say in the usual small talk. I wanted to ask them whether or not I should go to the meeting with Kallista's group. Something about it made me nervous. But I didn't want to share whatever this meeting represented with anyone else, especially not with them. I had this weird idea that a bunch of them would say that they wanted to come along too, and that would make me less special. I liked the idea that I would be a bit of a special guest.

The bell rang and children began to bubble out of their classrooms. Tilly and Percy came out of their classroom together again, heads bent together deep in conversation. The sight of them being close again made me happy. Even if they had acted strangely for a few days, it was nice to see Tilly making connections. I turned to look for Percy's mother and, sure enough, I found Tara in the crowd to the right. But, again, she didn't respond when I waved.

Percy rushed up to her and grabbed her in a big hug, and she smiled at him, and then they turned together to make their way through the horde of children and parents. Tilly rushed over and gave me a big hug as well. It took a few subtly swung elbows, but

I made my way through the parents around us so that I was able to say hello to Tara, to make sure that she knew I saw her. Neither of us was able to stop for long, but making the connection with her felt good.

The rest of the afternoon was sunny and warm, and I chatted with Tilly about the topics she was studying at school. When Otis came home I joined her in rushing to the door and holding him close. He laughed at us both and asked how our day went. Tilly started chattering about every incident from her day, which made him laugh again, and I felt my heart lighten as I watched them together.

I love my husband, I thought. He is a wonderful father, he works hard. What should I tell him about Nic? I felt the smile falter on my cheeks, but I made myself kiss Otis and welcome him home. I got him a bottle of beer as I started making dinner for the family.

We got through the evening happily enough, watching a Disney movie with Tilly until she was yawning on the couch between us and Otis carried her away into her bedroom.

"Poor dear," he whispered as he came back. "She was totally asleep before I even got to the hallway." He smiled.

That smile was something precious to me, but it seemed more fragile than ever, like a crystal model of a spiderweb. I stood up and put my arms around his waist, sighing as he stretched his around my shoulders and squeezed me close.

"Let's go to bed," he said.

In my pajamas, lying next to Otis under the covers of our bed, I took deep slow breaths, trying to settle the nerves that tickled my stomach. We had time now, and the evening had gone so well. Now I could let him know that I thought the builder down the street was a hunk and I had gone to speak to him. It would be okay. Right?

There was a moment of silence as I gathered my confidence.

"I saw a builder working on a house down the street," I added carefully. Otis shifted against me in a way that showed he had heard me, but he didn't say anything. "I asked him about getting a quote for the deck." I had my head held in close to his chest, and I looked up, wondering if I could get a glimpse of his face.

"I thought we were still too early for getting quotes?" I flicked my eyes back down. Now I didn't want to catch his gaze.

"I just thought it never hurts to get an opinion, and he is working in the area anyway." I let my voice drift off. My stomach was tense. "He was quite good looking."

Otis chuckled. "Yeah? Anything for me to worry about?"

"No, of course not." I laughed a little, but I felt as though I wasn't being fully honest with him.

"We're all allowed to have a bit of a peek from time to time I suppose." His hand squeezed my shoulder, and then I felt him stretch and reach up to switch off the light.

"Even if it's someone we've known for a while?" I murmured.

"What do you mean?" he asked. His voice was already sounding distant as he began to fall asleep.

"I'm just saying, we can peek at people we know, as well as at strangers."

"Sure, I suppose," he yawned. "Good night Pene," whispered his voice in the darkness.

"Good night love," I replied.

THURSDAY WAS POSSIBLY the slowest day I have ever experienced in my life. Tilly discovered that she had lost her shoes; the car wouldn't start at first and I was almost ready to call the automobile assistance association when it finally turned over. All the laundry had blown off the clothesline and fallen into the dirt, and catastrophe followed disaster through the entire day. I burnt dinner and as we went to bed, Otis asked if I was feeling alright.

"I'm fine," I answered, but I was beginning to wonder if the universe was trying to warn me about my future. *Or maybe it's punishing me for my past,* I considered as we lay in the dark, waiting for sleep.

"Did you hear from your new friend today?"

"What?" I blinked, wondering what he meant.

"That broker lady. Didn't you say you were making a new friend there?"

"Right, right. No, we didn't chat today. I guess I'll hear from her on Friday for the club."

I could feel him nod next to me.

"What about the hot builder, did you get some more secret peeking in?" His arm around my shoulder squeezed me.

"No!"

He laughed softly. "I'm just teasing! You're allowed to have a crush."

I lay in his embrace and considered what to say about Talia. I decided to try and see how he would feel about it in a more hypothetical way.

"Do you have a crush on anyone? Maybe someone we already know?"

"A crush?" He was silent for a while. "Not really."

"Not really? So maybe a little?"

"No, it's not really a crush, it's just..." He went silent again. I waited, hardly daring to breathe as I willed him to tell me what was going on inside his head.

"I have to admit, " he spoke slowly. "I've always thought Talia was quite pretty."

"You have?"

"Yeah, and she has been hanging out more often." His voice was low, and I suspected that he was worried about how I might react.

"Like you said, everyone's allowed a bit of a peek from time to time," I said, pressing a hand on his chest.

He laughed, relieved.

"Thanks for the permission, love!" He leaned over and kissed my forehead. His touch was tender and I felt my tension melt through my limbs. I slid my hand along the muscles of his chest, drifting lower and lower as I tilted my head back to meet his lips with my own.

"She and I nearly kissed after going to the art gallery," I murmured as his body pressed closer. He paused and I wondered whether speaking had been the right thing. How would he react?

In the darkness it was hard to see his face. What expressions might be crossing it right now? How was he taking my admission?

"But you love me, right?" he finally said.

"Of course I do," I replied, pulling his shoulders towards me.

Without speaking, he responded to my fingers and shifted over the top of me, the weight of him pressing comfortingly against me. He leaned back down to kiss me, softly, his lips felt warm and comforting. I breathed in deeply, smelling him as our bodies pressed together. Between him above me, and the bed holding me up, I felt contained and safe.

My hips began to shift from side to side. I could feel myself becoming slippery and my skin was getting hot. We both shifted our nightclothes and then he entered me smoothly. I sighed and clung on to him as he moved inside me, warmth and pleasure slipping through me.

We came together, quickly and then he moved off me, lying on his side of the bed with my arm caught around his shoulders. It wasn't the most outrageous or mind-blowing sex we had ever had, but I felt satisfied and close to him in that moment. I turned around so that he could wrap himself around me from behind before we both burrowed deeper into the covers and fell asleep.

I woke up feeling refreshed and alert the next morning, and Otis was already rushing to leave for work. It was Friday. Friday! I sat up and got out of bed in a whirlwind, almost beating the alarm. I had Tilly out the door and in school much earlier than usual. Her teacher looked extremely confused. I finished the day's chores as quickly as I could, stuffing clothes into any drawer that might hold them, leaving sleeves sticking out and catching in the drawers. The online reading only took me minutes, and I furiously typed out and submitted a response that I could only hope would be semi-legible when my lecturer got to it.

I checked my phone just after midday and grinned as I saw a text message from Kallista. It had the address and the time, 6pm in a community hall in the next suburb. I had to stop myself from hopping up and down in excitement.

I paced back and forth in the bedroom, wondering when Otis would arrive. I had tried on five different outfits, and I still didn't know which one was the most appropriate. The jeans and hoodie seemed far too casual and homebody for a night out, though it was certainly the most comfortable. I did have a nice purple dress that I had bought for a friend's wedding a couple of years ago, but it clung to me a lot closer now than it had then, and I didn't know if it was flattering or just embarrassing. There was a formal skirt and top, but they seemed too corporate. *What would Kallista be wearing?* She had looked so good in her formal clothes, and so confident in her daywear.

I decided on a loose summery dress in deep blues and bright yellows. It was comfortable, I liked the way it looked, but I hoped that it made me look a little less casual.

Where is Otis? I picked up my cup of tea off the dresser and took another sip as I continued pacing, placing it back as I returned the way I had come. My chest felt as though there was a small bird inside it, fluttering from side to side. There was a clunk as the front door swung open. *Finally!*

"Hi babe," I called as I swept out of the bedroom and into the kitchen to greet Otis. "Good luck with dinner, love you!" I kissed him on the cheek and sped out the front door.

"Have a good time!" I heard him reply just before the door banged shut.

I drove down the streets, following the directions from my phone, and I had to keep pulling my foot back from the accelerator. There was no need to speed, I was on time. But, always, I found my speed creeping up as I tried to get to the hall faster and faster. Then, I was there.

I PULLED over on the curb outside the hall's car park, looking across short cropped grass and open empty asphalt at the building. It was quite wide and low, built of dark wood and with an angled black corrugated iron roof. I was confused. The windows of the hall all seemed dark, and there were only one or two cars in the car park. Had I got the wrong address? Was this even the right place?

I pulled out my phone to double check the address Kallista had sent me, but it was correct. I was absolutely at the hall that she had told me to come to. I then checked the time, and yup, this was the right time. But the hall looked empty. *What is going on?*

Now what do I do, I wondered. I had dressed up for a night out. I had told Otis that I wouldn't be home for a while. I found that I really wanted to be out, to do something that wasn't making dinner or reading children's stories. I didn't want to just turn around and go home already!

I was just about to try texting Kallista and letting her know that I seemed to be lost, when a car pulled into the entrance to the carpark ahead of me. As I watched, it crunched through the car park and around to the back of the building, vanishing from my sight.

I felt like an idiot. *They're just all parked out the back!* I restarted my car and began to roll my own way around the back of the building.

When I got there, I found a cluster of cars that appeared to be deliberately trying to stay out of sight as much as possible. The drivers had been so keen to avoid their cars being seen that they had parked each other in, leaving only a tiny gap between each. *How strange,* I thought as I guided my own car up beside the one I had followed. I waited as the driver got out and then began to edge forward, following the example of the other cars and trying to get as close as I could to it.

The driver was a tall skinny woman with serious eyes and stern flat lips. She stood with arms crossed nearby and watched me park. As I began to climb out, she spoke to me in a clipped voice.

"Who are you? Why are you here?"

I was momentarily surprised. Why was she being so snippy with me? Wasn't this a social group, shouldn't she be pleased to welcome potential new members?

"Um. My name is Pene. I was invited here. For the meeting?"

"Oh, really?" The woman arched an eyebrow. "And exactly what do you know about 'the meeting'?"

From the way she spoke, I could tell that she didn't think of the event as a meeting. I began to wonder what else it could be?

"Nothing really," I admitted. "I met a woman named Kallista, and she thought that I should come along and see what it was like. She seemed to think it would suit me."

At the mention of Kallista, the woman's demeanour changed. She was still judging me, of course, but she uncrossed her arms, settling her hands on her hips, and she pursed her lips.

"Kallista invited you. I suppose that makes sense." She snorted, a most unpleasant noise when coupled with the way she was glaring at me. "You should probably come in then."

And with that she turned and strode into the back door to the community hall, her feet crunching on the loose stones in the car park. As I followed her, another car crawled around the corner and slid into the space next to my car, blocking the driver's side door from being opened.

Oh, that's just excellent, I thought as I stepped inside. *I couldn't leave now even if I wanted to.*

Inside I found out why the windows were dark. The group was meeting in a small room in the rear of the hall, and all the curtains were drawn, with chairs propped against them to ensure that not even a glimmer of light around the edges would leak out. About fifteen women were standing together near a collapsible table that had some small disposable plastic glasses lined up on it and few opened bottles of wine.

The stern woman I had met outside turned at the doorway and sighed.

"Would you like some wine?"

"Um," I hesitated. Given that I was in a situation with people I didn't know and I wasn't sure what would happen next, I wanted to say no to the wine. The nerves and my heartburn wouldn't work well together. But everyone around me was sipping at their glasses and laughing. How rude would it seem to refuse? Especially with this woman who had been so cold without provocation.

"Yes actually, that would be lovely." I wasn't sure why she had changed her tune, but things were beginning to look promising. I scanned the small room and saw Kallista on the far side, chatting with a short red-haired woman. Kallista looked amazing, just as she always did, wearing what seemed to be some sort of silk robe. The stern woman returned with a glass of red wine in each hand and held one out to me.

"Here you are."

"Thanks." I sipped the wine, enjoying the richness of it. "This is really good!"

The woman snorted and smirked. "Of course it is."

"You know my name, what's yours?" I asked, trying to sound light hearted.

"Lacey."

"It's a pleasure to meet you Lacey." I held out my glass to toast our formal introduction. Lacey rolled her eyes, but clunked the rim of her cup against mine. "So, what is this all about then if it isn't a meeting?" I still wondered how a group of people getting together didn't count as a meeting, but I had decided it was probably important to make as good an impression as I could for this first night. If I wanted to do something like this again, I'd need them to invite me back!

Lacey tilted her head to one side as she studied me closely. She took another sip of her wine. She stood with one arm across her stomach, supporting the elbow of her other arm, with the wine glass hovering in one hand near her shoulder.

"What do you know about it? How much did Kallista tell you?"

"Basically nothing."

"Hmmm." Lacey sipped again, running the tip of her tongue along her lips to catch a few drops of the red liquid that clung there. "Better for you to let her explain I think."

"Pene!"

Speak of the devil, I thought, as Kallista came rushing across the small room. Other women turned to see the commotion, and smiled. There were almost twenty of us now, a few more had come in while Lacey was getting me a drink.

Kallista grabbed me and hugged me, planting a kiss on my cheek.

"I am so glad you made it! And you even have a wine already, spectacular! You are going to fit right in!"

"I wasn't sure if I had got it right at first. I was outside wondering if anyone was here."

"Of course! I didn't explain how to come in, did I?" Kallista's forehead creased as she realised the mistake. I was just relieved to see that she did take it as her own mistake, and not some failing on my part. "I always forget that guests don't know the routine." She stepped around to stand beside me and curled an arm around my back, with one hand resting on my shoulder. "We prefer not to be disturbed you see, it's a bit of a private thing. That's why we make sure the windows are properly blocked and all that. You'll notice that the women are arriving at different times too, we try to space things out a little." She gestured with her free hand, the one holding her own wine glass, as another woman came into the room, smiling and moving over to catch up with her close friends. Someone had began to light sticks of incense around the room.

"That makes sense," I said, and it did. But it also seemed quite paranoid. What was going to be happening in this meeting that required such elaborate routines?

"Good, I'm glad you think so. I've been here for over half an hour already, greeting people, and I think we are probably ready to begin! You just take a space at the back and see what you think."

"Okay."

And with that, Kallista moved to one end of the room and turned to face the gathered women.

CHAPTER TWELVE

"Good evening sisters," she spoke in a voice remarkably full and loud. *It's the size of the room,* I told myself. *She's an exuberant person, so it's no wonder that she can fill such a small space with her voice easily.* Nevertheless, something felt unusual to me.

The conversations murmuring in the room quickly ceased, and women spread out to fill the hall. Everyone turned to face Kallista. I found a space at the opposite end of the room to her, near the back of the crowd alongside a young woman wearing pale makeup, black coated eyes and lips, and her hair bundled into two buns on her head. She smiled awkwardly at me and nodded in greeting.

"It is wonderful to see you all here again. We are Many and we meet, as always, in honour of the god, and in order to show our devotion to him. In return, we seek only that he share his bounty with us."

The god? Oh shit. I felt my heart drop into a pit in my chest. *It's a fucking religious thing? Oh my god, is this a cult?* Suddenly I understood why Kallista had not given me any details before I arrived, and why Lacey hadn't answered any of my questions. *Talia thought it was a scam, but a cult is even worse!*

It's some sort of fanatic thing. They're going to try and get me to pay them tithes and things, I bet. Oh my god, my car is blocked and I can't even leave.

I glanced over at the young woman next to me, but she seemed to be listening attentively. I resolved to listen politely for now, but once I went home I knew I wouldn't be coming back.

Kallista wrapped up her mentions of the god pretty quickly, and then asked the women to sit where they were. She modelled a pose and, although she didn't actually instruct the woman to sit the same way as her, I noticed that everyone did. I followed suit, placing my feet together and resting my elbows on my knees, hands clasped in front of me. I had expected the position to feel uncomfortable, but I was surprised at how natural it felt. The smell of soil and earth filled by nose, and I realised it must be the incense that was beginning to build up in the room. *What an odd scent,* I thought.

"First, as we do each meeting, take the time to visit with yourself in silence. We have all drunk from our cup, and so we can now begin to unveil ourselves. The first revelation is personal. Visit with yourself." With those words, Kallista closed her eyes and hung her head low, her long brown hair pulling forward over her shoulders and shrouding her face. I watched as everyone else did the same. Again, I glanced at the young woman next to me. Our eyes met and she shrugged, then closed her eyes and hung her head. I did too.

The darkness behind my eyes was quiet. I could hear the soft sound of other women breathing, the slight occasional rustle of cloth as someone shifted in position. I wondered what visiting with myself was supposed to entail. *What am I supposed to do?*

They didn't even tell me what to do. Do I just sit here like this? I wonder how long they expect me to do this. What would they do if I just got up and left? My muscles felt heavy, and I didn't try to leave. The idea of being so rude to someone who had invited me and given me a glass of wine, even if she had been hiding something; it made my stomach churn. And the physical effort of figuring out how to get my car out made leaving far too difficult a prospect to consider. *Okay, well, I may as well give this a try. They said it was about visiting with myself? What does that mean?*

I suppose I could visit my body? That kinda makes sense. And so I began to think about how my body felt, starting with my hands. I could feel them holding each other, and I noticed a small twinge in my left index finger near the finger nail, where I must have received a small cut at some time. From there, I thought through my arms, the way the muscles felt, the feel of the air in the room on their surface. Then I thought from my feet up my legs, noting the way my muscles pulled in the strange position we were sitting in. I felt my abdomen, the way it was curled over and crunching in order for me to hang my head. *You skipped some-where, didn't you,* said a voice in my head. I shook my head slightly. *You did. You moved through your limbs and then skipped straight to your torso. What's waiting at the top of your legs Pene?*

I felt confused at myself, hearing my own voice in my head telling me what to do. *Is this what visiting with yourself means?* I focused on the sound of my own breath in my nose. In. Out. In. And out. Then I thought about my sex. I didn't spend long on it, after all, I hadn't spent long on the rest of my body either. But I became aware of the cotton of my underwear pressing against my clit in this position. I became aware of the heat that came from inside me. I began to shift slightly as the sensations it felt grew stronger. I adjusted my focus to move my attention up my back and to my head.

It was as though I was sitting behind myself, running a second set of my own fingers along my first body. I could feel the sensation of them pass along my flesh, raising goose pimples where they passed.

"Thank you sisters!"

I blinked and sat back. Somehow, while we were all visiting, someone must have come through the room and lit candles around the floor. I wondered if they were allowed to do that in a community hall. Whoever had lit the candles had also turned off the lights, and now the small room seemed dark and cavernous. Even more sticks of incense had been lit in the corners of the room, stuck into small ceramic jars, and now thick sweet smelling smoke was curling like fingers around each us. I breathed deeply and instantly felt myself growing dizzy.

"When we visit ourselves, we extend our connection. Now it is time to strengthen those connections. We bond, we Many, sister to sister, in recognition of our mutual joy."

At Kallista's direction, we were arranged into a loose circle, facing each other. I had thought that I would sit with the pale makeup girl from the back of the room, seeing as we were both new, but one of the women next to me insisted on swapping so that we were separated. I would have tried to protest, but standing up and walking had been harder than I had thought, taking much more concentration than usual.

Lacey came around the circle and refilled everyone's glass with wine. She raised an eyebrow when she reached me, as if to ask whether or not I was going to participate.I put a hand on my stomach but then shrugged and held up my half empty glass. She tilted the bottle.

The circle ceremony was simple and actually quite relaxing. We would loosely take the hand of the woman opposite us and then sip from our glass and look each other in the eye. Then, one woman would introduce herself and recount what had been happening for her since the last meeting. My partner spoke first, and I realised that she had placed herself with me to demonstrate how the circle worked.

I was shocked by some of what she recounted to me. I had expected a simple summary of highlights from her life for the last few weeks, but she opened her heart to me fully. Her name was Melly, and she did talk about the highlights from her last few weeks, the date night she had spent with her husband to a very expensive restaurant, the weekend she had gone away to Kerikeri for a niece's wedding. But between these she also spoke of her concerns in her job, the ways she felt her colleagues were undermining her. She mentioned that she was extremely upset by her son's behaviour in school, insulting teachers to their face.

It was confronting, and I found it difficult to reciprocate when my turn came. However, she accepted my story of Tilly's school life and our path to renovating the deck without any judgement. I wondered if she expected me to talk about the darker side of my life as well, but I couldn't bring myself to mention anything. Talia's face rose in my mind, as did the builder, Nic's.

After we had spoken, we squeezed each other's fingertips, sipped from our wine glass again, and then moved on to the next woman.

I spoke to at least seven other women in that circle, and all of them were as open as the first. I was able to join them in the joy and peace they felt when they spoke of the good in their life, and I began to empathise and commiserate in the traumas. With one woman, I tried to say that the problem she was mentioning wasn't her fault, and that she would be okay, but she stopped me kindly.

"There is no need to fix this, Pene," she said. "These things happened, and these emotions are real. I am sharing them with you."

After that, I tried to focus on the sharing of emotion, rather than the problem itself. I even managed to tell the last woman that I was feeling a little guilty, because I had found a builder down the street attractive, but I hadn't mentioned it to my husband. She nodded and smiled and squeezed my fingers, and then the wine washed down my throat and warmed my limbs and I felt lighter. I breathed in the sweet incense and felt my eyelids flutter.

"Thank you sisters. Every circle winds us closer together." Kallista still spoke from the front of the room. I had watched her take part in the circle, but I was disappointed that I had not had a chance to face her. I was curious what she would have shared. I wanted to know more about her.

"We began with ourselves, and have expanded to one another. And now each of us needs to become one of the Many!"

Someone clicked a button behind me and a speaker crackled as it came to life. Then, music began to fill the small space. For some reason I had expected some folksy guitar, like a youth group hymn meeting. Or maybe some electronic dance music with a bit of celtic harmony thrown in. Instead the music was mostly drumming, simple rhythms that repeated over and over. A thin flute provided slight variation, with its winding high notes, and tambourines clashed periodically.

Kallista pulled out a tambourine herself and began hitting it in time with the music. The sound of the small cymbals emphasised the beat of the drums, and she began to twist in a slow and sensual dance. It was like watching a flame in slow motion, or a snake before a charmer. Around me the other women began to dance as well, each as serpentine as Kallista. *When in Rome,* I thought as I began to let my hips shift in time to the music, lifting my hands into the air.

I didn't notice the tempo increase, but I felt myself begin to sweat as our steps grew faster. That moisture made the thick incense stick to my skin as I danced, and I had to close my eyes to keep myself from over balancing. Stomps began to punctuate the music, scattered at first but in unison as the song continued. Strands of my hair fell across my face, but I didn't care, I tilted my head back with my mouth open. Someone poured wine into my mouth, and I swallowed it gratefully.

Our bodies bumped into each other, our arms twisted together in the hot air above us. The flickering glow of the candles' flames caught the drifting waves of incense that washed over me. I felt my breath rage in my lungs. The candlelight on the walls flickered and danced with us as we spun through the room, our passage pulling at the flames. The women around me cried out, wordless noises of ecstasy and joy, whoops of delight. I realised that I was joining in the calls, but I felt no shame in it.

I felt as though I had reached the highest peak of a great

mountain, a piercing pinnacle of rock that jutted high over a wide country of dark forest. Stretched out below my feet were entire worlds, flocks of birds, and even the clouds did not attempt to overawe me as I spun and spun and spun, my arms lifted high.

The song began to slow down again. The flute retreated from it's piercing heights, softening the drumming. The tambourines died away, and we were left, breathing deeply, standing together, with sweat on our foreheads. I grinned at the woman next to me.

"Sisters." Kallista spoke quietly now. She was panting, from the dance. "Oh sisters." She gestured at us to sit, and we all lowered ourselves to the wooden floor, stretching out as though we were sitting on the grass in a forest glade. I stretched like a cat and felt just as luxurious.

"Sisters, that was glorious. That was ecstasy! Thank you for your participation."

There was a rusting sound as the women nodded acknowledgement of each other.

"Now we will pause for a moment. Feel free to fill your glass again. Guests, it has been a pleasure to have you join us for this part of the evening, but what follows is for those who have committed to join us. We ask the god to fill your lives with ecstasy, and we hope to see your return to us soon."

Most of the women remained laying across the floor, though a low buzz of conversation began. One or two got up and moved over to the side table and poured themselves more wine. I considered it, but felt remarkably light headed. *How much wine did I actually end up drinking tonight,* I asked myself. I was completely unable to tell. *And what is in that incense?*

Instead of making my dizzy sensation worse, I decided that I would go quickly. As I walked to the door, Kallista materialised at my shoulder, grasping my arm.

"Pene, darling! What did you think? Did you enjoy yourself?"

"Yes, I really did." I was surprised to discover that I was telling the truth. I had expected that I would need to lie about it, just to get out without causing offence, but it really had been a good night. The dancing and wine had been fun, but the circle had actually left me feeling like I had got a lot of worries off my chest, and I was inspired by the way my partners had unburdened themselves. "I was a bit surprised to find out it was a religious thing though."

Kallista waved aside my objection with her free hand, as we stepped through the car park. I sucked at the cool fresh air greedily, as though It was fresh water and I had been in a desert for days.

"Okay, yes, I know that I should have told you. But did we rub it in your face? Really, we look at it all as a bit of a metaphor most of the time. There's no holy books, very few rules. And," she turned and held both my shoulders, her eyes inches away from mine. "We don't ask for a tithe." She winked. "I know that a lot of people find that to be an important part of these things!"

She turned her grip on my shoulders into a hug, leaning close. "I really do hope that you come back."

"Agatha!" I blinked as Kallista shouted while her mouth was still right next to my ears. "Sorry Pene. Agatha, let me say farewell!" Kallista swirled across the car park to gather the girl with the pale makeup into a hug as well. I couldn't hear what they discussed, but Agatha had a broad smile, so I guessed she must have enjoyed her evening.

Kallista urged me to join them. As I had to wait for my car to be unblocked by others who were coming out to shift their cars, I figured that I may as well.

"Before you both go, I have one more thing to say to you. You absolutely must not tell anyone what has happened here tonight."

What?

Clearly Kallista saw the look on my face, and she sighed. "I know that it sounds strange, but part of the joy that comes from being part of the Many is knowing that what we do here, the things that we share with one another, is personal and private.

Sometimes people think that it wouldn't hurt to share stories of our gatherings with their close friends, or the people they are in relationships with, but it never works." She shrugged. "So we ask that you simply don't."

I wanted to ask more questions, but Agatha was already smiling and declaring that she wouldn't tell anyone about the meetings, and so I found myself nodding along and agreeing. A car horn honked behind us.

Some of the women who had arrived later were moving their cars out of the way, but they had stayed in their cars with engines running. I didn't want to keep them waiting. I climbed into my car as soon as I could, and pulled out of the car park. I waved out the window at Kallista, who waved back enthusiastically before returning to the darkened hall.

As I drove home I was shocked to see the time. I had been in the hall for at least two hours! It made me wonder how long we were sitting in silence while we visited our selves, how long were we dancing? My legs ached, perhaps we were dancing for longer than I had thought?

As I crept through my dark house to get changed and slip carefully into bed beside Otis, I considered whether or not I would return. Especially if I was not allowed to tell him about it. As I closed my eyes and drifted into dreams, I knew that I would.

I FELT WARM. Darkness enfolded me. I was lying, wrapped in that warmth. I could feel someone next to me, and I reached out. I felt their back, their broad, strong muscles. My fingers slipped over them, halting by their arm then tracing along their side. I felt silken cloth at their hip, the muscle thicker here. I followed the silk, along the outside of their hip to their thigh. Hair shifted on the thigh as my fingers passed over and then pulled back up to cup their buttocks. It was so warm lying here.

They rolled over towards me, sending their own arm out to

search me out, resting on the curve of my waist. Their fingertips felt hot, leaving points of fire on my skin that flowed like molten metal as they began to push up towards my breast, shifting my tee shirt aside. The trails of flame circled my nipples and I gasped, the air in my throat felt hot too. I began to shift my hips slowly, in time with the rhythm of those fingertips.

My hand was pressed against their stomach, the path of rough hair that I found encouraged me to search further, to follow under the silk. Half awake I wondered if I should take my time, to draw out the sensation, but I couldn't wait and so I pushed my hand below, stroking through the thick hair I found there to the solid shaft of their cock.

"Oh yes," came a deep voice in the darkness. I knew that voice. I pulled on my husband's cock, feeling the smooth skin slipping under my hand, it's wide head nudging the bottom of my palm. As I tightened my grip and emphasised my rhythm, I thought I could hear drumming in time with my hand.

Otis' other arm dug beneath me, and I rolled a little on the mattress to allow him to surround me with his arms. His hand stretched around me, taking its place on my breast. The fingers pressed into my soft flesh, nudging and flicking my nipple. I groaned. His first hand, now free, rushed to my pussy, cupping my whole self at first, before one finger urged it's way between my lips and sought after my wet entrance. I felt as though I was spread wide open before him, sensation throbbing across my body, between his hands.

I felt his breath on my face and opened my mouth to kiss him as he leaned into me. His kiss was slow and forceful, and I savoured his tongue against mine. My pussy pulsed and my back arched as his fingers slid inside me, and the ball of his palm pressed into my clit. Encouraged by my body's response, Otis moved harder, but not faster. Deeper but not quicker. I rolled under him, hearing a silent music that drove us on.

My breath began to escape in small yelps of pleasure. Each one was followed by Otis' hand moving against me, it felt as though he was finding new spaces within me, filling me entirely. He shifted and I opened my legs to allow him into me. If his hand and fingers had felt as though they were filling me, his cock stretched me further. His hips moved on top of me, still with the same slow urgency, the deliberate desire that drove us on. I moved in time with him, and lifted my head to kiss him, my lips growing more fervent as his cock slid back and forward inside me.

Finally, as I gasped and held his chin above my face, still wrapped in the warm darkness, our rhythm began to increase and I felt my gasps begin to come out as sobs. I pressed my thighs into his hips, wrapped my heels against his backside as I tried to take him further inside. One hand curled onto his hip, pulling him faster and faster. His panting breath above me kept tempo with the slap of our bodies meeting.

My orgasm clenched my whole body and Otis bucked and rocked as he came with me. My hands pulled his head down to me, our foreheads touching as he emptied himself into me. We stayed in that position as our hearts began to slow.

A tinkling melody intruded on our moment and I tried to shake myself fully awake as Otis rolled off me and out of the bed. I stared up at the ceiling as he turned off the alarm on his phone and wiped his mouth.

"That's a much better way to wake up in the morning!" he said. He smiled at me. "Thanks for that love!" He got up and headed for the bathroom. "I'll be off pretty early for that hike, but I think I'll be home in time for dinner."

I grunted in response and waved him away. I wanted to burrow into the mattress and duvet, to enjoy the warmth for longer. The patter of footsteps down the hallway announced Tilly was awake too. I groaned.

"I guess I'm going to be awake now anyway."

It took me longer than I expected to wake up properly. I wandered through the house in a daze as I got Tilly some breakfast and got dressed. I watched my husband drinking a hot mug of coffee as he lounged on the couch beside Tilly, who was staring at the cartoons flickering on the TV. It had taken me a while to recognise that it was him lying next to me this morning. I had felt as though I was rising out of a dream, and he was a dream figure caught up in my bed with me. The foggy mind that last night's wine and incense had induced was lingering. It had been delicious.

But, my own cup of tea was growing cold as I watched him finish his drink and then move to gather up his backpack by the front door.

"It's been great girls, but I'm off. Have a good day!"

"We love you daddy!" yelled Tilly from the lounge. I blew him a kiss and then he was gone.

I sat in the kitchen trying to soak in the recent memories of my husband. The feel of his fingers as they brushed across my skin. The way his breath felt when he leaned over me, his lips so near to me, the panting air rushing from his mouth. But as I sat and ran my thoughts across him, I found myself returning to the drumbeat from last night. I shivered at the memory of the rhythm pounding down my skull and through my spine.

Maybe I need to do something today. Get out of the house, try to take my mind off things.

"Hey Tilly," I called out.

"Yeah?"

"Do you think we should see if Percy wants another visit today?"

There was a second's quiet and I could hear Tilly sucking in a huge lungful of air.

"YES!" she screamed.

CHAPTER THIRTEEN

Thankfully, Tara responded quickly to a text message and even suggested that we come and see them at their house again. That was lucky, because I knew that she couldn't drive and I preferred to have somewhere to sit down out of the sun. If she had suggested meeting at a nearby park I would have just had to bite the bullet and do it anyway.

On the way over, I thought about how I was going to her house and eating her snacks and taking up her time, for the second time in a week. Although she had suggested coming to her house, I felt as though I was becoming a bit of a burden. So I pulled over halfway to her house and ran into a supermarket while Tilly hummed in her seat. I found a simple bouquet of small white flowers and a box of chocolate biscuits. Hopefully that would help balance things out a bit.

"Tilly, come and see the slime I made!" exclaimed Percy as soon as we walked along the deck to their front door, and the children vanished in a flurry of stamping feet, leaving Tara and I standing by the doorway blinking.

"It looks like they already have plans," she chuckled. "Come in Pene, it is always such a pleasure to see you. How are you?"

I considered telling her how wonderful I had felt after

meeting The Many, but I remembered that she had seemed so suspicious of them the week before. I decided that it was probably better to avoid that topic.

"I'm doing really well, I woke up in a great mood." *My husband had plenty to do with that.* "Only now Otis has gone off to do a day hike and Tilly and I are all alone. I needed to get out of the house. Here, I got you a little something."

"These smell delightful," Tara said, with a broad smile. She lifted the bouquet closer to her face and closed her eyes, bathing in the scent. I hadn't really noticed it, but now that she pointed it out there was a lovely light fresh fragrance rising from the flowers, like a summer meadow at noon. "I don't get flowers very often."

She headed back through her lounge to her kitchen, inviting me to follow and make myself comfortable. In a moment she came back, with a tall clear glass vase half filled with water. She put the vase on a shelf to the side of the room and busied herself removing the plastic wrap from around the bouquet.

"I understand what you were saying," she nodded, with her back to where I was sitting. "It can be difficult for me to get out easily, and going out on a bright day just means that I can see even less than usual."

"Oh, I'm sorry, I hope you didn't-"

Tara laughed and lifted a hand to stop me. "It's alright, I know what you meant! I am lucky to be quite introverted I suppose. I'm happy sitting in my little lounge, reading books or listening to music. There!"

She stepped away from the vase. The white flowers seemed to glow in the dim lounge and it made me realise just how dark Tara must keep her space. But the flowers were like delicate stars in a night sky.

"They look lovely," I said, trying to hide my surprise. *I meant to bring a little gift, but they really stand out!*

"Thank you so much Pene, that really means more to me than you might realise."

She sat down in the other chair and I brought out the chocolate biscuits. She clapped her hands together and then selected one cheerfully.

"I must continue to ask you to my house!"

"Why are the flowers so important to you?" I asked, crunching into my own biscuit. "I'm thrilled that you like them, obviously, but it is only flowers after all."

"Look at this room," she said. "Does it look like the sort of space that a young mother lives in?"

I did as she asked. The bone shelves were still in their position dominating one end of the room, filled with black covered books that seemed to feature a lot of bones and skulls as decorations themselves. A large sound system sat near the TV, and a box of vinyl records sat next to that. The controller for a console game system was sitting on the arm of the couch near the TV.

"I mean, I don't want to be rude..."

"No seriously, does it look like a typical girly space?"

"Not really," I admitted. "It looks a bit more like a guy's living room."

She sighed.

"Exactly. I've never been very good at traditionally feminine things. Having a lovely vase of flowers to brighten the room makes me think it's something that I could do if I tried though."

"Is being a typical girly girl really important to you?" I asked. "You struck me as someone who is completely confident in their own skin."

Tara grinned. Then she pressed her lips together and shrugged. "It used to be the most important thing in the world to me, and I could never get the hang of it. Make up, dresses, pretty pink pillows." She grimaced. "I'm glad that I didn't keep the pink pillows."

I laughed with her.

"What changed?"

"My husband." Tara's face looked as though it was lit from within, like one of those paper lanterns that float up into the sky with only a small candle inside. "He helped me realise that I was good enough just as I was, and I stopped trying to force myself to meet the world's expectations." She looked over at the vase. "And now I just like to figure out the parts of being a woman that really work for me."

"Where is your husband?" I asked.

"He's in his workshop. Would you like to come see?"

Tara led me through their kitchen and out the backdoor. She held firmly onto a railing as she stepped down a narrow flight of stairs, leading me to an old door in the side of the house. I was impressed at how easily she moved, now that I knew she was blind. She barely paused or even lifted a hand to check where anything was. The door at the bottom of the stairs was in desperate need of a new coat of paint, and there was a hole in wood where a lock or handle should have been. But once I stepped inside I was blown away.

The workshop must have been an old garage or large laundry space. The walls were makeshift, but it was an expansive room, much larger than the lounge in my own house. The floor was bare concrete slab, cold and grey and solid. It was filled, from side to side and top to bottom, with old pieces of machinery and car parts, piles of metal and gears and chrome. But in the center stood a statue of a woman, standing with one arm outstretched towards the ceiling, and her head turned aside to look down her legs. She was naked, with a cloth held in her raised hand that draped around her body as it fell to the floor. Every inch of the statue was made of metal welded and joined together, including the draped cloth. Somehow the shapes of the machinery complemented the shape of the woman perfectly, and the total was one of the most beautiful artworks I had ever seen.

"That's incredible," I breathed.

"Cheers!" shouted a rough voice, and a tall broad man with dark hair that hung in waves just past his shoulders and a sharp nose stepped around the statue. He wore a black vest and his arms were heavy. He wore a black wristband on one, and the other was covered in black and red tattoos.

"This is my husband, Peyton."

"Nice to meet you! Your kid is the one Percy took a shine to right?" Peyton stomped over in his heavy work boots and ignored my outstretched hand to bundle me into a hug.

"Oh, uh, yes, that's me."

"Wonderful stuff! Love it when the kids get on well. So, you like her?" He turned back to his statue.

"Absolutely, it's amazing."

"Yeah, she's come out pretty good," he sniffed. "Still a bit of detail to add in the face, then I'll sell her on."

I spent the rest of Tilly's playdate in the workshop, discussing all sorts of things with Tara and her husband Peyton. They talked about the symbolism of the artwork that he was building, and how he drew inspiration from the literature he had read while skipping school as a youth. Tara said she tried to encourage him to look to various modern artists, whom I had never heard of, for new ideas and avenues to explore. She described their art in such vivid ways that I wanted to go and find them and experience them myself. The conversation was enlightening and I just wanted to sit and listen to these two explain their ideas for hours.

"She's based on older ideas?" I looked up at the figure. She was nearly eight feet tall, as best as I could tell, and the idea that she was based on old classical art was strange. Her skin was stainless steel, silvered and bent. Some parts of her reflective surface were dulled and discoloured by welding scars, and some of the heavier metals were matt and grey. But I had to admit, the shape of the eyes, the way Peyton had managed to curve the cheeks and lips while working with such rigid materials, had all added up to a remarkably life-like giant metal woman.

"Yeah, I mean," and he scrubbed a hand across the sandpaper roughness of his chin as he considered how to phrase what he said next. "Obviously the actual statue is just me trying to get a woman that looks like a woman. It's not abstract, right? But she's meant to be evoking some of the old mythology, a guardian, pure and stern. Athena and Artemis, you know?"

I nodded, though I wasn't exactly sure that I did. Tara seemed to recognise my lack of confidence.

"In Ancient Greece, some goddesses were strongly associated with protecting people, especially women. So Peyton tried to capture some of the way they were presented for this statue."

"See, she isn't armoured, but I've tried to use the metal to give her strength. See how I got the muscle definition in her arms and shoulders?"

He led me around the statue and pointed out these parts. I had to admit, they looked like strong muscles.

"See? She's meant to be tough."

"I thought that it would be interesting to use these car parts and electronics to create a modern fury instead, but Peyton thinks he needs a break from the underworld for a while."

"A fury?"

"An underworld spirit of vengeance," explained Peyton. "But as Tara says, I've just finished some work that was pretty heavily based on death and stuff, so I wanted to look at something else, something more positive. Here, I'll show you."

He led me to the back of the workshop, where he had a few benches set up against the wall. Curled shavings of metal covered the surface in sharp and glittery waves. Old pieces of gears, engines, wiring rose up from the surface like rock spires in a silver sea. But to one side was a round sculpture, a little broader than Peyton's shoulders. He lifted it and held it in front of him.

The sculpture was a bit like a shield, a large round curved surface, but it was covered in tiny figures and shapes. It looked almost like it had been embroidered, that was the size and detail of the shapes on it. A series of bones wrapped around the edge, creating a border, and a large face was in the middle, almost life size. The eyes in the face were hollow, open to a blackness behind. The rest of the 'shield' was full of structures that looked architectural, with spires and buttresses and archways, all tiny. It was as though a european cathedral had spread like a tiny rash across its surface. Skulls and miniature statues and rib cages decorated each little building.

"That must have taken forever," I gasped.

"Yup, this took quite a lot of my attention in the wee hours after Percy went to bed."

"Time he could have been in bed with me," teased Tara, elbowing him. He chuckled.

"Maybe, but isn't the end result good?"

"How did you come up with these shapes and designs?" I asked, reaching out a hand to gently trace the surface. Each part felt firm and yet fragile.

"I based it on one of those churches in eastern Europe made of bones."

"What?" I turned to him, and I could feel how wide my eyes had grown.

"Yeah, it's like a memorial to the fact that we all die. It's meant to be displayed on a wall. This is a death mask, and it's meant to make you feel as though you are sitting in a tomb. It's like 'Be grateful for what you have, enjoy your life, because eventually we all die.'"

"That is grim," I mumbled, returning my gaze to the shield. All the bones were really overwhelming me now. I wasn't so sure how much I liked it.

"I can see by your face that you understand why I didn't want to do a statue of an underworld goddess of revenge now! She would have been a fun project, but I needed to spend some time with something a bit more optimistic."

I nodded and turned back to the statue. "Yes, I can see why you decided to work on her. How long did she take?"

"About a month."

"Is that all?"

"Yeah, the execution isn't really the hard part, it's more a matter of sourcing all the materials once I have a concept in mind."

They told me about the business of art, the way they had to balance the work that they put in and the value they might be able to get back out of it. I asked them whether that balance meant the art was less meaningful, and they explained how many of the great works of art in the past had been created for a patron who told the artist what they wanted. Meaning could be created even in such circumstances. But they did admit that the balance was difficult.

Before we knew it, hours had passed and it was time to collect Tilly from the room upstairs and take her home. Before we could walk up the driveway, Peyton grabbed me into a big hug again. I was amazed at how gentle the big man's arms were. I could feel the power in them, they were so large, but Peyton was a sweetheart. Tara leaned over and kissed my cheek while she held my shoulder.

"Thank you so much for coming over Pene," she said. "I hope that we will get to spend more time together. And say hi if you see me out and about! Do please remember that emotions can rise and fall like the tide. Communication is always the best idea."

Peyton glanced between us but didn't ask what his wife meant. I felt my cheeks redden. The idea of this man, who I didn't really know, hearing about my personal life was something I didn't like. I wondered what the women in the circle would say about that. Would they expect me to be just as open with him as I was in the circle?

"Maybe we could go and get pampered a bit together one day," I suggested. After all, she seemed to enjoy having a bit of a feminine touch introduced to her life at the moment. "A massage and a manicure or something?"

"I've never really done that," she replied, her voice a little lower than I had expected. But then she nodded firmly. "Yes. Yes, I think that would be a great idea."

"You definitely should," chipped in Peyton. "I think you don't allow yourself to try these things, like you still don't think that you are allowed."

Tara sighed and smiled ruefully. "I think you are right. No matter how far I come, I still feel like someone will tell me that I shouldn't."

I think you should," I said, smiling at her. "And I look forward to us doing it together."

I TOOK Tilly home and we had a quiet afternoon. Once Otis came home and cleaned himself up, we had dinner and then played a simple board game, laughing and grabbing at letter tiles as we put words together. As usual, Tilly surprised me with the words she was able to spell.

Later, after I got Tilly to sleep, I walked out of her room into a darkened house. I moved down the hallway like a ghost drifting through shadows. I could feel myself separating from my body and I wondered if it was a real feeling, or if I had fallen asleep in Tilly's bed.

In our room, Otis lay in bed, reading by his bedside lamp. *She thinks that my emotions could take control of me, does she? She thinks I'm so weak that I would be swayed by a fleeting crush? No, I'm the one in control.* My blood raced as the thoughts flashed through my head.

I climbed onto the bed and crawled across the mattress to straddle Otis. He put his book down on his chest and looked at me, confused.

"Is everything alright Pen?"

I picked up the book and threw it to the side, onto the floor.

"Hey!" Otis began to complain, but I grabbed his wrist and pulled it up above his head. The motion moved my face lower, closer to his, and I leaned forward to kiss him. I kissed him hard, pushing against him, and forcing him back down to the mattress. His other hand headed towards me, so I grabbed that one too, then I bit his lower lip and pulled back.

He gasped and yelped, but I held on. His hips were bucking beneath me, and I could feel myself getting excited. I could feel myself beginning to throb, and I couldn't stop myself from writhing my hips against him. The friction was not enough, muffled by the duvet and our clothes, and I began to twist and turn, trying to satisfy my urge for contact.

I relented, and released his lip, enjoying the way he groaned in satisfaction as it was released. I shifted his wrist so that my one hand could hold both of his, then pushed my hand under the blanket, beneath my self, into his boxer shorts. I found his cock and chuckled slightly as I realised that it was still quite soft. *You weren't expecting this, were you sweetheart,* I thought to myself as I rubbed my hand across him. He was getting harder already. With my hand around him and beneath my hips, I was almost rubbing myself at the same time.

I withdrew my hand and kicked the duvet down the bed. Now Otis lay in front of me, spread along the bed, wearing only his boxers. His cock was poking out of them and I grinned. I released his wrists and stood up, undoing my pants and pulling my tee shirt off. Otis began to sit up and reach out for me, but I pushed a hand onto his chest and made him lie down again.

"This isn't for you," I said, and I smiled again at his look of confusion.

Once I was naked, I pulled off his boxer shorts and then straddled him again. Now his cock was at its fullest, pressing its heat against me as I sat on top of him. I reached down and maneuvered it between my lips, rolling my eyes at its heat, at the way it pushed on my hard clit. It slid across my skin, and I used him to bring myself closer, rubbing back and forth. He groaned and reached up towards me with his hands, but I leaned back and then slapped his hands away.

Finally, I couldn't hold back any longer. I could feel my orgasm waiting, but it wouldn't approach while I used him this way. I pushed his cock to my entrance and then gasped as it slid inside. My moan was long and deep as he filled me up. I held one hand to my stomach as I began rocking back and forward. Again, Otis lifted his hands, but now I was balanced on top of him. Not only did I push his hands aside, but I reached down and pinched his nipple with one hand. He squealed.

Now, I rocked hard. Faster. I bucked my hips against his, finding my own rhythm and pushing him down whenever he tried to make me move. Release was waiting, just beyond my sight, and I closed my eyes so that I could find it faster. I leaned forward, my breasts brushing against his chest, my nipples catching the hair on it as my breasts swung below me. My pace increased, rushing closer and closer to satisfaction.

Then, without warning, I crested the rise and my orgasm rushed into me, pushing down and through me. I felt my pussy clench onto Otis' cock, and my stomach tensed as I came over and over. I panted as my muscles began to relax and I was able to release his cock and lift myself off him. I rolled over and collapsed onto my side of the bed.

"Hang on," said Otis. "What are you doing?"

"What do you mean?" I replied dazedly. I was staring at the ceiling. I began to wind my hair around my finger.

"I mean, you just stopped. Why did you stop?"

"I'm done." My smile grew larger as I thought of the intense crescendo that had moved through me.

"I'm not though!"

"Oh." I blinked and glanced down at Otis' cock. It was still stretching up and away from his body, glistening in the wetness I had left behind. I looked up his body, eventually stopping at his eyes. "So, what are you going to do about that?"

"Do about it?" His eyes were wide. "I want to finish fucking you, that's what I want to do about it!"

"Oh. I mean, I was fucking you, you weren't fucking me."

Otis shook his head and gaped at me. "Okay! But I'd like to fuck you now then, alright?"

I sighed. "Yeah, okay. I got what I needed already."

So Otis moved over to kneel between my legs. I was still so

wet that his was able to enter me smoothly and he began to thrust as hard and fast as he could.I was just beginning to focus on the way he felt, only just beginning to feel as though I might be able to reach my crescendo again, when he groaned and shoved against me one last time. Then he rolled back to his side of the bed and sighed contentedly.

"You know, I really do think that you are the greatest wife a man could have."

"Love you babe."

Sleep came easily that night, but my dreams were strange. They seemed very real, as though I was walking through my house at night. But the rooms were full of people, men and women I had never seen, all of them watching me, naked. Their bodies reflected candles and starlight from outside, and I could see all the shapes and sizes of them.

CHAPTER FOURTEEN

The following week was a good one. I felt as though I made a lot of progress with my business papers, completing one report and continuing to contribute the mandatory online comments. I even received an email from my professor declaring that she was very pleased with the report after I submitted it! I poured myself a celebratory afternoon wine in honour of that.

I watched another episode of the mothers programme while I was folding some laundry, and I sent Tara a text afterwards, asking if she had started watching the show herself.

Yes, it is very funny! I've just reached the part where the psychologist mum has realised that she might have some mummy issues.

I laughed while I looked at my phone. That character spent almost a whole season in denial about her baggage, and the episode where she finally faced up to what she was doing was so good that I knew exactly where Tara was up to.

Still a long way behind me . i just watched another episode but cant tell you about it

Ill catch you soon then we could watch some together?

Good idea!

When Otis got home that evening he grabbed a beer out of the fridge and came to sit next to me at the kitchen bench. He raised an eyebrow at me then leaned over and clinked his bottle on my glass.

"A good day then," he asked as he took a sip.

"Yeah, I've been pretty pleased with things today!" I took a sip too, letting the pale yellow liquid wash across my tongue. I leaned over and rested a head on Otis' shoulder. He felt so warm.

Later that night I lay in bed staring at the ceiling in the darkness. I decided I needed to get out of the house with Otis. *It's all this domesticity,* I told myself. *Sitting around the house, cooking, cleaning. It's making me forget how much I want him, and that's why I keep finding myself feeling these things about other people. We need to go somewhere where we can unwind and relax together.*

First thing Saturday morning I told Otis and Tilly that we were going to spend the day at the beach. It was reinvigorating, the way Tilly smiled and ran around the house collecting her togs and some beach toys. Otis stepped up to me and held my hips with his hands, pressing his body against me, tucking his mouth into the curve of my neck.

"I haven't seen you in your swimwear in a while," he murmured, his lips feeling soft on my delicate skin. "I'll look forward to this." He lifted his mouth and kissed me, then slapped my butt as he walked off to get his own things together.

I packed a bag with some snacks and drinks to keep us going, and then, just as I was about to tuck my phone into a pouch on the outside I had a thought. I pulled my phone back out of the small space and unlocked it, but then paused with my finger hovering above the screen.

Is this really appropriate? Is this a good idea? Otis and Tilly came bouncing back into the room, carrying their own bags. I smiled at the sight of them, and then quickly typed in a text and sent it.

The beach was filled with people on the weekend, kids throwing brightly coloured balls, a few families flying kites, and people thronging the waves in front of the lifeguard station.

We pulled out a broad blanket and spread it on the grass beneath a wrinkly pohutukawa tree with zigzagging branches and hairy red flowers. The grass gently sloped down to the sand a few meters in front of us, but at least here there was a little shade. I began rubbing sunscreen onto Tilly and my own arms and legs.

"Looks like I'm just in time!"

Talia was walking across the grass from one of the car parks near the beach, carrying her own bag. She was wearing a black bikini and had a bright green wrap of light material wrapped around her waist, and the entire effect made her look like an hourglass.

"Aunt Talia!" shrieked Tilly and she raced over to grab Talia in a hug.

"It's a pleasure to see you too," laughed our friend. She dropped her bag next to the blanket and settled onto her knees beside us. "Hi everyone!"

"Hi Talia! I didn't realise that you were joining us," said Otis with a smile.

"I asked her before we left," I told him.

"Should I go then?" she asked, jerking a thumb over her shoulder and raising an eyebrow.

"No, it's always a pleasure to have you with us," Otis laughed.

I kept rubbing sunscreen on, and held out the bottle to Talia.

"Could you get my back for me?"

"No worries," she replied, moving over to start rubbing the thick white lotion onto my back and shoulders. Her fingers felt gentle and familiar as they moved across the shape of me, down my sides, and along the top of my swimsuit just above my bottom.

"Seeing as I'm sorting out your wife, would you mind dealing with me Otis?" asked Talia.

He moved over and I could hear him squirt the sunscreen into his hands. Although I couldn't see him, I imagined the way he would be moving his hands across our friend, sliding his fingers along her skin, and the curves of her body. I felt a familiar tingle begin to grow with the thought. I smiled to myself.

When all of us had finished running our hands over each other, and the sunscreen was on, Talia and Otis jumped up to chase Tilly along the sand. At first I thought I might join them, but the sun was so bright that my skin felt as though it was burning, and so I retreated back to the blanket and the shade under the tree.

There was a fresh scent on the air, salt and seaweed, and grass and dry dirt. It reminded me of the incense that had been so thick during the meeting with the Many. I frowned and blinked. *That's strange, the scents are nothing alike. Why would the smell of the beach today remind me of that meeting then?*

I lay on the blanket, it's rough fibre scratching at my thighs and shoulders, with my hands behind my head. I looked up into the tree, admiring the golden streaks of light that speared down from it.

The pillars of gold shifted as the leaves and branches moved. In fact, they seemed to rustle more than I would have expected in this breeze. Thick green foliage covered the tree in a dense coat, shrouding me in shadow though the sun and sky seemed bright beyond. One branch swayed slowly lower, and then rose a little, before bending down once more. It looked as though something heavy was moving along the branch, forcing it to bend almost to breaking point. I began to think that maybe I should move our blanket, before the branch broke and fell on me, or before some stray cat fell out of the tree. Then the wind gusted, blowing the leaves aside for one moment, like a curtain being pulled away.

Crouching on the branch, staring down at me, was a short, hairy little creature, with bulbous muscles and skin. Tufts of hair burst from it's chest and the back of its arms. It had huge eyes and a squashed nose, and it's heavy lips were pulled back on it's wide mouth as it leered down at me. It was like Frederick's statue come to squat, ugly life.

I shrieked in fright and flinched away, lifting my hands to ward off the creature. I could see Otis turn to look at me from the sand. I began to point into the tree, to let him know something was there, but when I raised my eyes I could see that the tree was completely empty. The leaves seemed more spread out now, and it was easy to see the thin branches inside the canopy, and even glimpses of the blue sky.

"I thought... I thought that I saw something in the tree..." My voice trailed off. *What had happened?* I shook my head slightly, then took a deep breath.

Laughter bubbled over from the sand and I rolled onto my side to see what the others were doing. Tilly had led the charge into the low rolling waves of the beach, shrieking and jumping over each low white curl of water. Sunlight sparkled around her like an aura made of diamond pieces. *She is so small and perfect,* I thought to myself as I smiled.

Otis was close behind her, hunched over in the water and flicking splashes of seawater at our daughter. Tilly squealed and spun in the water, her shoulders lifted high as though she might be able to pull herself into the air above the cold water. I could hear Otis' laughter across the sand.

Talia was following them both, and her waist seemed somehow more slinky than before. Her black bikini covered less of her from the back and I watched as her buttocks clenched when the water splashed up against her. She reached up to tie her curly hair into a bun, high on her head, and I watched the skin on her back shift as she moved her long arms. *I wonder if she looks like that while she's working on her murals?*

I suddenly found myself thinking of a mental image of Talia, dressed in paint covered overalls, hair bound back behind a mask that protected her from inhaling the fumes from her pile of spray paint cans. Beneath the worn denim straps over her shoulders she had on a tight red top, and as she worked and stretched against the wall in my imagination her body seemed ready for someone to reach out and hold.

I blinked and focused on the trio out in the water. Otis had begun splashing Talia now, and her shrieks and laughter were mixing with the sounds of seagulls drifting on the breeze above us. Talia bounded away through the water, each step making her breasts bounce within the swimsuit. Otis followed and leapt at her, grabbing her around the waist and carrying her under the surface with him. They both stood up, water pouring off them, with huge grins. Otis must have let go of her under the water, but she leaned over and shoved him in the shoulder so hard that he went tumbling back into the water again.

As the afternoon wound on, I enjoyed watching my little family playing in the surf. When Otis walked back over to the blanket where I was waiting, he asked me what I had seen. I felt silly, and avoided describing the vision I had had.

"Nothing really, I thought there was something in the tree."

"Like, a bee or something?"

"Maybe. Maybe I was falling half asleep, and had a mini nightmare," I said, as I searched for an explanation for the ugly little vision I had had. "Anyway I think it might be time to go."

He placed a comforting hand on my shoulder and nodded, then kissed the top of my head before packing away our things, and getting Tilly ready to leave.

Tilly was easy to get to sleep that night, exhausted from running around in the salt and sand. I pulled up the blankets around her shoulders and leaned down to kiss her forehead. *Sleep well little one.* As I walked out of her room, I made sure the small night light on her clothes drawers was on, glowing with a gentle light that shifted from pale pink to deep green.

As I walked down the dark hallway to my bedroom, I found myself thinking of Otis and Talia in the water, the way drops of light had traced the curves of her shoulders and waist and hips, and others had dripped from his nipples as he stood waist deep in the ocean. The cold of the water was hard to imagine as a ball of heat grew inside me.

By the time I stepped into the bedroom my skin felt as

though boiling water was flowing just beneath its surface. Otis was just pulling on a worn old tee shirt and pulling the blanket back from the bed. He looked up at me, catching my eyes.

"What?" he asked.

I walked around the bed and grabbed my husband, pulling him close to me. His hands held the small of my back and I pressed his chest against me. I reached up and pushed my fingers through his hair, pushing his face to mine, meeting his lips with a kiss that was long and slow and hard. As I kissed him I saw images of Talia leaning close to me in the shadows after the art gallery. Instead of dampening my flame, I felt myself burning brighter, and I pulled away from the kiss and gasped.

Otis placed a hand along my jaw and leaned back into the kiss, pulling my hips to him, and I could feel how hard he was. His cock tried to push its way out of the smooth fabric that contained it, and I slid one hand down to hold his shape, rubbing my hand up and down along his length. Now he groaned into our kiss, pulling back to draw a shuddering breath.

I knelt down in front of him, pulling his boxer shorts down along his thighs and leaving them around his ankles on the floor. His cock was standing out from him, straining as though it might try to reach out to me itself. Otis' hands moved around my head and guided me closer, and I let his cock slide along my cheek, until my lips reached the base. I slipped out my tongue and gently traced along his balls and up along his shaft, licking back out to the head. I ran my lips over it and then slid his cock into my mouth. I moved back and forward, enjoying the feeling of my husband inside me, and pushed a hand down the front of my pants so that I could find some relief for myself at the same time.

I was soaking wet and I enjoyed the slick feeling as I ran my own fingers between my lips, teasing myself and then finding the hardness of my clit. I began to rub it, softly and first, but harder and faster as I continued, matching the rhythm of my mouth on his cock. I imagined that it was someone else's hand, someone else's tongue that was stimulating me while I worked on my husband.

I wanted to be laying on the bed, pillows holding me up while Otis was above me, one of my hands behind someone else's head as they buried their face in me and drew orgasm after orgasm out of me. I imagined Talia's curls between my fingers, and then convulsed on my bedroom floor, Otis' cock popping out from my mouth as I came. I felt the gush around my fingers and my legs quivered with the effort of staying upright.

Otis reached down and caught me under my arms, pulling me to my feet. His cock bumped into my stomach as I caught my balance and I reached out to grab it. He turned me and the backs of my legs caught the bed, then I fell onto my back.

I lay spread out along the bed, looking up at my husband standing over me, between my legs. He looked down at me with fiery eyes and his hands reached out to grab my shoulders. I reached up to take his hips in my hands, aware of his cock moving ever closer to my entrance, gasping as it's heat began to move along my lips. Otis bore down on me, kissing me as I pulled him closer. I pulled back.

"What are you thinking about?" I asked, looking up into his eyes. He blinked.

"What do you mean? I'm thinking about... you know..." He glanced down towards his cock, and shifted his hips so that it pressed against me again. I groaned and slid aside.

"I'm thinking about your hands," I said, sliding my own up and down his sides. "I'm thinking about how slippery sunscreen feels." I dug into his skin with my fingers.

"I don't-" he began, but I pushed him sideways and rolled over, scrambling on top of him.

"Does it look good?" I asked, one hand on his chest as I straddled him. His cock was pressed against me perfectly, and I tingled with anticipation. His eyes were wide.

"You look great," he said, confusion in his tone.

"When you see us from behind, I mean." I raised myself up

and turned around so that I was facing away from him. With one hand holding onto his leg, I reached down between mine to find his cock, running my hand along it's hardness for a moment, before guiding his head to my entrance. I heard his breath as I slid down, taking him inside me. I sat in place, enjoying the way he filled me, then began to lean back.

I had to move my legs so that I could support myself comfortably, but I wanted my shoulders and back close to him.

"Touch me," I ordered him. His hands reached up, fingers running over my shoulders and down my sides. As I began to rock backwards and forwards on him, his fingers began to seek around my sides, under my arms, searching for the soft curves of my breasts. I rocked faster, one hand moving down to rub my clit, moving lower to feel what his cock felt like as it entered me. I wondered what it would be like to see Otis' cock sliding inside someone. Someone who wasn't me.

"Does it look good when you are behind us?" I asked again.

"Who?" gasped Otis.

"Anyone. Women," I said.

"It's amazing," he replied, and pulled down my skin with his fingernails, leaving trails of fire in my skin. I imagined what Talia would have felt as he ran those fingers along her skin, and came again, my whole body spasming and shivering on top of Otis.

As I regained myself, he grabbed my hips, pulling me into a rhythm on top of him. He moved me forcefully, and I couldn't tell if I wanted to fight him or not. He pulled me down, his fingertips curling into my hips as his cock thrust up and into me. I could feel every pulse as he came inside me, setting off a wave of pleasure that melted under my skin from my head down my neck and breasts through my arms and fading at the tips of my feet.

Slowly, with weak limbs, I climbed off Otis and rolled into a pile on top of the blanket on my side of the bed. Otis lifted himself on one arm and leaned over to kiss my cheek. Then he climbed off the bed and went into the bathroom. As he got ready for bed, and sleep began to pull at my eyes, I had a swarm of thoughts circling in my mind. *Is it so bad that I enjoy the image of Talia fucking my husband? I think that he enjoys it too. It's hard to be sure. What would she think? Maybe she would be just as excited as he is? Would it be so bad if it actually happened?* But sleep could not be held off any longer

CHAPTER FIFTEEN

The rest of that week I was insatiable. I kept thinking of the way Talia had smiled and laughed with Otis in the waves, and then pulling him into our bedroom, where I would hold him down and run my hands along his body. I would press my lips against his and pull him into me, until I burst with satisfaction.

As well as that, I ran into the builder down the road, Nic, once or twice. He didn't have much to say, but his brilliant eyes would stare into mine and I would feel myself blush, excuse myself, and then retreat to my bed and reach my hands down, using my fingers to caress and rub myself until I felt satisfied. The release I gave myself would tide me over until I was able to get Otis alone again.

But in the back of my mind all that time, was the thought of going back to Kallista's meeting. She had texted me a day or so after the first meeting to see if I had enjoyed myself, and to ask whether or not I would like to come back. I told her that I was definitely interested. But I was still worried that it would turn out badly.

As the date for the next meeting approached, I felt a ball of tension grow in my belly. I began to get more nervous, snapping at Tilly over small things and then stooping to apologise to her. I found that the desire for my husband that had been growing so strong suddenly became more binary, which surprised me. At one moment I would be desperate for him to take me to our bed and fuck me, but then the moment would pass and I would prefer to be left to read a book.

I was glad when I ran into Tara after school, literally bumping into her when I began to rush off with Tilly's hand in my own and I didn't check where I was going.

"Ooof!" came her voice as I rebounded, startled.

"Oh my god, I am so so sorry!" I reached out and grabbed her shoulders, trying to stop her from falling, although she had clearly kept her own balance anyway.

"That's okay," she said, pressing a hand to her forehead and blinking. "Are you in something of a rush?"

"You know, I'm actually not," I admitted. I tried to figure out why I was racing away with Tilly just to get home and go back to my online course while we waited for Otis. "I don't really know what it is this week, but I've felt as though everything is just a step to take towards something else. Do you know what I mean?"

Tara smiled. "Yes indeed! Sometimes it feels like our whole lives are just a scramble to bustle along the busy tunnels of an ant's nest."

"Exactly!"

"How about we take some time out then?"

"What do you mean?"

"There's a playground in the park not far from my place. We could go and let the kids play for a bit. Maybe even go past the shops and get them an icecream?"

I looked down at Tilly next to me, her hand still clutched in mine. She wasn't paying attention to whatever it was us adults were talking about; instead she was watching the other kids go racing by on scooters and bikes, screaming with excitement. *She deserves a bit of fun,* I decided. *After all, we all do from time to time.*

"Let's do it!"

We gathered up Percy and began walking to the park. Tilly and Percy went skipping ahead of us, pointing at birds in the trees along the footpath and jabbering like a pair of pigeons when they found a driveway covered in some child's chalk drawings. Tara and I kept walking as the children checked out the mural, and then they came running after as.

"How is that statue that Peyton was making going? It seemed pretty much finished when I came by the other day."

"Yes, it really is. Peyton is such a perfectionist though, he has started staying up extra hours into the night, just looking for flaws to fix."

"Oh dear, up into the night? How late? How many flaws does he keep finding?"

"None!" Tara shook her head and then tucked her hair behind her ear. "There were plenty to find when he was in the thick of making Tiz, and he would do what he could and then get tired and declare that he was done for the day. But no he finds nothing and is sure he's missed something, so he won't quit until at least eleven o'clock most nights."

"What an odd dedication to the craft." I laughed, hoping she would realise that I didn't mean it negatively.

She smiled too. "Yes, I have tried telling him that he's a dope, but he just says that Tiz deserves nothing less. He's always been like this as he finishes a project."

"That's actually quite sweet."

We arrived at the playground and Tilly began trying to climb up a ladder of metal loops, then jamming her legs over the bars and hanging upside down by her knees. Tara and I found a bench and sat down, stretching our arms along the back of the wooden planks and sighing in the shade of a broad tree.

"I don't know where you both come up with ideas like that guardian," I told her absently. "I would never look at a pile of junk metal and think that it could all be put together so beautifully. And with such a sweet idea behind it, a guardian for someone."

"It's not so hard once you start. Imagination is like a muscle, you just have to exercise it." Tara pointed at our children. Percy was laughing as he climbed around the outside of the playground and Tilly ran along the bark beneath him. Tilly was stretching up and trying to tag him with her hand, but he kept managing to pull himself out of reach at the last second. I could just hear him shouting at this distance, "You'll never get me lava monster!"

"They don't need to exercise it. They get practice every day. But you and I?" she gestured to herself now. "We have to make time to use our imaginations or they fade away."

"I think I use my imagination," I began, but she didn't seem convinced.

"Everyone does. But how often do you go out and expose yourself to new art, new ideas? How often do you create something that no one else has ever dreamt of?"

I felt annoyed. Tara had been very kind to me, but this felt like an attack, what made her think that she knew me this well?

My feelings must have come through in my face, because Tara leaned forward and laid a hand on my arm. "I'm sorry, I don't mean that to sound cruel. It's something that everyone has to be aware of, not you in particular. We grow up and we find someone to love and we have children, and it's all satisfying and cozy, but it isn't something new."

I realised that I had been feeling that way recently, even without Tara's comments, and told her so.

"You see? So Peyton and I always make time to go to galleries, and watch unusual movies and television, and seek out strange music. You know, we try to look for new ideas on purpose and then that helps us come up with our own when we create."

"That does sound good. Have you seen anything recently that you would recommend? My best friend took me to an art gallery exhibit launch a few weeks ago."

"That's perfect! I went to one recently myself. It was really wonderful to see so many different views and experiences on display." She sniffed slightly and murmured to herself as she continued thinking. "You already came to a gallery opening, so you've seen some new art. How about 'Synchronicity?'"

"What's that?"

"A movie that Peyton and I watched the other night. We found it in some out of the way subcategory on Netflix. It's about this scientist who thinks he has found a way to travel in time, and then he falls in love and is betrayed, but actually he wasn't travelling through time exactly..." she trailed off, waving her hands in the air, and then grinned. "It's hard to explain. But it really was a good one for encouraging us to think of new ways to interpret the world!"

"It sounds complicated." I wasn't sure if I wanted that. I had thought that my life was quite simple, but small changes were already leaving me feeling more overwhelmed than I had anticipated. Maybe complicated just wasn't for me. Maybe I need to find ways to simplify my life.

"I suppose. But life is complicated," replied Tara, unconsciously answering my own internal thoughts. "And sometimes we just don't see what's really going on. It's so hard to be truly aware and present, even when we think things are working as we wanted."

I thought about everything that had been happening to me recently. The way I was feeling about Talia and Kallista and Nic. The way I kept treating Otis so hot and cold. My lack of focus when it came to my business course. *Oh god, I haven't checked on that properly in so long, didn't I have a report that I was supposed to be completing and submitting soon?* I resolved to check as soon as I got back home.

"I suppose you're right. I feel like taking some time to think through and check what is really going on is something I need to really take on board these days."

"I can tell you this much," said Tara. "You are really sitting with me in this park on a sunny day while our children have a great time."

I smiled at her. "It's pretty good, right?"

She leaned back and lifted her face to the blue sky. I knew that she wouldn't be able to see in the brightness, but a smile spread across her face too as it was warmed by the sun. "It really is."

I WAS WOKEN in the middle of the night that Friday, by a knocking on the front door. It was a strange sound, by turns loud and rapid but then soft and infrequent. As I rolled over and sat up, my sleep filled brain slowly processed the noise, until finally it was able to identify what was happening. *Someone doesn't want to be a nuisance, but also wants to wake us up. But they also don't want to wake us up.* I got out of bed and padded across to the hall, down through the orange glow of Tilly's nightlight to the kitchen, and through to the front door. The world was dark outside. The person knocked again.

Carefully I unlocked the door and pulled it open a few centimetres.

"Yes?"

"Thank goodness you're up!" It was Talia standing outside the door, with wide eyes and hair that looked more wind tossed than usual. "Is it okay if I come in?"

"Yes, of course. I wasn't actually awake you know." I pulled the door the rest of the way open and stepped back as she moved inside. She shivered and rubbed at her shoulders.

"Why are you here? And what time is it?"

"I have no idea." She scrubbed at her eyes with the heels of her hands and slumped down at one of the stools by the kitchen bench.

I looked at the microwave and saw 12.23 glowing in square numbers on it's display.

"It's after midnight. Is everything okay? Where have you been tonight?"

I pulled a tall glass out of the cupboard and filled it with water from the tap, then handed it over to her. She smiled at me and took a long gulp and then drew a deep breath.

"I just went to see a new group at the Cellar," she answered after she had steadied herself. "It was a lovely show, they do this sort of sea shanty music? Very catchy." Her head wobbled a little. "And I drank a lot of wine and then on the way home I thought, What are Pene and Otis doing right now? I bet they don't feel as sick as I do." And as soon as she said it, her eyes bulged a little and she hunched forward.

"Oh god, don't be sick, don't be sick!" I leapt to another cupboard and shoved my hands in looking for a mixing bowl to catch any vomit before it could cover the bench.

"I'm okay!" Talia puffed out her lips. "I was a bit off there for a second, but I'm okay now. So I got the driver to drop me here!" She spread her arms wide, as though she had just completed a magic trick, with her smile just as wide. I had to laugh as I walked around to hug her shoulders.

"Oh Talia, that's really sweet. We're all asleep though, you know that. We don't have wild Friday nights anymore."

Talia tilted her head back to look at me, those deep eyes suddenly so serious. "I think I'm over the wild friday nights myself." She lifted a hand and rested it on the back of mine where I was holding her shoulder. I swallowed.

"Shall we set you up on the couch?" I asked as I stepped back slightly. "I'll leave you a bowl and we'll chat in the morning."

Talia smiled again. "Yes please. I like it when I wake up in this house."

After arranging a blanket from the hallway cupboard over my friend and checking to see that she had her face sideways so that she wouldn't roll onto her back, I turned off all the lights and went back to my own bed and my husband. He was snoring, lightly and in a strange rhythm, but I snuggled in next to him and slid my arm over his chest.

As I waited for sleep to come back to me, I felt closer to him than I had all day. I didn't know what it was that was warming me again but it felt good, especially as I had found my tension all week had led me to feeling disconnected from him. I felt a familiar tingle begin to grow and let my leg seek out his. I breathed deeply, slowly, as I felt the hair of his leg catch against my skin, as I pushed it gently back and forward.

I heard his breath change, small grumbles acting in the back of his throat, as his body turned slightly. I reached my hand down, seeking him out, and found him immediately, hard and pressing against the shorts he was sleeping in. I pulled at the elastic band, tucking my fingers underneath and wrapping around him, the warmth of his skin flooding through my veins. He reached out to me now, his hands catching at my breasts, my shoulders.

I rolled away from him, and smiled as I heard his muddled confusion. He was still mostly asleep, and his instincts didn't know what was going on. I held his hands against me as I turned and then moved back towards him, and his hardness traced across the curve of my buttocks. I reached down to guide him inside me, sighing as I felt his pressure relieve the pressure that had built below my stomach. I heard his quiet moan as he pressed deeper.

Will she hear us, I wondered. The darkness lay over us, heavier than the blankets that we moved beneath. The faint rustling, and our breaths blowing from our mouths, seemed louder than fireworks to me. But I knew that Talia would be fast asleep now anyway, even if our noises had been loud enough to pique her interest. The cold disappointment of that realisation sat in my stomach, conflicting with the warmth of my husband.

In the darkness we rocked together, his hands caressing me from behind, mine holding his to me. I pulled in lungfuls of air that brought a fresh clean feeling washing over me, keeping rhythm against the heat that drove inside me.

All too soon Otis clung harder and pressed deeper, and I felt his warmth burst, bringing a glowing heat that spread out and up my neck, until I was sure my cheeks were on fire.

I was barely conscious of him pulling away, as the sensation swaddled my mind and I fell into a dreamless sleep.

WHEN I WOKE in the morning, I was alone. I was confused for a second. Where's Otis? My hand was resting on his side of the bed, as though it had been on his chest and then he had vanished, letting my hand drift down to settle on the sheets below. I sat up on my elbows and looked around the room, twisting my neck and stretching out my muscles.

"Babe?" I called out softly. I could hear some murmuring from the kitchen and lounge.

I padded down the hallway, pulling up my old faded pajama pants that were threatening to slip off my hips entirely. Otis was in the kitchen bustling around a set of mugs on the counter. He smiled at me and gestured at one of the mugs, then leaned over to kiss me quickly as he picked up the others. He walked off towards the lounge.

I could hear the high pitched voice of one of Tilly's favourite cartoons, an annoying young white rabbit boy. *Oh, poor Talia! She'll have a terrible hangover!* But when I walked in, she was leaning on the arm of the couch, with Tilly curled up in her arms, and the blanket tucked around them both. Talia looked for all the world like someone who had never been more entertained than by this rabbit arguing with his baby brother in their garden.

Otis walked around the back of the couch and handed one of the mugs to Talia. She almost rolled her eyes in ecstasy and mouthed "Thank you!" to Otis. He smiled and touched the top of her head and then walked back over to me, sipping at his own mug. He slid his arm around my waist and squeezed. I leaned my head onto his shoulder. *Does it matter that I don't feel worried when he touches her like that?* It was so casual and so familiar. I pulled my lower lip between my teeth. *Does that mean that I don't love him any more? I was so excited to feel his touch last week. But then I had felt so turned off by him. Was it all a sign that I was done with him?*

"When did this one show up?" he whispered into the top of my head.

"You don't mind do you?" I hadn't even thought about that. If he was upset by the sudden arrival of my oldest friend, he wasn't showing it, but it must have been strange for him to wander out of his room in the morning and discover her on the couch.

"Of course not. I just hope she's alright. Nothing bad happening that caused her to come running over to our place?"

"No, she just had a big night and got drunk and wanted to come to see us."

"How sweet," he chuckled and sipped at his tea again. I squeezed him back and then stepped away to perch on the other end of the couch. Tilly barely looked at me, her wide eyes fastened on the TV screen. Talia glanced my way though, through eyes rimmed in thick black smudges of make up. I began to giggle and then caught myself.

"Feeling alright?" I asked carefully, watching for winces on her face.

She nodded. "Tea is good."

I stretched out along the couch, my feet pressing into the pile of blankets over my daughter and friend. I felt warm bodies underneath and then a foot pressed back onto me. It was too big to be Tilly. I smiled at Talia and she smiled back. Then she let her head drift down to her shoulder and her eyes closed. *I guess she still needs some sleep,* I laughed to myself. I looked over the back of the couch to where Otis stood smiling down at us all. *And I do still love him. So why do I feel this way?*

CHAPTER SIXTEEN

My feelings remained erratic all through the rest of the week as I waited for Friday night and the next meeting of the Many. I knew that I was feeling a sense of anxiety about returning, but I knew I wanted desperately to get back as soon as possible. It was the same conflict that I was feeling about Otis, desire and fear. I poured myself a small glass of wine each night, hoping that it would soothe my nerves and let me sleep without my mind racing.

As I drove my car into the carpark on Friday night and slid up next to the other tightly packed cars, my teeth were almost chattering. I turned off the engine and stepped out, drawing a deep breath as I walked towards the darkened door and windows.

Something growled at me from the left of the building and I spun, lifting my heads to defend myself. In the row of trees that lined the fence just beyond the end of the hall, a large shape was squatting in the shadows. The sunset was washing the car park in deep reds and darkness, and whatever it was that lurked there seemed gigantic. I swallowed hard and stepped sideways.

If I can get inside, I'll be okay, I thought, holding a hand out sideways as if I could pull myself towards the hall faster. I stepped slowly, hoping not to trip on the bottom step. Just as I felt it's concrete edge bump against the side of my shoe, the form darted out from the shadows, tearing across the carpark between the cars that were packed tightly in. It caught me by surprise, and the evening light cast long shadows on strange angles, but I would have sworn that it was a huge cat, with yellow fur and covered in small black splotches. *A leopard? That's ridiculous.* I blinked and rubbed my eyes. *I must be seeing things. Maybe I'm too worked up about this meeting.* I clambered up the steps quickly, one hand on my chest as I tried to restrain my breathing.

As soon as the door opened, my nerves vanished. Kallista came out to greet me, with wide arms and a broad smile.

"Penelope, you look an absolute dream!" she declared as she wrapped her arms around me. She stepped back and slipped her arm into mine as we stepped inside. "I am so sorry that I haven't been able to see you at all this month, work has been so busy. But, that's part of the benefit that this regular get together offers, isn't it?" she laughed in a voice like bells.

"I think so. I'm looking forward to getting to know some of the other ladies better as well." I accepted the glass of wine offered to me in the hall by a woman I recognised from last time but whose name I couldn't remember.

"I look forward to getting to know you too," the new woman said. Kallista patted her on the arm and then swirled away amongst the ladies.

"She is a bit of a whirlwind, isn't she?" I asked, watching as Kallista left.

"Absolutely," laughed my new companion. "She's always been like this, chaos and beauty. I think she's admirable."

"She has certainly been very successful in what she does, maybe I need to be a bit more chaotic myself!" I sipped at the rich dark wine.

"We all could use some more chaos, that's for sure," agreed

my friend. *Was her name Ness,* I thought, trying to remember so that I wouldn't seem rude.

Kallista left the hall and I looked around at the women gathered there. They wore all sorts of clothes, telling me something about the lives they came from. Some were in tie-dyed loose fabrics, some were in their black and white corporate clothes. All were smiling and chatting. I made some small talk about my week with Ness, and learned that she worked in a clothing store nearby.

Kallista came back in with Agatha bundled under her wing and got her a glass of wine. I recognised her as the other newbie from the last meeting. The young girl ended up standing with Ness and me.

"You came back too?" she asked me.

"Yeah. I had a great time last time. How about you?"

"Obviously," she replied, but with a broad smile. "I haven't stopped thinking about it. I could have come for another meeting the next day!"

"Me too! There was something freeing about it!" I took another mouthful of my wine.

"It's called Catharsis," said Ness. "One of the main things the Many try to achieve here. If you expel all your thoughts and emotions, and process them, then we have done our job."

"I think it's working!" I said. *The Many. I wonder what it means? I've been thinking the name all month, and never questioned it until now.*

"Welcome ladies, can we gather around please!" Kallista had taken her place at the front of the hall. "We are in for a treat tonight! There are no new guests tonight, although we do have Agatha and Pene returning from last time." There was a murmur from the women in the hall. "So, we can let loose a little more than last time." She sought out my eyes. "Don't take offence you two, but we do try to take into account when there are newcomers. You still have a lot to learn about our little group!" Small giggles broke out around me. Someone had lit plates of incense around the room, sending up slow swirling columns of thick sweet smoke.

"Without further ado, please take your places." She settled down into the same seated position that she had instructed us to take at the beginning of the last meeting. "We meet, as always, in honour of the god, and in order to show our devotion to him. In return, we seek only that he share his bounty with us."

We all took our places as well. I felt much more relaxed this time. Even the awkward position of my legs felt more natural than it had last time. I felt less self-conscious about the prayer that Kallista seemed to be giving. It was her thing, and it guided this group, but that didn't mean I had to really take it seriously. And still no one had asked for any money! Talia must have been over reacting.

"First, as we do each meeting, take the time to visit with yourself in silence. We have all drunk from our cup, and so we can now begin to unveil ourselves. The first revelation is personal. Visit with yourself."

At the same time as those around me, I lowered my head and closed my eyes. This time the 'visiting' felt easier, smoother. I thought through the muscles of my body, experienced the sensation of my skin. I thought through myself and felt my awareness of my body separate from the body itself. I felt as though I were running my fingertips along my own shoulders from behind, then down my sides. The hairs on the back of my neck and arms began to stand up. I relished the feelings that I could take the time to focus on. As I breathed in, my nostrils were over whelmed with the sweet floral incense.

All too soon, Kallista prompted us out of our reverie and directed us into the circle. I began with Ness and surprised myself at my own ease with revealing my deepest thoughts and emotions. I had thought that I would be sharing so much positivity. The last few weeks had felt so good while I was in them. But instead I found that I was talking about the way I had felt judged by Tara, how I felt as though she didn't think I was grown up enough to decide what I did with my own life. I said that Otis was boring me in his regularity, and realised the truth of it as I said it. *Why hadn't I said that to myself before now,* I wondered. I mentioned my confusion about how Talia had been acting. The circle moved on and I spoke with three other wonderful women, all of whom shared deeply and honestly with me.

Then, I shifted one more space in the circle, and I was sitting with Kallista.

"Pene, I'm so pleased that I get to circle with you." As always, her smile was large,and her eyes were bright. She was dressed in a long black dress with thin straps and a billowing skirt. Her hair was pulled forward over her shoulder in a tight braid.

Kallista told me about her concerns running the group. She described the way she felt nervous when addressing a group of powerful women, especially when so many of them would ask her questions that she might not know the answer to. She admitted that it was only her belief that the god would guide her responses that got her through.

I did find it hard to listen to her speaking about the god. She always said it like that. "The God", never just "God". I wondered why it was so different here. Of course, the group was meeting in his honour, but I had hoped to basically ignore that side of things. I still didn't think that a religious group was something I wanted. *But, I am here,* I thought to myself. *I'll try to keep an open mind.*

When it was my turn, I told her about my time since the last meeting, and how I had been feeling really good, but that my positive experience was tempered by warnings from a friend since before the last meeting. I expected Kallista to explain why I shouldn't listen to that friend, or to be offended, but she just nodded and accepted what I said completely. It made me want to hug her.

After our part of the circle ended, she leaned over and squeezed my shoulder.

"It sounds like you have some conflicting ideas and feelings that you will need to resolve. Let me know if there's anything I can do." And with that small personal touch we moved on, each sharing ourselves with someone else. I found that I was opening up much more in this circle, and it was building a gratifying sense of release, as though I had been drained of something poisonous.

"Thank you sisters. Every circle winds us closer together."

I smiled at the woman I was facing and we both stood up and turned to face the front of the small hall. Kallista was walking to take her position at the front, making eye contact with each of us. It felt as though she was standing right next to me, though long meters separated us and there were other women in between. The sweet perfume of the incense felt as though it was seeping into my head, soaking into my brain.

"We began with ourselves, and have expanded to one another. And now each of us needs to become one of the Many!" She lifted her hands into the air. "And tonight there are no new faces, so we can be truly vulnerable." And then she reached down to push the straps of her dress to the side, allowing the whole dress to slither down her figure to the floor.

As the speakers crackled into life, the rhythmic music starting to echo off the walls, I was struck into stillness. Kallista's body was totally exposed, and I couldn't tear my eyes away. She hadn't been wearing any bra or underwear, and now she was completely naked. Her skin was clear and smooth, and the small darkness of her pubic hair drew my gaze. I swallowed. She began to dance, sinuously winding her arms and swaying her hips. The movement pulled her small breasts slightly, and her hard nipples shifted with them.

All around me was the rustle of clothing being removed. I blinked and looked around and saw even the grumpy woman from the last meeting, Lacey, had pushed her shirt over her head and stepped out of her skirt. I saw large breasts that hung low, I saw stomachs that wobbled, I saw legs with stretch marks. Some had large bushes of hair covering themselves, many were trimmed and controlled. But no one hesitated, no one felt as though their body was unacceptable. The lights were low, and the wine was warming my veins and fogging my head. I decided that I would join them.

As I pulled my own clothes off, bundling them in my hands to pile at one side of the room, I looked around for Agatha. She was my only reference point, the only other person who was remotely in the same position as me. I wondered if she had been scared off by this.

But no, she was already completely naked too, and lost in the music. Her arms held high, she was stepping in rhythm with the drums and spinning round and round. Swirls of incense traced her form, like spirits trying to dance with her.

I have never danced like that before. The air on parts of my body that would normally be covered made my skin feel more sensitive than ever. I felt my pulse in my core and looked forward to getting home to Otis. The bodies of the others were a warm presence around me. As I moved in the middle of the room, I couldn't avoid bumping into them, my hands resting on their shoulders, their bottoms brushing past my hips. My skin quivered and my breath came in shallow sighs as I lifted my arms to the beat and felt my body respond to the rhythm.

Even though my eyes were closed, I could see Kallista's eyes before me, dark as soil and deep as a cave, watching me, watching me move.

When the dancing came to an end, I knew my cheeks were flushed bright red. I could feel my pussy aching to be touched, and it made me squirm as I pulled my clothes back on. Everyone's face was as red as mine, and I saw a few eyes that were glazed over. I wondered if I could make it back home, or if I would need to pull over somewhere dark and relieve the tension myself.

"Thank you for joining us in these more open circumstances," said Kallista. She stood at the front of the room, still naked, her skin electric with the heat and sweat of the dance. Her eyes saw all. "But we must ask you both to leave before we continue into the final parts of the meeting. Thank you for being here Pene, Agatha." She clasped her hands together in front of her chest.

"Thank you so much," exclaimed Agatha. As we left the room, still straightening our clothes, I thought I heard a strange clattering noise from a door behind the wine table. I paused and looked closer, but the table was surrounded by women pouring themselves new glasses of wine. I looked at the door behind them. *Was that a light showing underneath the edge of the door? And, perhaps, were those shadows moving into it?* Feet stepped into my line of sight, and I looked up into the stern face of Lacey.

"You need to leave now Pene," she said, holding her wine glass precariously in crossed arms.

"Yes, I know," I smiled, trying to soothe her. I thought I heard one more clatter, like coconut shells banging hollowly together, but then Lacey shooed me out of the hall and into the car park with Agatha. Together we stood in the chilly air and waited as the cars were maneuvered back and forth so that we could leave.

"That was much more intense than I had expected," I mentioned to Agatha.

"I know. Wasn't it great!" she replied. Her eyes shone, even in the darkness of the night outside the hall.

It did feel great, I told myself. *It felt amazing! Like the whole world was compressed down to fit inside my body.* I turned to look at the hall, it's windows dark, hiding it's secrets from us. *But Tara may have had a point. What happens to someone who completely lets themselves live in their emotions and whims?*

I shook my head, worried about the way the sweet thick incense and large glasses of wine had made me suggestible. Dancing naked with strangers wasn't my usual way of spending an evening!

The memory of Tara's warning sat in the back of my head as

I drove home. I felt uneasy about what had happened in the meeting. Clearly Kallista was more serious about the religious aspect of things than I had realised. I didn't know how to feel about that. I had never really considered what I thought about religion. *Gods weren't real, were they?* The moon hung low in the sky, bathing the road in silver light, watching me all the long and cold drive home.

My earlier excitement had faded, faster than I expected, and by the time I crawled into bed next to Otis, I didn't want him anymore. At least, I didn't want his sex, I didn't want to grapple with him and feel the fire from inside myself. Instead, I rolled sideways and shuffled back against him, pulling his arm around my shoulders like a blanket. The heat we built between each other was soft and comforting; not an inferno, but life-giving. I fell into sleep.

CHAPTER SEVENTEEN

*B*y Monday my thoughts were hard to pin down. I had so much swirling around in my head that I would find myself pouring a glass of water and not noticing that the water had filled the glass completely and was now overflowing. *Maybe I should ask to see Kallista,* I thought. *Maybe we need to have a bit more of a discussion about what's going on here.*

I sent her a message but she said she was busy the whole week. *I suppose that's not surprising,* I admitted to myself, but then she sent through another message explaining that she had an appointment to meet someone at Avagadro's on Wednesday and she might be able to squeeze in a chat with me after her meeting.

Tahnk you that sounds good I replied.

That morning I strolled up to the café feeling better already. Just the thought of getting to sit down and enjoy Kallista's company again made me feel much less uprooted. It made me feel as though I was settling into calm waters, where I might be able to rest and relax and let the sun shine down on me. Then I saw her.

Kallista was sitting at a table near the tall windows at the front of the café, leaning back so far that I was sure that she was about to slip off the seat entirely and onto the ground. The sunlight made her dark hair sparkle as though tiny jewels had been strung through it. I smiled.

On the other side of the table though, was Lacey. I nearly tripped as I stepped through the wide doors. *What is she doing here,* I wondered angrily. *If there's anyone I'm less interested in sharing my meeting with, it would be her.* As always, the woman's face was sour. She looked as though she had been sucking on a lemon. Neither of them had noticed me however, and I did wonder if maybe I should leave and pretend something else had come up.

I drew a deep breath and made myself walk over to their table. I had come here to see if Kallista could help me understand why I felt so confused about what had been happening. I needed to ensure that I took advantage of her attention and figured things out.

"...too big for this hall, and it is far too public," Lacey was saying as I got close enough to overhear what they were saying.

"It is a fine line to tread, between keeping the rites sacred and sharing with others, but we do want the Many to grow–"

"Hello Pene," interrupted Lacey. She had turned her head and narrowed her eyes at me like a cat who had spotted a stray walking onto her territory.

"Good morning guys," I said, offering a smile for Kallista as she turned around. She stood up out of her chair and leaned forward to give me a warm hug.

"So lovely to see you Pene! I'm sorry that I didn't have much time to spare this week, and you seemed quite in need of someone to talk to."

"I didn't know my time was so unimportant to you," muttered Lacey.

"Should I go?" I asked, unsure how to respond.

"Whatever," said the other woman, waving me into a seat. She picked up her coffee cup and turned away as she took a sip, looking across the other customers seated at the tables further inside.

"I'm glad that you reached out to me," said Kallista, guiding me into a seat and pouring a glass of water for me. She frowned. "I should have ordered a wine earlier, I did know you were coming."

"That's okay."

Kallista smiled. "But you called for me to help when you were having a tough time. I feel so honoured! What is the problem?"

"I don't know if it's a problem, really," I began, glancing over at Lacey. The sharp woman was pretending to look away, but I wondered how likely it was that she would be eavesdropping. *Do I care what she hears? Will it make me vulnerable to her?*

"It's just that the meetings have made me feel..." I paused, searching for the right words to describe the floating burning sensation that had begun to fill my head most days. "Eager. Free. Does that make sense? It's sort of scary."

Kallista nodded and reached out to take both my hands in her own.

"The first steps into a new world are always scary. And that is what this is. Your eyes are opening to possibilities that you didn't even know existed. Suddenly you see that there are more options for your life than you had ever dreamed! And the size of it is intimidating."

I nodded. "And the fact that it is all on me. That's a lot."

"It is," said Kallista, tilting her head slightly. Her eyes were wide and serious as they studied me. "But it is the only real choice. We have to be responsible for ourselves."

I took a deep breath.

"It would help if I could tell Otis more about it."

Kallista's hands slid back to her side of the table and she bit her lip.

"Is that your husband?" Lacey's voice cut in.

I grimaced but nodded again.

"Typical," she snorted.

"Don't you see Pene, if you tell him everything, then you aren't really taking responsibility for yourself are you?" Kallista's smile was beginning to peek back from her cheeks.

"I guess not?"

"No, certainly not! But you will spend time with him, and as you make more choices for your well-being, I am sure he will notice the benefits." She leaned over the table and her eyes sparkled. "How often do you take responsibility for yourself?"

"I thought we were just saying that I am only just starting to understand-"

"No no no," laughed Kallista. She tossed her head, shifting her hair. "I mean, getting to grips with your *self.*" She waggled her eyebrows and grinned.

"She means mastubation," said Lacey with a straight face.

"Oh!" I coughed and felt my cheeks begin to glow. "Uh, not often," I admitted. "There has been some inspiration recently however..." I looked down at the table, but couldn't stop the smile that stretched onto my face.

"New inspiration?" Kallista raised an eyebrow.

"Just... just someone I see around sometimes. He's very good looking."

"I approve," said Kallista. She reached down to her bag and pulled out a sleek black phone. "I want to make sure that you are really doing things properly. Do you have one of these?"

She swiped through her phone and then leaned forward to show me what she had on it's screen. She had opened a website and there was something black and smooth and curved there. I had to twist my head and squint to try and figure out what I was looking at.

"Oh my god," I said when I realised what it was.

"The best toy on the market!" said Kallista.

"I could never," I said, a hand over my mouth.

"What? That's a ridiculous thing to say! Every woman needs something like this, to ensure that they are getting good orgasms on demand!"

The idea of being able to guarantee my pleasure did sound appealing, but I had never considered getting any sort of sex toy. *Isn't my husband supposed to be enough for me, what sort of person am I if I can't be satisfied by what he brings to me?* I thought about how I had been feeling recently, and wondered if I had to admit that he did not satisfy me. The idea made my stomach tense.

"Pene, my question is, do you have anything even close to this? I'm guessing that the answer is no from your reaction."

I shook my head. I couldn't help but notice that Lacey was rolling her eyes at me.

"Oh Pene. We need to fix that. Here," and she poked at the screen quickly. My phone buzzed in my handbag sitting on the ground beside my chair. "I've sent you the link and I'm not letting you leave until you've ordered one with express delivery."

"Express," I laughed nervously.

"Absolutely!" Kallista's eyes were wide and shining. "You don't understand what freedom awaits you!"

Under those burning eyes I had to dig out my phone and click on the link that she had sent me. The toy appeared on my phone, and I could feel myself beginning to blush again. I dug out my credit card and entered the number onto the checkout of the website, while I had to try to ignore Lacey and Kallista watching me in silence, sipping on the last drops of their drinks.

A waiter came by to ask them if they wanted refills just as my order was confirmed and the screen popped back to the listing, displaying the whole black and silver phallus shaped toy across the whole screen. I heard the poor young man stutter as he must have caught a glimpse of it from over my shoulder, and I could feel my head shrinking into my torso.

"Well done," Kallista congratulated me after the waiter had gone. "You are about to experience a wider, wonderful world."

The next day, when I got home from dropping Tilly to school, there was a small white cardboard box sitting on the front step in front of my door. I got out of the car and walked over to it, as slowly and cautiously as a bomb squad engineer. I picked it up in both hands and carried it inside, setting it gingerly on the kitchen bench. Then I got a bottle of water out of the fridge and poured myself a tall glass, before sitting down on a stool and staring at the box.

What is in that box, I wondered. Oh, I knew what it would be, obviously. But I was wondering why it was that Kallista had insisted that I buy one, right there in the café? She seemed to think that it would result in me getting to live a better life somehow. How would that happen? What connection could a vibrator possibly have to whether or not I'm having a good life?

I gulped down the water. Then I got up and went around to the other side of the kitchen bench and pulled out a knife. I stabbed it into the crease at the top of the box and slit open the tape holding the flaps of the box closed. I put the knife back away in the drawer before I took hold of the box lid though. I paused and breathed in and out. Then I opened it.

There was a second box inside the first, and it slid out with a faint rustle of cardboard. It looked expensive, and sleek, like a really high end cellphone. As I opened the second box, I felt my pulse quicken. The vibrator was set into a purpose moulded black interior that had a velvety texture. There was a slippery instruction booklet sitting on top of it, which made me laugh. *Who needs instructions for this?*

I reached in and lifted it out of the insert, cradling it's heavy length in my hand. I could feel my pussy beginning to respond to the feeling of it in my hands. It felt as though the device had a battery that was sending a low trembling wave of electricity into my hands and up my arms, and then down and past my belly.

I turned it around, looking at it from all sides. It was covered in soft smooth black rubber, and it felt almost like real skin. As I slid my fingers up it's side, curling them around the shaft, I shivered. There was a chrome coloured stripe up each side, but the surface was surprisingly warm. I found three buttons at the base, and pressed the top one.

The vibrator began shaking, gentler than a nervous mouse and quieter than a fly in another room. I pressed the top button again, and again, and the speed and noise increased each time.

Eventually I didn't notice it increasing any more, but the vibrator was humming and taking much more strength to hang onto by then. I pressed the second button, and the vibrator introduced rhythm, stopping and starting in pulses. The beat changed with each press of the second button. When I pressed the bottom button, the device began to slow down, until it was turned off again.

There was a loud knock at the front door, and I nearly threw the vibrator into the air. I managed to fumble and grab at it before it clattered across the counter, and I stuffed it back into it's fitted box, then spun around on the stool. I patted my cheeks with my hands, wondering if they appeared as hot and red as they felt.

I opened the door and felt my heart lurch sideways in my chest. Nic, the builder from down the street, was standing there, staring directly into my eyes with his piercing blue ones. He stood with tanned arms crossed, the veins along his forearms standing out heavy against his strong muscles. His scruffy beard was begging me to reach out and run my fingers through it. I stepped back.

"Good morning," he grumbled, blinking and looking from side to side.

"Hello," I stammered.

"I was just running late for a final check down the road, and I realised that I hadn't come to see about that job you had in mind?" He was scratching the back of his arm now.

"Oh. Yes. Um" I could hear myself scrambling for time as I tried to restart my brain. *Job, what job did I have in mind?* The only job I could think of right now was the one that had me lying down on the bed in front of him and discovering what his body would feel like as he pressed down on top of me. "Oh, the deck."

"Yeah, that sounds right."

"The thing about that is, we haven't actually managed to get our finances sorted for that yet, and I don't know if we are going to be able to do it." I swallowed and twisted my fingertips in one another.

Nic nodded and I saw his eyes slip over my shoulder. They widened and he blinked and then smirked.

"I'll give you my card and you can let me know when you're ready," he said, reaching into the back of his dusty shorts to pull out a faded leather wallet. He handed the card to me. "I'm sure you'll have a good afternoon."

I stood on the doorstep, holding his simple business card in both hands, watching him trudge back across the driveway to where his van was parked. He climbed into the front and waved at me as he started it up with a bang and cloud of smoke, and then pulled away.

I closed the door and turned slowly, where I saw the vibrator had been left on and had shaken it's way out of the box and was slowly edging across the counter. *Oh my god,* I realised. *He must have seen it!* I felt so exposed that I might shrivel up and die.

What would he think of me? I considered what he might have thought and felt my breath grew heavy. *How might he picture me in his mind now?* I imagined him watching me as I used the toy, and clenched.

I stormed past the counter, snatching up the toy, and dashed into my bedroom, where I flung the covers back and began pulling my clothes off. My pulse was racing faster and faster as I got each item off, each movement bringing me closer to the moment when I could experience my brand new toy.

I lay back on the sheets, fully naked, stretching out to enjoy the fresh feeling on my skin. Then I lifted the toy and lay it on my stomach. I pressed the button and it began to hum. The pressure was like being tickled, but so much more pleasurable. I let the length of it press down my stomach, towards the soft skin where my leg met my hip. I could feel myself beginning to open up.

As my breath caught in my throat, I smelled sweet flowers, just the same as the incense that had caressed my naked skin at the last meeting. It melted my muscles and I traced my lower lip with my tongue, feeling my skin prickle with anticipation.

I imagined what Nic would say if he knew that this is what I was doing so soon after he spoke to me. I imagined him standing in the doorway to the bedroom, his eyes watching my body shiver, watching as I moved the toy closer and closer to my self.

As it pressed at the edge of my lips I gasped and closed my eyes, imagining that it was Nic's hands that were pressing on my skin. The movement made me feel warmth spread out from my stomach and my pussy throbbed. I pressed in with the toy, feeling the way it stretched me open, its vibrations easing me wider. As the toy moved further inside me, I shuddered and gasped, nearly losing my hold on it as I shook. The vibrating shaft lay along me, pressing on my clit and I felt my entire body squeeze as every muscle tightened.

What if it short circuits, I panicked as I felt my orgasm wash over my skin and then burst from inside me. My fingers were soaked but I kept moving the toy, over and in and out. Nothing zapped me from inside, and so I kept moving, kept drawing my orgasms out from within, until I could move no longer and my legs lay jelly-like on the bed.

As I lay in the bed, staring at the ceiling, trying to catch my breath, my thoughts darted around as badly as they had during the meeting with the Many. *I get it,* I thought. *She wanted me to know that relying on one person for everything can't work. I can rely on myself for more of this if I need to.* I thought of Nic, walking away from me at the door. *Maybe I can rely on more than myself.*

CHAPTER EIGHTEEN

I kept messaging Tara for the next week. Otis was never going to be as interested in the TV show we were watching and I needed someone to joke with about it. She had managed to catch up to me on it, and we would text each other when we had time to watch so that we could watch at the same time and send comments to each other.

I was disappointed that we didn't manage to actually spend much time together in person, other than brief greetings when picking up the kids after school. I wanted to ask her what she though about my realisation that one person couldn't be everything for someone. I wanted to ask her whether Peyton was everything for her. But I didn't think I could do that through text messages. *Maybe when we arrange that manicure, I'll be able to ask her more about her relationship.*

A week after my toy arrived, I was driving home after dropping Tilly at school when something darted across the road in front of me. At first I thought it was a large dog, a great dane or something. All I noticed as I slammed my foot onto the brake was the brown fur, and it's size. The animal vanished through the bushes next to the road on the left.

"Jesus!" I exclaimed, my arms jutting out straight and solid as fence posts, while my knuckles gripped white on the steering wheel. I snatched a look in the rearview mirror, but luckily there was no one else on the road. Licking my lips I eased off the brake and accelerated enough to pull the car over to the curb. I looked at the bushes next to the road, which still rustled. *Should I check on it?*

I hadn't actually hit the animal, so I didn't need to worry about it being injured. But maybe it was lost or something? It had run so fast, and risked itself so strangely. Most animals wouldn't have risked coming that close to a car. I looked to the right, to see if something was chasing the animal, but saw nothing.

Alright, I can spare five minutes at least, I supposed. I unbuckled my seatbelt and stepped out of the car.

The leaves still shook and rustled as I approached the bushes. I pushed the branches to the side and stepped forward into green shadow.

Movement to my right. I turned and snapped my way through the twigs and bracken. A glimpse of dark brown fur, almost invisible, it's colour and texture blending into the rough trunk and knotted branches all around. I walked closer, wincing as thin branches whipped at my face and arms,forcing me to squint and close my eyes.

I felt space around my face and opened them again.

He was standing a few meters away, framed in the hollow between some of the small thickly-leaved trees. His smell struck me all at once, like a wind from an animal-filled pit, musky and earthy and heavy. Somehow I was reminded of the incense that the Many burned during their meetings. My senses were swimming and I felt dizzy.

At first I thought he was a man. A tall and strong man, wearing dark furry clothes, which would have made me laugh if his presence wasn't suppressing any thoughts that tried to form in my head. His shoulders were broad and strong, and his chest and stomach were uncovered. They conveyed strength and power and solid muscle, though not the preening self awareness of a body builder. His eyes were deep black holes in a face that smirked at me. It was an expression that knew the effect he had on me, and enjoyed it.

He stepped forward and I gasped, my throat shaking. His legs moved strangely, and I took a closer look. They bent backwards and forwards, as though he had extra knees. The sight made my blood cold. I realised that the furry clothes were simply his own fur, growing from his hips into a thick coat over his thighs and further down. His cock was free too, and it swung ponderously between his legs as he moved closer. I felt my eyes widen as I considered it's length, nearly to his knees. It swung softly, but the thought of it growing hard made my mouth dry and my stomach clench.

The leaves under our feet were thick and browned with age, rotting into the soil below and filling the space beneath the canopy with a heavy smell like freshly dug gardens.

Twigs crunched beneath his hooves and I blinked and frowned and began shaking my head. *Hooves? How could he have hooves?* He grimaced and pulled a branch out from the tightly coiled horns that hugged his skull. *Horns!?* I began to laugh, rapidly and softly. I was rubbing my thumb over my fingers with my hands held at my sides. *This is fucking unreal. It's not real! I need to get out of here!*

I stepped backwards and his eyes narrowed. I saw his muscles tense and felt a shiver of fear slip down my spine.

"Leave me alone," I cried and I spun to dive through the branches, crashing through the boughs as I desperately raced back to my car. It was my worst nightmare, trapped in the undergrowth while roots seemed to rise out of the ground and clutch at my feet, while branches were stabbing at me and scratching my arms. I was sure I would be poked in the face, but still I ran.

I burst out of the undergrowth and scrambled around the front of my car, throwing myself into the seat and starting the car. Just as the engine caught and I shoved the car into gear, I saw movement in the trees, a tall figure behind the leaves. Black eyes watched me. The tyres actually squealed as I drove away as fast as I could.

I sat at home for hours that day. I couldn't concentrate on anything. Laundry went unwashed, the breakfast dishes sat in the sink, attracting flies. I poured myself a glass of wine as soon as I got home, although I did feel a bit guilty about it. The clear yellow liquid set my tongue ablaze and the warmth soothed my tense muscles as I sat in our dining room and stared out the window. Every now and then a shadow would shift, or a bird would swoop past, and I would flinch away.

It had seemed so real, but there was no way that it could be. The man wasn't even human! He was like the tiny white statue in the art gallery, but huge and hot and staring at me through the dense leaves. I swallowed. I had been seeing things when I saw Fredrick's statue too, I reminded myself. I must get myself under control.

I almost forgot to get Tilly, only realising that I was going to be late when I went to refill my glass in the kitchen again and I caught sight of the time in the microwave. I had to text Tara and ask her to wait with my daughter until I got there.

"I am so sorry," I exclaimed as I rushed up to Tara and the two children. Tilly and Percy were running around his mother in tight circles, shrieking with laughter. Tara chuckled herself and waved aside my apologies.

"It's quite alright," she said. "Percy absolutely adores Tilly, they've been a treasure. What happened? Is everything okay?"

"Yes, it is." I felt annoyed that Tara was looking for a reason for me to be late. *Wasn't it reasonable to just say, I was going to be late? Why did I need a reason? Did she think I wasn't trying hard enough to be a good mother.* "I had a bit of a shock this morning and it's left me out of sorts." I wished I didn't feel the impulse to explain myself to her.

"That's not good." Tara stepped closer to me, her eyes

searching for me behind their red lenses. "Do you want to talk about it?"

"No, thank you." I didn't want to talk about it, not with her. I would hold on to the shock and instability until I could reveal it to the others in the circle.

"Okay." Tara stepped back a little, tucking her hands into the belt that encircled her. It had a silver skull buckle on the front. "Do remember that I am always happy to chat about anything that's on your mind, not just the show. I enjoy it." She smiled at me.

I smiled back. The irritated sensation was lessening. *After all, I told myself, she hasn't actually outright said that she's judging me. Maybe I'm just over-reacting. I'm probably still shaken up, and over-sensitive.* "Thanks. Come on Tilly, let's go and clean up the house before daddy gets home."

That evening I felt much better. I was able to make some baking soda volcanoes with Tilly before Otis came home, and he took over the messy science while I made some spaghetti for dinner. I poured myself a glass of wine to drink as I cooked, and another for Otis and I to go with our meals. Tilly watched a movie with us and was in bed before we knew it. Otis and I lay in bed next to each other, reading. I slid my foot over to his legs, running it up and down him, flicking the hair on his leg as I passed by.

"Are you in the mood?" he asked.

"I could be," I replied.

He groaned softly. "I'm really exhausted babe, I don't think I can rally tonight."

"Oh." I pulled my foot away. "I'm sorry."

"I'm sorry too, but I really just need to get a good sleep, alright?"

"Sure."

Otis turned off his bedside lamp and wormed into his pillows. It was almost insulting how quickly he was snoring. *Is he so disgusted by me?* I visited with myself, exploring my body and my feelings as I lay in the dark room. I hadn't wanted sex actually, I had just wanted to feel closer to my own husband after a stressful day. *Why was he being so stand-offish with me?* Again, I had the feeling that he was not interested by my body. I felt a spark of anger in my chest, but I tried to ignore it and go to sleep. *Why was he trying to keep away from me?* A cold hand gripped my heart. *Was he thinking about Talia?*

THE NEXT EVENING I sat in the kitchen, watching a pot of soup boiling on the stove. I sipped at my glass of red wine, while Tilly played with her dolls in the lounge in front of the TV. She'd been happy to sit there there since I got her back home from school thankfully, which had left me to sort out the laundry and dinner. Though, to be fair, I had left a pile of laundry on one of the easy chairs instead of sorting it and putting it away. I'd been too busy enjoying some music, spinning through the house with my earphones in. It had been good to get some expression and release into what would otherwise have been a very boring day.

Behind my daughter, Otis was reading a novel on the couch. He licked his finger and turned a page, then glanced up at me.

"Are you alright there love?"

"I'm fine," I said, still watching steam rise from the bubbling orange liquid. I sipped from my glass again.

Otis tutted and got up from the couch, walking through to stand beside me. He put his arm around my waist.

"Are you sure? You seem distant."

I shrugged.

We stood at the kitchen bench for a while longer, me leaning over the bench, him beside me. The soup hissed as it boiled.

"It's just, you don't seem to come in to hang out with Tilly and I much any more."

"What do you mean 'any more'? I've been hanging with Tilly all afternoon."

"Sure, sure."

I didn't like his tone. It sounded like he was trying to pacify me, as though I was some toddler having a tantrum. *Why did he think this was a tantrum, I was literally telling him what I was doing?*

"It's just, it's not only tonight. You've been quiet a lot recently. And you've really been drinking a lot of wine."

"Am I not allowed a glass of wine after a long day now? Thanks dad." I stared into his eyes as I took another sip from the glass. The red wine was spicy and thick on my tongue, then warm and filling as it slid down my throat.

"How many have you had today?"

I snorted and returned my attention to the soup.

"I want to understand sweetheart. Something seems to be going on. You're acting differently."

"I'm just not wearing a mask anymore. And why should I?"

Otis blinked and sighed. "I'm sorry you felt like you were wearing a mask before. I thought you were happy with your life."

"My life is fine." I sniffed a little. "It's just that we could have so much more, and we accept the same old routine." I turned to him, reaching out to hang one arm behind his neck, drawing him closer. "Why don't we do something outrageous? Let's break the rules." My eyes were coals, so hot did they feel.

Otis swallowed and tried to smile, but I could see that he was worried. "What rules?"

"Any rules!" I frowned and stepped away from him. "Anything to get out of this routine!"

Suddenly I was hot and yearning for him, my whole body craving his fingers and touch. I wanted him to take my shoulders and kiss me, to drag me away from Tilly and to fuck me as hard as he could. I lowered my head, but looked up at him, my breath deep.

Otis stepped up to me and cupped my chin with one hand, and then drew my face up so that he could kiss it. The kiss was soft and long. It was a kiss that said 'I love you'. But it was not a kiss that said 'I need you now'. After he pulled back I licked my lower lip.

"I think the soup's about ready."

His brow creased as I stepped away to serve dinner. We ate in silence. After I got Tilly to sleep, we both fell asleep in bed, lying next to each other with barely a handspan between us and yet so very far apart.

I HAD to wear sunglasses to drop Tilly off at school the next day. The sun seemed far too bright and it made my eyes hurt. Tilly's high pitched voice jabbing into my ears didn't help much either. I walked to the school gates with her hand in mine, and then bobbed down to give her a hug before she went running into the grounds. *Thank goodness. I need to go home and get some pain killers,* I said to myself. As I turned around, I nearly bumped into Lei.

Lei was one of the mothers at the school who I sometimes passed the time with while we waited for the kids to come out of class. I noticed that she was carrying a stack of paper brochures in one hand, and had a broad smile beneath slightly concerned eyes.

"Good morning Lei," I said warily.

"Hello Pene! It's so good to see you! I'm glad I caught you before you had to shoot off again." Lei's smile only grew wider with each word.

"I do have to shoot through though, as you say, so I'll see you-"

"It's just that we're doing a bit of a fundraiser for the school, to replace the netball hoops, and we really need a few more people to make it successful. I was wondering if you'd be keen to contribute?"

I had to concentrate to avoid my shoulders sagging.

"I would Lei, but I don't know if I'm really the sort of-"

"We're doing a mum's night out."

I paused. *A night out?*

"What would a mum's night out consist of exactly?"

"We've booked out a movie theatre, and you get one free drink with your ticket. Only $30 per person!"

It wasn't exactly cheap. But still, more nights out of the house sounded good.

"What's the movie?"

"Diamond Joe. You know that new one about..." And here Lei had to glance about, to ensure that there were no school children close enough to over hear her. Her cheeks began to glow a little red. "... about a male stripper?"

I grinned. "Oh yes, I have seen ads for that one! Now, that could be a good night out for the mums!"

Lei smiled, but her eyes still looked worried. I got the impression that she knew the movie would be a good drawcard for the mums at the school, but that she wouldn't have picked it for herself.

"Look, I can't get a ticket now, but can you give me the details? I might be keen."

"Absolutely!" She held out the brochure and I took it for a closer look. These had clearly been put together by her, or one of the other mums. They were simple and straight to the point, with a few stock images to try and make the brochure look a bit more interesting, all on a sheet of A4 folded in half.

"I'll let you know."

I sat in the car looking at the details for the fundraiser. The movie was scheduled for later in the week, which explained a lot of why Lei had looked so nervous. She must not have the numbers she thought she would and now she was rushing to get more mums along. I tried to remember if I'd seen any notices about the fundraiser in the last few weeks but, honestly, I'd been marking emails from the school as read without even opening them recently. They were always so long, and I just wanted to put my feet up with a wine and relax.

A free drink and a movie about a stripper, huh? I tapped my finger on my lips. *I think this could be a fun night. But I'll need an accomplice.*

I pulled out my phone and typed in a text explaining the night. Then I began to scroll through my contact list.

First I looked up Talia and began to type in a message to her. A night out with her sounded like a great idea, and one with a few drinks and semi-naked men dancing on the screen just made me even more excited to make it happen. But then I paused. *Is Talia really going to want to come to such a mummy thing? It's a school fundraiser for god's sake!* I breathed out through my nose disappointedly then skimmed down to Tara instead.

would you like to come to see diamon joe on thursday?

I had a reply before I had even managed to put the brochure away and start the car. Tara must have been sitting with her phone nearby. I felt bad for moment. *Should I be calling her more often?*

would love a nite out of the house, but too tired this week. Thank you

it's fundraiser for school, lots of mums. Are you sure? I texted back.

*Yes, but thank you :) *

What now, I thought. Then an idea struck me. I flicked my finger along the screen and sent another invite out. By the time I got home, Kallista had replied.

Sounds like a great nite out babe I'd love to come! Count me in

I let Lei know she had two more sales.

CHAPTER NINETEEN

The night of the movie rolled around and I told Otis to make his own dinner as I walked out the door and drove to the cinema. As I pulled into the carpark, I saw Kallista waiting outside the cinema doors. She was dressed in a slim black suit that emphasised her legs, and her open shirt collar made her neck look absolutely enticing. I shook my head as I walked over to her.

"Good evening Pene! You look absolutely ravishing tonight, I could just eat you alive!" said Kallista with a sparkle in her eyes.

"Thank you, I was just thinking to myself that your suit really suits you." I realised what I had said and cringed. Kallista laughed.

"If you did that on purpose, love the joke. If it was a mistake then that's even funnier!"

I grimaced.

"Don't worry about it," said Kallista, reaching her arm around my shoulders as we walked through the automatic glass doors to the cinema. "I'm just glad to see you."

We walked up a wide flight of stairs and into the lobby, where Lei and Tracey and about forty other middle aged women were laughing and talking while sipping on tall glasses of bubbles.

There was a woman whose name I couldn't remember sitting at a small circular table by the top of the chairs, and she asked our names as we came closer.

"Oh yes, here you are," she said as she crossed our names off a list in front of her. "And these tokens will get you your first drink. Please feel free to get another, a proportion of the profits for the night go to the fundraising!"

Kallista held up the small blue circle of plastic that the lady had given us and raised an eyebrow at it. Then she caught my eye and smirked.

"Come get a drink," she insisted.

The free glass of wine was very generous. We could choose from either red or white! *How decadent,* I laughed to myself. However, there was also a special cocktail that the cinema had made just for the night, and I watched as someone else collected theirs and headed off into the lobby with her friends. The glass was tall and curved, with something thick and orange filling it, under a head of foaming cream. Our two glasses of red wine arrived moments later and I nudged Kallista after she had handed over our plastic discs to pay. "Check that out!"

She turned to look, sipping at her wine. She scrunched up her nose and smacked her lips.

"It looks absolutely sickening," she said. She swirled the glass in her hand. "And this is far too sweet." She sighed. "Still, at least this one was free. I'll pay for something half decent next." She took a large mouthful of the wine.

"It does look sickening," I agreed, watching the radioactive orange drink disappear into the crowd. "And I want it!"

"If you want something, you go and get it babe, that's my motto" said Kallista, swallowing her wine with a grimace. She growled. "This is terrible. I need a better drink." And with that she swallowed the rest of the wine in one gulp and returned to the bar.

I got myself one of the cocktails, though it meant that I had to carry a glass in each hand. Once she had her new wine, a thick dark red that cost her nearly twenty dollars, Kallista and I found a space in the lobby to wait for the doors to open to the cinema. I saw a few women that I recognised from school, and Theo with his husband Luke. We exchanged nods of acknowledgement, but every time one of the faces I knew began to walk over, Kallista would take my arm and begin walking to another part of the lobby, ostensibly to examine a movie poster or check out some of the potted plants. The first time I assumed it was just an unfortunate coincidence, but the second time she murmured, "Ugh, I am not here to hear some woman gush about her crotch-goblins while I enjoy an overpriced glass of wine."

I tried not to meet the eye of Sarah, the woman who we had just avoided. I thought about what Kallista had said. *She has a point,* I told myself. *We are here on one of the few nights out that we actually get to ourselves, we've got some lovely drinks in our hands, why should we waste time thinking about our kids? We're here to remind ourselves of who we really are!*

The door beyond Kallista opened and the crowd began to shuffle in it's direction. I clinked my glass against Kallista's. "That's right! Let's go see some hunks get half naked!"

A few of the women around us turned as they heard Kallsita whoop. I saw their eyes, some judgemental, others simply confused, but then Kallista strode forward, teeth flashing in an aggressive smile, and led the way into the dark cinema.

"I have my hands full, did you have our tickets?" I asked Kallista as we moved down the aisle beside the rows of plump seats inside.

Kallista snorted. "Who cares? These seats look good." She gestured towards the middle of the row we cwere standing by, almost halfway down the cinema but closer to the screen.

"What if someone comes? Someone else will have those tickets, surely?"

"Pene, let me explain something to you." Kallista turned and her silhouette was lithe and beguiling. I could see only twin pinpricks of light reflecting off her eyes, and the impression of darkness that was her mouth.

"The world is full of things that are no fun. It's our duty to make sure we wring every drop of happiness we can out of it. If someone else has tickets they can try to fight me for this spot, but I want these seats."

And then she moved down the row, taking little care not to bump the legs of the people who were already sitting in it. I took another gulp of my wine and then followed her. *I mean, it's only seats at the movies. What's the harm really?*

We settled into the seats and Kallsita leaned over to me, until our shoulders were touching. Her skin felt like molten gold, hot and smooth and invigorating. She was facing me and so I turned to hear what she was going to say. Her eyes stared into mine and her lips were moments away.

"I'm really looking forward to this movie starting," she began but before she could say anything else, a voice from behind shattered my small, focused world.

"Hey, those are our seats."

Kallista's brows twitched as she leaned back from me.

"No."

"Excuse me?"

"I said no, these aren't your seats. Go away."

I could feel something passing over me, something passing from Kallista to the women standing next to us in the row, as though the air had taken on weight and was pressing against us.

"I'm pretty sure that-"

Kallista stood, slipping that thin body upwards like a snake rising from a basket. She stepped forward, bringing her hips and legs closer to where I sat. I swallowed.

"I'm pretty sure that, whatever those tickets say, you'll be happy to just sit down where you are. You might even find it more comfortable in the long run to move to a different row."

She shouldn't be saying that, I heard a voice in the back of my head. It had to be my own thoughts, but they seemed to be coming from far away. I just wanted to shrink lower in my seat.

It's not hurting anyone. But these are their seats.

They'll be fine sitting somewhere else.

But they wouldn't have to if she had just followed the rules.

Who says following the rules is always so good? Annika always wants everyone to follow the rules, and I would hate to be like her. I settled back into my seat as the other women edged back down the row and Kallista sat back down next to me. She reached over and lay her fingers on the back of my arm.

"There now, where were we?"

Though her fingers felt like small dots of flame on my skin, the voice in my head had unsettled me. As the movie screen spread out before us began to shine, pounding music filled our ears. Muscular men in tight trousers and their skin glistening with sweat began to dance and discuss the ludicrous plot that moved one them from one display of skin and muscle to the next. The ladies in the seats around us shrieked and laughed, thrilling at the chance to let loose. And through it all, Kallsita's fingers moved in slow spirals on the back of my skin.

She shifted until her shoulder touched mine again. I wanted to turn my face to her, I wanted to hear her breathing close to me, to feel the warm air on my lips. I wanted to reach out to her. But the voice had unsettled me, and I couldn't.

When the movie ended, Kallsita and I stood and left the theatre, smiling and laughing with the other women, flushed faces and broad grins surrounding us. I managed to speak with her about the movie, and she said that she had enjoyed it. She said she found it stimulating then closed her eyes and wriggled, running a hand down her hips. The movement made me suck in a gulp of air.

Kallista gave me a hug outside the complex, then waved as she walked away. I watched her leave until I couldn't see her anymore, then turned to get into my car. However, someone else was walking towards me from the cinema. I paused, wondering if it was Kallista on her way back, but this figure was silhouetted by the lights of the building, and seemed much larger, curvier, and with bigger hair than my new friend.

"Hello?" I called out. "Look, if you were upset in the cinema, I'm sorry, but we were just trying to have a good night ou-"

The woman walking towards me began to dance, lifting her hands high above her and jutting her legs out at right angles.

"What are you doing?" I stepped backwards towards my car.

Now the woman began a high wailing sound, clearly some sort of melody, but loud and unsettling. Something moved in her hand as she came closer step by awkward bouncing step.

I decided that I didn't want anything to do with this bizarre woman, and so I turned to race over to my car. Once I reached I glanced back over my shoulder, and saw the woman was racing towards me now, fully visible under the tall lights of the car park. She wore a light fur and her hair stuck out in all directions from her face. Her eyes were wide and barely seemed focused on anything, as though she was deep in some sort of trance. Her mouth was wide and the song continued, but her hands were outstretched like claws as she rushed towards me.

"Fuck!" I yelped as I pulled the door open as fast as I could, dove in, and slammed it shut behind me. I ducked down, looking out of the window. The woman kept running closer and threw something towards me. A handful of small writhing snakes slammed into the window, shaking the car and making me flinch lower.

I waited, horrified at the thought of what this woman might do, but nothing happened. The sound had stopped. Cautiously, I opened my eyes. There was nothing outside except an empty carpark. A cat was sitting near an alley mouth by the cinema, far away, but the only living thing in sight. I even cracked the door open and looked at the ground by the car, but no snakes were there either.

I've drunk too much, I decided. *That's why I'm imagining things so realistically. I'll have to be extremely careful while I drive home.*

My pounding adrenaline and shocked emotions led to quite a strange drive. I felt a ball of fire below my belly, but it was unstable and glowing in bursts. Sometimes it felt as though I just wanted to pull over in a dark car park and slide my hand between my legs, and other times the fire died, leaving me cold. It was quiet and dark when I pulled into the driveway, a street empty and lonely. I carefully unlocked the door and made my way to my bedroom, where Otis was snoring softly. I crawled in next to him and reached out a hand to touch his side. The fire had left me completely.

THE NEXT MORNING I lay in bed until Otis had gone out, staring at the ceiling. Tilly even tried to get me out of bed, but I just told her to go and make herself some breakfast. I tried rolling over to go back to sleep and then decided that the world wasn't going to leave me alone, just because I wanted it to. I sighed and got out of bed, got Tilly ready for school, and dropped her off.

I managed to convince myself to open my laptop in the lounge so that I could check my online courses, but I ended up staring at the screen for half an hour before I even logged in. I could tell how long it was because the computer had a small clock in the corner that I watched the whole time. *Why am I so out of it? Where has my oomph gone all of a sudden?*

I managed to get to the end of the day, finishing the bare minimum amount of work that I had to do on my course, and arriving just in time to pick up Tilly. When we got home I stuck on her tablet and went to the kitchen. *Finally,* I thought as I poured myself a decent glass of red wine. I picked it up and breathed in the smell of it, moaning a little at the pleasure of it. The thick liquid caught on the slick glass sides as I swirled it around. *Heavenly.*

By the time Otis got home, I was feeling much better than I had all day. I had spread out along the couch and I was flicking through my social media feeds as I sipped my way through the glass of wine.

"Good evening love," he said as he shut the door behind him and put his bag down on the dining table. He glanced around the room and frowned.

"Hi," I called out, looking at Rachel's latest photos, which were all of her swirling around a dancefloor with a big ballgown on. *Should I take up dancing,* I wondered.

"Um, have you forgotten?" asked Otis as he stepped into the longue and reached over to tousle Tilly's hair. She made an annoyed noise.

"Forgotten what?" *Is it a class she's been taking, or was Rachel at some sort of ballroom dancing event?*

"My parents are coming to our house for dinner tonight."

I blinked. I had forgotten. I looked around the lounge, with toys pushed to the sides of the furniture and a pile of laundry waiting to be folded and put away still stacked on one of the chairs.

"What time?" I asked as I sat up on the couch.

"In about an hour I think," said Otis. "Did you have a plan for dinner? You know how fussy my mother can be."

I certainly did know. I pursed my lips and narrowed my eyes, then took a sip of my wine.

"It's fine, we'll just order something in." I lay back down on the couch.

"Shouldn't we clean up?"

I waved a hand in the air. "You feel free to clean up if you want. It's about time Annika got to see what life is really like."

Otis stood over me with a blank expression on his face, and then walked over to pick up the pile of laundry.

"Come on Tilly, help me clean up the house for grandma and grandpa."

"Okay," she sighed.

The two of them had the house looking much neater by the time Annika and Larry arrived. I took a quiet thrill in the look on Annika's face as she came in, her eyes wide and her mouth slightly downturned. She didn't know what to do when I wasn't bending over backwards for her. *Get used to it,* I thought. *I'm not doing things for other people any more, I'm doing things for me.*

"What's for dinner?" she asked in her high voice as she sat at the dining table awkwardly. I realised that she was trying to sit on the chair without having to actually touch either the chair or the table.

"I thought we'd get in some thai takeaways. Would you like some wine?" I held up the half empty bottle of red.

"Take aways?" Annika's voice rose slightly.

"I haven't had thai in a long time," said Larry with a smile. "Sounds great!"

I smiled at Annika as I poured her a glass, looking directly into her eyes.

"I'm glad you agree Larry."

Dinner was delicious and filled my mouth with heat and sweet sauces, and did a great job of keeping me from having to talk. Otis and his father filled the silence best, though Tilly was as keen as ever to contribute her own stories, about school and friends and her favourite shows.

"Pene, thank you very much for having us over for dinner."

"You're welcome Annika." I stuck a piece of well sauced beef into my mouth and relished the flavour that burst from it as I chewed.

"It must be very difficult to keep the house looking presentable at the moment, with your renovations?"

"Renovations?" I wasn't sure what my mother-in-law meant. I glanced over at Otis.

"We haven't actually started renovations yet mum," he said. "Actually, have you heard back about that loan babe?"

I waved my hand at him. "Yes, of course. Kallista was very efficient."

"Then why hasn't work begun," asked Annika.

"I am speaking with multiple builders, canvassing our

options." I was pleased with my response, and rewarded myself with another sip of wine. They didn't need to know that so far I had only spoken to one builder. My plan was still to talk with others.

"Good work," said Larry as he leaned back in his chair and laid both hands over his belly. He looked as satisfied as an old cat.

Later in the evening, after Otis had left to take Tilly to bed, Annika licked her lips and drew her breath. Clearly she was building up her nerve for something. *Now what*, I wondered.

"Pene, we were wondering if you would all like to come to the botanic gardens with us tomorrow?"

That wasn't at all what I had expected. In fact, given a hundred years in which to relive that moment over and over again, I didn't think I would ever expect that question.

"The gardens?"

"Yes, Larry wants to see the new season's roses, and I..." She trailed off and looked around my house, not quite grimacing but I could tell she wanted to. "Well. I just want to see Tilly exposed to some natural beauty from time to time." She smiled at me. "We could make it a family picnic."

There's no real reason that I can't manage a simple weekend lunch with Annika and Larry, I thought to myself. My stomach burned and I had to swallow to settle the sensation. *They're my husband's parents, and my daughter loves them. Just do it Pene!*

When Annika suggested that she and Larry would need to leave and get an early night in bed, I didn't argue with her. Even though Larry immediately started asking why a trip to the gardens for a picnic lunch would mean he couldn't get a sleep in, I just smiled and agreed and helped them gather their things and get out the door. Once it was shut behind them I turned and leaned my back on it, sighing and smiling.

"What is going on with you?" asked Otis. He was standing at the kitchen bench, his wrinkled forehead showing his concern.

"What do you mean?"

"You've been acting so strangely. And tonight? I know that you don't like having to meet my mother's standards, but you basically ignored her completely. That's not like you."

"Maybe it is going to be more like me."

He twisted his mouth. "Why?"

"Because I should be allowed to do things the way that I want to."

He nodded. "That's fair. But it seems like the way you want to do things is meaning you don't want to do them my way."

"What?"

"You've pulled away from me a bit more recently." He sighed. "It's not much, but it's been happening in different places and times." He shook his head. "I feel like something is changing, and I don't know if I'm part of the change."

"Don't be silly," I told him. I walked over and gave him a quick kiss on the cheek. "Let's get to bed."

CHAPTER TWENTY

We pulled up at the botanic gardens and Otis turned off the engine and began climbing out. Tilly began to get out too, and the pair of them gathered up the chilly bin of picnic food that we had packed. I sat in my seat for a little longer, taking deep breaths to prepare myself.

"Come on babe, are you ready?"

"Yes, I'm good!" I slid my seatbelt off and got out of the car, enjoying the feeling of a cool breeze that was pushing across the cricket grounds next to the gardens. The broad flat green grass stretched out to the trees in the far far distance. A circle of young men in sparkling white cricket uniforms were out on that grass, enjoying their game in the sunshine. I wondered if we could go and watch them play instead. Tilly came around to where I was standing and took my hand, and then we followed Otis towards the Botanic Gardens building themselves.

The entrance to the Gardens was through an old collection of Victorian greenhouses, large iron frameworks built with the arches and decorative shapes that you might expect of that older building style. Their frames were painted in thick white paint, and filled with heavy glass panes that were clouded by a thin layer of condensation from the steam within. Even during the coldest winter months, these greenhouses managed to maintain a smothering humid warmth.

Beyond these claustrophobic buildings, as I knew from previous visits, broad flower beds and gravel pathways led through a series of rolling fields and beneath dark trees. It was a beautiful place to spend an afternoon strolling and admiring the plants, or stopping for a picnic.

Just as we were about to go through the doors into the main greenhouse, Otis paused and frowned. He looked around the car park behind us and scratched at his chin.

"Is everything okay hun?"

"Yeah," he answered slowly. "I asked Talia to come along today. She said she'd meet us here."

"That was a nice idea." I smiled at the thought of Talia walking through the beautiful gardens with us. But then I paused. "Won't your parents mind?"

"Oh no, they're used to us having friends come along to events every now and then. Remember they didn't mind Xavier turning up to help out with Tilly's birthday a year ago? Or was it two years ago?"

I suppose that's true, I thought as Otis took out his phone to send Talia a message. *We do have friends come to family events.* But I felt as though something had changed recently. Having Talia come along wasn't quite the same as having a friend join us used to be.

"How did this plan come about?"

"She sent me a message this morning, about the new kitchen shelf she had installed to hold her favourite mugs. I mentioned we were coming out this weekend, and seeing as she lives nearby I figured I may as well ask her along." He kept his eyes on the phone in his hands.

Just as Otis finished sending his message, and tucked his phone back into his pocket, Talia came bursting out of the doors behind him and wrapped him into a hug from behind.

"Hey there!" he yelped as she wiggled him back and forth,

and he patted her arms around his chest. Then she released him and swooped in on me, gathering me into just as enthusiastic a hug.

"Hi Talia!" I managed to squawk out before she let me go.

"Hi guys!" she grinned, then reached out to give Tilly a high five. "How are you doing little miss fantastic?"

"I'm great Auntie Talia!" beamed Tilly in response.

"Glad to hear it! Shall we go find the mouse eating plants?"

"The what?!" shrieked my daughter before Talia grabbed her by the hand and they both ran into the building. I stepped over to Otis and took his hand in mine, strolling next to him into the greenhouse.

"I think that was a good idea you had," I murmured as the heavy air fell over us. *Maybe I should have known that she would be okay with domestic things like fundraisers and picnics.*

Inside the greenhouse, Otis and I trailed along behind Talia and Tilly, who were giggling with one another as they leaned over the low curved concrete walls that held the flower beds. Next they stopped by a small pond, with a waterfall that trickled a few feet down rocks into a surface covered with broad lily pads. Large heavy green leaves swung overhead in the hot air and I had to take off my jacket. I could feel my cheeks growing redder in the hot air.

"Your cheeks make you look like you've done something naughty," laughed Otis as I tucked my arm through his. I slapped his shoulder.

"Leave me alone," I smiled.

"Hey, I like it when you misbehave," he said, his eyes piercing into mine. I grinned but looked away.

At the end of the greenhouse, a few tens of meters ahead of us, a couple was standing, watching us. I recognised Annika's severe haircut and squared my shoulders. *I can do this.*

As we got closer, Tilly noticed her grandparents and squealed then ran over to them. Larry leaned over to ruffle her hair, but Annika didn't seem to notice her own granddaughter bouncing around her. *For goodness sake,* I wondered. *What have I done wrong now?*

Talia stood up from the bright orange flowers she was smelling and took Otis' other arm as we crossed the final space to my in-laws. As we got closer, I could see Annika's eyes above her stiff smile were focused on Talia.

"Hello dears," she began, wiping her hands unconsciously on her sides. Tilly grabbed Larry's hand and dragged him back along the path we had just come down, pointing at particular plants and flowers that she thought were interesting.

"Hi mum!" said Otis, but she didn't even glance at him.

"Hi Anni–"

"And who is this young woman?" asked Anniika, cutting me off in the middle of greeting her.

"I'm Talia!" exclaimed Talia, letting go of Otis to reach out and shake Annika's hand. *Is that too personal,* I wondered. I remembered how close we had behaved, at the beach, when she had slept on our couch. It felt natural and comfortable to me, but suddenly I saw it through it Annika's eyes. *She must think something is wrong here.*

"Hello Talia." Annika squinted as she burrowed through her memories. "Oh yes. Otis has mentioned you before, I'm sure. You helped organise the wedding?"

"Yes I did! I was in charge of catering."

"That's right. I'm sorry, I don't remember much about the catering. I felt sick quite early in the meal, so I spent a lot of time outside getting some fresh air, rather than trying to eat anything."

"I'm glad you feel better now."

Annika's mouth twitched, but she turned her attention to me now.

"So, why did you invite your friend along to this family picnic?" That stiff smile had returned as she looked at me. She took her time emphasising the word family.

"Actually, it was Otis' idea to have Talia join us," I replied.

"Oh!"

I have to admit, I do like that shocked expression on her face.

"Yeah, I just thought that, seeing as she lives so close by, Talia might like to come along."

"So sweet," smiled Talia.

Yes, that expression is definitely one that I'll enjoy seeing more often, I thought as Annika struggled to hide a grimace.

After walking through the greenhouses for twenty minutes, with Tilly leading the way and Annika trying to avoid any conversation deeper than "What a pretty flower," we began to reach the end of the traditional buildings.

We followed the path past tall thick trees with huge angular leaves that hung over our heads. The path reached an alcove at the end of the current wing of the greenhouse and then looped around to return along the other side of the beds. A set of broad grey stones were set into the rich soil, clear of the low bushes and flowers. Tilly hopped up and onto the stones, and began to walk across.

"Tilly, what are you doing?" snapped Annika. I blinked and frowned, wondering what was wrong.

"What?" Tilly froze, turning on the third stone to look at her grandmother. Larry and Annika were both stepping smartly over to her, reaching out their hands. Talia and Otis were further behind us, reading a wooden sign in a flower bed together. They looked up at the same time when they heard Annika's voice.

"Is something wrong?" I asked, following my parents-in-law. Tilly was looking confused, her eyes darting between the faces closing in on her. I could see her flinching away, and I was getting angry.

"She's jumped into the garden!" snapped Annika. "Isn't it obvious?"

"Isn't that a path?" I asked. A hand touched my shoulder from behind.

"What's happened?" asked Talia. Otis was reaching past his

parents to pick up Tilly. Father and daughter shared wide bewildered eyes that were a perfect imitation of one another.

"Tilly was stepping on those stones, and Annika doesn't want her going through the garden."

"Aren't those stones a path?" asked Otis as Tilly gripped her small arms around his shoulders.

"The real path is only a few feet away," said Larry. "Seems weird to have a path in the garden when people can just walk on the real footpath right there, doesn't it?" He stroked his fingers over his mustache as he spoke.

"It's not a big deal," said Otis. "I would have thought they were a path too Tilly. But let's just stay on the main path at the moment." She nodded and he put her on the ground. "And maybe we don't need to react quite so strongly next time?" He raised an eyebrow at his mother, and she pursed her lips. For a moment I could feel my temper rising as I wondered if she was going to argue, but then she nodded.

"Great. Let's go find somewhere to eat, I'm starving." Otis took Tilly by the hand and led the way along the path towards the exit. His mother followed closely behind.

Talia took my hand and squeezed. I squeezed hers back, then realised that Larry was still watching us. His forehead creased and he opened his mouth as though he was about to say something, but then closed it again and set off after the others. I let go of Talia's hand.

Oh man, one more thing that she's going to hold against me I bet.

We set up a picnic blanket beneath a broad tree with gigantic roots that twisted around each other like some sort of giant sea monster, if the short green lawn was the sea. The breeze rustled the leaves above us and cooled my skin. *This is fantastic,* I thought, *even if I do have to put up with Annika.*

Tilly ran off to climb up the roots of the tree and hide in it's dark and gritty crannies. My mother in law frowned, but managed to restrain herself from complaining as she unpacked some cheese and crackers and plastic glasses. As Otis brought out the peanut butter sandwiches we had whipped up just before leaving, Annika also pulled out a bottle of wine.

"Will anyone have a small glass?" she asked as she twisted off the lid.

"Sure!" said Talia.

"Sounds good," I agreed. Otis got out our thermos of tea and some simple metal mugs that he used when he went on his hikes.

Talia leaned back on the red and blue tartan blanket that we had laid out on the grass. She sipped from the cup that Annika had given here. "This is nice, thanks for asking me along," she said, reaching over to pat Otis on the knee. Annika blinked.

"Just check out the statues!" Talia added, pointing with her cup. Across the gently curved grass lawn, a huge figure carved from dark grey stone lurked. It seemed to be a woman, judging from it's long geometric curves of hair and hips, but it was so cylindrical and square that saying it was a robot could have been just as appropriate. Other similar squat figures were sitting around the whole lawn.

"Yes, just look at them," sniffed Annika. "Ugly little brutes if you ask me. I've been hoping that they get removed ever since they were added a few years back."

Of course Annika hated anything that challenged the carefully controlled environment of these gardens, I thought to myself. I considered the various trees and shrubs and flowers that filled the beds and glasshouses. *Surely they would burst out of their confines if they could. Everyone wants to break free from the bounds they are confined in. Don't they?*

"Oh, really? I quite like them. Really challenging the status quo, you know what I mean." I tried not to giggle at Talia's comment.

"Hmmmm." Annika narrowed her eyes.

"I suppose the girl has a point," said Larry, just before he crunched down on a cracker with cheese.

"Maybe. So, Talia, what have you been doing with yourself

this week?" asked Annika, now all full of innocent inquiry and carefully posed indifference.

"I've been working on my latest art commission actually."

"Something challenging like these grey people here, is it?"

"No, not really," laughed Talia. "I've been painting a mural on the side of a dairy down by the Hills."

"A nice neighbourhood," said Annika.

"I do hope that your mural is something appropriate to the location," murmured my mother in law as she took another sip from her cup. I took another sip of my wine and coughed to clear my throat.

"I never worry about being appropriate to my location," laughed Talia, shaking her head so that her curly hair bounced around her face. "I just want to make something epic, that people look at and feel something deep in their core. I'm doing a lot of space art at the moment!"

"Space art?" Annika looked as though she had just been given a plate full of raw lemon to eat. "What does that mean?"

"You know, nebulae, galaxies." Talia pushed aside the hair from her forehead. "I really want to make people feel like they are part of something bigger than themselves, and powerful and beautiful." she looked over at me and smiled. Her eyes shone.

"I don't really know about all that," murmured Annika.

"Da-ad," interrupted Tilly, trudging across the grass and slumping down next to Otis. "I'm bored." She rolled over onto her back and stared up at the blue sky full of puffs of cloud.

Otis laughed. "Alright you. Let's go and have a bit of an explore, shall we?" He stood up and reached out to take her hand. She stretched up from the grass and he lifted her up into the air, completely off her feet. Tilly laughed loud.

"Did you know there are bird statues hidden between some of the gardens here Tilly," he asked as they began to set off towards the distant shrubs and bushes that filled the gardens.

"No! How big are they? Can I climb on them!"

"No, you should be sticking to the path!" called Annika. "You might break the flowers!"

I saw Otis lean down to whisper to our daughter as they left. If I strained my ears, I could just make out what he was saying. I wondered if his mother could hear him too, and whether he was speaking loud enough for her to hear on purpose.

"Sometimes it's fun to get off the path, right love?"

Thankfully, Annika decided to chat with her husband while we continued to nibble on the food, and I was able to lie down and relax, staring at the clouds in the same way Tilly had. I was surprised when Talia lay down with her head on my stomach, but it felt comfortable, quiet and close. I began to run my fingers through her hair, twirling the ends around my fingertips. The leaves above us rustled.

For a moment I felt my stomach clench as I imagined seeing a small ugly figure hiding in the branches, but these branches were wide and leaves so small, that I could see through the whole tree and be sure that nothing was hiding inside. The thought of that thing made my stomach clench and I sat up, shifting my friend from her spot.

Larry frowned. "Is something wrong?"

"No, " I shook my head. "I just had a dizzy spell." I rubbed my head and took a deep breath. Otis and Tilly were walking back across the lawn, my little girl running in circles around her father as they approached. "It might be time for me to head home though."

Larry shrugged, but nodded.

We began to gather our things into the picnic basket and chilly bins that we had brought. Tilly went scrambling back up the roots of the tree, which made me nervous, but we could see her at all times and there was clearly nothing there. Nevertheless, I made sure that I was always as close as possible in case I needed to run over and protect her. Talia and Otis folded up our blanket, and Larry stood with all of their things in his hands.

We headed back to the greenhouses in a group, Otis chatting

with his father about the plants that he had seen with Tilly. He was trying to learn about as many plants as he could, he wanted to identify them in the wild on his hikes, especially any that could be used for food or medicine. The idea of being able to live off the land during his long treks made my husband very excited.

We reached the exit of the greenhouses and looked at the car park spread before us. Annika leaned over and bumped her cheek into mine as a farewell, and Larry made an awkward attempt to shake Otis' hand without putting down the large blue plastic chilly bin. Annika nodded at Talia and gave a big kiss to Tilly before our group split.

They walked off to the left and we all climbed into our car, Talia included. *Where is she going?* I turned around in my seat to speak to her, which let me see Annika standing by her car somewhere behind us, looking back at our car.

"Why did you get in?" I asked Talia.

"I figured you guys would at least drop me home, right?"

I looked out the window at Annika again. She was rubbing her face with her hands.

"Of course we will," I smiled.

CHAPTER TWENTY-ONE

I stood with the other parents outside the children's class after school. My mind had been full all day and I wasn't really paying attention to anybody else around me. I was so confused. Was it fair of me to treat Talia the way that I had been treating her? It was almost as though I had been relying on her comfort with myself and Otis in order to make Annika upset. That was just using my friend, which couldn't be an appropriate thing to do. But I also had been thinking about her more and more since we had gone to the art gallery and nearly kissed. Maybe I had only imagined the desire that night, but she had been acting far more intimate than I had expected ever since. Or had I just been more aware of it? I had been much more aware of the warmth she made me feel.

And then THAT made me wonder if perhaps I was falling out of love with my husband, the man I had built this life with. I had a child with him, we had managed to buy a house with the help of my parents. Surely the foundation we had built was strong, and our marriage would stay that strong?

I thought about the way he had made me feel at the gardens, watching him play with our daughter. I did love him, I was sure.

I wasn't just using him as a means to pleasure myself while I thought of someone else.

No, I admonished myself. *You have a new toy to use for that.* Why had I let Kallista talk me into buying such a ridiculous device for myself? I didn't need a vibrator like that! I was more than satisfied with my sex life as it was beforehand. I tried not to remind myself that I had only ever thought of Nic the builder when I used the toy. I tried not to remind myself just how often I had used the toy already.

It had all started after I met Kallista I realised. Ever since I had seen her at the art gallery my feelings and emotions had begun to ebb and flow like a storm tossed sea. She had opened a door somehow, a door to a world of emotions that I hadn't realised existed inside myself. It was a terrifying world but I didn't want to shut that door again.

And that's why I've been seeing strange things, I told myself. *Those half-animal creatures. I'm over stimulated and over emotional and just over... everything! I need to calm down and just be honest and appreciative of everything in my life.*

Appreciate everything, like Talia, who I'm not appreciating at all. Instead, I'm just using her. My thoughts wrapped over and under each other in knots, just like the knots I was teaching Tilly to tie in her shoes. Round and round, the rabbit through the hole. I sighed. I didn't know how I was going to resolve any of this.

The bell rang and I straightened my shoulders, pulling my lips into a smile, ready to greet my daughter. Quickly she came out of the door, holding on to Percy's hand, like she did most days now. The pair came rushing over, waving and grinning, and I felt the tension ease out of my shoulders. It became easier to stand straight, but I crouched down to grab Tilly into a huge hug. Percy stood just next to us, looking around.

"Hi Percy. Have you two had a fun day at school today?"

"Yes thank you," answered Percy in his serious way. His smile broadened as he looked over my shoulder. "Hi mum!"

I turned as I stood up, taking Tilly's hand in my own. Tara

was walking up behind us all and Percy nipped over and took her hand. She smiled and waved in our direction.

"I assume that's you Pene?"

"Yes, it's us. How are you?"

"I've been very well thank you. Would you and Tilly like to come to our house and play this afternoon?"

"Mum, can we, please, monkey mumma?" begged Tilly.

I was about to say no, but then I closed my mouth and frowned. It's not as though I had anything particularly pressing to do at home, I'd spent the whole day sitting on the couch or the kitchen stools or the side of the bed, pretending to do chores but really just going around and around my worries in my head. Maybe Tara would be able to give me a new perspective on it all.

"Actually, I wouldn't mind a chance to get some things out of my head, if you don't mind?"

"I'm sure I can offer you a friendly ear at least," smiled Tara.

"Then let's do it my little number one," I told Tilly and the four of us set off along the path that led to their home.

The kids ran off as soon as we went inside, and Tara settled me into her small lounge as she gathered some tea and biscuits. It felt good to be waited upon. I sank into the soft cushions of the chair and wriggled my shoulders. *Yes, this was very comfortable.*

"So," said Tara as she set a steaming cup and saucer on the small table between the chairs and then sat in one herself. "What's been getting on your mind that you want to talk about?"

"It's just that I've been seeing weird things." I felt so silly even bringing this up. Maybe it made me sound like someone who was losing control of themselves! "First I thought I saw a dark figure following me around a few times, then I saw a little creature watching me in a tree while I was at the beach," I paused and bit my lip, wondering how Tara was reacting to what I was saying. She was looking at me with a clear gaze, not giggling or frowning at all. She was just listening. I decided to continue.

"I've thought I saw a spotted cat, a big one, like a leopard or cheetah but it must have been a dog or something. And a woman dancing around with snakes! I've been quite frightened by them all actually. And there was this huge man who wasn't a man. He was particularly frightening. But also, kind of exciting?" I knew it didn't make sense, but it was true. I felt embarrassed and coughed then picked up my cup of tea.

"I'm sure we've all had daydreams like that before," laughed Tara. "Dangerous and new things make us feel alive, it gets our adrenaline pumping. Everyone needs a little adventure and excitement sometimes, don't they?"

I nodded and thought about how excited I had been while having sex with my husband and thinking about Talia. *Was that dangerous and new?*

"But what do you mean he was a man who wasn't a man?"

I described the figure to her, his hair, his size, his hooves and horns. I was surprised to find that my heart started pounding and the hair on the backs of my arms stood up just at the memory of the figure. A cold ball began to form in my stomach.

"It sounds like a satyr," said Tara, though she wasn't smiling any more.

"What is that?"

"A satyr is a half-man, half-goat creature, a follower of the ancient Greek god Dionysus. He's the god of wine. Satyrs are hard to control, and indulge their whims at all times. Drinking, sex, whatever urge takes their fancy, they will try to do it. But why were you dreaming about satyrs?"

"I think I saw a statue of one at an art gallery recently," I said, unsure whether Tara would remember bumping into me.

"I did too," she nodded. "But the one I saw was small and cheerful, like a child. That's the way they are often presented these days, with all the danger stripped out of them. It seems unusual that you would be dreaming of a giant scary one." She chuckled. "So it was the same gallery that we must have both been to!"

"It must have been," I nodded, then returned to the main topic of our conversation. "I think maybe it's because I've been having scary and exciting feelings recently."

I explained to her about the feelings I'd been having for other people recently. I told her about the way my old friend had seemed like she was going to kiss me, and how I had met a new friend who inspired heat in me whenever I looked at them. She was sympathetic, but also asked me if I had thought that I would go my whole life never being attracted to anyone ever again after I married Otis.

"No, I suppose not. I mean, realistically, I imagine it's natural to find someone attractive."

"Exactly," said Tara. "We all see people who we think are good looking, and sometimes they are people that we know. Sometimes it's the fact that we know them so well that helps them appear so attractive to us!"

"And sometimes they are just some builder down the street," I murmured, looking at the cup of tea perched in my fingers.

Tara laughed. "Yes, I think sometimes it is exactly that!"

"So, you don't think I'm falling out of love with my husband?" Just saying the words out loud spiked my heart with an icicle of fear.

"No, of course not! The only way to know you are falling out of love with your husband is if you don't feel like you love your husband. It's got nothing to do with anyone else." She sniffed and tilted her head a little to one side. "Have you talked to your husband about all this? Do you think you don't love him?"

I sipped at my tea and let the hot liquid sit on my tongue as I considered. I thought about his face, his smile, the feel of his hands. I remembered his laugh and the sound of him playing with Tilly. I shook my head. "I'm not falling out of love with him."

"There you go, no worries!" she said. "But I am not surprised that you've been having this sort of problem. I think that group you joined up with would be designed to bring deeper feelings to the surface, usually to knock you off balance."

"What?" I was stunned to hear her change the topic so quickly. I was confused. "I was talking about my feelings, not the group." *I'm not supposed to talk about the Many at all.*

"I know, but like I said the other week, these groups can make your emotions feel really powerful. It's intoxicating stuff."

"It was a good intoxicating," I said hotly. I thought of the freedom I had felt while the drums had been beating, the way I felt as though no one was judging me at all. I remembered how comfortable it had been to talk with the women there, to reveal my thoughts and feelings to them in the circle. "You know, it was going to that meeting that has helped me feel comfortable opening up to you about these things."

Tara raised her hands. "I'm not attacking you Pene. I'm really glad that you felt happy enough with me to open up, I'm glad I can help."

"It feels like you're trying to tell me that I've been making bad decisions." I slouched lower in my chair, avoiding her eyes. I knew I was acting like a grumpy teenager, and it made me flush with embarrassment. It cleared my throat and tried to sit up straight and meet her eyes.

Thankfully our conversation turned back to the school, and what events were coming up that Percy and Tilly were excited for. I didn't want to share any more with her, I was sure she would just explain to me how I was letting myself be led astray. *Ridiculous,* I told myself as I gathered Tilly up and we began to walk back to our car, parked near the school. *They haven't asked me for any money at all! They aren't some sort of scam or cult that are trying to lure me in and steal my belongings. All that suspicion that everyone was telling me about was totally unfounded.*

BY THE FOLLOWING Friday I was so glad to get away to the next meeting at the hall. I wanted to know I was in a space where there were people who understood how I was feeling, who shared my desire to enjoy my life instead of worrying all the time about the future. I was used to the darkened windows now, and the sight of the cars filling the car park made me relax. As I walked into the small hall I exchanged smiles and greetings with many of the women there. Even Lacey managed to nod at me in recognition. *I'm really getting the hang of this,* I thought.

My self visitation went well that night. It allowed me to slow down my thoughts, as I realised that they had been tumbling over and around each other like a litter of puppies. *I don't need Tara trying to explain what I'm thinking to me,* I decided. *I just need some space and support to untangle it all myself.* As I held myself still and focused on breathing slowly and regularly, I was able to start lining up my thoughts in order. It allowed me to see them all in turn, instead of feeling as though my emotions were reacting and bouncing off each other.

By the time Kallista called us into the circle, I felt serene. I felt as though my face was the surface of a pond deep in the forest, undisturbed by wind or rain. The smoke of the incense that was drifting through the hall felt light and smelt like fresh leaves. I felt the peace suffuse my skin and I smiled at the first woman I was placed with.

We shared ourselves and our feelings gratefully. She was eager to explain how her husband had been especially attentive recently, bringing her gifts when he was late home from work. I murmured an appreciation for how happy she seemed. On my turn I expressed how Otis seemed to be finding his attention drawn elsewhere, to other hobbies and even other women, and how I wished that we could re-establish the sort of connection that this woman had with her husband. She winced in sympathy but placed a hand on my knee as we sat by each other, rubbing in small circles.

After the circle, I felt excitement flutter in my belly. I hadn't realised just how much I was looking forward to the dance. The scent of the incense carried some spice with it, cinnamon or aniseed, I couldn't quite place it. Kallista stood at the front of the hall, surveying us with a solemn expression.

"We began with ourselves, and have expanded to one another. And now each of us needs to to become one of the Many," she said, in a soft voice. I wasn't sure what was going on. Normally she was more enthusiastic, full of joy and grins. But tonight she seemed more serious.

"We will be vulnerable, and we will be open. But tonight, with our new friends ready to fully embrace the god, we will not pause before the final rituals."

There was a sigh from the assembled women, a sound that I couldn't understand. Were they surprised by this announcement from Kallista? Was she changing the rules and expectations of the meeting? Or were they pleased to hear this, was it what they had been waiting for? I saw Lacey at the side of the room, and she wore a broad smile. Clearly, she was pleased to hear the announcement!

I searched out Agatha. She was looking at me with a questioning raise of an eyebrow but, when I shook my head slightly to show that I didn't know what the final ritual was either, she just shrugged and turned back to Kallista.

"First, we dance." As the speakers came to life and drums began, Kallista continued speaking. "We release what has built up within us. Release our tensions and worries, release the overwhelming emotions, release our tempest selves, until what is left, is nothing." She slowly undid her dress, slipping it down to her feet, and then began to dance. She stepped from one position to the next, pausing in between. Her arms drifted around her head as she held each pose. It was like watching a mannequin, one that melted into a new position every few seconds. All around me the women removed their clothes too, and joined in the slow dance.

As my clothes fell to the floor, I shivered in my skin, exposed to the air. I joined in the dance, moving slowly as the others did. Each step felt like the movement of mountains. My mind escaped from my body and I felt as though I was floating through a black void. I was surrounded by drifting clouds of colour like nebulae. There was a thud, as all the women's feet struck the floorboards at the same time, a synchronicity that shook me back down to my body. We spun around each other, our pace quickening. I smiled as hands brushed past me, as hips slid against my own, our skin tingling and prickling in the dim light of the room.

I escaped myself again, lifting higher in the darkness. This time I smelt the loam of a deep forest, the wet leaves and fresh water of a stream. Hints of the spice lifted into my mind from the incense around us. I felt clean, even though I felt dirt all around me, I felt pure. The simultaneous stomp of feet again brought me back down. This time it had come quicker, and the rhythm was building. Now the crash of our feet fell once more, accompanied by wild yelps and cries. I could feel my nipples were hard, and I was biting my lip. It was all I could do not to grab them myself, to press them and get some sense of the relief I craved. I gasped as one of the dancers passed by close enough that her hair brushed them, the sensation crackling through me like electricity.

There was a change in the sound of the room. The drumbeat continued, broken up by the sound of flute and the tambourines. But now the yelps and cries included deeper more guttural sounds. I opened my eyes and stumbled. There were men here with us.

CHAPTER TWENTY-TWO

I paused in my movements, shocked to see these men, but the press of bodies soon picked me up and spun me through the crowd. Now I was aware of the sweat that slicked the bodies around me, and the way that the hot air lay heavy on my head, stifling my breath. Incense flooded my nose, the scent stifling my thoughts.

The men spun in time with the music themselves, and they were naked also. Some of them were lithe and muscular, with trimmed hair and beards, while a few were older. The older men were scruffier and carried a little more weight, but they moved with the same passion, stomping in time with the music. Some of them had eyes open, fire burning from within, while others closed theirs, caught up in the beat.

Their nudity scared me at first. I couldn't look away from their dicks, which swung around their thighs as they danced. As I watched, each began to grow harder as the men slipped between the dancing women. I saw one man dance behind Lacey, his cock brushing across her buttocks. I saw her back arch and her mouth open wide, as he reached around to cup one of her breasts. Her arms were stretched up in her dance and one came down to catch the back of his head and pull his face closer to her.

One man moved past me, but he didn't seem to see me. His cock was huge and hard, almost glowing in the candlelight. He was turning and stepping, arms raised in pleasure. As I watched, one of the other women reached out and caught hold of his cock, squeezing and tugging. I saw him gasp with the joyous shock of contact.

The music grew faster and my pulse began to quicken. All around me the yelps and stomps of the beat began to turn into gasps and sighs. To my right, Kallista was leaning back against a man with a greying beard, her small breasts pressing out and begging to be sucked. His arm wrapped around her hip, pressing down her stomach, with a hand tucked between her legs. Her legs were slightly opened, and she bucked on his hand in time with the drums. She turned her head to kiss him, his other hand around her neck. Both her hands were pushed behind her back and I couldn't tell what she was doing to him.

I moved among the bodies as many slowly lowered themselves to the floor. The smoke from the incense was so thick that it hid many in half-shadow, and flooded my senses with spice and sweetness.

Agatha was on her knees in front of a slim young man with long dark hair. She was pulling on his cock as she sucked on it. She seemed totally engrossed in his shaft, her eyes staring up past his firm stomach to his face, as he pushed his fingers through her hair. I watched the muscles of his hips and stomach shift and tense as he shoved his cock further into her mouth and she ran fingers across his balls and around to his arse.

A hand reached out to me, tracing across my stomach. I flinched and turned. My eyes widened as I realised that it was Lacey who was reaching out to me from the ground nearby, and not one of the men. Her eyes were smouldering and she was rocking back and forwards on top of a broad shouldered man lying on the floor. He had her hips in her hands and he was pulling her in motion on top of his own hips. I could see the full shape of her breasts outlined above him.

"Join us?" she whispered.

What should I do? I was caught like a bee in a spiderweb, frozen in a moment of time while my thoughts raced. How should I react to all of this? What should I think of the Many, if this is what happens in their meetings? Could I be a part of this? What would it mean for my relationship with Otis? What would Talia think? But all these thoughts burst into light at Lacey's voice and then faded, shrouded by the spreading incense that fogged my mind. I felt the shiver in my spine and the heat that was spreading along the surface of my skin, and I wanted to feel more.

Slowly, I knelt down next to the pair and looked over her body. Her skin reflected the orange candlelight and her nipples made dark points on her breasts. The man beneath her wore an expression of concentration as he tugged her hips. Now that I was closer, I could see the dark tangle of her hair where it met him, and it made me aware of my own aching pussy. I leaned closer.

Lacey lifted her head to me and kissed me. Her lips were so much softer than anything else I had ever experienced before, and the sensation was luxurious. Her hands reached out to me, slipping over my shoulders and drawing me closer. I reached out with one hand too, brushing my fingers over her nipples, and sliding my hand down her side. I paused as my hand met the man's, his fingers rougher and thicker than Lacey's, which were currently brushing down my back as I let her tongue into my mouth. But then he shifted, releasing her a little, lifting his hand to cover mine, to encourage it down her side. My hand lay between Lacey's skin and the man's hand now, part of their movement, part of the way she was thrusting on him.

My pussy felt desperate for touch and I leaned closer to the pair next to me. My skin burned, and I pulled my hand out from it's warm space and ran it across Lacey's stomach. Her muscles were hard, though her skin was soft. Faint hairs tickled the palm of my hand and I followed them lower until I pushed my fingers through a thicker collection. I wondered if she could tell how nervous I was. I was sure that my hand was shaking.

My fingers sought out her clit, her hard center, suddenly aware of how new this all was for me. I paused and swallowed.

"What do I do?" I whispered as my hand moved closer."

"Silly. Just treat it like your own," she whispered back.

I could feel the man's stomach by my hand as well as I pressed and rubbed at Lacey. She broke off from my mouth and bent over the man, groaning deeply and riding harder, faster. I pressed further into the wet space where the two joined and found the hardness of his cock, sliding into her slick entrance. The pressure was building inside me until it felt as though I would explode.

"God yes," screamed Lacey as she convulsed and shuddered on the man. She clutched at his shoulders, nearly knocking me aside. I pulled my hand out and looked around me as Lacey and the man kissed deeply.

All around me were men and women in various positions and states of sex. Some must have finished, like Lacey, because they were stretched out on the floor, tangled with their lovers and with relieved and relaxed faces. Fingers dawdled across chests, or down stomachs.

Other were still fucking, concentration and closed eyes defining their faces. Kallista lay at the front of the room with her legs wrapped around a man who was fucking her with strong strokes, his hands to the sides of her shoulders, her hands raking down his back as she gasped. Agatha was on hands and knees with one man fucking her from behind, his fingers digging in to her hips, while another man stood in front of her. She couldn't concentrate on him though, the man behind her was thrusting so hard that she kept dropping the cock from her mouth.

As I watched, the man with Kallista grunted and tensed as he orgasmed. He held himself still as he collected his wits and then carefully lifted himself off her. Kallista lay on the floor, arms and legs spread out, and then lifted her head. She caught my eye and winked, and then kept scanning the room until she saw another man nearby. He was rubbing himself, clearly still hard, and she beckoned him over, turning her hips so that he could slide himself inside her more easily.

The music still pounded around us. I had forgotten that it existed. I was still on the floor, and my pussy still needed release, so I shuffled my legs around until I was lying down with my knees up and reached down to rub myself. I started slowly, building up pressure and speed quickly on my pebble, letting a finger drift down to the wetness between my lips.

"Would you like help?" Gentle voices spoke by my ears. I kept my eyes closed and nodded. Other hands joined mine, and softly slid inside me, pulling me open, taking over for my own hand. Hands reached out to grip my breasts, pinching the soft skin, rolling my nipples in their fingers. One finger ran across my mouth and pressed inside, and I let my tongue lick it. The hands were everywhere and I was drifting outside of my body again, expelled by the overwhelming sensation. There was no way that one person could provide this sort of sensation, it was too much. No one person could have this many hands, touch me in this many places. No one person could urge me to climax quite like this. It was as though I was deep in the darkest parts of a forest, surrounded by yowls and sounds of the wildest creatures that could exist, eyes upon me from every angle. There was no light, and no normal sound, just tambourines and yawps. I was racing, trying to find my way through the darkness.

As I passed through trees and felt them all reaching out to me, the rough branches turning to hands that traced my skin, I felt my orgasm rushing to meet me. I connected with it just as I left the deep darkness, bursting from their shelter and and facing up into endless stars in the night sky. My orgasm fell on me like a downpour of cool water, flushing through me and bursting out of me. I heard the crowd of people around me murmur and sigh in appreciation of my joy. The hands retreated, leaving me warm and unwound on the floor.

I lay catching my breath and staring at the plain white ceiling of the hall. Around me the sound of skin slapping on skin continued. I propped myself up and looked around, enjoying the sight of so many people caught up in their ecstasy. Groans and gasps filled the air, and the drumbeat pounded like all our heartbeats. Now that the first rush of excitement was fading, I could see condom wrappers lying on the floor amongst the revellers.

The door I had noticed at the last meeting creaked open. The light from the far side seemed blinding in the dim candle light and I had to shield my eyes from the glare. Someone seemed to be coming through. *Was that where the men had come from,* I wondered. *Who are they?* Suddenly I felt very exposed. I realised that I was lying naked on the floor when there was a group of men I didn't know having sex with these women. *Who was looking at me? Oh god, who had been touching me?*

A shadow moved in the light, and a clacking sound rang under the drumbeat and the sounds of the others. *I heard that noise last time,* I realised. The dark shape resolved and appeared to be a goat being led into the room. It had a thin cord around its neck.

Kallista walked through the crowd, still utterly naked, and took the cord from the hands of the man who had led it in. The candlelight reflected off her damp skin. The air smelt thick with the sex that filled the room and I was having trouble breathing. I was light-headed. Cries and yelps echoed from the walls, the crack of skin connecting with skin. I pulled my knees up to my naked chest and hugged onto them. I was feeling overwhelmed with sensation, and nausea was building at the bottom of my gut.

Kallista and the goat walked through the crowd, hands reaching out towards them from the knotted figures that sprawled across the dark floor. The limbs seemed red and black in the light from the flames lining the walls, stretching up from a writhing tangle of skin, eyes pinpoints of reflected light that spun in the mass. I couldn't see Kallista anymore, the light was too dim, and bodies blocked the view.

I pulled tighter and swallowed, trying to clear my head. My eyes were sore from the smoke and incense in the air, musky. It made the air seem like a solid presence around my head, seeping through my nose into my lungs. There was a loud noise, louder than any cry that had come already that night, and it tore across my mind. I lifted one hand to rub my face and tried to peer through the room.

Something seemed to be happening on the far side of the hall. Most of the people present had moved over to that side, and they were gathered in a mob, still moving in regular rhythmic routines. I crawled across the floor, to see what was going on.

Kallista emerged from the crowd, walking directly towards me. Her eyes were fixed on me, twin lighthouses in the tempest, and I felt secure as she approached me. She reached out her hands to help me stand. Just as I lifted mine to accept her help in standing, I saw that her hands were covered in shining darkness and I flinched away. Her smile flickered, her twitching to a frown, and for an instant I wondered if she would yell at me. The smile returned in all the time it took to blink, though her eyes seemed narrower.

"Is... Is that...?" I stammered as I stared at her hands. It was hard to be certain in the candlelight, but I thought that the substance covering her hands, stretching up her arms to the elbow, dripping from her wrists, was thick blood. I licked my lips and lifted my eyes to meet hers again, feeling the hairs on my back stand on end.

She tilted her head and let her hands fall to her sides.

"It is what it is. The god demands sacrifice, but offers so much in return."

"It's b... It's b..." I couldn't say the words aloud. *Blood. What on earth would blood be doing here?* I looked over at the pile of bodies on the far side of the hall. *Where did the goat go? What were they all doing?* One of the figures rose from the struggling pile, and lifted something to his mouth, pulling at it with his teeth. Darkness ran down his chin, and painted his chest. *Oh god, where had these men come from?*

Kallista stepped sideways, between myself and the man, hiding them from me. Her eyes met mine again as she peered out from under her brows.

"Pene?" she asked. There was no actual question, but the way she spoke my name carried multitudes in it's harmony.

"I'll be okay," I murmured, pressing my hands to my stomach. I rolled onto my legs and climbed to my feet. "I'll be okay, I just... I'm a little overwhelmed right now."

"Come and have some wine," suggested Kallista, gesturing to the table at the side of the room.

When we reached it, she poured out two large glasses of heavy red wine, one for each of us. I took a long sip and then gasped and coughed and put my glass on the table.

"What's the matter?"

"It's just that it's so dark and thick and..." My voice trailed off. Was I trying to accuse them of slipping blood into the bottles? What did I think was going on? Were they vampires?

Kallista chuckled and sipped again at her glass before pouring me a fresh glass of white wine.

"Here. This might not be quite so on the nose."

The wine did help. It made my mouth seem cleaner, and it washed down my throat and into my stomach before the cleansing sensation moved out along my limbs, leaving me calmer. I realised again that I was standing in the room naked, with people I didn't know. I looked back at the hall and realised there was no way that I would be able to retrieve my clothes until everyone else had stopped. From the grunts and moans, it didn't seem as though they were looking to stop any time soon.

"You seemed quite tense. Are you feeling better now?"

I nodded.

"I suppose you have some questions then?"

I looked over at Kallista. She seemed such an approachable and friendly person. Her smile was comfortable and easy and it spread across her face at a moment's notice. She spoke to everyone as though they were the most important person in her world at that moment. But here she was, naked, leading a group of women into what seemed to be an orgy and animal sacrifice. I shook my head slowly and gestured at the hall with my wine glass.

"What is this?" was all I managed to say.

Kallista frowned and sipped from her glass again.

"We are an ancient group," she began in a soft voice. "We have existed, in one form or another, for hundreds of years. I was introduced to the group about twenty years ago, and I suppose I found it as overwhelming as you do at first. But, over the years, I have grown to love my times with this group. The rituals help me." She leaned closer. "We can truly reveal ourselves here. With one another, we need hold no secrets. Do you understand how truly freeing it is to be your whole self?" She searched my eyes as she spoke. "Once we are part of this communion, we are like butterflies pulling ourselves free of the chrysalis we hid in most of our lives. We can dance on the wind!" Her eyes shone with a fire that I hadn't seen before. It wasn't the reflection of the candles, it was a deep belief, a fervour that drove her onwards.

"I get it," I replied, nodding. "I do. Or, at least, I thought I did. The last couple of meetings were wonderful. I loved the sense of myself that you all encouraged in me, and the circles are amazing. Even the naked dancing made me feel free at one level. But tonight?" I pointed back into the middle of the hall with my head. "I don't understand tonight."

"The god does ask certain things of us," answered Kallista with lowered eyes. "I find that it's not worth trying to explain this part of the ritual to outsiders. They don't understand, or they refuse to countenance it. But once you are here, if you experience it yourself, you begin to understand."

She hooked an arm into my elbow and turned me to face the crowd. Many more people were finished now, laying across the floor, breathing deeply and silently, their heads and arms resting on each other's naked forms.

"The god is a god of life, and of love, and of connection. But if he is to enrich these parts of our own existence, we must present our offerings of these things. This is an important part of our ritual."

"I didn't expect there to be men here."

"I know, and it is shocking at first."

"Who are they?"

"They are followers of the god from our brother group. They worship the god themselves, and on some occasions our rituals cross paths. You don't think we would allow just anyone to be a part of these rituals would we?"

"How often do they cross paths?"

"Well," she said, letting the word drift on as she waggled her head from side to side, a sly grin spreading across her lips. "More often than not, sure... But did you feel unsafe? Did anyone do anything you didn't want them to do?"

I sipped at my glass as I considered the question. I wanted to say "that's not the point" but as I thought about it I realised that no one had gone any further than I had been comfortable with. *Comfortable with in the moment, don't you mean,* said a voice in the back of my head. *And is that really the same thing?* It wasn't my own voice. It sounded very much like Tara was standing behind me, whispering in my ear. *I tried to warn you,* the voice said. *It is easy to let your feelings and emotions carry you to places that you didn't expect. Is this what you want?*

I opened my mouth to answer but Kallista spoke first, squeezing my arm with the hand that was still crooked around my elbow.

"Of course, what is light without darkness?" I became freshly aware of the blood that covered her arms and was now smeared on my skin. "What is a god of life, without the acknowledgment of death? So, there must be death. And we must all be touched by it. It marks us for the god, as those who belong to him. In that moment of death, he becomes one with us, he drives us, he possesses us. With him, we act, there is death, and then he brings new life and ecstasy back to us."

"Is it even legal?" I asked.

"Of course!"

I didn't believe her.

The others were beginning to get up from the floor and make their way over to stand nearer us, and so Kallista withdrew her hand and moved forward to begin talking with some of them. The music began to wind down, and before I knew it we were left in silence. Some people began to gather their clothes up from the floor, and so I searched for mine as well.

"Thank you for joining together, my sisters and brothers," Kallista spoke loud and clear to all. "Truly, we have experienced the pleasure our god wishes for us tonight! Please, allow yourself to come back to your body before leaving. Do not be in a rush to disengage here and reconnect with the world outside. That said, be well, see you next time!"

Cheerful pockets of conversation began to pick up through the hall as everyone gathered their belongings and began to dress. Laughter was common, especially when someone turned on the lights and we were all momentarily blinded. A few people had been caught still undressed and they grinned and chuckled, while others remained naked without a care. Many were picking up new glasses of wine and chatting near the table. I was amazed to see a few men and women standing with arms around one another. I wondered if they were couples, or if this was just how the group behaved on these shared ritual nights.

I looked for Agatha, wondering if she was as off balance as I was. She seemed happy when I found her. She was dressed already but her cheeks were still flushed and a fire was beginning to burn in her eyes.

"Were you expecting this?" I asked.

"Not at all! But I have to say, I thought it was incredible!"

"Didn't you think it was too much?"

"No." She paused, and gave full consideration to what I was saying. "No, I don't think so."

"Did you... do anything?" I asked, already knowing the answer but wondering what she would say.

Agatha grinned and lowered her head. "Oh yeah!" Her answer burst out of her.

"Don't you have a boyfriend though? What would he think?"

Agatha blinked and her mouth gaped slightly. "I... That hadn't occurred to me."

"Maybe you shouldn't tell him," I suggested, horrified that she hadn't even considered what this evening would do to her relationship. The nausea I had felt before returned. *What would this do to Otis and myself?*

I drove home slowly after the meeting, wondering what I would say to Otis. By the time I pulled into the driveway in the dark, I had resolved to tell him the truth. We had been dancing and it had been freeing, and then things had gone further than I expected. I nodded to myself, sitting in the front seat of a motionless car. It was the best way.

I walked through the dark house and went to the bathroom where I prepared myself for bed. I knew that I was delaying the conversation, but I still took my time, brushing my teeth much more thoroughly than I usually would. Eventually I couldn't put it off any further and so I walked into the bedroom.

My husband was curled under the blankets, snoring softly. I lifted the blankets on my side and slid between the sheets. Otis mumbled and rolled over onto his back. I watched his face.

Just as I was about to reach over and shake his shoulder, there was a tapping noise from the bedroom door. Tilly was standing there in her pajamas, clutching a lizard soft toy up near her face. When she saw that I had seen her, she came quickly across to the bed and then clambered across the top of the duvet and buried herself between Otis and myself. He reached out and wrapped an arm over her and she closed her eyes, snoring herself within seconds. I couldn't help but smile at my ridiculous family. I snuggled under the covers and went to sleep too.

CHAPTER TWENTY-THREE

he next few days passed quietly as I tried to process everything that had happened. I took Tilly to school, and I did the household chores. Otis was happy as he rushed out of the house in the morning, with a quick farewell kiss for me, and he unwound with a beer and games on the X-Box in the evenings. But on Thursday, my day was different.

I had only just got home from dropping Tilly at school, where she had insisted that we arrange another playdate with Percy. I had sat down in the lounge with a pile of laundry that needed to be folded and sorted and put away. I turned on the TV and looked for one of my shows, something to have on while I worked my way through the laundry. *I'll get to the clothes in a moment,* I told myself as I lay back on the couch.

The women on the show met up for coffee with each other and complained about their husbands and children, but in amusing ways, and I giggled and dug deeper into the luxurious cushions. My eyes felt heavy.

There was knocking from the front door, and I jerked out of my doze. On the screen one of the main characters was standing in her business suit, soaked from head to toe, while her boss's boss tapped one foot in front of her. I decided that I would need to take it back a scene and figure out what had happened. But first, I stood up and went to the front door.

Is this a courier or something, I asked myself as I walked through the kitchen. *I don't think I ordered anything?* I smelt freshly cut wood on the air. I pulled open the door.

"Yes?"

Nic the builder was standing on the front step, his hands held together in front of him. He was still wearing a black singlet, which showed off the way his muscles were strong and tight along his shoulders and arms. His bright eyes were watching me closely.

"Good morning," he said, shifting his head so that his long dreadlocks fell to one side.

"Uh," I said as I stood frozen in shock.

"I'm sorry it's taken so long to come around. I had another job that needed sorting before I had any spare time. Can I come inside?"

"Uh, sure," I mumbled and I stood aside. He kicked off his heavy brown work boots and left them beside the door then stepped inside. He was wearing thick woolen socks below his thin but powerful legs. They were heavily tanned from working outside. I coughed as I realised that I was looking over his body as he walked past me.

"So, it was some renovation to the deck that you were looking for, right?"

"Uh, yes." *For the love of god woman, what is going on with you?* I followed Nic as he walked through to the lounge and pulled open the ranch slider. He stood at the open doorway, looking over the deck.

"Hmmm," he said.

"What?"

"It does need quite a lot of work."

"Really?" I knew that Otis thought so, and we had been talking to Kallista to get the money for it, but for some reason I was intrigued by Nic's opinion. I had discussed it for hours with

Otis, but this man's thoughts were all I wanted to hear about right now. I clutched my hands at my chest and peeked out past Nic.

"Yeah, see those supports?" Nic leaned over and put an arm around my shoulders to help guide my vision, pointing with his other hand. I saw the support posts he was pointing at.

"Yes." I felt the warmth of his arm on my shoulder. I could barely see, I was so obsessed with the contact of his skin with mine. I could think of nothing else. My head was flooded with the scent of damp undergrowth and pine needles.

"Yeah, those will need replacing pretty soon. And we'll need to get in some temporary supports or some of the roof might come down." He turned to look at me as he explained what he would need to do.

I looked back into his eyes, my cheeks burning. His eyes were dark and intense. His face was a breath away from my own.

"But of course, anyone could have told you that," he said. "Maybe there's something else that I could do for you while I'm here."

His hands behind my shoulders pulled me closer to him and his lips met mine. He kissed me intently, with strong lips and his confident tongue searching it's way to my own. I felt myself begin to settle into his arms, pushing my hands around his sides. I sighed at the feel of his firm muscle beneath his clothes. The buzzing sensation below was back. Then I opened my eyes and tried to step away, placing a hand on his chest. *God, he's so strong.*

"I can't, I'm married."

"I think you can. I think that, actually, you want to." He stepped closer again, reaching out a hand to my hip. I felt myself twisting to accommodate his hand.

"I don't know," I began, trying to get my thoughts in order.

"I do," he said again, pulling my hips to him.

"Yes," I murmured, my blood racing. I began to melt under his mouth, the way he sank onto me brushing aside my meagre objections. I wanted him to touch me, and I gasped as his hands picked me up and drew me against him. His fingers were so strong and firm, and they pressed into my back and sides. His tongue pushed into my mouth and it's warmth began a fire inside me.

Nic pulled away from my mouth, leaving me waiting for him to return, breathing deeply. He gripped my shoulders and moved me back to the kitchen bench, away from the front door, his face stern. The muscles in his arms were bunched up as he moved me. The bench ran into my bottom but he kept pushing, and I tumbled onto my back on the bench. I began to sit up on my elbows, but he pressed me back down. There was a rustle of papers as the pile of junk mail on the end of the bench was swept to the floor by my arms. There was a box of tissues sitting right next to my face and I shoved it away after the junk mail.

I felt his fingers fumbling at the button to my pants, and I reached down to undo it for him, only for him to slap my hand aside.

"Lie down," he instructed curtly, as he finished undoing my pants and pulled them down with my underwear. He left them bunched around my ankles, and then pulled my knees apart, exposing my pussy to him.

I was burning up and I wanted to feel him touch me, to slip inside me, but I also knew that we were in the front room, not far from the front door, and someone walking by might be able to see me. I tried to roll over so that I could stand up and move somewhere more private, but Nic grabbed my thigh and pushed me back down.

"I said stay there," he growled, and the animal noise sent a shiver that rushed from the top of my head, down my spine, and ending up quivering through my clit. I need him to touch me now.

He placed his hands on the soft skin at the tops of my inner thighs, his rough worn palms scratching and sparking on my skin. The sensation made me squirm and I rocked my pussy towards him, but he didn't respond yet. He squeezed my skin, digging in with his nails until I squeaked.

Then he lowered his head to my pussy and slid his tongue between my lips, slipping up to my clit and then down again. Each movement made me gasp, and the intensity of his tongue on my most sensitive area brought tingles to my fingertips. At the beginning of each movement his tongue pressed around the edges of me. I wanted to draw him inside, each movement rocking me against the smooth flat surface I lay on.

Moments before I was about to come, Nic stood up and looked down at my figure lying before him. I felt exposed beneath his bright piercing eyes, and pulled my arms across my chest. He pulled one arm away, and then began to pull my top up from my stomach. I wriggled, trying to pull the top back down. He released my arm for a moment, just long each to grab the bottom of the top and wrench it up, tangling my arms in it and covering my face. Now fully exposed he leaned down and took one of my hard nipples between his teeth, biting down.

I squealed and writhed under him, trying to get my arms out of my top as the pain sluiced through me. My tangled legs made it hard to get leverage, and then Nic released me. I felt his hands grasp the cloth above my head, gathering the material into one hand so that it became a handle for him, trapping my arms and hiding my face. He slid his other arm under my knees and then lifted me off the kitchen counter.

I felt cold air on my naked body as he carried me through the room. The sensation of floating made my pulse quicken, and I felt my flesh prickle with goose pimples. I held my breath and tensed my stomach, praying that he wouldn't drop me. I had no idea where he was taking me, and I worried about him carrying me too near the windows. *What if the neighbours saw me? What would they say? What if they told Otis?*

Suddenly the world jumped and I nearly screamed. Nic had let me go and I was falling, but then I landed on something soft and bounced slightly, before shifting as Nic's weight joined me. *Where are we,* I wondered.

Nic's hand landed on my thigh and moved up towards my pussy, where he turned his fingers and pushed them inside me. His fingers reached further, deeper, pushing the flames higher. I felt his body above me, though I could see nothing. My breath began to come in rhythmic pants, matching the speed of his fingers, pressing in and out of me, his palm covering my clit and rubbing against it.

As I moaned and felt the pressure building inside me, as Nic's hand moved and drew me closer and closer to my climax, I noticed that his other hand had released my top. I felt him fumbling with the neck of the top, pulling the elastic up over my chin and revealing my mouth. I gasped again, breathing in the cool air deeply after being stuck with the stuffy warmth that had been trapped in the top with me.

I was surprised that he stopped moving the top once my mouth was free, and so I began shifting my shoulders in an attempt to move it up the rest of my face. The sound of Nic's hand slapping my cheek was a loud crack, and the pain that shot over my skin numbed me. I felt my pussy grip onto his fingers as an orgasm made my muscles tense.

"Stay still," he said again. I nodded slightly. My body slowly relaxed, and his fingers began to slip in and out of me again. I could feel how wet they were now, slippery and slick.

Again, I became very aware of his body leaning over me, and I could tell that he was moving, rearranging his position, though I couldn't see what he was doing. Then, I felt a hot thick shape at the edge of my mouth, tracing my lips. I allowed them to part and accepted him inside.

His cock filled my mouth and I was amazed at how thick it was. I had to pull my lips further back in order to open wide enough to take it in. His cock sat on my tongue, hot and salty. I tried to suck on it, to run my tongue around its size, but it was so hard to move, and he was still pounding my pussy with his hand.

He began to thrust at my face, pushing towards the back of my throat. I could feel myself struggling to breathe properly, but I didn't want him to stop. As he pounded both ends of me, I felt the fires rise within me again, until an inferno burned out from my core, and I began to buck underneath him as my muscles jerked through another orgasm. After I stopped moving, he pulled his cock out from my mouth and I sucked in a lungful of air again. Then his fingers slid out of me and I felt him position that thick cock right next to my pussy. My lips were throbbing, pressed and stretched by his rough pounding hand, and I wanted him inside me.

I groaned as his cock began to press on my entrance, the wetness of my orgasms allowing it to spread me open and move inside me with ease. I felt like I was being pulled apart, stretched until I could accept the whole man inside myself, until I could take him within me.

His hand settled over my collarbone, thumb to one side of my neck, fingers curled around my throat on the other. He pressed down and my breath caught, my gasps and moans curtailed into rattling gulps. He began to fuck me, his hips slapping on my thighs. I had to bend my legs to allow him in, restricted as they were by the material around my ankles.

The rhythm built harder and harder, the slap of his body on mine setting a beat that my pulse began to mimic. I tried to suck air down as he fucked me, dragging the air past his hand that clenched around my neck. Each breath felt like cold water, shocking against the fire that burned inside filled my body. I could feel the texture of his hands, rough hands, used to working hard. I couldn't see, but a blackness began to encroach on the edges of my vision anyway. Sparks glittered on the sides of my sight and I felt my body begin to go limp beneath the insistent rhythm of Nic, fucking me like I was a toy under his command.

Just before I passed out, Nic's cock pushed me over the line, and I felt my being wash out of my self. With that final orgasm, I was complete. I was finished. I was ready to let go and fall away into the darkness that was enveloping me. As my will vanished, I felt Nic grunt. His hips shoved into me and I felt him filling me. It was as though he had stripped me down and emptied me, and then replaced my being with his own.

I shudder and sighed as he pulled away from me, releasing my neck from his strong grip, withdrawing his cock from my pussy. I felt the loss immediately. I felt abandoned in a cold pile. I moved to try and get comfortable on the soft surface he had put me on. Though I could breathe again, the darkness remained. My top was still bound around my head. A satisfied sleep crept around me and pulled me down into its depths.

I stretched and rolled over on the couch cushions, shifting my head on the firm arms. My neck made a series of cracking noises as my bones shifted into a more comfortable position and I rolled my shoulders and smacked my lips as I sat up. The lounge was empty, a basket of laundry sitting next to me, and the TV was ready to begin playing my show. I frowned and squeezed the bridge of my nose. *Where did he go?*

The room was filled with a gentle floral smell. The door was open to the garden, and fresh air was wafting through. I stood up and walked through to the kitchen. The breakfast dishes still sat in the sink, but there was no sign that I had been bent over the bench. Some junk mail and local newspapers were still sitting next to the box of tissues at the end of the bench.

When I got to the front door I pulled it open and stood just outside, looking up and down the street. The sun was shining and the street was empty. I looked for the van that I had seen Nic driving around in, but there was nothing, not even someone walking a dog.

I shut the door as I walked back inside, and then I crouched down and ran my hands over the carpet just inside the door. *Is that a footprint,* I asked myself as I felt along the soft fibres. *Is that a hint of mud from his work boots?* The fibres bent and sprang back into position as I slid my hand over their surface, but there was nothing that I could be sure of. Maybe the marks were just shadows, so faint that I couldn't be certain.

I poured myself a glass of water and stood in the silent kitchen, sipping slowly. The cold liquid soothed the fire and confusion that was swirling in my chest. After I finished my drink, I was able to clean up the dishes and sit down in the lounge to fold laundry. I tried to put the encounter out of my mind. It was difficult.

After completing the laundry I began thinking about what had happened. I spent far too long remembering what it had been like to lie down in front of Nic, to see the strength in his muscles as he pushed me down. To watch his arms tense, to see his abdomen tighten. I began to shift my hips as I thought about his cock, rising up from his hurriedly shoved aside jeans.

But before I got caught up in the memories, I glanced over and noticed the time showing on the microwave in the kitchen.

"Shit," I exclaimed. "I need to get Tilly!"

I was running late.

CHAPTER TWENTY-FOUR

I ran through the empty spaces between the quiet classrooms, berating myself in my head. *What are you doing,* I yelled internally at myself. *How could you let yourself get so distracted? God, I hope she's not upset.* I tore around the last corner and saw her.

She was standing under a tree in the courtyard outside her classroom and Tara and Percy were there with her. She and Percy were chatting, heads held close together and Tara was on her phone, but Tilly glanced up as I emerged. Her face grew hard, and she glared at me.

"I"m so sorry sweetheart, I got caught up this afternoon," I began to explain, panting as I caught my breath. I wasn't sure if it was guilt, embarrassment, or just the run that made my cheeks grow warm.

"You're late," she grumbled, crossing her arms.

"I know I am, and I'm really sorry," I said, crouching down and opening my arms to her. It took her a moment to decide whether or not to accept my hug, but in the end she tumbled into my embrace. "Thank you so much for waiting with her," I said over my daughter's shoulder to Tara. "I should have texted or something, but I just jumped in the car and raced over!"

"It's not a problem," she replied with a smile. She tucked her phone back into her bra. "You know Percy loves to spend time with Tilly. Speaking of that, I think it's about time for another proper playdate! Shall we come to see your house this time?"

"That sounds lovely," I agreed, and we made plans for the two to come by on the weekend.

While I drove Tilly home, I was very aware of the silence in the back seat.

"Are you alright love?" I asked.

"What happened?" she said in reply. "I'm supposed to be your number one."

"Oh, I know, I just got a bit caught up doing chores and forgot to leave on time. I'll make sure it doesn't happen again."

She just hurrumphed at me in reply.

Tilly refused to leave the kitchen while I made dinner. I poured myself a wine to distract myself from the sound of whining dolls in the video that she watched on her tablet, sitting up on the bench by me. Just as I finished preparing the meal and pouring myself another glass, Otis came home.

"Hello my ladies," he called loudly from the doorway, though we were not far away. He swirled into the kitchen and bundled me up for a kiss.

"Watch it, you'll spill my wine," I laughed.

"Alright alright, you drunkard," he teased, before rushing around the bench to tickle Tilly. "How's my favourite little treasure eh?"

"No, daddy, don't!" squealed Tilly as he wiggled his fingers on her sides. After she managed to stop laughing, she pointed at me. "Mummy nearly forgot to pick me up after school today."

"What?" Otis raised an eyebrow at me.

"Oh, it's fine. I was running late, I lost track of time."

"Fair enough," he grinned.

As we lay in bed that night I didn't want to close my eyes. I lay with my hand resting on my husband's hip, as he curled up beneath the covers. His breath kept a calm rhythm in the darkness, in and out, while I tried to think through what was happening to me.

I didn't want to close my eyes, because I didn't know what I would find there. How much of my recent memory could be trusted? I felt sure that something else was happening. Maybe these memories were real, maybe they really happened, but even so, something unusual had happened to me. I was scared that if I closed my eyes, some new uncontrollable situation would unfold, and I would fall further into a world I wasn't sure I meant to be a part of. Eventually, I could not fight my eyelids open any longer, and I drifted to sleep.

I lay in bed, the soft feeling of sleep slipping around me. It felt like pillow stuffing brushing around me. I wondered if I would ever get to sleep, or if I was doomed to lie in bed all night, worrying about my husband. I decided to get up and get a drink of water.

I walked out into the hallway and noticed that there was soft green light shining under the edges of the walls. The carpet felt thick and lush and cool against the soles of my feet. *Shouldn't the light in the hallway be orange?* I stepped through the doorway and onto the polished marble of the kitchen. As I walked out from the marble archway, the moon came out from behind a cloud and bathed the scene in it's silver glow. The colour of the moonlight and green glow from the shrubs that clustered around the sides of the plaza blended beautifully, creating a pleasant light that lifted my spirits.

Spiderwebs of twisting branches created a grille that enclosed the plaza, with only two gaps. One the marble archway I had entered by, the other an archway formed out of thick foliage on the opposite side of the plaza.

I frowned. *When did the kitchen bench get swapped for a marble altar?* The altar was basically a block of stone, broad and pale, sitting to the left of me. It was wrapped in carvings, depicting women and men dancing, twirling cloths around and between each other. The carvings made me smile.

I heard a clunk from the other entrance. When I turned, he was standing there. The same figure I had found in the bushes weeks ago. A satyr, just as Tara had described. Not the small fat smirking creature that I had seen in the art gallery, but tall and strong and dangerous. My heart began pounding, my breath grew shallow.

"Who are you?" I stammered. The figure said nothing, but stepped closer.

He was still naked, still covered in thick dark hair around his waist and down his legs. His muscles were still broad and power-ful. His black eyes were somehow even darker than before, pools of endless night. He took another step.

"Why are you here? This is my home." I stepped backwards as nerves twisted in my stomach. I placed both hands on my stomach, trying to calm myself. The tangled sensation moved lower, between my legs, and I gasped. My skin grew hot.

The figure's cock began to lift away from his legs, thickening and hardening. My eyes grew wider as it rose to stand rigid and full, the skin dark and stretching. Veins rose from within. I felt my pussy begin to beg for that monstrous cock, I wanted to feel it spread me wide open. *But my husband. What about Otis?* The thoughts were wisps that drifted far to the back of my mind as the figure stopped up to me and reached out to grasp my shoul-ders. His firm fingers pressed against my skin and all my thoughts fled.

He lifted me entirely off the ground and placed me on the altar, sitting on it with my legs over the side. Then, he gripped the neck of my tee shirt with one fist and yanked, ripping the clothes from my body. I yelped as the fabric pulled around me, and then clutched my arms over my exposed breasts. He leaned closer and pulled my arms apart. He was so strong. I tensed my arms, trying to hold them in place but I couldn't stop him. He looked down at my body and leered. I hated to admit it, but the fire in his eyes caught a flame in my stomach. I shifted my hips and pressed my thighs together.

He let go of one arm and used his free hand to push me back until I was lying down on the stone. It was cold, and it made my skin rise into goose pimples. He pressed down on my chest between my breasts, his thick fingers holding me on the cold surface. Then he released my other hand, and reached between my legs. Again, with one swift strong movement, he tore away my underwear. I tried to squeeze my legs together again, but he was standing too close, right between my knees, and I couldn't force my thighs closed. I felt the thick hair on his legs scratching the soft skin inside my legs, near my pussy. I moaned as his cock lay down on top of me, hot and heavy. The base pressed on my clit, it's weight separating my folds. I could feel his skin slide against my wetness. The shaft lay along my stomach. I was panting now, pushing my hips closer to him.

He leaned down and kissed me hard. I wrapped my hands in his hair, curling my fingers around the coils of the horns that were half-buried inside. His lips were firm and insistent, and I pulled him closer.

He stood up again, still with the lazy smile on his face. *At last,* I thought, as my pulse raced. I could barely see, I was so over-whelmed with anticipation of the pleasure to come. But just when I expected him to slide his cock inside me, he pulled my shoulder and turned me over on the stone, forcing my breath from me. My hips rested on the edge of the altar, my knees on the ground. And then it came.

His cock was bigger than anything I had ever experienced before. I caught my breath and was holding it, trying not to move as the thick shaft stretched me wide open. It pushed at me, and I groaned as it forced it's way deeper, probing me. The pressure grew all through me, and even my fingertips were throbbing. I felt the cold stone against my cheek, the heavy weight of his hand between my shoulders. My breasts were pressed beneath me. Then he began to thrust.

Each movement sent a jolt of sensation shifting from my pussy, through my core until it reached my extremities. Then, just as the shock began to fade, he would thrust against, sending fresh waves inside me. The stone that had felt so smooth now seemed harsh against my skin, tiny claws scratching over my nipples, rubbing them raw. I felt tears slip from my eyes at the pain, but I bit my lip and held on.

The pounding grew faster and faster, and I began to cry longer with each thrust, until I was sure that I was screaming in one long endless open mouth of pleasure and pain. My thighs were slamming into the altar, and my head shook as I moaned and gasped. The repetitive slap of his flesh on my arse kept the rhythm. I had to close my eyes from the pressure building inside me.

Before the pressure built strong enough that I would explode, the figure heaved against me, so hard that I screamed again. That devastating cock shook inside me, and I writhed under it, like I was being stapled in place by it. My pussy tried to grip that thick shaft as I came, every muscle tensing and pulling into one ball of release. Even as I tried to relax, I couldn't. Fresh spasms would roll through my muscles, wringing every drop of my passion from me. Finally I was left, drawing in long rattling breaths as I tried to get my bearings.

I felt his huge hands withdraw from my skin and the sudden cold air was unwelcome. He slid his cock out of me, and the chill on my entrance was a new intensity, setting my heart racing again. I tried to turn over to see him, but my limbs were shaking and I could do no more than turn my head. I caught a glimpse of movement, but I was so drained that my eyes began to close. I pushed at the stone beneath me and felt my hands sink into it, as though they were pressing into foam bubbles.

In the distance I heard a soft electronic melody. It rose in repetitive cycles and I buried my head further into the pillow, pulling the duvet up around my shoulders.

"Turn it off," I grumbled.

"Sorry babe," said Otis as he rolled out of bed. "I've got an early meeting. Tilly should be up soon."

I rolled over and stretched. My muscles ached and I felt as though I had been sleeping on the bare floor. As I twisted myself, I heard my spine and neck crackle as the bones resettled.

What a dream, I told myself.

By the time Tara and Percy arrived on the weekend, I was more eager to see tham than Tilly. I really wanted a chance to sit down with Tara and discuss the Many with her. I had been so annoyed when she had said that the group and their meetings were encouraging me to let my emotions control me, but after the last meeting I was worried that she might be right. I needed to ask for her advice. I was terrified that it might even be too late.

Otis left early in the morning for another hike, kissing me on the cheek by the door as I stood in my dressing gown and sipping at a hot cup of tea.

"See you tomorrow!" he chirped then he heaved his bag onto his shoulder and walked out to the car. I went to shower and get dressed and then sat in the kitchen next to Tilly on her tablet, waiting for Tara and Percy. As I waited, I ran through a list of things I wanted to ask her in my mind. Once they arrived and we had sent the children off to play with the lego in Tilly's room, I sat Tara down in our dining room and poured a glass of thick red wine.

"Would you like some?" I offered, proffering the glass to her.

"No, thank you." Tara winced slightly. "You know that it's only eleven in the morning, right?"

"Yes, but sometimes you just need a little something to get you through the day, right?" I kept the glass and took a sip. It clinked onto the table as I put it down and I blew out my breath in one go. "Tara, you're a woman of the world."

Tara smiled awkwardly. "Sure, I guess you could say that?"

"You know about strange groups, and weird ideas, and you and Peyton are so artistic and everything." I waved a hand in the air between us, trying to summarise the way she and her husband were able to weigh in on discussions about anything. They seemed to already have considered every idea that came bursting into my mind like a firecracker, new and inspiring. Now I needed to use their knowledge to help me grow.

"You tried to warn me about the meetings I was going to be part of. Last time we spoke in particular."

"Absolutely. You said they've been helping you open up to people though? So they've been good."

"Yes, they are exhilarating," I said huskily. Then I coughed and took a sip of my wine. "Why was it that you wanted to warn me about them again? Surely being in touch with my emotions is a good thing."

"I've had experience with groups that like to go a little under the radar." Tara leaned back and stretched on her chair. "I think that they recognise someone who flies under the radar every day in me. But anyway, there are a few different groups operating around here, and really they are all harmless as long as you know what you are doing with them."

"If they are harmless, why did you warn me?"

"I do say they are harmless only if you know what you are getting into. One of these groups is about bringing your emotions to the top of your mind, bringing them to the surface. That means that you aren't hiding anything from anyone. It means that you wear your heart on your sleeve."

"Aren't those good things? Surely, if we all let each other know how we are feeling, the world would be a better place?"

"Absolutely! And that's why I say that they aren't a big problem! We should all be more conscious of our feelings indeed. However, if you aren't used to it, if you aren't prepared for it, it can cause problems."

"Like what?"

"If you aren't used to your emotions, you can let them begin to make your decisions. You can begin to think that you have to take an action, just because it feels right in the moment."

I remembered the feeling of hands on my sides, of soft material cushioning my body while my head was wrapped in my own clothes. I took a sip of my wine.

"It's important to express emotions, but also to process them and to consider them. Which, when it's done right, is the whole point of those sort of groups! Have you been finding that?"

"They certainly give you space to feel your emotions." I leaned forward and rested my arms on the kitchen bench. I took a deep breath and glanced around to make sure that the children weren't playing nearby. I had to gather my strength to be able to tell Tara. Kallista had made it so clear that I wasn't to talk about the meetings with others, I felt as though she was looking over my shoulder even now.

"To be honest, that's part of why I wanted to talk to you. At the last meeting I..." My hand was shaking slightly, so I placed it palm down on the bench. "I think I may have gone too far."

"Oh." Tara's eyebrows came together in concern. "How far is too far exactly?"

"You have to know first, that the meeting includes some dancing."

"Okay."

"And, sometimes the dancing, is... Um..."

Tara tilted her head and smirked. Her eyes glittered. "Is it maybe dancing with less clothes on than usual?"

I felt my cheeks flushing red. "Yes, that's one way to put it."

"Yes, I know how these things work. Go on."

"Okay, so last time we were dancing, and then these men came out to dance with us."

"Are men not there usually?

"What?" I blinked and stared at her. "No! Did you think that we were dancing naked with a bunch of strange men at all these meetings?"

'No. But aren't you explaining to me that you were dancing naked with strange men at the last one?"

I spluttered and coughed and then took a sip of wine to settle myself.

"I know one of the groups that approached me dances naked with men and women all the time. It's most of the reason that they exist. They try to sell it as performance art, but there's a few layers beneath that facade I can assure you! So, what happened with these men at your meeting?" Tara's eyes were heavy and knowing. She knew exactly what I was going to say, and she was just waiting for me to actually say the words out loud, to make them real.

"So some of the women at the meeting... They had sex with the men."

"And did you?"

"No, but I let a lot of people touch me."

Tara turned her head questioningly again. "Define touch."

"They... well... Just touching, but then their hands were everywhere until... You know..." I was looking down into the dark red liquid that filled my glass. *Shouldn't this be emptier by now,* I wondered.

"I see."

"Yeah."

"Is that all?"

"Not really."

"Not the best situation to find yourself in." Tara sighed and frowned, but worry creased her forehead as she leaned a little closer to me. "Does your husband know?"

"I haven't told him."

"You probably should. All the problems in the world seem to me to be caused by a lack of communication."

"I couldn't do that to him." The thought of telling Otis what had happened at the meeting sent a spike of ice into my stomach. His hurt eyes flashed up into my vision, and I shook my head slightly to try and dislodge the image.

"You've already done it," said Tara. "Now you're just lying to him really."

"I haven't lied!"

"No, but it's a big deal and he should know about it. Did you say it wasn't all that happened?"

"Yeah." I sighed again. The words felt like rocks in my chest, and it was difficult to pull them up through my throat to expel through my mouth. I was surprised that I was finding it so hard to break the rule about telling someone else, now that I had decided I had to do it. *This would be so much easier in the circle,* I thought to myself. Then, the little voice I heard before spoke up again, asking why that was. *What was different? Was it just that in the circle you are talking to people that you don't see outside of the meeting? Maybe you should have realised that it would be harder to talk like this to someone who you saw more often, who might actually have an impact on your daily life?*

CHAPTER TWENTY-FIVE

efore I could say anything else to Tara, Percy and Tilly came rushing in from her room, shouting and snatching at each other.

"Hey hey hey, what's going on here?" I snapped.

"Percy won't play with me and he's been saying that I'm silly because I wanted to play mums and dads with my dolls, and he's not being nice and it's not fair!" My daughter's voice was a ragged tumble of complaints.

"Percy?" asked his mother.

"Kind of, but she won't let me choose who to be in the game, and when I said that I wanted to do some drawing, she said that I wasn't being a good friend!"

"Sounds to me like we need to find a compromise," said Tara. I closed my mouth sharply. I had been about to tell Tilly to do whatever her guest wanted. If Percy wanted to draw, then she needed to draw. Instead, I listened to Tara.

"Tilly, Percy says he wants to be able to choose who to be. Can you let him do that?"

"But he said he wanted to be the brother, but it's mums and dads, not brothers and sisters!"

"Okay, but if he can't choose, maybe he won't want to play at all. Could you change the game a little bit for him? Then you guys could play together."

Tilly pursed her lips. "Maybe."

"Would it be better if you guys did some drawing first? Then you would have some time to think about what you want to do next?"

"Okay." Tilly nodded and looked down.

"How about you Percy? Is that compromise going to work?"

"If Tilly does some drawing with me first, I don't mind being the doll that she says."

I raised my eyebrows. "Oh? How come?"

"She would have done what I wanted to do for a while, so it seems fair that I would do more of what she wants. And I'd get my thing first."

"That sounds really kind Percy," I said. "What do you think Tilly?"

My daughter nodded, with a small smile beginning to appear on her face.

"Great! Now, how about you two go and play while I keep talking to Auntie Tara, okay?

"Okay!"

There was another swirl of wind as the two bustled back to the bedroom, already shouting happily at each other once again.

"Thanks for stepping in there," I said to Tara.

She waved aside my comment. "It was nothing! Now, you were about to tell me something juicy I think." She grinned and leaned a little closer.

"Oh right." I screwed up my face, wondering how she would react. "The other day I got a knock on the door and it was that builder."

"The same one?"

"Yup."

"I thought he hadn't been around for weeks?"

Tara's comment made me pause. *When was the last time I had seen Nic before he showed up on my doorstep?*

"He was there then. I think." I put one hand to my forehead and blinked. "Although, maybe I was just dreaming, or something. I have been seeing strange sights recently..." I cleared my throat. "Anyway, he came in to check out the deck so we could start planning renovations and one thing led to another and..."

"Really? Here?" Tara looked around the kitchen. Her eyes widened and she smiled. "Where on earth did you manage that?"

I nodded towards the counter where we were sitting.

"Oh my god!" Tara leaned away from the counter. "You could have warned me!"

"Consider this your warning," I chuckled.

Tara leaned forward slightly and shook her head.

"I am amazed that you are doing all this. It seems so much further than I expected. What is driving you?"

"I don't really know." I put a hand on my forehead and leaned forward, trying to think through my own emotions and actions. "It's just that... I've never been allowed to act this way. This isn't what I'm supposed to be doing. And it's like, now I have a chance." I lifted my head and looked into Tara's eyes. I could feel the way my eyes were hot, and tears were beginning to form in the corner. I wanted her to understand! "So now I can do something that I never thought I could do. And it feels good! So why shouldn't I? It's my chance to be in control of my life."

Tara leaned forward and breathed softly through her nose.

"I can't answer that for you. Maybe you should do it. That's entirely about you and your well-being. But I do have one question that I want to ask. If you are going to always do things that you have been told you cannot do, are you taking control of your life? Or are you still just bound to the decisions and ideas that you were raised with?"

I considered what she was asking in silence.

"What do you mean? I'm doing what I want."

"Are you though? Is this really what you want? Or are you just doing the opposite of what society expected? Is that any less controlled?"

"I know I want it, it feels so good."

"Of course it does. Lots of things feel good in the moment. That's what these groups are all about, letting you actually find out what you are feeling. So many of us in this world don't have enough time or awareness to do it! But shouldn't you also then think about your feelings and make a decision about what you really want, instead of just reacting to them? Again, are you in control, or are your emotions?"

I licked my lips as I sat back on the stool and tried to process what Tara was saying to me. What was it that I really wanted? Not just what felt good as I did it, but what did I want for my future? Did that match what I was doing now?

I thought about Otis. *I loved him. He was so kind, and he was a great father for Tilly. Was I saying that marrying him had simply been something I had to do because it was expected of me?* I shook my head as I took another sip of my wine. *No, I had married Otis because it was what I wanted. We had discussed it together. We had reached that decision together. And the pain that stuck it's fingers into my heart when I considered telling him what I had done reminded me that I didn't want to lose him.* I sighed.

"I'm not sure what I really want in the future," I admitted to Tara. "But I do know one thing. I want that future to be made with Otis. I want to discuss it with him, and to make it happen with him."

Tara smiled. "Maybe it will look a lot like this. But I'm glad to hear that you will need to discuss things with him."

I nodded and lifted my wine glass to my lips and then grimaced. "It's really too early for this. I think I'm going to make myself some tea. Do you want some?"

"Yes please."

Otis came home early on Sunday afternoon.

"How are you babe?" I asked as he came in, his cheeks still red and his clothes sweat stained. I wrinkled my nose, but made myself step closer to him so that I could give him a welcome back kiss on the cheek. He swung his face around to kiss my lips, and I bounced away.

"Ew! Not when you're all gross like that!"

"Sorry!" he said quickly. He rubbed a hand over his face. "My goodness, it's nice to get out and work up a bit of a sweat in the forest, but it feels awful afterwards. I'm going to go get a shower." He dropped his backpack and now-empty water bottle on the floor at the end of the kitchen bench and headed off down the hallway.

I looked at the empty doorway that my husband had just set off through. To my right, Tilly was playing with her dolls, talking quietly to herself as she moved them around, waving them at each other as they spoke.

"Tilly," I said softly. "Are you alright there?"

"Yes mum."

"You know how to turn on the TV if you want to watch a cartoon, don't you?"

"Can I watch the TV?" exclaimed Tilly excitedly. Normally I would have said no, it was a sunny day outside and she didn't need the screen time.

"Sure," I said, as I began to stroll down the hallway.

I walked into our room and saw Otis' clothes piled in the corner of his side of the room. The shower was running in our ensuite, and steam was beginning to leak around the edges of the door. I slid my top up and over my head, then placed it on my side of the bed. Then I unbuttoned my pants and pushed them over my hips until they slid to the floor. I picked them up and put them on the bed too. Still watching the door to the bathroom, I undid my bra and dropped it onto the pile of clothes and then kicked off my underwear.

I stood naked in my room and breathed in deeply. The sunlight warmed my skin, and I felt as though a breeze was gently caressing me from shoulder to thigh, from foot to finger.

My skin tingled and I shivered and smiled. Then I opened the bathroom door.

I could see Otis standing in the shower, behind the glass door to the cubicle. Drops of water washed down the sides, blurring his form, and covering the sound of my entrance with their hiss. I pulled open the door. Otis turned, with soap on his chest and shoulders, eyes wide in surprise.

"Pene?"

I stepped inside, pressing my body against his slippery soapy body. My breasts slid up against his chest, and I could feel his nipples press into my soft skin. I reached out to put my arms around his shoulders, causing the water to spray back towards me. My face ran with the hot water and it rolled across my skin, joining with the heat that I felt growing in my core. I leaned in to kiss Otis.

His mouth opened to mine and we sank into one another. My tongue slid around the edge of his mouth and met his coming the other way, warm and slick. I welcomed him into me, enjoying the feeling of him penetrating me. At the same time his soapy slippery hands were tracing down the curve of my back and squeezing onto my butt, bringing me closer to him. The hot water washed over us both.

I could feel his cock stretching up against my leg and he had to turn in order to give it room to grow. I smiled against his mouth and reached down, grasping it tight and squeezing the base. I began to pull on his cock, striking a rhythm that matched the sway of my body against him. I uncurled my fingers and allowed the tips to stretch down beneath his hardness, drifting over the soft round shapes below. Otis moaned against me, taking my lower lip between his teeth and pulling on it.

He brought his hand back from my shoulder and lifted my breast, catching my nipple between his fingers, then pressing the fingers together, squeezing and tugging at my nipple. It was my turn to moan and squirm in the hot shower, my breath husky in the steam.

Between my legs, Otis ran his finger along me, sliding it into me and then out again, mimicking the way his tongue probed at my mouth as we kissed. I pushed my hips forward and growled low in my throat.

"Do it." My voice was deep and rough. I felt Otis smile and he slipped his fingers into me. My legs began to shake as I spread them wider, allowing him to move inside me easier. My knee spasmed and I reached out one hand to support myself on the shower wall. His moved inside me as though summoning a wave from within, and I could feel my reserves building. All the while, hot water ran down my body, and steam swirled around my face. I could feel the sweat building on my skin as the heat inside swelled.

My clit tingled as he moved, his strong arm pressed along my stomach and his shoulder against mine. I buried my face in his neck, tasting him in the water that gathered, feeling his breath on my shoulder. The waters rose, higher and higher, boiling hot and ready to overflow.

As I came, shuddering and spasming, I felt my orgasm washed away by the shower. I felt drained, like a tank that had been unplugged, empty of everything that I could bring to the experience. That was when Otis grabbed my shoulder and spun me around. I grunted as I took his direction, still reeling from the sensation that had cleansed me. Once he had me facing away, Otis pushed me forward with a hand on my shoulder, and then spread my open with his other hand. I felt the head of his cock pressing at my entrance.

Slowly, with my pussy stretching wider as he pressed into me, Otis entered me. I bit my lip and hung my head as his cock filled me up where I had felt empty only moments ago. Now it was as though I could feel nothing else.

He began to rock back and forward, his hands clenching onto my hips. This rhythm was faster than the one he had made with his hands, the tempo more insistent, the feeling more that he was using my body for his own pleasure. As much as I had felt resplendent as he had pleasured me, there was something deep and instinctually arousing about the way he was being pleasured by my body now. I grinned as I heard him groan, and then he pounded into me two more times, slow and solid movements as he emptied himself deep inside me.

We held that position for a few moments more as the water poured over us. I stood up carefully, feeling dizzy from the heat, and from my own climax. I turned back around to fce Otis, hanging my arms on his shoulders.

"Thanks for joining me," he gasped.

"Mmmm, thanks for doing that thing you do so well," I murmured and kissed him again.

Together we soaped each other down, cleaning ourselves from any leftover evidence of our dallying. I noticed his cock thicken slightly and twitch, but it didn't rise to full attention again so quickly.

The rest of the day went well. Otis declared that we should take a family walk, something that we hadn't done in a long time. So we gathered our clothes and put on some good shoes. Tilly looked gorgeous in a woolen hat with woolen viking horns on it. I smiled as I straightened it.

"Look at you, my little raider!"

"Muuuumm," Tilly complained. "Don't call me a raider."

We strolled out of the house and started heading down the street. As we approached the house that Nic had been working on, I felt my throat clench a little. I reached out to hold Otis' hand. *Wait, should I have just left his hand alone? Will he think that something is wrong now? No, surely I'm allowed to hold my husband's hand while we are taking a family walk! Unless, do I normally hold his hand?* Trying to second guess my behavior and act naturally, when I hadn't thought about what my natural behavior would be, was causing me difficulty. I held my hand still, though I could feel my shoulder twitching.

Down the street, across the main road and through the small group of shops we walked, our little family strolling in the sunshine. Tilly ran ahead and ducked through a hedge into the park, while Otis and I had to scurry around the hedge in order to keep her in sight. She dashed off to a small playground and climbed up it's ladder, brightly painted in shining primary blue, then paused at the top where a board of wood had been screwed over the entrance to the slide.

"They've broken the slide!" she yelled, furious. I laughed.

"Oh honey, there must be something wrong with it," chortled Otis as he walked over and reached up to lean against the playground. He was just able to reach Tilly's feet, and he rubbed her shoes in an attempt to soothe her. She stomped in frustration, though she did avoid his fingers.

"But I wanted to go on the slide!"

"I know sweetheart, " Otis continued. "Sometimes we want things that we can't have. At least, not right away. I'm sure they'll fix it soon."

Tilly harrumphed and spun around to clamber off the high platform to where she could start swinging along the monkey bars. I hung back from Otis, who followed her and whooped as she wobbled from one end of the rungs to the other.

"Sometimes we can't have what we want, not right away," I murmured to myself as I looked around the park. I hugged my hands to my shoulders, shivering a little, though the sun was beaming down on us. Tall thin trees towered around the park.

I watched Otis catch Tilly as she dropped from the bars, screaming with laughter, and then hold her upside down over the tossed bark that was strewn beneath the playground. He made me smile. She made me smile too.

Tilly pulled her father over to the swings and made him lift her into the rubber seat then push her. She held onto the chains and leaned backwards, nearly falling off the seat. I dove forward, reaching out to catch her.

"She's alright babe," said Otis, putting a hand up to hold me back. Tilly pulled herself up as the swing came back and then he pushed her, sending her flying forward again. "She's just having a bit of fun."

"It may be fun, but it looked like she was going to fall right on her head," I said to him in a low voice, so as not to upset her.

"I get it," he agreed. "But we've got to trust her. She's holding on and she doesn't want to fall on her head. I mean, would you want to take a fall like that?" He looked over at me, his green eyes piercing me to the quick.

I licked my dry lips and shook my head.

"Of course not," he answered himself. "No-one wants to fall, even if it is exciting to get close to the edge sometimes. Besides." he shrugged, watching our daughter squealing on the swing again, pushing her forward. "If the worst comes to the worst, then it's our job to help her up and make sure she's okay. Right?"

"Right," I said.

Tilly grew bored of the swings pretty quickly, and climbed down. I took her by the hand.

"Alright family," I said with a grin. "Shall we head home now?"

"Home?" exclaimed Otis. "But the sun isn't even close to the horizon! I want to go on an adventure, what do you think Tilly?"

"Adventure, adventure!"

"That's not really what I thought we were doing," I began to say, but Tilly was running off across the park screaming "adventure, adventure" over and over, while Otis was smiling at me and shrugging as though he had no idea why she was acting that way.

We followed the path out of the park and down the road to the river, which we walked alongside for the next half hour. As I walked with my hand in my husband's and my daughter rushing along the boardwalk, I felt at home in the natural surroundings. Though there was a path here, it was designed to follow the edge of the estuary instead of control it, and the waves lapped softly alongside us. Birds circled and called. Other than the path we walked on, there was no sign of civilisation or it's expectations.

At the far end of the public walkway, the path opened out

under large bowed trees to reveal a thick muddy mangrove estuary. Overlooking the squat green bushes and the black mud that clogged their roots, was a broad rectangular building with tables and umbrellas set out in front. A broad wooden deck, large enough for dozens of people to wander past one another with plenty of space, was built out into the estuary. A few couples were leaning on the railing, talking quietly and watching the tide slowly rolling in through the gnarled trunks of the mangroves.

"Would you look at that," said Otis, pretend surprise plastered across his face. "There's a pub down the end of this path!"

"Yes yes, very funny," I said.

"Can I have some chips and a milkshake?" asked Tilly, jumping up and down and clapping her hands together.

"What do you think mum?"

I looked at my daughter and her giant puppy-dog eyes. From there I looked up at my husband, a cheeky dimple popping into his cheek.

"I suppose we may as well while we're here."

"Yay!" shouted Tilly and we all went inside for a treat.

Otis had a tall glass of dark beer, and Tilly got her milkshake. We shared the chips. Although I lingered on the wine menu, in the end I folded the sheet of cardboard closed and ordered a lemonade. Otis raised an eyebrow at me but didn't say anything.

"You see, we should be going on more adventures like this," said Otis after taking the first sip of his beer. "We deserve some more fun in our lives I think, we've been working too hard and worrying too much."

"I don't think we should stop worrying," I said. If anything, I was beginning to think that I hadn't done nearly enough taking care and worrying recently. Thinking longer about everything I did was going to become more necessary.

"I mean, we can keep it in mind. We can come back to it. But we also deserve a chance to put it aside once in a while, to enjoy some time together."

"I do like that," I agreed, holding up my tall thin glass. "To our time together."

Otis tilted his beer slightly, connecting with mine with a ringing clink. Tilly lifted her milkshake in both hands and thumped it against ours.

"To our time together," we all said, and smiled at each other. We drank our drinks and then enjoyed our walk back along the river towards home, followed by sparrows and fantails in the trees.

After putting Tilly to sleep, Otis and I sat down in the lounge. He picked up the remote control, but I took it from his hands and put it back down.

"What's going on?" he asked.

"I just want to say, I love you deeply and I don't want to give up anything we have together," I started. My heart was fluttering at the top of my chest.

"I love you too," Otis began to reply, but I held up a hand to stop him.

"That said, I've been having feelings recently, and I think we need to talk about them."

"What do you mean?"

I explained that I had been feeling attracted to a builder I had seen on the street. How the sight of this man had made me burn and squirm. I told him that I had had extremely realistic fantasies about the builder fucking me, and I hoped that I was correct in my conclusion that I had not crossed any lines in reality. Then I told him how I had started to feel about Talia. I told him how we had nearly kissed after the night at the art gallery. Then I told him how turned on I had been by the thought of him touching her.

"I have to say, I am pretty attracted to her as well," he admitted in a soft voice. "But that's only normal, isn't it? People can still find others attractive, even if they are happy with what they have?"

I nodded then swallowed thickly. "My meetings got more intense than I expected last time."

"Oh?" Otis looked confused, unsure why I was seeming to change the subject. I looked down as I continued to speak, explaining in a low voice that the meeting had included naked dancing, and then at the last one there had been men, and that I had enjoyed their touch.

"You liked it?" came his reply, his voice deep.

"Yes," I whispered. "I don't know why I let myself get so carried away. I'm so sorry."

"Thank you for telling me." He reached out and laid his hands on my shoulders, his fingers pressing into me. He shuffled closer on the couch, and leaned in to kiss me. His touch was firm and slow and strong and I responded instantly, my breath leaving my lungs in a rush. "I have to admit, you telling me that turns me on."

"I never want to go behind your back." I thought about what he had said, the way he felt with his hands on me now. "Did you ever think that, maybe, sticking with one thing is just what is expected of us?"

"What do you mean?"

"Did you ever think, maybe, that we could have more?" I stared into my husband's eyes, falling into their green irises.

"Do you mean, more than all this? Or swapping this for something bigger?"

"Like I said, I don't want to lose you at all. But maybe, if we were careful, we could add someone?"

We stayed up late, cautiously revealing our inner thoughts to each other. By the time we went to sleep, only one question really remained. What did Talia want?

CHAPTER TWENTY-SIX

The next day, I decided that it was time to speak to Kallista. I knew that I didn't want to come back to the meetings any more. Overall, they had opened up a door for me to understand more of my own deep feelings and I would always appreciate that. The Many had shown me not to just do what I thought I was supposed to do with my life, but instead to explore what I wanted from it. But they had opened it too far. I could see that there would be no way for me to control what had been uncovered if I kept going to the meetings and just allowing sensation to guide my actions and responses with no reason to rein it in. Walking with Otis and Tilly had grounded me. I wanted to be with my family, I wanted those unleashed emotions to help me connect with the people I really cared about, not to guide me away from them.

I felt like I was lost in the woods, circling through glades and hills, passing the same trees and landmarks. I had been content in my suburbs, mown lawns and fenced properties, with no awareness of all the wilds and adventures that existed just beyond my awareness. How could I be content with such a small horizon? I had to get beyond my fences.

But then I had been drawn towards dangerous lands, when

hidden chasms could open beneath my feet if I rushed too fast, and predators could be hiding behind any tree. There had to be a balance, where I could experience these wild places without abandoning my security, my safe places?

So, I sent a text to Kallista.

Hi, can I talk to you about the meetings? It's important

I was amazed to get a reply within seconds.

I'm really busy this week, can you come to the hall a bit earlier on Friday?

I stared at the screen of my phone. The small black line of my cursor blinked on and off in the reply box. What could I say to her? Could I just say that I was going to quit through a text? It felt like I was breaking up with someone through a text message.

But the idea of going to the meeting early to explain to her that I didn't think I could keep going... I knew that I would find it hard to resist the pressure to change my mind and to stay. *Oh gosh, what if others start to arrive? What if Lacey is there early too, to help set up? She seems to be involved in a lot more than I thought.*

I wondered how Lacey would treat me the next time I saw her. She had always been so stern, so gruff. She had been just one degree away from rude to me the entire time I had known her. But she had reached out a naked arm to me and embraced me, she had reached into my private spaces and brought out my climax. *Would she smile at me now? And how would I react if she did?*

My breath caught in my throat as I tried to decide. My fingers moved slowly, and I almost didn't know what they were typing until after the words appeared. Thumb shaking, I hit send.

Yes, I will see you before the next meeting.

It was time to see which way the winds were blowing.

THE DAY of the next meeting arrived. As I drove up to the community hall I tried to remember the first time I had driven along this road. It had been three months since the first time I had come, since Kallista had first convinced me to step outside the well-worn tracks that I was used to. And what had I found? Glorious light, vistas I could never have dreamed of, but also hidden crevices and perils that lurked in the darkness. I sniffed and blew out a nervous breath. *I can do this.*

The community hall looked different in the daylight. The walls were brighter under the sunlight. The front of the hall had large open windows that glinted in the light. I could actually see into the front rooms now. As I slowly drove around to the back, I could see colourful pieces of paper inside, covered in drawings by young children inside the windows. I saw a poster board covered in small dark rectangles that I could tell were photos. Who else was using this hall? Were they as lost as I was?

Around the back of the hall there were already a few cars parked on the gravel. There was no one outside though. I thought I saw a glimpse of someone reaching up one of the windows inside, and pulling the curtain across. *I don't want to be trapped if others arrive,* I thought to myself. *I'm going to be leaving way sooner than them.* I pulled over away from the other cars, making sure to turn the car so that I was facing back out into the main car park, ready to leave.

So, who is here? I looked across the cars and tried to remember if I had seen any of them before. One was a very plain white sedan. Nothing remarkable. Another was a lime green hatchback, the sort of thing that I might have thought was cool when I was younger, before I had had to make compromises in my choice of car to accommodate my family. I had no idea who they belonged to at all.

I closed my eyes for a moment, and then took a breath and stepped out of the car. I felt as though someone was watching me the entire time it took me to walk across to the entrance. I put my hand on the door but then paused. *Do I have the right to just walk in?* I knocked cautiously on the wooden door.

"Come in!" came Kallista's voice from inside. "We could use a hand with the chairs!"

I came in to find Kallista moving through the small hall and closing the curtains. As I had suspected, Lacey was there too, helping to pull curtains across all the windows in the room. I was surprised to see Agatha bringing bottles of wine out of the back room and placing them on the table. It was the same doorway that had seemed to contain something that glowed under it's edge. It was the same door the goat had come from. But now it was just a plain door on the side of the room.

The room that would contain the meeting later in the night looked so normal right now. The table with the wine was just a cheap plywood thing with fold out metal legs. Agatha smiled at me as she flung a black sheet over it and straightened the corners.

Lacey glanced at me. I tried to smile at her as I caught her eye, but she just looked back at the curtains and then began shifting chairs from the center of the room to hold the curtains back, tucking the ends under their legs and wedging them against the wall.

"I'm so glad you're here," said Kallista as she strode across the room. She took me by the shoulders and kissed me on both cheeks then began walking towards the back room where Agatha had brought the wine from. "Come with me."

She took me by the elbow and hustled me through to the other room. It turned out that the other room was a small kitchenette. The strong scent of incense pressed against me as I walked in. Agatha was hunched over in front of a small old fridge, pulling out bottles of white wine. I could see a box of red wine in the cupboard behind her. She glanced up as we came in, then smiled and moved around us with the bottles clustered in her arms.

Kallista gestured to a tiny table and chairs on the side of the room, beneath a worn out calendar with a photo of a mountain next to a clear blue lake, then sat down herself. The source of the incense smoke sat between us, a thin red sticks, glowing at the tip as a coil of thin smoke lifted into the air. I coughed. It was strong.

"So, what is so important that you need to talk about?"

"Is this where those men came from last time?" I asked, dodging the question for a moment while I organised my thoughts.

Kallista waggled her hand side to side. "They were in one of the front rooms for their own ceremony first, then they came through to join us."

"Are they there now?" I turned in my seat, examining the other door to the kitchenette. It was slightly worn out and enticingly closed.

Kallista laughed, tinkling like bells. "No! They don't tend to spend as much time as us on connecting with ourselves and each other I think. But, they are not us, they have their own protocols to follow. As long as the god is pleased, I can't complain."

"And as long as we are pleased too, right," I leaned closer and winked.

"Absolutely!" laughed Kallista again. She smirked and looked into my eyes. "But my sweet Pene, it's not the men that you are here to ask about is it?"

"I suppose not." I squeezed my left thumb with the fingers of my right hand. I wasn't sure what to say. In the end, I just had to say it out loud. "I don't think I can keep coming to the meetings though." I put my hands down on the surface of the cheap table, looking down focusing on my fingers.

Silence filled the room.

I risked a peek up, to see how Kallista was taking my comments. Kallista's eyes were narrowed, and she was no longer smiling. She pursed her lips.

"You don't think you can keep coming?"

"No." My voice was soft.

"I suppose we can't make you," said Kallista slowly, teasing apart the meaning of what I had said. It was as though I had read out a particularly confusing crossword puzzle clue to her and was waiting for her to answer it. "But it seems rather strange of you to come to us, to be part of our connection, to participate in all our rituals, only to decide to leave."

I looked back down.

"After all, we took you in. We gave you something to live for."

"I already have plenty to live for," I whispered. She was still not yelling, but I was scared that she might erupt at any minute. I was very conscious of Agatha and Lacey in the next room. Lacey scared me. What might she do?

"That sad little husband of yours? Your quiet life of parent teacher meetings and vacuuming?" she snorted. "We want more for you. We know there can be more for you! Why would you reject us?"

"I appreciate that you've opened my eyes to more, because you have. But I felt something dangerous at the last meeting–"

"Of course there is danger!" Kallsita's voice cracked and her eyes flashed. "If there was no danger, then how could there be excitement and passion? If you weren't risking the loss of something important, are you truly offering anything to the god at all?"

"Why do I need to offer anything to God? Why can't I just live my life for me?" I coughed again.

"God? Capital 'G', God?" Kallsita leaned back, her eyes widening in confusion. "Is that what you've thought we worship? You think we are just another group of weird christians?" She shook her head. "Oh no child. We are far more than that."

"If you are, then why wouldn't you let me tell Otis about it? There's a group of men in the next room, couldn't he have joined them?"

Kallista scoffed and shook her head, allowing her long dark hair to fall in a curtain past her face.

"The god doesn't work that way. That's no sacrifice. What are you giving up for him if you want to bring your husband with you?"

I heard the thump of feet at the door and jerked my head around to look at who was there. Lacey was standing in the doorway, her eyes low, her mouth set in a line so straight it could have been used as a building level. My stomach felt nauseous and I tried to swallow to settle it, but it continued to churn..

"What's all this?" she asked as she crossed her arms. I felt as though the door beyond her was pulling further and further away from me and my head wobbled.

"She wants to leave."

Lacey sneered at me, anger twisting her fine features into something harsh. She looked me over, clearly unimpressed. *Sheesh, this from a woman who had wanted me to finger her last time we were around each other.* I clenched my fingers.

"I've told you many times that you are too willing to let in newcomers. Tell them about the evenings yes, invite them to come along, sure. After all, the god needs more followers. But you throw them in too deep too quickly, and they drown."

"It's the only way to find out if they're going to be able to swim," said Kallista, still leaning forward with her eyes on me.

"What have you told her?"

"Nothing yet. She was just asking why her husband couldn't be part of the Sated celebration."

Lacey laughed once, sharply. A cruel smile flickered over her lips.

"One of the Sated? What a joke." She stepped further into the room and I leaned away from her. The movement made her snort again. "The Sated aren't just any men, Pene. The Sated have renounced everything that they once were, they have no connections left to the world at all. I suppose your husband could join, but then you would never see him again." She tilted her head with a small smile again. "I mean. You would see him at the rituals. And maybe I would sometimes. Maybe Kallista. You see, he wouldn't remember you anyway."

What she was saying made no sense. What was the point of such a thing, and how would they not remember their own wives? Who would agree to this? I blinked as my head swayed and I tried to bring my thoughts into order.

"You're wondering how the god finds people willing to do this?"

I nodded. Speaking was too difficult right now. I coughed and sniffed. The incense was coating my throat. I felt like vines had fallen around my arms and shoulders, holding me still, and were now tightening around my throat.

"There are so many people who are following the path of indulgence deeper into a pit. Being given any slight hint of a rope to climb out of it can bring many keen devotees."

"All of this is besides the point," interrupted Kallista. "You want to leave. I'm afraid I don't think I can allow that."

"What?" Although I had expected something like this I was still shocked by her statement. I knew that she would be upset. I thought that she would try to keep me here, but to say that she wouldn't allow me to leave? *What gives her that right?*

"No, I think we will keep you here tonight. Lacey, we have some of the god's personal wine don't we?"

Lacey rolled her eyes.

"Oh really? You'll just try to dose her? And what if we miss a dose somehow?"

"I would make sure to pick her up each week."

"Excuse me? What the hell do you mean you would dose me?" I could feel anger and fear writhing in my stomach like worms of fire and ice. The two emotions bubbled up and gave me strength to speak, to move. The two women glanced at me then ignored me again. I felt my jaw drop at the absolute dismissal.

"I have a much simpler idea. We kill her."

"What?" I shrieked and stood up, knocking my chair over as I did. I lifted my hands up defensively, but Lacey just gestured for me to sit down again, "I'm not sitting down! You can't *kill* me!"

"I agree Pene, there's no need for that. Lacey, relax, the Many don't need to be that desperate. After all, we aren't breaking any laws, are we?" Kallista smiled at me, as if I would be reassured that the woman who was talking about drugging me or poisoning me only seconds before was someone I would want on my side.

These women are totally crazy, I realised. My breath was heavy in my lungs and I felt my heart racing. *I have to get out of here.* I watched Lacey closely, and as soon as I thought that she was focused on Kallista, I made my move. I bolted at the door, lunging as hard as I could. Lacey was waiting for it though, and she spun around and flung her hands out, fingers curled into claws as she snatched at my arms and shoulders. I managed to shove my way past them, and Lacey actually began to fall over as she came off balance.

"What's going on?" said Agatha from where she stood next to the wine table as I came clattering out of the kitchenette. Her eyebrows were creased in confusion.

"Stop her!" screeched one of the women behind me, anger bending their voice so much that I couldn't identify which of them it was. I was looking at Agatha as she heard the voice, and I saw her face grow hard as she grabbed a wine bottle like a small club and began to run towards me.

Shit, I yelled internally. *I'm closer to the door, I hope she's not as fast as me!* I crossed the room in an instant, praying to get outside and into the car before Agatha could hit me with that solid glass bottle. *I can't believe she's reacting like this,* the thought flashed through my head, somewhere far below my instinct to get away. *She was a newcomer at the same time as me. How did she get so deep in this already? She grabbed a bottle as a weapon without even thinking!*

Oh god, I'm going to have to get in my car, and start it, and drive out, without her smashing that thing through a window. I grabbed the door handle, but the large white door began to shove in towards me before I could turn it.

"What the-" I yelped as I was forced backwards, stumbling and tripping over onto my rear end. Two women were standing over me in the rectangular space that led outside. I recognised one of them, Melly. She was the one who had sat with me in my first circle, who had shared with me about something so important to her life. She had inspired me to open up more, setting me on the path to something larger than myself and the world I had limited myself to.

Melly looked at my face with a curious expression and then her eyes rose over me. I sighed and turned onto my elbow, reluctantly looking behind myself as well. Agatha was standing over me, clutching the wine bottle in one hand and cradling it with the other.

"She isn't to leave," said Agatha. I looked back at the two who had just arrived. My muscles felt like wet cloth, dragging down towards the ground. They nodded, stepped through the doorway, and pushed the door closed behind them. Even though the fresh air from outside smelled sweet and light, my brain was still swimming and I felt myself tilting sideways as my eyes rolled shut.

CHAPTER TWENTY-SEVEN

I was kneeling in the middle of the hall. My clothes had been taken off, but my memories were hazy. Had they taken them off me? I could remember pulling them over my head, and folding them before placing them on the floor by the door. But why would I have done that? Surely they must have stripped me, as some sort of punishment? I focused on keeping myself upright. The weakness in my neck meant that I was constantly on the edge of toppling over.

I shut my eyes so that I didn't have to meet the eyes of any of the women who were arriving as I knelt. The room was warm, thanks to the candles they had lit. Many many more candles than usual. I hoped that the plumes of incense would provide some sort of shield for my nakedness but I knew I was fooling myself. I wanted to look around, to see if any of the women would be sympathetic, to try and gauge if any of them would be willing to speak on my behalf.

But the first women who had arrived had ignored my sobs and pleas. They had seen me and then avoided their eyes. They spoke in hushed whispers to the women who were already here, and then tutted and shook their heads. The gossip spread as each person approached the others and learned about my betrayal. I had soon realised that I would find no respite there, and had shut my eyes. *What's so bad about not wanting to come back to a simple meeting?*

I still didn't know who had won the argument about me. I was sure that Lacey wanted me dead, which was horrifying and unsettling. I had no doubts that she knew how to do it and get away with it. Something about the way she acted said to me that she was a cold bitch who had planned all manner of ways to get away with terrible things. I looked over at her through the corners of my eyes and gasped as I saw the thick curling white horns that sat in loops on either side of her head, like the heavy horn's of a ram. I stared back down at the floor.

I didn't know if Kallista still wanted to drug me. After bolting from the kitchenette I hadn't been able to catch her eye. I was hoping that she had won the argument, because at least then I would be alive. I hoped. I drifted to my left and then caught myself and swayed back upright. *If she was going to drug me, when would it happen? Was she waiting for all of the Many to arrive first?*

"Welcome sisters." Lacey's voice rose out of the murmuring voices, and they died down. I tried to slow down my breathing. *If she's taken control of the meeting, I am in a lot of trouble.* I hunched lower over my knees.

"As you can see, things are a little different tonight." I could hear the smile in Lacey's voice. There was a resonance that slunk through my ears and down my spine. "Normally we meet together and bring out our deepest selves, so that we can connect in genuine community with one another. But tonight, we find a different way to share our connection."

I heard her footsteps approaching on the bare wooden floor.

"Tonight, we are upended. And so we will begin our night in revelry, in ecstasy, and by coming together to give sacrifice. We will end the night with ourselves." Lacey slid her fingers around my chin, cupping my face and lifting it up. I had my eyes scrunched closed, but I couldn't keep them that way. I had to see. Her face was centimeters from mine, her green eyes glittering in the candlelight.

"So let us begin."

The drumming began with an intense rhythm that I had not heard before. All around me, the women whooped as they removed their clothes and handed bottles of wine to each other. I bowed my head to look at the floor again, but I could see them dancing out of the corners of my eyes. Their movements were unlike the dancing I had seen before. Now they moved in jagged lurches, screeching and yelping to punctuate their movements. Wine splashed onto the floor and ran down chins and curved over naked breasts. I was sure I saw women drinking the wine off each other.

My breath began to come in short bursts. I was nearly panting. The women were coming closer and closer to me in their whirling dance, a spiral that stomped around me, their eyes rolling back in their heads, and grins pulling their lips back to expose their teeth. I remembered the sight of the goat, disappearing behind a pile of naked bodies, and then Kallista rising from the pile, covered in blood. Some began to reach forward with curved fingers like talons. I closed my eyes again, and grunted as someone shoved into me, knocking me over. I lay curled up on the floor on my side and waited to see what they would do to me.

There was a commotion from the doorway. Scuffling, clumping footsteps, raised voices.

"... going on? I just want to speak to Aggy, why are you being so rough?"

"What is going on back there? Who is that?" Lacey's voice pierced the drumming and noise. The music was turned down, and the whirling dancers paused, looking at one another with frowns and raised eyebrows.

"We found this man creeping around the hall, trying to look through the windows."

"A peeping tom?"

"Exactly. We thought it appropriate to bring him in. We think he needs to know what happens to someone who peeks on women when they want to be undisturbed."

"Guys, I wasn't trying to peek on you, I just want to speak to Aggy. I thought she was here. What the hell, why is there a naked woman on the floor!?" The short man at the doorway, with his arms held behind his back, looked around with his mouth hanging open. "Why are you all naked!?"

I felt my cheeks burning as I imagined what this must look like to this man. My rear end would have been pointing at him as he entered the room, and he would have had a pretty easy view of me. It made my stomach turn.

"Ben?" I recognised Agatha's voice. There was murmur from the other women and the sound of footsteps crossing the hall towards the entrance.

"Aggy! Thank god you are here. I was so confused!"

"I told you not to be here. This isn't for you."

"What's that supposed to mean? Why on earth are you all naked?"

"Get out Ben."

"I'm afraid it's not that simple Agatha." This time I did recognise Kallista's voice. "We have very strict rules about who can be a part of these times. Once the ritual is begun, the god is very unhappy at interruption. Bring back the drums."

With her short instruction, the sound of drums rose again, accompanied by the clattering of cymbals. The women began swaying again, red wine dripping down their arms and chests. I saw many had their heads rolled back, or their eyes closed.

"Sisters!" called Kallista."Spin like the wind! Crash like the seas!"

And all at once the dance returned, the woman leaping and twisting in a circle around myself and Agatha, Ben and Kallista. Kallista walked over to Agatha in the low light, running a hand down her cheek. She leaned forward and kissed the younger woman gently on the lips.

"Join the dance Agatha. Lose yourself. There is no singular woman here, we are Many."

Agatha smiled and bowed her head, then spun on her feet and whirled off into the crowd around us.I lost sight of her in the dance, so rapidly were they moving. They stomped and raised their arms, and yelled. It was like we were surrounded by a single entity, made of many heads, and innumerable arms reaching out to us.

Kallista was holding on to Ben's arm. He looked lost. His eyes were wide, and his face had fallen. He too was trying to find Agatha in the crowd of women, but unlike me, he still thought that he would be able to find her. I knew better. Agatha was gone now. There was no Agatha in this dance. There were only the Many.

Kallista leaned forward and kissed Ben. Her naked figure shone, with drops of wine running down her shoulders, reflecting the candle's flame. She reached around his body and pulled him closer to her. He tried to resist, lifting his hands away from her skin and trying to lean away. But he couldn't pull back for long and I saw him begin to respond to her, moving his lips against hers.

I felt a presence in the room and turned my head. I couldn't see anyone, but I felt sure that the half-man, that satyr, the same one from my dream, was here. I felt the same way I had then, as though it's powerful figure was standing behind me, watching this all.

She stepped back just as his hands lowered down to her hips. There was a broad smile on her face, the smile I had found so enticing when I had first seen her. It was a mischievous smile, a smile that promised games and excitement.

Then she grabbed his upper arms and threw him towards the dancers, sending him stumbling and tripping into the middle of their movements. There was a gutteral sound as the women dove towards him, fingers clutching at him, teeth flashing. I saw Agatha next to him, her mouth fastened on to his neck. His mouth was opened wide, but I couldn't hear if he was screaming over the music.

But the women leapt over me in their rush to get to him and I found myself on the outside of their writhing mass. I blinked and looked around. As far as I could tell, none of them were looking at me at all. I took a step towards the door, and then another. Still no reaction. So I turned and sprinted out, managing to grab my own clothes from where they sat in a tidy pile on the floor as I did. I thanked whoever was watching over me that I had such good luck.

I banged the door shut behind me and pulled on the jumper and pants that I had grabbed. I jammed a hand into my pocket and grabbed my keys. *Yes! I knew parking off to the side was going to pay off!*

I ran across the gravel car park to my car and jumped in, spinning the key and stomping on the accelerator. *Come on, come on.* I gritted my teeth and then realised I was in someone else's car. I shook my head, trying to shift the fog that was making hard for me to think clearly.

If this is someone else's car, where is mine? I pulled my key back out of the ignition, noticing now that it had not actually fit into the ignition where I had been shoving it. I jumped out of the car and spun in a circle. *I have to move quickly! They'll be after me any minute! Or haven't they noticed me? No, surely they will be after me!* I looked back at the doorway to the hall and yelped as I saw some movement in the dark opening. As I flinched down I realised that my car was the one right next to me. *I'm an idiot!*

This time I paid close attention to the key as I pushed it in, leaning forward and tipping my head around the steering wheel to ensure that I could see what I was doing. Tilting my head that way made me feel dizzy. I turned the key once, twice, and then just before I was going to jump back out and try to run all the way home, the engine turned over. I let out a triumphant yell and then raced out of the car park. I looked in the mirror and saw a giant black cloud rising up over the hall like some sort of tornado. I tried to keep the tears inside so that I could see what I was doing as I drove home, lurching away from parked cars and stopping far too soon at intersections. *What's wrong with my reactions?* I felt as though I could barely control myself, which only made my panic worse.

When I finally made it home I sat in my car in our driveway for a long time before I could face getting out and going inside. Had that really just happened? Had I seen what I thought I saw? Were they really saying that they were going to kill me? I tried to laugh off the idea, but I couldn't. It had seemed so certain to me, their expressions, their angry eyes. *Did I think I saw horns on Lacey?* I rubbed my face with both hands, trying to scrub the incense and fear from my mind. If they were just pretending, trying to scare me, then they certainly knew how to do it effectively!

I held onto the sides of the steering wheel and leaned forward until my forehead rested on it.

What was I going to do now?

I SPENT the next few days in a state of constant vigilance and mild panic. I kept expecting to open the front door and find Kallista standing there, with her deceptive smile and her beguiling ways. But Otis noticed my unease and came to hold me whenever I was beginning to feel overwhelmed. He would walk up behind me and wrap his arms around my waist, nuzzling his mouth into the back of my neck.

"Hey love," he would murmur, his breath warm on my skin. His fingers squeezed me. "Why are you so tense?"

"It's nothing," I replied, running my fingers along the backs of his hands.

After two days, I received a text message from Kallista.

Hi Pene! Such a shame that I didn't get to talk to you before you left. Don't worry, I'll make sure I catch you soon

I read the message with an icy sensation in the pit of my

stomach and then stuffed my phone into a drawer in my bedside table, refusing to look at it again that day.

I found it hard to get to sleep that night. Otis was snoring softly beside me, but I couldn't get comfortable. I would turn over and punch my pillow, and stick one leg out and then pull it back under the duvet, and nothing helped. I just couldn't get comfortable. Then I heard noises from the lounge.

I got out of bed and tip toed towards the hall, peeking out past my bedroom door. A soft light spilled from the lounge, and I thought I could hear water trickling from somewhere in the house. There was a clonk that made me jump. I turned to look back through my bedroom but nothing was behind me.

The clonk sounded again. I was sure that it was the sounds of a hoof on stone. *Not again,* I thought, my heart pounding. I looked back down the hallway. A tall shadow was standing by the door to the kitchen. *No!* I ran back across the bedroom, diving back into my bed. I pulled the covers over my head, feeling silly, but I couldn't think of anything else to do. I felt like a small child hiding under the covers from the monsters in my nightmares.

Otis rolled over as I bounced on the mattress and flung his arm over my back. He rolled up against me, twisting his legs amongst mine. I felt as though he was armour around me. With his presence protecting me, I finally settled into sleep.

The next day, after school, I stood outside the classrooms, trying to keep an eye on the buildings around me.

"Is that you Pene?" called a voice behind me, and I jumped. "Whoa! Are you alright?"

I turned with wide eyes and then felt my shoulders sink as I relaxed when I saw Tara walking closer.

"Thank goodness, it's you. You would not believe the weekend I've had!"

"Really? I thought you were having a lot of good times recently? Did something go wrong?" Tara pushed her red glasses back up her nose a little.

"Just a little. First, I decided to get out of that group."

"You know, I'm actually very glad to hear that! I had a feeling that it was working poorly for you."

"So, I went to the meeting early to explain that I didn't want to come back."

"What? Why would you do that?"

I paused.

"Why would I go back?" I repeated Tara's question out loud. It seemed ludicrous to me. *Of course I had to go back. How rude would it be if I just bailed and never came back?*

"Yes. I mean, you don't owe them anything. If they have a problem, they can get in touch with you. Why waste your time?"

"I would be letting them down."

"But that's their problem, not yours."

I had never thought of it that way. I rubbed my mouth with one hand as I thought about that point of view. Before I could reply to Tara, the school bell rang and children began to tear out of the classrooms around us.

Tilly and Percy came rushing out also, both of them latching onto me and Tara.

"Would you like to come over for a cup of tea, and let me know what happened?"

"That would be great," I smiled. *Yes. Getting out of my house and my own thoughts would probably help to settle my nerves.* "Tilly, shall we go over to Percy's house?"

"Yay!" screamed my daughter.

So we joined Tara and Percy in the walk back to their house. We went through a narrow path on the far side of the school field, and came out on a quiet suburban street. We turned and followed the footpath, Percy holding on to his mother' hand. We chatted about the children's day as we walked, hearing about the life cycle of butterflies, and the way that the class had built a wall of butterflies out of paper, and caterpillars out of toilet rolls. Before long, we were at their house.

CHAPTER TWENTY-EIGHT

I sat in the lounge as the children ran off to Percy's room and began systematically taking it apart. At least, that's what it sounded like they were doing. Tara stayed in the kitchen and began gathering things to make cups of tea. I noticed that she got out three mugs and I felt my breath flutter in my chest. *Who else is coming?* I suddenly found myself wondering if Tara was going to bring Kallista here. *Am I in a trap?* My fingers clenched onto the arm of my chair.

"Is someone else here?" I asked, trying to keep my voice light.

"Peyton should be home soon," replied Tara as she stirred a little milk into each mug. I felt like an idiot. *Of course he is.* She carried my drink through to me and left it on the small table between the chairs.

"Actually, he's nearly finished that statue you saw him making! I think he'd quite like to show it to you."

She went back to the kitchen and brought in her mug, leaving Peyton's steaming on the kitchen bench.

"Now, why don't you tell me what's wrong?"

And so I did. I explained to her that I had decided to leave the group because my emotions were running too strong for me to control and I was worried that I would do something I truly regretted. I showed her the text from Kallista asking me to come early to the meeting. I explained that Kallista and Lacey had both agreed that I couldn't be allowed to leave, although they had argued over what should be done to me.

"Wait, you say that you think one of them suggested killing you?"

"Yes! You can see why I'm so terrified!"

"I can, but how likely is it that this group of women would actually kill you?"

I pressed my lips together and then caught the lower one in my teeth.

"It's pretty crazy," I admitted. "But I swear that's what I heard."

Tara was leaning forward with her elbows on her knees and her hands held together in front of her face.

"I believe that it's what you saw, and what you heard. Did you say that they suggested drugging you?"

"Yes."

"And you said that they had lots of incense burning, even when you arrived early?"

"... Yes." Could what she was insinuating be right? Had they been drugging me, sending me into some sort of paranoid daze? Tara nodded. She could see that I was considering exactly what she had suggested.

"It's something to consider."

"But what if I was right? What if they really are that dangerous!?"

"I don't think that they are. As I've mentioned, many of these groups tried to get me to join them when I arrived. This one certainly seems to be one of the more troublesome ones, but I wouldn't expect them to actually reach such a violent level."

"You could have told me about this."

Tara frowned and raised a hand to calm me. "It's not until I see these messages, and hear your description, that I recognise what you have been involved with. I am sorry I didn't think to give you more explicit instruction to not take part." She sipped from her mug. "Would you have listened to me? After all, I did give you some warnings."

I leaned back in the chair. She was right. "I don't know. I probably wouldn't have believed you. I mean, I didn't believe you when you did say a little."

"Exactly. Did anything else happen?"

I went on to explain that I had been naked on the floor and that they had reversed their ceremonies. That made her suck in her breath and raise an eyebrow.

"What?"

"It's just," she sighed and paused to gather her thoughts. "Reversals are never a good thing. Something intense was happening there."

"I'll say" I described how Ben had come in and distracted the women, giving me a chance to escape. As I began to describe what had happened to him, my voice caught and tears began to prick at my eyes.

"Do you honestly think they killed him?" Tara asked me. I could hear the tone in her voice, gentle and motherly, but also cynical.

"I don't know." My memory was so foggy, and even as I described what I thought I had seen, I felt my own disbelief rising. *That's ridiculous,* I told myself. *You know it is.*

But I wanted to try and defend my reaction to Tara. "It seemed like they did. But that's just me becoming paranoid about this all, isn't it?" My heart was pounding. *How did I get mixed up in this?* It was all so unreal, it couldn't possibly be real.

Tara leaned back and sipped at her tea.

"Do you want us to go to the police?" she asked, raising an eyebrow behind the mug held by her lips.

I sighed and squeezed both hands on my head. "No. I can't imagine that they'd believe me. Even a few questions from you, and suddenly I can't be sure what I saw." I could feel my brow creasing as I tried to summon up memories of the night in the hall. Was I even naked? I thought I was, but now I thought I could remember the denim of my jeans poking at my knees while I knelt on the floor. "I can't think that there would be any point."

"I may still be able to help."

There was a clatter along the deck and then the door banged open. Peyton stepped through, pulled a black bandanna off his head and chucked it on the table.

"This mine love?" he asked, picking up the mug of tea.

"Sure is!"

"Cheers babe." Peyton came swaggering into the lounge and nodded at me. "How's things Pene? Sorry if I stink, I've been out at work all day obviously." He took a sip of his tea and said "Aah-hhhhhh, that's just what you need when you get home."

"Babe, Pene's been having a bit of a problem. I think we might be able to help her though."

"Yeah, what sort of problem?"

He leaned on the back of her chair with his arms crossed. She filled him in, and his smile slowly turned to a frown.

"Shit, they do sound like trouble. What did you think we could do?"

"If Pene's okay with it, I thought we might set a guardian for her."

He pressed his lips together and nodded. "Not a bad call. Who would do it?"

"I wondered if Tiz was ready."

He nodded again, more slowly. "I think she is. Come on, let's go take a look."

Peyton led the way down to his basement workshop. As we walked, I wondered what Tara meant by a guardian. As she had spoken, I had thought that maybe she knew someone who could be something of a bodyguard or private investigator for me. But then she mentioned her husband's statue. What on earth did that mean? When we got to the workshop I had to clutch my hands around my sides as I looked at it. The statue stood tall and shining, proud and complete. She was beautiful.

"What do you think?"

"I love her," I said. "She's just so stunning. And I love how you have combined so many strong and industrial elements to create something so beautiful. Strength and beauty together, you know?"

He grinned. "I knew you got it!"

Tara came up beside me and rested her hand in my elbow. "So, Pene, I want to know if you are willing to let me do something a little strange." She led me across to one of the few stools in the workshop while Peyton began wiping down his statue, clearing off any remaining grease or fingerprints. Her chrome surfaces gleamed.

"What's this strange thing?" I asked once we were settled.

"It's an idea I've had that might keep you out of this group's hands. I would set a guardian to watch over you and protect you. I might need to see if I can do something about this group, after what you said about that man. But the first step is making sure that you aren't in danger."

I wondered whether I could believe Tara. I knew that I did trust her, despite my paranoia about being followed. Tara was a rock of truth in a shifting uncertain world. But did I believe that she could do this? What did setting a guardian even mean?

"Tell me about it."

"I would need you to come and sit with Tiz while I burnt certain herbs in here. I'd recite particular words, introducing you to Tiz and binding her to you. Would you let me try?"

"I mean, I'll let you do it, though I don't know that it will do anything. Do I need to take the statue with me after that?" I couldn't imagine what I would do with such a massive thing. Could I hire a truck and crane to collect it? Where would I put it near my house?

"No, she won't need to be physically near you."

Thank goodness, I thought. *It sounds more reasonable than what-*

ever has been going on in those meetings. Maybe it will let me put them into my past, where they belong. "Alright, let's do it."

The ceremony took nearly forty five minutes to set up. Tara spent much of that time burrowing in old drawers for packets of the herbs that she said she needed. She opened up old creaking books and scoured their contents for the right words to use. In the meantime the children came screaming through and Peyton made them peanut butter and strawberry jam sandwiches before they catapulted back into Percy's room.

Then we went back down to the workshop, lighting sticks of incense and candles, burning the herbs in broad bowls. The smoke made my eyes water, and I nearly sneezed.

Tara positioned me at the statue's feet, then began to walk in a circle around us both, reciting short phrases in a language that I didn't understand. Around and around she walked, until my back and thighs were beginning to ache from sitting so long. I tried to stretch my back, so that I could sit without complaining. Tara kept walking, around and around. I was beginning to recognise the phrases she was repeating, and I even began mouthing themself, though I still had no idea what the sounds meant.

As the words came and went, I began to feel the pain in my body less. I felt like I was smearing out across the room. I was blurring with the smoke and incense, drifting through the workshop. I thought that I could see myself, sitting at the base of the beautiful statue Peyton had made. The statue was like a weight set in the middle of the room, bending everything towards it. I looked at the smile on it's beautiful face.

The statue turned her head and opened her eyes, staring straight at me. Those eyes burned with red fire.

I gasped and leaned forward, all my awareness snapping back into my body.

Tara walked by and placed a hand on the back of my head but did not stop. I stayed where I was, leaning over my crossed legs with my head bowed as she circled another five or six times and then she stood in front of me in silence.

I raised my head and tried to restore my regular breathing. I met Tara's eyes and she smiled, pulling me to my feet. I grimaced as blood rushed back into my legs, and I had to stamp back and forwards to try and get past the pins and needles. I turned and looked up at the statue. It's eyes were smooth pools of metal, shaped by Peyton. They couldn't open. It was a statue, it couldn't move. I mustn't've seen what I thought.

"What happened?" I asked.

"You and Tiz were introduced. She is going to watch over you for me." Tara smiled, took my elbow, and led me out of the workshop. At the doorway I stopped and looked back one last time. I wasn't sure, but was the statue in a new pose now?

I gathered up Tilly and we said goodbye to Percy and his parents. Peyton grabbed me in a mighty hug as he did so often.

"Take care," he growled into my side. "And let us know if Tiz helps you out."

I nodded. Tilly and I walked back along the footpath that led between some houses and back to the school, on our way back to my car. The sky was beginning to grow dark. *That's strange,* I thought.

"It's dark already? How long were we there?" I said out loud.

"Three hours mummy," said Tilly as she skipped along the path beside me. We were nearly back on the school field.

"What?"

"Yup. We've been learning about how to read clocks, and I read the clock in Percy's lounge, and it said four o'clock and now it said seven o'clock, so that means we were there three hours."

I stared at my daughter for a moment, then patted her head and kept walking.

Three hours, wow, time really flies when you are occupied with something like that, I thought to myself, then turned to look back down the path as though looking back to Tara's home would give me clarity in what had happened.

A tall figure stood in the shadows at the beginning of the path. Their silhouette in the dusk meant I couldn't see who it was, but their shoulders were broad and there was something strange about their legs.

Oh god, I thought and then turned to face forward, rushing Tilly past the classrooms and out the other side of the school to the car. I strapped her into her seat and climbed into the driver's seat, then raced home as quickly as I dared. When I glanced in the rear view mirror I was sure that the figure was standing by the classrooms, watching us leave.

DINNER PASSED QUIETLY THAT NIGHT. Tilly seemed exhausted after her long play session with Percy, and I was lost in my own thoughts. Otis skewered a piece of chicken on the end of his fork and placed it in his mouth, chewing carefully.

"It's very tasty love, thank you."

He kept chewing, swallowed, and then picked up his glass of juice, sipping a little. I heard a tapping on a window in the lounge and jumped, spinning to look through the lounge. Otis raised an eyebrow.

"Pretty sure that's a branch babe," he said.

I blinked and nodded and then looked back down at my plate, pushing a piece of chicken through the creamy sauce from one side to the other.

"Is everything alright?"

I nodded, still watching my dinner.

After dinner we cleaned the dishes and got Tilly ready for bed. Otis took her to her room and I could hear him reading her a story. I stood in the kitchen with both hands on the bench, watching the front door and keeping an eye on the lounge. Nothing was going to get by me tonight. My phone buzzed on the counter, vibrating as a text message arrived. I snatched it up, and stabbed at the screen to unlock it.

It was just a message from Talia, asking if Otis and I were free for the weekend because there was going to be an art exhibition that she thought we might like to see.

I sighed and put the phone back down.

Eventually Otis came back into the kitchen and walked up behind me, putting his arms around my hips and nuzzling his lips into my neck.

"She's asleep. Come on, let's get you into bed so you can relax."

I let him lead me back to the bedroom, switching on all the lights as I went and peering into the cupboards as we passed them. I made him go into our bathroom and check that it was empty before I began to get changed in our bedroom.

"Seriously, what's happening?" he asked as he came back. "You really are all tied up in knots."

"I don't even know where to begin." I said as I sat on my side of the bed.

"Lie down, " instructed my husband, and he got me to lie face down on top of the duvet. Then he climbed on top of me, straddling my legs. I saw him reach over to the bedside drawer and pull out a bottle of body cream. He put some on his hands, rubbed them together, and then began massaging my lower back.

I sighed as he worked at the knots in my back, as he slid his hands up to my shoulders and worked to release the tension there also. Although my fear that Kallista would track me down didn't dissipate, I felt safe with Otis near me.

As his hands moved across my skin, I felt my fear begin to lift from me like a mist, and my body felt as though it was sinking deeper and deeper into the bed. My eyelids fluttered closed. I tried to talk to Otis as he asked me questions, but sleep overthrew me.

I woke up with a start and sat up. I had heard something. My bedroom seemed blue and dark. I patted myself down and looked around me to see where I was. Otis must have moved me, because I had been lying under the blankets. I looked around the room, trying to see if anything was out of the ordinary.

Otis was breathing gently on his side of the bed. Everything else seemed to be in the right place. I couldn't hear anything else.

There! A very soft thud, like someone had bumped a hollow log far in the forest. *Where did that come from?* I swung my legs out of the bed and tip toed over to the hall door. *Was she here now? Had she come to get me?* I didn't feel afraid anymore. I was surprised that she would have waited for night, instead of coming to my home during the day, but I realised it made sense. No one would see her at night.

There was another thump as I looked through the darkened corridor. *Did I turn off Tilly's nightlight?* I still couldn't see anything. As I looked closer at the doorway to the kitchen I realised that the soft light that edged through was more green than blue. That seemed so inconsequential, and yet I knew it meant that something was wrong.

Clonk.

The figure stepped through the doorway, ducking slightly to bring his head under the lintel. My breath stopped and I pressed my hands to my stomach. Tiny pinpoints of light reflected from his dark eyes.

But before he could take another step, I heard a different noise. It was like a whispering, a susurration of voices murmuring over one another. The sound of them wove through my ears like serpents or insects, and I saw a golden beam of light rise from a single point in the floor. It illuminated the tall figure and I saw him rear back, his well defined muscles shifting like slabs as he did so.

From within the beam of light, a figure rose. She was sleek and silver, and her hair shook like a curtain of liquid mercury. She glittered in the light and stepped forward to place a shimmering hand on the dark figure's chest. I saw her mouth move, but I couldn't hear what she said, the whispering voices that filled my ears were too numerous.

The figure frowned and attempted to step towards me again.

The silver woman reached down and grabbed the tall naked figure's cock, squeezing. His eyes bulged and he gritted his teeth. Then she released him and he sank to his fur covered knees, clutching both hands to his groin. She leaned over him and spoke again. I still couldn't hear her.

This time he nodded, and he tried to stumble back through the green light of the kitchen. The silver woman turned to face me. She smiled and so I smiled back. Then I blinked, and the hall was empty and dark. The regular blue light of the moon and stars outlined it's edges. There was nothing there.

Tilly! My thoughts clattered through my skull and I rushed down the hallway to check on my baby. She lay contented beneath a blanket with cartoon princesses smiling all over it. An old toy kea was tucked into her arms. *Thank goodness,* I thought. *She's okay.* I smiled and brushed some hair off her forehead and then left, heading back to my own bed.

CHAPTER TWENTY-NINE

I curled my body up against Otis reaching my arms around his comforting body. I lay so close to him that my skin grew hot. It was like we were one form, cruelly split into two separate parts. I ran my hand along the skin of his stomach, pressing against him, wishing that we could be rejoined. As my hand moved, the sound of his breathing changed, growing rougher and faster. His hips moved back against me.

I slid my hand down his stomach and under the elastic of his boxer shorts. I was in no rush. I took my time feeling how the dark bush of curls scratched at my fingers, before I moved further, finding the hard smoothness of his cock, rising at my encouragement.

I wrapped my fingers around him, feeling warm and cocooned in our blankets, pulling at his cock slowly but steadily. He groaned beside me and pushed his arm back, searching for me. I leaned closer, and his hand caught on to my hips, pulling me against him. I felt his cock swell as he touched me. I kept pulling, leaning closer to kiss the back of his neck gently.

With a grunt, Otis rolled over, forcing me to let go of his cock. Now facing me, he reached out for my face, running his fingers down my cheek and chin, running around the curve of my breast under my tee shirt. As he traced his finger along my side, we moved closer and kissed, our lips meeting like continents, slow but sure.

The kiss continued, our lips moving constantly. Otis's tongue slipped into my mouth, and I welcomed him into me. I wanted us to return to our singular being. I moaned as his hand reached my pussy, slipping his fingers between my lips and exposing how wet I was. He began to slide his fingers deeper inside me and I decided that if he was able to be inside me, I should be inside him. I pressed my tongue forward, around his, until it began to move into his mouth.

His fingers built their rhythm and pressure inside me, driving my breath in gasps as we kissed. I reached down to pull on his cock again, sighing at the feeling of it's hot skin on my palm.

Otis shifted again, moving above me. I shoved my pajama pants down and opened my legs, allowing him to kneel in between. Only now did he seem to open his eyes, to waken up into the experience we were having. He smiled down at me.

"I love you babe," he said. Then his cock pressed against my entrance and spread my lips further apart. I caught my hands around his shoulders as he entered me and we became one form again, as we were always meant to be.

He thrust into me with a steady pace, matching my heartbeat. I pulled my fingernails down his back, willing him further and further inside me, feeling every part of me that his cock could reach. All too soon I felt him tense and shudder as he came inside me, and the sensation pushed me to my own release, clenching my pussy around his length and sending sensation rolling along my skin.

Otis leaned down to kiss me once more and then rolled back to his own side of the bed. His naked backside peered at me, making me giggle, before I pulled the duvet up to cover myself, hiding it from view. I curled back into my position around his body and fell into a deep sleep.

. . .

"I THOUGHT we should get away this weekend," said Otis over his bowl of cornflakes.

"Oh? What did you have in mind?" I spooned a small pile of the crunchy brown flakes into my mouth. "Talia thought we should go to an art exhibition." I coughed, holding a hand in front of my mouth as pieces of cornflakes caught in my throat.

"That's a nice idea! But I thought we could take a family walk along one of those short hikes and spend the night in a hut? Pretty exciting thing for Tilly to do with us!"

"Hey, if you're keen, that sounds good to me," I smiled.

So we gathered up some things during the morning. Otis packed a hiking backpack for himself and advised me what to put in mine. I was amazed that he had some dehydrated food and low weight utensils just sitting in the backs of the cupboards, ready to go.

"So, you say Talia was keen to hang this weekend was she?" said Otis. "Shall we call and see if she wants to come on the hike as well then?" He was carefully looking into his backpack as he said it, tucking in some food pouches.

"Yeah, why not," I answered, with a tingling in my stomach. I pictured Talia's smile and it made me smile too.

Then, once we were all packed and prepped, he made a few calls to check if the hiking hut had a space and used his credit card to make a booking. We bundled Tilly into the car and headed out. On the way we drove past Talia's house and picked her up. She had a woolen bobble hat on her head, which made me giggle, and she was dwarfed by an absolutely shockingly large backpack.

"Are you sure you need all of that?" I asked as she struggled to swing it off her shoulders and into the back of the car. Otis was watching through the rearview mirror with a worried expression on his face.

"It's fine, I always bring this much. It's only a short hike right?"

"Only a couple of hours I think," agreed Otis.

She managed to wrestle the pack in and then came around to take her seat next to Tilly in the back. Tilly grinned at her.

"Hi Talia!"

"Hi babe!" said Talia, leaning in to give my daughter a hug. "I can't wait to see this hut we're going to stay in, how about you?"

"Same!"

Otis drove us along the motorway and took a turnoff I had never used before, winding through narrow rural roads and passing fewer and fewer houses as we went. Then we were there.

I was amazed at the walk. I hadn't realised what it was that Otis was suggesting that we do. We began in a small gravel car park just outside some farmer's fields, and we walked through the muddy ground, trying to avoid the cows. They stared at us blankly while they slowly chewed on their mouthfuls of grass. But soon the fields gave way to a beautiful stream that trickled over rocks and around bends with a delightful tinkling sound. The track followed the stream back into the hills, and the banks grew steeper and steeper.

As we left the broad open fields and entered the dark damp overhanging forest alongside the river, my heartbeat grew stronger. Out here in the trees I was feeling much less able to defend myself, easier to be surprised. The idea was not pleasant. My dream about the silver woman had made me feel more secure than I had felt in a long time, more settled, but I couldn't shake the idea that Kallista might be following me even now. *That's ridiculous,* I told myself. *Why would she follow you all the way out here? Surely she would just wait back at your house.* I blinked at my own conclusion and shuddered.

"Are you okay Pene?" asked Talia, striding up next to me in her thick rugged boots, with hiking stockings under her shorts.

"Yeah," I said as I trudged along the damp leaf-covered path that was beginning to wind further and further up the side of the hill. "I'm just feeling a little claustrophobic I guess."

Other than my lingering paranoia, the path was beautiful. Being surrounded by tall trees and loud birds made each step feel light, despite the heavy pack resting on my shoulders. The sun was strong and warm and illuminated us all from a broad blue sky and I felt as though my smile was so wide that it would split my face.

This was right. This was the balance. A path that only existed because others had trod it before, but it was still wild. We could still make our own way if we choose, and sometimes we did, passing through the forest and clambering amongst the roots and tree trunks, when we thought the path wasn't going to be the best option. Here we could find ourselves.

Talia reached out and took my hand, but said nothing. She smiled at me, and we walked together through the shadows beneath the spreading branches overhead. A tūī spun across the path, dipping between the boughs and settling over our heads to warble it's song. Her fingers woven in mine eased my pounding heart.

Otis had to pick up Tilly before we arrived at the hut because she started complaining that her legs were too tired. Once the path began to look more well-tended, she jumped down and began to run ahead along the short grass. She shrieked with delight when she saw some wooden signs covered in thick green paint telling her which way to go. Talia, Otis and I all grinned at each other. Otis was massaging his shoulders and rolling his arms.

"She's getting pretty heavy huh?" I asked. He just grinned and shook his head.

The hut was stunning. It was a small building, but well-made of solid wooden planks. Inside we found a pile of chopped wood and a small wood burner. Next to the main communal space were two rooms full of bunks with cheap thin blue mattresses stacked to one side, ready to be thrown on the beds. We all chucked our bags on the bunks and explored the rest of the hut. There was a long drop toilet outside, and a small kitchen with three sinks, and taps with small pumps that we had to move in order to pull water through.

Outside, the trees were kept back from the edge of the hut, leaving a clearing of short green grass for Tilly to run around and around in circles on. I stood watching the trees for a long time. Was that a tall, broad-shouldered shape standing in the shadows? Had it returned, was it still watching me? The sun reflected off something in the trees, a flash of cool light, and I was sure that there was nothing there. Talia touched my shoulder.

"Are you okay?"

I turned to look at her. Otis was standing with her, concern in his eyes. I smiled at them both and called Tilly over from where she was doing rolls on the grass.

"I'm fine. Let's see what else we can find."

We followed some signs that led towards the tall banks of the stream that I thought we had left far behind and were delighted to discover a swimming hole. It had a small soft shorebank, rather than slippery rocks dropping immediately into the cold water. Tilly splashed on the bank up to her ankles and kicked water out into the darker deeper pool.

"Oh wow! I didn't know that this was here," said Otis.

"Did you bring anything to swim in?" asked Talia.

"No, I didn't. How about you Pene?"

"No, I relied on your suggestions," I teased.

"I guess we won't be able to go swimming this time," he sighed.

"Oh, never say never," murmured Talia, as she turned to walk back to the hut. Otis met my eyes and raised his eyebrows. I just smiled back at him.

We passed the afternoon playing card games with Tilly and filling the hut with our laughter. At one point, while Otis was teaching Tilly a more complicated game, Talia walked up behind me and grabbed my sides, resting her chin on my shoulder.

"Wanna come for a swim?"

"I didn't bring anything to swim in though," I protested. I turned around to talk to Talia, but she didn't step away. I could smell the apple scented shampoo she must have washed her hair with that morning. Her eyes looked up at me.

"That won't matter, come on." She took me by the hand and began to lead me out of the hut.

"We're just going to go for a swim," she called out when Otis glanced over at us. "You can have a turn later."

He winked and returned to the game with Tilly.

We strolled down to the swimming hole together, Talia still holding on to my hand. I felt her fingers pressing on mine, and the sensation tingled along my arm. When we got to the swimming hole, she began to pull her top over her head. I saw her breasts press against her sports bra, outlining the hard points of her nipples as her body stretched to take it off. I sucked in a breath and looked away.

"But how will we get dry?" I asked.

"There's enough time to drip dry if we need to," said Talia. She was shaking her hair out now that she had removed the woolen bobble hat, black waves shimmering around her face. She was topless and the curve of her breasts made my own ache to be touched. She met my eyes and smiled. "Besides, I do have one of those micro-towel things. It's always helpful to be able to dry stuff off on a hike."

She bent over to push her shorts and stockings down, kicking off her hiking boots, and then straightening up fully naked before me. I couldn't help myself, looking across her body, admiring the way her curves shaped her hips, the black curls of hair between her legs. She crossed her arms, lifting her breasts slightly on top of them and tilted her head at me.

"Well?"

I guess I'm getting naked, I thought to myself, and I began pulling off my own clothes. At first I thought that I would feel embarrassed, getting naked around a friend of mine, someone who might judge me or laugh at me. But I realised that Talia wouldn't treat me that way, and my confidence grew as I got more naked. I straightened up and put my hands down by my sides, not quite sure where my hands should go. I shifted their position once or twice.

Talia looked me up and down and smiled.

"Come on!" she cried as she jogged down the bank and into the water. "Whoa," she yelped, as splashes of cold water leapt up from her legs and left glittering droplets on the skin of her ass and back. Her hair swung across her shoulders. I ran down after her, diving into the chilly water and feeling the stream fold around me, driving goosebumps across my flesh.

We swam in the pool for nearly an hour, diving around each other, splashing water at each other. Occasionally we would drift closer to each other, craving the warmth of each other's bodies as we floated in the cold stream. I found a rock under the water that was perfect to perch on, with my shoulders just breaking out of the water and into the air.

Talia swam over to me, placing her hands on my thighs as she balanced herself in the water by me. Her mouth dipped under its surface, but her eyes were locked on mine. I felt her fingers shift along my skin as the current pushed and pulled at her. I felt my lips part and my breath stalled in my throat. I focused on her lips as her face lifted from the water, and drifted closer.

Her face was centimetres away from mine when she spoke, softly. "I'm getting cold. Shall we go back?"

"What?"

"I'm ready to go back." She turned in the water and began to swim back to the soft sloping bank, lying on her back in the water. Her pale breasts were just below the surface, the darker skin of her nipples shimmering and blurred by the water passing over them. I felt a regretful throb between my legs as I realised that she was serious.

We both climbed out of the water and she pulled out her micro towel to dry off. I couldn't help but watch as she ran the pale blue material over her skin, wiping away the beads of water that gathered under her breasts, and along the trail from her belly button down her stomach. Then she straightened up and did a little hip shaking dance, one of the most delightful sights I had ever seen.

"All dry," she called and tossed the towel over to me. I was tempted to tweak my own nipples as I dried my chest, to spend more time rubbing and drying my pussy than I truly needed to. The pressure was building and even the slightest touch sent shivers through me.

But soon we were both dressed, our soaking hair wrapped to one side, and walking back along the track to the hut.

ALTHOUGH A FEW OTHER hiking groups showed up during the afternoon, it turned out that none of them were staying overnight. Each of them sat with us to chat, ate some food that they had brought with them, but then gathered their things and left to return the way that they had come. By the time that Otis brought out his small portable gas cooker, it was clear that the hut was going to be ours alone that night. *That's convenient,* I thought to myself.

We fed Tilly and tucked her into her sleeping bag on a bunk that was near the door so that she knew where we were. After the long walk up into the hills, and the excitement of being somewhere so unusual, Tilly dropped to sleep within moments. I walked back out into the living area of the hut, where the sunset was painting the walls golden. Darkness swelled in the forest around the hut, pressing in on the remnants of the day. I shivered a little.

"It's getting cold."

"Come here," said Otis. He had unzipped his sleeping bag so that it could be used like a blanket. He lifted one side of it for me to nuzzle in next to him, wrapping it over my shoulder along with his arm. We sat together for a short time, listening to each other breathe.

Soft footsteps approached. We turned to see Talia standing nearby. Her eyes reflected the last fires of the sun.

"Mind if I join you two?" she asked.

I turned to Otis and found he was watching me already. He smiled. "I like the idea."

I turned back to look at Talia. She had supported me through some of the most unusual things that I had ever experienced. She had seen me in my let loose partying days, and stuck by me in my quieter family days. She was an amazing artist, and one of the people I wanted around me all the time.

I lifted the blanket, making room for her to snuggle in between myself and Otis. Her hips pressed up to me, and her head rested on his chest. We all had to lie down a little more to stay comfortable, and I felt shivers of electricity run along my skin as our hands and bodies moved and settled.

We lay like that until the sunlight had truly gone, and the only light remaining was a small torch that Otis had placed on the wooden table in the middle of the hut. Even the wind was still. I could hear my heartbeat, every rustle of the blanket.

I looked across at Otis. He was watching me in the shadows. Below his face was Talia, laying back against him, watching me also. I leaned forward towards them both.

THE END

You can keep informed of any new writing by A. J Richards by emailing author.ajrichards@gmail.com

ACKNOWLEDGMENTS

My partner Andy encouraged me to try and write something with a bit more heat than I would usually try, and this novel is what I came up with. I am generally quite introverted, and so it was certainly a challenge when I started! However, I am very pleased with how it came out, and the feedback I received from early readers, so I hope you have enjoyed it too!

My inspirational friend Steff helped me with the technical details of getting a book self-published, and always encourages me to try and write more. As a very successful author, she really doesn't need to spend her time helping me, and it would be some small acknowledgment of her support if you were to go to www. steffanieholmes.com to see if her books are your cup of tea as well!

Kat is a wonderful editor for me, cleaning up the mistakes in my writing and pointing out when someone's keys magically shift around from place to place between scenes. In all likelihood, anything that still seems wrong was my fault for ignoring her.

Kaysey was a new reader for me with this manuscript, and she was a great one. She ripped through the story at a furious pace, and gave me some really good thoughts about the book as a whole. One day maybe I'll write something more to her particular tastes and see what she thinks of that!

A. J. Richards lives north of Auckland in New Zealand with their partner, their two daughters, and a small menagerie of household animals. The whole family loves when A. J.'s eldest daughter visits too.

They grew up as a voracious reader of science-fiction and fantasy, often to the annoyance of their unheeded family. Becoming an author was a childhood dream, alongside being a paleontologist, or a rock star.

You can keep informed of any new writing by A. J. Richards by emailing author.ajrichards@gmail.com